THE SCUTTLERS

DETECTIVE WATTERS MYSTERIES BOOK 4

MALCOLM ARCHIBALD

For Cathy

This book is dedicated to Detective Sergeant Charles Foote (1939 – 2019) of the Tayside Police.

PRELUDE
DUNDEE, SCOTLAND

FEBRUARY 1864

WALTER ABERNETHY TURNED THE FALSE KEY IN THE KEYHOLE and gently pushed the door. When the hinges squealed, Abernethy paused for a moment and hugged the shadows, feeling the rapid patter of his heart. Only when nobody appeared did he step inside the room, with his distrustful companion a few feet behind.

Without a word, Abernethy moved to the back wall with the thin beam of light from his bull's eye lantern bouncing in front of him. The room was devoid of personality, characterless as if waiting for human occupancy to give it a soul. The furniture attempted to make up for the lack of life by providing bulk: a heavy oaken four-poster bed, clumsy wooden chairs, and a Jacobean-style table that seemed to be carved from a single block of wood.

"Door," Abernethy said, and the second man closed the door and pulled the bolt across.

"Here," Abernethy handed over the lamp and began to roll back the carpet. The second man helped until they had cleared a third of the floor, exposing the wooden floorboards beneath. Abernethy held out his hand, and the second man produced a chisel, which Abernethy used to lever up four floorboards. The first made a slight noise that caused him to stop, while the next three were silent. He laid them at his side and examined the floor beneath the boards.

"Lathe and plaster," Abernethy said softly, "Pass me an auger." The second man produced an auger from the bag he carried. Very carefully, Abernethy drilled holes in the floor, forming an eighteen-inch square and brushing away the dust with a gloved hand.

"Ready?" Abernethy asked.

When the second man nodded, Abernethy put pressure on the square within the holes, pushing until the entire section gave way, to fall into the room below with a crash like the end of the world.

"Jesus!" The second man blasphemed as Abernethy waited for the dust to settle. Reaching inside the bag, he produced a knotted rope, tied one end to the closest leg of the four-poster and climbed hand-over-hand into the darkness below.

"Light!" Abernethy breathed, and the second man shone the lantern, so a pencil-thin beam of light illuminated the room.

"Over here!"

The room was empty except for a desk and a large green safe. A pile of blank notepaper on the desk bore the heading *Royal Hotel, Dundee*. Ignoring the desk, Abernethy crouched at the front of the safe, tested the mechanism with a series of keys, and then set to work.

"Hurry," the second man glanced behind him, starting at non-existent sounds.

"Quiet!" Abernethy hissed. He placed his ear to the safe. "These things need time."

As Abernethy worked, the second man watched, hoping to pick up some tricks of the trade. He grunted in satisfaction as

Abernethy gave a slight nod, turned both his keys, and opened the door.

"Here we are," Abernethy said, looking at the contents.

A small cashbox stood next to a larger canvas bag, with a thin pile of banknotes at the side. Abernethy scooped everything into a soft leather case that the second man produced from his bag.

"I'm watching you, remember," the second man warned. "If you try to gull me, I'll tell Himself."

"I know what you're doing," Abernethy sounded bitter.

On the second shelf, a diamond necklace wore a small label, which Abernethy read.

Mrs Annabelle Gordon, Room 16.

"Sorry, Mrs Gordon," he said, "you've lost your prize jewels." He showed the label to the second man. "What do you think?"

"I'm no scholar," the second man said, indicating his inability to read.

"Of course not," Abernethy said. "Come on, let's get out before somebody hears us." Reaching into his pocket, he produced a plain biscuit and crushed it, sending a cascade of crumbs onto the floor. "My calling card," he said.

"You're a bloody idiot," the second man commented.

"Maybe, but at least I can read."

They left the same way they had entered, closing the door behind them, and climbing out a back window before clambering down a waterspout. When they reached the back of the hotel, they walked through a dark close to Union Street, where streetlights forced caution upon them.

"This way." A smirr of rain carried the salt air of the German Ocean as the second man led them to Mint Close.

"One more to rob, and we're finished," Abernethy reminded.

"No, wait!" The second man pointed to a draper's shop in Reform Street. "We'll do that as well."

"It's not on the list, James," Abernethy hissed. "I can feel the bluebottles are close." He looked around, listening for the portentous tread of polished boots.

"Himself gave us the beat times," James said. "We've plenty of time for an extra. Follow me!" Climbing up a lamppost, he stretched across to the flat roof of Spence and Company, one of Dundee's leading drapers. A cupola graced the roof, and James scraped away the putty from a pane of glass and looked down.

"I don't do petty theft," Abernethy said. "I'm a professional."

"You do as I say." James relished his temporary authority, "or I'll tell Himself you refused to co-operate. How'd you like that, eh? An old Demon like you?"

"You're a bastard," Abernethy said.

"Come on!" taking a length of rope from his bag, James secured it on the roof and dropped it into the darkness below. "You first!"

Abernethy looked around the shop in contempt as James forced open the office door and peered inside.

"Here's the desk," James said. "There's nae safe for you." Forcing open the drawer, he swore. "Maistly just browns - copper coins - but I dinnae care a boddle. We can spend them, tae," he scooped the cash into the leather bag, laughing. With a glance over his shoulder at Abernethy, he pocketed a pound in silver. "Come on, Abernethy, help yourself."

"We're wasting time," Abernethy said. "We have a timetable."

"Your timetable can go to the devil!"

As Abernethy watched, James lifted half a dozen items of clothing, helping himself to a coat and waistcoat. "Here," James opened a box and hauled out a dozen pairs of men's underwear. "I could do with new drawers," he laughed high-pitched and stripped off his clothes there and then.

"Oh, for God's sake," Abernethy said as the second man

dropped his stained and threadbare underwear on the floor, stood naked for a moment with the lamplight playing on his pale, thin body, and pulled on a new pair of drawers.

"Come on," Abernethy urged as the second man fastened his trousers with clumsy fingers. "We have one more job." He did not crumble a biscuit here, for petty theft was beyond him.

Still laughing, James grabbed the bag, swarmed up the rope, waited for Abernethy to follow, untied the knot, and returned to Reform Street. "Lead on Abernethy, and I've got my eye on you, remember."

CHAPTER ONE

POLICE OFFICE, BELL STREET, DUNDEE

JANUARY 1864

CHIEF CONSTABLE DONALD MACKAY TAPPED BONY FINGERS ON the desk. "What do you know about Mr Muirhead, Watters?"

"He's a shipowner, sir," Sergeant George Watters replied. "He's the managing owner of at least two of the Dundee Greenland Whaling Company's vessels."

Mackay tapped his fingers again. "Anything else?"

Watters shook his head. "No, sir. Mr Muirhead has never come to my attention. Why, sir, have we caught him shoplifting?"

Mackay ignored the attempt at humour as his pale blue eyes fixed on Watters. "He's come to your attention now, Watters. I want you to find out everything about him."

"Yes, sir. Why is that?"

In response, Mackay tossed a file across the desk. "Read that, Sergeant." He waited as Watters opened the buff folder and scanned the contents.

"A small vessel, *Toiler*, sank on her passage between Stromness and Dundee," Watters said. "And the owner, Mr Muirhead, has her insured with two separate companies. Do we suspect scuttling, sir?"

Mackay leaned back in his chair. "You're the detective, Watters. Take the file away, dig a little, and come back to me with your conclusions." He waited until Watters reached the door before calling him back. "Oh, and Watters, there has been an increase in the number of burglaries recently."

Watters turned around. "So I hear, sir. Thefts from hotels and shops, I believe."

"That's correct. Look into it, will you? Deal with the scuttling case first. I doubt that will occupy you for long, then look into the burglaries."

"Yes, sir," Watters said and made to turn away.

"Oh, wait, Watters, I have another matter to discuss with you."

"Yes, sir?" Watters knew that Mr Mackay would not have let him off so easily.

"I may wish to increase the detective establishment of the force." Mackay leaned back in his chair, pressed his fingers together, and watched Watters' reaction through his cold northern eyes.

"Yes, sir?"

"What do you think of that?"

"We could always use another couple of men, sir," Watters said. "Much of our time is spent inspecting pawn shops for stolen goods and giving evidence at court rather than detecting crimes."

"I'm glad you agree," Mackay said dryly. "I have the finances for only one position, with two officers in mind. Both will join you shortly. Use them, assess their attributes and weaknesses, and report back to me."

"Yes, sir," Watters said.

"I can only afford one more man," Mackay reminded, "so they are in direct opposition to one another."

———

Watters returned to his desk in the duty room, where Constables Scuddamore and Duff were scraping their pens over a seemingly endless pile of forms and routine paperwork. Both looked up as Watters slid onto his chair.

"Keep working, lads," Watters said. "We've got three jobs now. One is to look into the recent burglaries, and the second is a scuttling case."

"And the third, Sergeant?" Scuddamore asked.

"We're nursemaiding a couple of Johnny Raws," Watters explained about the possible augmentation of their numbers.

"Two more men?" Duff grinned. "Well, they'd better be good. Do you know who they are, Sergeant?"

"Not yet."

"I hope they're experienced officers and not starry-eyed young hopefuls who think policing is romantic and exciting." Scuddamore dripped ink from his pen-nib onto the topmost document on his desk, swore and reached for his blotter.

"Which case are we going to concentrate on, Sergeant?" Scuddamore asked.

"The scuttling," Watters said. "With luck, we should get that out of the way in a few days and then we can look at the thefts. I don't know when these new men will come." He flourished the Muirhead file. "This rubbish is all about Mr Muirhead, whom Mr Mackay suspects of scuttling one of his vessels. I'll read this thing and see if it's of any interest to us."

"I've never worked on a scuttling case before," Duff said.

"Most are insurance frauds," Watters told him. "A shipowner over-insures a vessel, takes her out to sea, and sinks her. Mr Mackay wants us to see if this vessel, *Toiler*, follows that pattern." He looked at the empty mug beside his blotter. "I work better with a full mug of tea, though, Scuddamore."

"Aye, these new lads had better be good at making tea,"

Scuddamore said, standing up. "I want none of that wishy-washy coloured-water stuff."

Only when Scuddamore filled Watters' mug from the teapot that sat permanently on the grate did Watters open the file and study the contents.

"Right, lads," he said at length. "This looks like a simple case of scuttling, but I want your opinions."

Duff and Scuddamore left their administrative work without hesitation and pulled their chairs closer to listen to Watters.

Watters sipped at his tea. "*Toiler* was a small, elderly vessel without much value, so it seems strange to insure her. According to this account, she was only thirty-five tons, and she sprung a leak off the Redhead by Montrose."

Scuddamore nodded. "Yes, Sergeant."

"The report here claims that as the water within *Toiler* rose, the crew abandoned her fifteen miles off Bodden, and rowed to Montrose." Watters looked up. "That sounds fairly straightforward until we reach the speculation that the master, or one of the crew, either forced out the bow plates or bored holes in the hull."

"Is there any justification for the speculation, Sergeant?" Duff asked.

"Perhaps," Watters said. "*Toiler* was heavily insured; she was worth perhaps £300, but Muirhead insured her for £925, with two different companies."

Duff grinned as he sipped his tea. "That sounds plain enough then, Sergeant. A shipowner with a poor-quality vessel looking to make a quick profit. Who's the owner?"

"Muirhead," Watters said.

"Keith Muirhead?" Scuddamore asked.

Watters checked the file. "The very same."

"But Muirhead's one of the most successful merchants in Dundee," Scuddamore said. "He's got no need to scuttle a vessel for a few hundred pounds. He must be worth tens of thousands. He lives in a palace out by the Ferry." The Ferry, or Broughty Ferry, was a salubrious town a few miles east of Dundee and the home of many of Dundee's elite merchant class.

Duff grunted. "That's how these people get rich, Scuds. They take every advantage, twist every law to suit themselves, and bleed the poor to line their wallets."

Watters put down his mug. "We're not here to judge the man's morals, Duff, only to see if he's breaking the law. "I want to find out all you can about Keith Muirhead. Scuddamore, you talk to his employees and see their opinion of their master. Duff, go to his bank – the Tayside Bank – and speak to their new manager, a fellow called MacBride. Look at Muirhead's bank balance if Mr MacBride allows."

Both detectives rose at once, happy to escape the drudgery of administration.

"I'll talk to the insurance companies," Watters said. "With luck, we should wrap this up in a couple of days. With a lot of luck, by tomorrow."

The Dundee Maritime and Household Insurance Company boasted that it had offices across eastern Scotland. Its Dundee office was in Dock Street, on the second floor of a building a hundred yards from the Dundee Perth and London Shipping Company and only a biscuit toss from Muirhead's Greenland Whaling Company.

Although the common close was unassuming, the insurance company's name was inscribed in gold lettering on the door, and the reception hall was brightly lit, with a smell of polished wood and brass. The young man behind the desk greeted Watters with a smile.

"Yes, sir? May I help you?"

"I am Sergeant George Watters of the Dundee police, and I wish to view the insurance policy of the vessel *Toiler*, owned by Keith Muirhead."

The clerk looked nonplussed for a moment. "I am not sure if I am allowed to do that," he said.

Watters had expected such a response. "Then fetch somebody who has the authority," he ordered. "I'll wait," he consulted the silver watch that Marie had given him on their third wedding anniversary, "for five minutes, and then I'll start to look myself."

Within three minutes, the clerk returned with an older man in a wing collar.

"It's quite against company policy," the older man said. "Quite."

Watters leaned over the small wooden half-door that barred entry to the office's inner Sanctorum, snapped open the bolt, and stepped inside.

"Show me where you keep your files," Watters said, "and I'll search myself."

"It's against company policy," the older man repeated, pulling at his collar as Watters strode inside the office and looked around, with his cane balanced over his shoulder and his low-crowned hat pushed back on his head. The room was large, with three tall windows overlooking the street below, four desks for the clerks, and a fireplace. A heavy, glass-fronted bookcase dominated one wall, and wooden pigeonholes another.

"Here we are," Watters pointed his cane at the rows of pigeonholes, each containing bundles of documents tied with white linen ribbons. "Do you file by ship name or company name?" He removed the documents from one pigeonhole. "I'll empty these on the floor if I don't need them."

"Oh, no." The elderly man put his thin hands on Watters' arm. "No, sir, you mustn't do such a thing. These files are confidential."

"I only want one," Watters said. "The policy that concerns Mr Muirhead's *Toiler*."

The elderly man pulled at his collar again. "Over here," he submitted at last. "We file by the client's name, and Mr Muirhead is under M."

Watters walked with the elderly man to the third column of pigeonholes. "Thank you, Mr…"

"Gallacher," the elderly man seemed equally reluctant to part with his name. "Edward Gallacher."

"Thank you, Mr Gallacher," Watters delved into the three pigeonholes under the letter M. The contents of the first compartment were of no interest, but the next had a dozen documents neatly tied together with a strip of linen. "Are these all Mr Muirhead's vessels?"

Mr Gallacher considered before answering. "Yes, Sergeant Watters."

Watters lifted the bundles. "I'll borrow these as evidence and return them when the case is closed." He gave an ironic bow. "Thank you, Mr Gallacher."

Gallacher nearly tied his hands in a knot as he watched Watters carry his documents out of the office. "Please don't forget to return them, Sergeant Watters."

The second insurance company was in Edinburgh, only an hour and a half's journey by rail but a different world from the boisterous, smoky streets of Dundee. Watters admired the neo-classical architecture of George Street as he searched for the office, which was at street level, with marble columns surrounding the door. Once past the uniformed commission-aire, he found the clerks even less helpful than their Dundee counterparts.

"Dundee Police?" A middle-aged man with greying whiskers stared suspiciously at Watters. "This isn't Dundee, you know."

"I know," Watters said, perusing a familiar set of wooden pigeonholes. "Do you file by ship name or company name?"

"Our clients each have a personal file," the clerk tried to

prevent Watters from pushing past. He glanced at the commissionaire for support.

"Ah, thank you," Watters said, extracting the documents under Muirhead's name. "I'll return these when the case is closed." He paused at the door. "One more thing, Mr…"

"Edmund Fairbairn."

"Mr Fairbairn. Could you describe Mr Muirhead to me?"

Fairbairn pulled at his whiskers. "I did not meet the man. My assistant, Mr Beaumont, dealt with that enquiry."

Mr Beaumont was a sandy-haired man with steady blue eyes. "I remember Mr Muirhead well," he said.

"Could you describe him to me?" Watters asked.

Beaumont furrowed his forehead. "He was a well-set-up gentleman, with a very upright stance." His frown deepened with the struggle to remember. "Mr Muirhead was nearly military in attitude and very tall. Taller than you and me."

"How old?" Watters asked.

"He was a young man. I would say in his middle thirties," Beaumont nodded. "Yes, perhaps thirty-five or thirty-six." He nodded to emphasise his words.

"Did Mr Muirhead come in person? Or did he send a clerk?"

"He came in person," Beaumont said.

"Thank you, Mr Beaumont. I may return to ask you more questions," Watters said.

He returned to Dundee in a thoughtful frame of mind for aspects of the case that were unclear.

————

"Right, lads, how did you get on?" Watters leaned back in his chair, with the winter rain hammering at the window beside him.

Scuddamore shook his head. "I found nothing unusual,

Sergeant. I spoke to a dozen of Mr Muirhead's employees, including his secretary, and none of them had a bad word to say about the man." Scuddamore consulted his notebook. "The comments include phrases such as "excellent employer," "a true gentleman," and "always polite." He smiled. "They do say he is careful with money, but that is the mark of any merchant in Dundee."

"Thank you, Scuddamore," Watters said. "How about you, Duff?"

Duff shook his head. "The bank manager did not release the books to me, Sergeant, but he said Mr Muirhead's accounts were extremely healthy and showing an annual increase. I need a magistrate's order to view the figures."

Watters nodded. "We're not at that stage yet. Would you say that Mr Muirhead does not need to scuttle his ships, then?"

"I would say that he does not, Sergeant," Duff agreed. "There was one thing that I thought unusual, though."

"What was that, Duff?"

"Mr MacBride told me that Muirhead's accountant, a fellow Mackenzie, opened a new account for him last week and put in six hundred pounds."

Watters smiled. "Six hundred pounds? That is interesting, Duff. That's the same figure as the Scottish and English Mutual paid out."

"Yes, Sergeant."

"Was the account in Muirhead's name, the company name or Mackenzie's name?"

"Mr Muirhead's name," Duff said.

"In that case, gentlemen, we have an investigation on our hands," Watters said, with a smile. "I do not believe that Mr Muirhead insured his vessels twice, and in a few moments, I'll tell you why. Pour the tea out, Scuddamore, and make it strong."

Scuddamore grinned and brought over three mugs with the tea black as tar. Watters added a stiff dram of whisky from a bottle he had in his bottom drawer.

"Real peat-reek boys, from an illicit still in the Angus Glens. If you drink it naked, it will lift the skin from your throat." He tasted his tea, coughed, and added another drop. "We're back on a case, lads, not just our normal petty theft and drunken brawls."

"Yes, Sergeant," Scuddamore said.

"Well," Watters held up his mug. "Here's to us, lads, wha's like us?"

"Damned few," Scuddamore said as the three mugs clinked together.

"And they're a' deid!" Duff said, grinning.

They drank, gagged, and drank again.

"Now, Watters said, "here are the insurance documents for *Toiler,* one from the Dundee Maritime Company and one from the Scottish and English Mutual." He laid both on the desk. "I want you to read both and tell me what you think."

Scuddamore scanned both documents. "The Dundee Maritime is dated earlier," he said. "April 1856, while the Scottish and English Mutual is October 1863, just a few months ago."

"That's one thing," Watters said. "Anything else?"

"Mr Muirhead signed both," Duff said, "but with different signatures. And the Dundee Maritime is for only £325 while the Mutual is for £600."

"That's strange, don't you think?" Watters asked. "The later one, when the ship is older, for nearly twice the amount, and with different signatures."

"The Dundee Maritime says K. L. Muirhead, and the Mutual says Keith Muirhead." Duff reread the names.

"I don't think the same person signed both documents," Watters said.

"Do you think somebody forged Mr Muirhead's signature?" Scuddamore asked.

"I do," Watters said.

"Why would they do that?" Scuddamore asked.

"That is what I intend to find out." Watters sipped more of his tea. "Or rather, that's what we will all find out."

CHAPTER TWO

"FORGET THE SCUTTLING FOR A MINUTE, SERGEANT. HAVE YOU
seen this?" Scuddamore nearly threw the poster onto Watters'
desk. "They're all over the town."

"What is it?" Watters unfolded the paper and read.

Fellow Irishmen!
Now's the time, and now's the hour!
For too long, Ireland has struggled under British oppression. Now the
Fenian Brotherhood has arrived to remove the colonial chains and free
Ireland. We call upon all True Irishmen who love the Shamrock and the
Green to gather in Dundee.
Eirinn go Brách.

"What the devil?" Watters shook his head. "The last thing
we want in Dundee is trouble between the Irish and the
Scots."

"I agree, sir," Scuddamore said. "I thought we'd seen the
last of these troublemakers, and here they are again."

"I met some of these lads when I worked in London,"
Watters said. "They are a formidable crew. Best look into it,

Scuddamore, but don't forget the scuttling case is our priority."

Watters looked up as two uniformed constables approached them. One man was about thirty-five, tall, broad-shouldered, and erect. The second was smaller, slighter, and looked more nervous than Watters expected from a policeman.

"Here come the Johnny Raws," Scuddamore said quietly, putting a sheet of blank paper on top of the poster.

"Good morning, gentlemen," Watters said as the two constables stopped six feet from his desk. "What do you want?"

The tall man acted as a spokesman. "Mr Mackay sent us, Sergeant. He said you have to assess us as possible detectives."

Watters looked them over before speaking. "Do you have names, Constables?"

"Yes, Sergeant," the taller man said. "I am Constable Richard Boyle, 236, and this is Constable Shaw, 239."

"Well Constable Boyle 136, and Constable Shaw 239, here's what I want you to do." Watters pointed to the kettle that sat on the grate. "We need hot tea ready at all times, so that's your first job. I am not getting you out of uniform until I see how good you are."

Constable Shaw looked disappointed as Boyle checked the kettle and refilled it. Watters waited until Boyle placed the kettle on the grate.

"The second thing," Watters said, "is to look at this document Detective Scuddamore has brought in." He dragged the garish poster from under its folder.

Both prospective detectives read the poster. "It looks as if the Fenians are organising something in Dundee," Shaw said helpfully.

"You're right," Watters encouraged. "What do you know about the Fenians?"

"They're an organisation in Ireland and America," Boyle said. "They want Ireland to be separate from Great Britain."

Watters leaned back, aware that Scuddamore was listening to every word. "Where do you think we might find the Fenians?"

Shaw and Boyle looked at each other for inspiration.

"Ireland?" Shaw hazarded.

Watters hid his impatience. "Boyle said that. Where in Dundee might they be found?"

"Where the Irish have settled," Boyle said.

"Which is?" Watters felt as if he were drawing teeth.

"Scouringburn, Lochee, and Hilltown," Shaw said at once.

"Quite so," Watters said. "Those are the areas in which I wish you to operate today and tomorrow. Do your normal duty shifts in uniform, then wear civilian clothes and tour these areas, listening for any signs of subversion or Fenianism."

"Double shifts?" Shaw asked.

"Double shifts," Watters replied, watching their reactions. He did not want any man who was shy of working long hours. "Now I'm sure Sergeant Murdoch has already allocated you a beat."

"Yes, Sergeant," Boyle said.

"Then get on it," Watters watched them walk away.

"That will keep them out of our way for a while," Watters grunted, "and maybe they'll find out something useful."

"Maybe, Sergeant," Scuddamore said, "but I doubt it."

———

Red streaks between the early morning grey clouds promised a windy day to come. Watters hefted his golf bag, selected a club, and squinted along the fairway. "I was surprised to see you here, Mr Muirhead. I thought you were a member at the Balcumbie Club."

Mr Muirhead smiled. "I would be, Mr Watters, but the Dundee Artisan allows me to tee off earlier. Besides, the rates are lower." His clubs looked well-used, even shabby. "I am happy to find a partner so early on a January morning."

"I grab a round whenever I can," Watters squared off and swung, sending his ball soaring down the fairway. It bounced twice, then rolled to within a yard of the green.

"Nice drive," Muirhead said. "I can just about make out the ball." He squinted up to the sky. "It's still too dark for accurate golf, but the course is quiet at least."

"Any earlier, and we'd have to carry candles," Watters said.

Muirhead swung mightily, with the ball soaring along the fairway, to land with an awkward bounce and finish in a patch of rough.

"Hard luck," Watters sympathised. "You seem to be having a run of bad luck just now, losing *Toiler* as well."

"*Toiler?*" Muirhead hefted his bag and began the trudge along the frost-hard fairway. "Yes, that was a strange one. It seems her bow plates just opened up, and she went down in fifteen minutes. We were fortunate that nobody was lost."

"That's always the prime concern," Watters agreed. "*Toiler* was insured, wasn't she?"

"Oh, yes," Muirhead said. "All my vessels are insured." He smiled again. "I'm fortunate that the insurance office is only a step from the company offices."

"That will be the Dundee Maritime?" Watters asked, helping Muirhead find his ball in a tangle of rough grass and winter-brown bracken.

"Yes," Muirhead sounded disinterested. "Where's that damned ball? I know it landed here somewhere!"

"I believe that some shipowners have a second insurer as well," Watters pointed his club to Muirhead's ball.

"Yes," Muirhead said, shaking his head. "My ball's in a

damned bad lie. It will be a devil of a job to get it near the green from here."

"It's a friendly game," Watters said. "Kick it to a better lie. I won't look."

Muirhead frowned. "I don't do that," he said. "I'll try from here." He swung and shook his head when the ball travelled six inches and settled back in the rough. "Stand back, Mr Watters, and I'll try again."

Watters watched as Muirhead hacked at the ball, with every attempt moving it a few inches closer to the green. Eventually, the shipowner succeeded and finished with a beautiful putt that placed the ball in the hole.

"You won that one," Muirhead said.

"I did, Mr Muirhead," Watters agreed. "Did *Toiler* have a second insurer?"

"*Toiler*? No. Are you in the insurance business, Mr Watters? If so, I'm afraid you're wasting your time. I've been with the Dundee Maritime a long time and am perfectly happy with them."

"I've heard that the Scottish and English Mutual is equally good," Watters said as they lined up for the next hole.

"It may well be," Muirhead swung first, with his ball travelling two thirds down the fairway. "That's a better drive."

"Would you consider using the Mutual?" Watters swung, with his ball landing a hands-breadth from Muirhead's.

"I've never heard of it," Muirhead said. "Are you here to play golf or to sell me ship insurance, Mr Watters?"

"I'm not an insurance salesman, Mr Muirhead," Watters said, as they strolled up the fairway with their feet making slight indentations on the grass. "I'm a policeman. Sergeant George Watters of the Dundee Police."

Muirhead looked sideways at Watters as he lined up his next shot. "Are you, indeed? Are you investigating me, Sergeant Watters?"

"I am investigating the loss of *Toiler*," Watters said.

"Why is that?" Muirhead drove the ball onto the green, watching it bounce and roll back to the edge of the fairway.

"*Toiler* was insured with two different companies, to a value far in excess of her worth, and sank in calm seas." Watters placed his ball a little behind Muirhead's.

"I think you are mistaken, Sergeant," Muirhead said. "I only ever insure with Dundee Maritime and never above the value of my vessels." He chipped his ball beside the hole. "There, that's better. No, Sergeant Watters, I don't believe in wasting money on excess insurance premiums, and I'd never risk the lives of my men by deliberately sinking a ship."

"Nice shot, Mr Muirhead. I am afraid *Toiler* was insured with two different companies, sir. Dundee Maritime and the Scottish and English Mutual. I will bring the documentation to your office later today, and we can discuss matters further there."

"That would be best," Muirhead gave Watters a stern look. "Then I can show you that you're talking nonsense. Shall we say eleven o'clock?"

"Eleven o'clock it is," Watters watched Muirhead sink his shot, then followed suit. "A tied hole, I believe."

Muirhead glanced at the sky. "The weather's breaking," he said. "I shall have to get to work, Sergeant Watters. Eleven o'clock, then."

Watters watched Muirhead walk away, a man in his late thirties with a snap to his step.

————

"Golfing, Sergeant?" Duff asked as Watters placed his clubs in the corner of the room.

"Golfing with Mr Muirhead," Watters said, pouring himself a mug of tea. "I'm meeting him at eleven in his office."

"Are you going to arrest him, Sergeant?"

"If I think he's guilty, I will," Watters said. "At the minute, I am unsure. There are too many imponderables in the case. Anyway, golfers who lose rather than cheat are unlikely to fiddle their insurance companies."

"Is that why you played golf with him?" Duff asked.

"You can find out a lot about a man's character on the golf course," Watters said.

"What am I doing today?" Duff pushed his pile of paperwork away in a gesture of contempt.

"You're on pawnshop patrol," Watters tasted his tea, pulled a face, and added another half-teaspoon of tealeaves. "Weak tea is suitable for children and old women," he said. "If the brew doesn't stain the spoon, it's no good to anybody."

"Yes, Sergeant. Do you want me to do your normal pawnshops as well as my own?"

"Well volunteered. It's time you learned the Dock Street area." Watters handed over a closely printed sheet of paper. "This is a list of property stolen in Dundee over the past week. You know the drill. If you find anything, arrest the pawnshop managers, and bring them in, together with the items. Theft is a bigger threat than violence and more prevalent than scuttling. Boyle and Shaw here will help you," he said as the two prospective detectives walked over.

Shaw glanced at the list. "There are hundreds of items here," he said. "How will I identify them all?"

"You won't," Watters said. "Read the list and find the most distinctive, then look for them. You'll never identify one white shirt from a score or a pewter mug from a shelf-full, but if something has distinctive markings or a watch is engraved, then you have a chance. Selective detecting, Shaw; concentrate on what you can do, rather than wasting time on the impossible."

"Yes, Sergeant." Shaw wrinkled his nose in distaste.

Duff read through the list again. "A lot of this property is high value, Sergeant. Will the thief find a pawnshop able to sell it?"

Watters shook his head. "That's the property the thieves took from the Royal Hotel and the shop break-ins. I doubt any Dundee pawn would touch the expensive jewellery that's easily identifiable. It is more likely the cracksman will sell it in Edinburgh or Glasgow, but keep your eyes open anyway."

"Yes, Sergeant," Duff said.

"Here's Scuddamore. Take him with you. You'd both better all learn the area."

"Take me where?" Scuddamore poured himself a mug of tea. "It's cold out there today. Playing golf later, Sergeant?"

Watters glowered at him. "I played this morning, Scuddamore, when you were still lazing in bed."

———

Muirhead's Greenland Whaling Company's office fronted onto Dock Street, with a splendid view of the packed shipping in King William the Fourth Dock. Watters stepped into the reception area and stopped at the ornamental brass railing between him and the two busy clerks. He held a leather case in his left hand and his lead-weighted cane in his right.

"I'm here to see Mr Muirhead!" Watters rapped his cane on the counter.

The first clerk was about eighteen, with thin shoulders and slicked-back hair. He eyed Watters up and down. "Mr Muirhead doesn't see anybody without an appointment," he said.

"I am Sergeant George Watters of the Dundee Police. Pray, tell Mr Muirhead that I am here." Watters held the clerk's gaze until he scurried away to fetch his master.

Muirhead greeted Watters with a smile and an outstretched hand, which was unusual for a man that Watters had recently accused of scuttling a ship. "Come in, Sergeant Watters, and we'll get this nonsense cleared up."

Muirhead's office was large and plain, with oak-panelled walls and two tall windows overlooking the docks. Muirhead ushered Watters to a comfortable leather chair on one side of his desk, seated himself on the other and rang a small brass bell. "Tea, Sergeant? Or coffee? I feel it is too early yet for anything stronger."

"Tea would be most welcome, Mr Muirhead," Watters said, looking around the office. Save for the desk, two chairs, and a single glass-fronted bookcase, the only items in the room were ship models, a clock, an old-fashioned harpoon, and a barometer.

"Are these your ships, sir?"

Muirhead's eyes brightened. "Yes, they are, Sergeant." He stepped across the room to the ship models. "The steam paddle-steamers are *Toiler* and *Travail*, the sail-powered coasters are *Teresa* and *Tamerlane*, and the whaling vessels are *Guinevere*, *Arthur* and *Lancelot*." He paused beside the largest of the models. "This beauty is *Lancelot*, only launched last month, a steam-whaling ship and the pride of my fleet."

"She's a beauty," Watters caught Muirhead's enthusiasm. "You must have invested a great deal of money in building her."

"I have," Muirhead agreed. "Hunting the whales is a very chancy business, Sergeant. One good voyage can make a man, and one unsuccessful trip can break him. That is why I spread my money around in different ventures, although whaling is my primary concern."

With her three masts and sturdy construction, Watters could only admire *Lancelot's lines* while Muirhead explained his situation. "Some of the smaller, one-man or one-ship whaling companies live on the edge of disaster with every voyage," Muirhead said. "For them, even the capture of a single whale can make the difference between profit and loss, success or failure, the continuance of business or bankruptcy. I am in the fortunate position of being able to spread the risk between my different vessels and various business interests."

"I see, sir," Watters said. "I am afraid I must return to the reason I am here, Mr Muirhead."

"Oh, yes, this insurance nonsense," Muirhead reluctantly left his ship models and returned to his seat. "Let's get that cleared up." He looked up as a smart, young man entered the room. "Could you fetch us a pot of tea, please, Killen?"

"Yes, sir." Killen gave a small bow and withdrew.

"I called around at the Dundee Maritime after our golf this morning to pick up the original documentation," Muirhead said, "but it seems you beat me to it."

"I have the documents with me," Watters said. "I believe you have the copies?"

"My secretary looked them out for me," Muirhead indicated the papers on his desk.

When Killen brought the tea, Muirhead had him pour two cups and then handed over the insurance documents to Watters. "There you are, Sergeant, all in order."

Watters compared the copies with the originals. "Exactly the same, sir," he said. "I notice you sign as K. L. Muirhead."

"Always," Muirhead said. "My middle name is Lancelot. When I was younger, it embarrassed me to have such an unusual name, but now I use it as an extra form of security. Not many people know what the L stands for, you see." He nodded to his ship models. "That's why my whaling ships have Arthurian names, and I plan a Gawain in the near future."

"May I see some of your recent correspondence?" Watters asked.

"Of course," Muirhead sounded slightly irritated. He rang the bell again and ordered Killen to bring him his secretary.

"This is Mr Forbes, my secretary," Muirhead said.

Forbes was a tall, thin man who looked down at Watters from a long nose.

"And this is Sergeant George Watters of the Dundee

Police," Muirhead completed the introductions. "The sergeant wishes to see a selection of my signatures, Mr Forbes. Could you fetch some, please?"

"No, no," Watters said. "Just show me, Mr Forbes. I'll come with you." He was quite aware that Forbes could bring a selection of innocent signatures. He accompanied Forbes to an adjacent office.

"I'll look myself," Watters said. "Where do you store copies of Mr Muirhead's correspondence?"

Muirhead was a prolific letter writer, with everything duplicated and neatly filed. Watters selected twenty letters at random over the past five years and found the same signature on each sheet of paper. "K. L. Muirhead."

"Thank you, Mr Forbes," Watters said. "I may call on you again."

"Yes, sir," Forbes gave a small bow.

"Well, Mr Muirhead," Watters returned to his previous chair and half-finished cup of tea. "I do not doubt that the Dundee Maritime Insurance documents are genuine, as is your signature."

"I am glad to hear it, Sergeant," Muirhead said dryly.

"That leaves us with these," Watters produced the documents from the Scottish and English Mutual. "Which are for your vessels and bear your signature."

"Let me see these!" Muirhead held out his hand. He glanced at each document. "These are certainly for my vessels," he said, "but that is not my signature."

"That's what we thought, sir," Watters said.

Muirhead looked up. "Well, who the devil would wish to double insure my ships?"

"That's what we hope to find out, Mr Muirhead. Do you recognise the signature? The style of writing, sir?"

"Devil a bit of it!" Muirhead said. "What possible profit can anybody make from such a scheme? The money would come to the company." He looked up.

"When the insurance companies pay the money," Watters said. "Would they pay it directly to this office? To Mr Forbes, perhaps?"

"No, sergeant," Muirhead said. "Any monies are sent to my accountant, Mr Mackenzie."

Watters wrote the name in his notebook. "And what should Mr Mackenzie do with the money, Mr Muirhead?"

"Why, he should pay it into my account, of course." It was evident that the barrage of questions was irritating Muirhead.

"Are there any circumstances where he could open another account?" Watters asked.

"No," Muirhead said. "Although I give him a free hand. I have known Bill – Mr Mackenzie – since we were at the High School together."

Watters nodded. "Thank you. Could you supply me with the logbook and the Articles of Agreement – the crew list - for *Toiler*?"

"The logbook went down with the ship," Muirhead said. "But I am sure that Mr Forbes has a copy of the Articles. He keeps one to pay the wages." Muirhead rang his brass bell again and ordered Killen to fetch the list from Forbes.

Watters checked to ensure the crew's addresses were added and tucked the sheet safely inside his case.

"Thank you, Mr Muirhead," Watters decided he had asked sufficient questions for a friendly interview. "I appreciate your co-operation." He packed away the insurance documents in his case and reached for his hat and cane.

"I have a question to ask, Sergeant Watters," Muirhead said. "This extra insurance affair. Did the money come from my accounts? Have I been charged with these unnecessary expenses?"

"I am afraid I don't know the answer to that, sir," Watters said. "You'd better ask Mr Mackenzie."

"I'll be sure to do that." Muirhead gave a small smile. "Am

I off the hook, Sergeant? Do you believe I am scuttling my vessels?"

Watters jammed his hat on his head. "No, sir, I do not believe that you scuttled *Toiler*."

"Then tell me, Sergeant, why somebody is insuring my vessels, sometimes for more than they are worth?"

"That, sir, remains a mystery," Watters said.

CHAPTER THREE

The police headquarters at Bell Street was busy as always, with uniformed men arriving for their shifts or marching out for their regular beats. Two men struggled with a well-known prostitute, and one constable nursed a bruised face after attending a domestic dispute between husband and wife. Sergeant Murdoch looked up when Watters came in. "Afternoon, George," he said. "About time you appeared. Mr Mackay has been asking for you this past two hours."

"I've been busy. What does Mr Mackay want?"

"There's been a robbery at Sinclair's the Jewellers in the Nethergate," Murdoch said. "Mr Mackay wants to talk to you about it."

"I'll see him right away," Watters said.

Mr Mackay had his office on the top floor of the building, with a view to the prison next door. He looked up when Watters entered, put down the pen he had been holding and immediately began to speak.

"Have you got your men onto the burglaries yet, Watters?"

"Yes, sir, I have them working on tracing the stolen items." Watters removed his hat and held it under his arm.

"Good," Mackay grunted. "Any results?"

"I'll find out in a few moments, sir. I've been concentrating on the scuttling case." Watters removed his hat and placed it under his arm.

"That should not take long," Mackay said. "Find out who the insurance company pays the money to, and you have your man."

"It doesn't appear to be as simple as that," Watters said. "There are complications."

"Never mind that now," Mackay waved away Watters' words. "The scuttling is in the past; it's done with. This spate of robberies is more important as they are ongoing. I want you to concentrate on them."

"I don't think the scuttling was a one-off," Watters said.

Mackay leaned forward in his chair. "Is *Toiler* sunk?"

"Yes, sir," Watters said.

"Was anybody drowned?"

"No, sir."

"Then it's a simple case of insurance fraud. Put it to the bottom of the pile and deal with it later. These burglaries are becoming serious, Sergeant, so I am ordering you to prioritise them."

"Yes, sir," Watters said.

"Go to Sinclair's Jewellers and find out what happened," Mackay said.

"Yes, sir," Watters turned around and marched out. Not until he returned downstairs did he vent his feelings in a sequence of words that should have blistered the ears of anybody listening.

"Temper now, Sergeant," Murdoch leaned against the corner of a door, puffing on a curved-stemmed pipe.

"I feel I'm making progress on the scuttling case when the old man takes me off and sends me to deal with a jewellery theft!"

"I know," Murdoch said quietly, puffing smoke into the air. "How much was the ship worth?"

"What?"

"The ship, *Toiler*, how much was she worth?"

"About three hundred and fifty pounds," Watters said.

"Well, this particular jewellery theft is worth two and a half thousand pounds, and it's only one of many. Mr Mackay is doing you a favour by steering you away from the scuttling." Murdoch removed the pipe from his mouth to add tobacco. "Anybody who catches the jewel robbery may be in line for a promotion, and wouldn't Marie like that? Especially with her new baby."

"Two and a half thousand pounds!" Watters repeated. "That's twenty years wages."

"I know," Murdoch thrust the pipe back between his teeth. "That's why Mackay wants you to find the thief. He could have sent Lieutenant Anstruther."

"Anstruther couldn't find a puddle in a wet November," Watters said.

"Maybe aye, maybe och aye," Murdoch added more smoke to the air. "But you'd better prove that you are better than him."

The Nethergate was one of Dundee's principal streets, stretching from the City Churches and the High Street until it became the Perth Road and the western highway out of town. The term gate was from the old Scots word gait, meaning a street rather than a place of entrance. With shops at street level and residential tenements above, the Nethergate was bustling with shoppers and crowded with traffic. Sinclair's, the Jewellers, was on the north side, a short step from the prostitute's haven of Couttie's Wynd. Watters saw Jim Bogle, one of his preachers, his informants, standing in the shadows of the Wynd, and nodded.

I'll speak to you later, Jim, my lad.

Mr Sinclair was inside his shop when Watters arrived, with Scuddamore and Duff hurrying in a few minutes later.

"Look what they've done, Sergeant Watters, look what

they've done to my shop!" Sinclair was nearly in tears as he showed Watters the damage. "I had the door double-locked and iron shutters on all the windows. What more could I do?" He held onto Watters' shoulder as if about to collapse. "I ask you, Sergeant Watters, what more could I do?"

"I see they entered through the ceiling," Watters looked at the mess in the back of the shop, with pieces of plaster and timber scattered on the floor.

"Yes," Sinclair said.

Watters prodded his cane at the square hole in the ceiling and pulled at the length of knotted rope that hung from the flat above. "You," Watters pointed to the youngest constable of the half dozen who swarmed in the shop, a man in his early twenties with clear, intelligent-looking eyes. "I don't know you: what's your name?"

"Constable Macpherson, sir, number 147."

"Are you new to the force?"

"Yes, sir."

"Well, welcome to the Dundee Police, and don't call me sir. I'm only a sergeant. Has anybody been up there yet?" Watters pointed to the hole in the ceiling.

"No, Sergeant," Macpherson replied.

"I thought not," Watters said. "Duff, you and Scuddamore take over down here. Check the shop for anything the thieves may have left behind and get these blasted uniformed men away. Post two outside including this Macpherson fellow and send the rest back to Bell Street."

"Yes, Sergeant," Duff said.

"What a bloody mess," Watters said as he climbed up the rope to the house above the shop. As he expected, the burglars had left nothing behind. There were no tools except the rope, no items of clothing. Nothing. Watters checked the front door lock, grunted, untied the rope, and dropped it into the shop below.

"I'll speak to the neighbours," he shouted to Scuddamore through the square hole.

"Yes, Sergeant," Scuddamore was on his hands and knees, sifting through the mess for any clues as Sinclair continued to lament his bad fortune.

The flat above Sinclair's was one of ten in a common stair or a close as the Dundonians termed it. Watters inspected the lock, saw it had not been forced and checked the floor for footprints in the dust. There were two, one without any tread and one a half print of a worn boot.

Two men, then, one wearing rubber over boots to deaden the sound and the other less professional and not successful, judging by the state of his footwear. That's a start.

Watters rapped on each door of the close and spoke to the inhabitants, asking if they had seen any strangers in the area recently.

"Strangers? There are always strangers here," the nearest neighbour viewed Watters with suspicion. "People coming and going all the time."

"Did any of them pay particular attention to the empty house?"

The woman screwed up her face. "The landlord has been trying to make that place respectable these last few weeks." She shook her head. "We used to have a right bad lot in there, Irish, you know, so he's improving it and raised the rent to attract a better class of tenant." She sniffed and looked Watters up and down as if assessing him to see if he was suitable for her close.

"Who is the landlord?"

"I don't know," the woman said. "I know that the factor is John Munro because he's the factor for all the houses in this closie."

"John Munro. I'll speak to him," Watters scribbled down the name. "Thank you. Have there been any interested parties recently?"

The woman frowned and then nodded. "Yes, a few."

"Do you recall any of them?"

"No, they were just people. Quite respectable men mainly, compared to the rubbishy lot we used to have here. I remember that one was a policeman." The woman smiled, with her eyes softening a little. "I hope he gets it. I would feel a lot safer with a policeman in the close, particularly as we're so close to the women in the Wynd." She lowered her voice. "A lot of them are flashtails, you know, hoors!"

Watters nodded. "I am aware that many prostitutes live in the Wynd. Now, this policeman? Do you remember his name or number? He'll have his number on his collar, just here," Watters indicated the spot.

"No, he was quite a handsome chap, though. And well-spoken. I think he was a sergeant or even a lieutenant."

"Thank you," Watters said. If he could find the police officer, he might glean more information.

Attracted by the voices, the other tenants of the close gathered round to give their opinions and advice. "I'll send a police officer to take your statements," Watters promised as he squeezed through the crowd and entered the shop. "Did you find anything, Scuddamore?"

"Not a great deal, Sergeant. The thief picked the locks to get access to the display cases. He knew what he was doing and left no clues, sir." Scuddamore said, "And he was either hungry or very relaxed."

"What makes you say that?"

"Look, Sergeant," Scuddamore pointed to the floor. "Biscuit crumbs."

"Biscuit crumbs?" Watters crouched on the ground. "So they are." He collected a small amount and placed them in a bag. "Sergeant Donaldson found crumbs at the Royal Hotel break-in as well."

"I remember that, Sergeant," Scuddamore said. "Maybe the thief is so nervous that he has to eat something."

"Maybe so," Watters said. "I rather doubt it, though. I suspect it's deliberate." He stood up. "We'll keep the crumbs in mind. Scuddamore, go to the close above and take everybody's statement. Ask if they've seen a police officer looking at the flat and try to get his name. Mr Sinclair," he looked around. "Where's Mr Sinclair? Ah, there you are, sir. How much is missing? Do you have a list for us?"

Sinclair had recovered some of his self-control. "Yes, Sergeant," he said. "I've got everything written down."

"Good," Watters took the list. "I'll have the details sent around the country, and we'll check the local pawns and fences tonight, although I doubt we'll find much in Dundee." He touched Sinclair on the arm, "are you insured, Mr Sinclair?"

The question steadied Sinclair further. "Yes, Sergeant. Yes, I am insured."

"Then I suggest you put in your claim," Watters said. "I also suggest you improve the security of your shop, or any future insurance claims will be invalid."

"What more could I do?" Sinclair asked.

"Put iron plates on the ceiling and floor," Watters said, "or the next burglar will follow the same technique. If they can't get in the doors or windows, they'll come in from above or below."

Sinclair nodded vigorously. "Yes, Sergeant, I'll see to it right away."

"You do that," Watters said. "And maybe employ a dog."

"A dog?"

"Nothing daunts a thief more than a dog. Employ a couple of dogs, a large one with lots of teeth, and a small terrier that barks the alert. A dog is better than a padlock and more reliable than a human watchman." Watters paused. "Watchmen can be bribed or coerced to look the other way."

Having given his advice, Watters had a last scout around the shop. The light reflected on something small on the ground, and he stooped to pick it up. It was a rectangle of thin metal, less than half-an-inch long.

"Is this from your stock, Mr Sinclair?"

"Let me see." Sinclair hurried over, anxious to retrieve any of his stolen goods. "No," he shook his head in disappointment. "That's cheap metal. We don't stock anything of such inferior quality." Sinclair examined it. "You see how it has broken off? That's part of a small buckle. A lady's shoe perhaps, or a pair of braces."

"Thank you, Mr Sinclair," Watters put the piece of buckle safely in his pocket. "I'll keep hold of this for just now."

Duff was watching. "Is that another clue, Sergeant?"

"It may be Duff, or maybe a customer dropped it." Watters lifted the rope he had detached and left the shop. "Come on, Duff, we have some investigating to do."

"What do you think, Sergeant?" Duff stopped outside the shop, where Sinclair could not hear him. "What do you think happened?"

"Two men, Duff. One was a professional who knew exactly what he was doing. At some time over the last few days, he checked the house above the shop, got an impression of the lock and had a false key made. I suspect he came in the guise of a prospective tenant."

"Does the agent keep a list of viewers, Sergeant?"

"You can check, Duff," Watters said. "One of the prospective tenants was a police officer, which might help. Last night, our cracksman returned to the house, wearing rubber overshoes, and with a companion who wore old, worn shoes, a man who is not a success in his profession. He bored the holes to weaken a section of the ceiling, scrambled down the rope, picked the showcase locks, took the best of the jewels, and left the same way. I want to know how many professional thieves in Dundee could do that and who viewed the house."

Duff scratched his head. "Do you think Mr Sinclair was involved, Sergeant?"

"You mean another insurance fraud? Mr Sinclair stealing his own stock and claiming the insurance as well? That's a possibility. I am not discounting any possibility." Watters passed the rope to Duff. "Find out about this rope, Duff. See if it's special in any way and if we can trace it."

"Yes, Sergeant."

"I'm going to speak to the factor of the close," Watters said, "and we'll find out which policeman was interested in renting the house above the jewellers."

John Munro was a plump man with a friendly demeanour and hard eyes. He greeted Watters with an outstretched hand, invited him into his office and produced a pile of documents about the house.

"I'm the factor for the entire close," Munro said. "That residence, 1/1 – the first house on the first floor - has been troublesome for some time, indeed, with a succession of less than reliable tenants." He lowered his voice as if imparting a great secret. "Some of them were Irish."

"Ah," Watters nodded. "Irish."

"I imagine you know all about the Irish, Sergeant." Munro put a finger alongside his nose. "You'll deal with them a lot in your line of work, I imagine."

"My wife is Irish," Watters said blandly. "She's from Dublin."

"Oh," Munro looked away.

"Now, Mr Munro," Watters did not pursue the subject. "Did you keep the names and addresses of the people who were interested in this house?" Watters asked.

"Yes, Sergeant." Munro fumbled through his papers and produced a list.

"Thank you," Watters scanned the names. He knew the cracksman would have visited to inspect the house and get an impression of the lock. However, he would have used a false name. Although some criminals attempted to be very clever by assuming the same alter-egos, in this case, none of the names was familiar. "I see you have a man pretending to be a police Lieutenant," Watters pointed to the name. "Lieutenant Kinghorn."

"Pretending?" Munro said. "I am sure it was no pretence, Sergeant," Munro said.

"Describe him to me," Watters demanded.

Munro looked blank, as Watters had expected.

"Did you meet him?"

"No, Sergeant."

"We have no Lieutenant Kinghorn in the Dundee Police," Watters said. "Who would have met this fellow?"

"The counter clerk," Munro said. "Lieutenant Kinghorn would pick up and sign for the house keys, then return them when he had viewed the property."

The counter clerk had experience in dealing with all the riff-raff of the city. He met tenants daily, from the honest and respectable to the shifty-eyed rogues who would smile as they lied and deceived. He grunted when Watters asked about Lieutenant Kinghorn.

"He seemed a decent fellow," the clerk said. "He was tall, as policemen are, and as far as I remember, he was quietly spoken and polite." The clerk reread the name. "Not all our customers are like that."

"Could you describe him to me?"

"No. He was only another possible tenant. I see twenty a day." The clerk ran a jaundiced eye over Watters. "He was taller than you, sergeant, and dressed in his lieutenant's uniform."

"Thank you for your help," Watters said. He expected no more. Why should anybody recognise a stranger they passed in the street or one customer out of a hundred? In his experience, the average person's descriptions were widely inaccurate at best, and only after gathering half a dozen at least could he create a general impression.

Watters walked back to the police office, swinging his cane.

He had learned a little and made a start towards discovering the identity of the cracksman, with the broken buckle and the two footprints. Watters swung his cane and watched an invisible golf ball speed down the Nethergate. He had a hunch, no more, that there was a connection between the scuttling and the thefts, but for the life of him, he could not see how. At present, it was only a policeman's suspicion, the result of years of experience.

CHAPTER FOUR

DUFF PLACED THE ROPE ON WATTERS' DESK. "IT'S A LENGTH of a foreganger, according to the foreman of Wilson's rope maker's yard."

"A foreganger? What the devil is a foreganger?" Scuddamore asked.

Duff smiled, happy to educate his colleague. "A foreganger is the line that attaches a whaling harpoon to the much heavier whaling line. It's flexible," Duff twisted the rope in his hands, "and sufficiently strong for the whale not to snap it."

"Who do we know with a whaling connection?" Watters asked.

"Mr Muirhead," Scuddamore replied at once.

"Coincidence? Or not." Watters poured himself a mug of tea. "Mr Mackay ordered us to leave the scuttling aside," he reminded, "but we'll keep it in mind, gentlemen."

Scuddamore opened his notebook. "I spoke to everybody in the close," he said.

"Paraphrase your notes." Watters sipped at his tea. "I don't want chapter and verse, only the main points."

"Yes, Sergeant. All the people in the close knew about the empty house. They told me that about twenty prospective tenants had viewed the house, including one man who they said was very shifty and one tall police officer."

"Lieutenant Kinghorn, who does not exist," Watters said quietly. "I suspect that was our cracksman, posing as a policeman." He finished his tea and placed the mug on his desk. "Get back to work, lads. Check the pawns, ask about anybody pawning jewellery or watches, and see what you can discover about this cracksman. There are few such skilled men in Scotland, and we know this cracksman didn't work alone. Somebody will know something, either about the disposal of the stolen goods or the preparations for the robbery. Ask, probe and question, boys. Keep pushing, and something, or somebody, will break."

Watters held the foreganger, his only tangible link between the robberies and the scuttling. He had heard that some detectives solved cases with a flash of inspiration. In his experience, such things did not happen. He solved murders and thefts through patient, inch-by-inch investigative work and understanding how the criminal mind worked. He would tour his network of informants and see what they knew and build up the evidence slowly and carefully. Finishing his tea, Watters rose from the table.

"Is that you off again, Sergeant?" Lieutenant Anstruther asked.

"Yes, sir." Watters reached for his hat and cane.

Anstruther towered over him, threatening because of his height, although he seemed to avoid Watters' gaze. "I'm also investigating some robberies, Sergeant. If you find anything significant, let me know. We can pool our results."

"Yes, sir," Watters was surprised to find Anstruther so cooperative. "That's an excellent idea."

Anstruther took a step back. "So far, we've had little success."

"We're in the early stages, sir," Watters said. "I'll let you know if we find anything significant."

———

The men hunched around a battered circular table, talking together as they sank their pints. "This beer is like old bilge water," the bald headed-one said, wiping the froth from his lips.

"I've tasted better black strap in Shanghai," a squat, pock-marked man commented, half-emptying his glass in a single draught.

"You lads won't be wanting any more then," the third man was taller, with a scar running down his face and the remnants of an army tunic on his back.

"You're not getting out of paying your whack that easily," the bald man said and jerked his chin as Watters stepped into the public house. "Here's trouble. That man's a bluebottle as sure as my name's Dan."

"Aye, the tall man said, "who stole the donkey, eh? Who stole the donkey?"

The three watched as Watters entered. "Well, Betty," Watters leaned over the bar as Arbroath Betty washed the glasses in preparation for the evening's trade. "You know everything that goes on in Dundee."

"Some things, Sergeant Watters," Betty agreed. She looked up, with her broad face suspicious. "What are you looking for this time?"

"Information about the theft at Sinclair the jewellers," Watters said.

"Oh, that," Betty said offhand. "Look around you, Sergeant. Does this look like the sort of establishment a cracksman would use? She indicated the three men at the circular table. "My customers are dockers, Greenlandmen, Baltic seamen, labourers and shipbuilders. I don't deal with upmarket folks like solicitors, merchants and cracksmen."

Betty's public house sat on Dock Street and was usually busy with seamen and maritime workers. She had renamed it

Betty's Welcome, with the name painted in scarlet letters on a yellow background and presided over her customers from a raised floor behind her bar.

"People talk, Betty," Watters said, "and you listen. Has anybody said anything that you may have inadvertently overheard?" He produced half-a-crown and held it up between finger and thumb.

"I hear many conversations," Betty said. "Most of them lies about ships with fast voyages and bigger lies about faster women."

"Did you hear about Sinclair's robbery?" Watters allowed the coin to slip down his thumb until he closed his fist on it.

Betty eyed Watters' hand. "I may have," she said.

"What might you have heard?" Watters turned his back to view the customers. The three men at the circular table quickly looked away, with the scarred man snorting with laughter.

"Who stole the donkey, eh?" The bald man muttered to the contents of his glass.

The scarred man grinned and began to sing.

"When I was a little boy, and so my mother told me,

That if I didn't kiss the girls, my lips would grow all mouldy,"

Betty shook her head. "I heard it was a foreign gentleman who done it," she said.

Watters raised his eyebrows. "What sort of foreign gentleman? Tell me all you heard, Betty."

"I heard he come from overseas," Betty said. "Germany, France, Austria or some such place." She screwed up her face. "Aye, that was it, Austria."

"Who said that?" Watters asked, returning his attention to Betty while keeping his fist closed. He tried to imagine why an Austrian cracksman would rob a jeweller's shop in Dundee when Edinburgh, Glasgow or even London offered much more prosperous targets.

"I don't know," Betty put out her hand hopefully, "but that intelligence is worth a half-dollar, surely?"

"He came from overseas, did he?" Watters placed the silver coin on the bar, then clamped his hand back on it. "You know more than you're telling me, Betty."

"What I told you is worth half a crown." Betty insisted.

Watters removed his hand, and Betty scooped the coin into her apron. "There was one of yours involved," she said.

"One of ours?"

"A bluebottle," Betty explained. "A policeman."

Watters' heartbeat increased. "I know that the cracksman pretended to be a policeman."

Betty turned away. "If that's what you choose to believe."

Watters sighed and fished a florin from his pocket. "Money's tight, Betty and I've got a new mouth to feed."

"That's not my affair," Betty said. "You should learn to keep it in your trousers."

"Tell me about this policeman."

"Show me your silver," Betty countered.

"Goodbye, Betty," Watters spun the florin in the air. "Thank you for your intelligence."

Betty watched the silver coin as Watters adroitly caught it. "The cracksman was working with the bluebottle," she said, "and with a third man."

Watters tried to keep the concern from his face. "I see," he said. "Does this policeman have a name?"

"Of course, he has a name," Betty held out her hand for the florin. "Everybody has a name."

"Do you know this policeman's name?"

"Kinghorn," Betty clutched the coin triumphantly. "Lieutenant Kinghorn."

"Thank you, Betty," Watters walked away, knowing what he had learned was very disturbing.

The three men at the table watched Watters leave, with the scarred man continuing with his song.

"I found myself a Yankee girl, and sure she wasn't civil,
I stuck a plaster on her arse and sent her to the devil."
"Who stole the donkey?" The bald man asked as his companions cackled with laughter. "Who was it, eh?"
What bloody donkey? Watters wondered.

Eddie the Cabbie shook his head. "I don't know nothing about a foreign cracksman, Mr Watters. I never heard anything."

"There were at least two of them, and possibly three." Watters stood at the cab's nearside front wheel, looking up as Eddie sat on his driver's seat at the stance. The waterman, whose job it was to water the horses, hovered out of earshot. "One might have been foreign, and the other could have been a policeman."

Eddie shook his head once more. "That means nothing to me, Mr Watters. I've never heard the lads mention any foreigners in town. None except the German merchants, and they've been coming here for years."

"How about the robbery at Sinclair's?"

"Oh, I heard about that, Mr Watters," Eddie said.

"Tell me what you heard."

"The cracksman broke in from the house above," Eddie removed his bowler hat to scratch his thinning hair. "I heard that right enough."

"Did you get a name, Eddie? Anything I can use?"

Eddie glanced around the cab stance as if he thought the waterman could hear his conversation. "I heard the cracksman was a ticket-of-leave man who had returned before his time."

Watters lifted his head. A ticket-of-leave man was a convict who a judge had ordered transported to Australia, served part of his sentence, and gained limited freedom. If he returned before he completed his full sentence, the authorities would send him back to finish his stretch, often with a few years added. "The cracksman came from overseas, then," he said.

"Yes, Mr Watters," Eddie said. "I suppose he did."

Watters fished another shilling from his pocket. "Thank you, Eddie." The cracksman came to Dundee from Australia, which made much more sense than an Austrian criminal in Dundee. Watters nodded; that was a valuable piece of information. Now he had one more regular informant to see, and then he would try the prostitutes.

Swinging his cane, Watters strolled beside the docks, watching the ships getting ready to sail. The worst of the winter was behind them, and as soon as the northern ice eased, the vessels for Riga and other Baltic ports would slip out of the Tay. The whaling fleet was also preparing for the season, ensuring the hulls were double planked to resist the pressure of the Arctic ice, the metal bow plates were in place, and the internal bracings sufficiently strong. The shouts of sundry mariners came to Watters' ears, reminding him of his time at sea with the Royal Marines.

"Jim, my friend!" Watters shouted as he saw Jim brushing down a horse outside a stable.

"Mr Watters," Jim started at Watters' approach. "I never saw you coming, Mr Watters or I'd have come to meet you." He looked around furtively. "I'm meant to be here, Mr Watters. I've started a new job as a groom. I'm trying to keep inside the law now."

"And I'll help you, Jim," Watters said cheerfully. "No more following young women or looking through windows in Couttie's Wynd, then?"

"No, Mr Watters. I don't do that sort of thing anymore."

"I'm glad to hear it," Watters fondled the horse's muzzle. "Maybe a smart lad like you can help me, Jim."

"Maybe I can, Mr Watters, but I don't know much now. I just work and go home."

"Maybe, maybe not, and maybe you still listen at open windows and hover outside doorways to hear what people are doing." Watters took a practice swipe with his cane, watched an imaginary golf ball soar into the distance and returned his attention to Jim. "The jewel robbery at Sinclair's," he said. "What do you know about it?"

"That wasn't me, Mr Watters," Jim said at once. "I don't do jewel robberies. That was a cracksman and a local lad that done that."

A local lad. Thank you, Jim.

"Now, Jim, I did not accuse you," Watters took another practise swing. "That was a better shot, don't you think, Jim? Did you see how far the ball travelled?"

"Yes, Mr Watters. It was a good shot," Jim said, continuing to brush the horse.

"A cracksman and a local lad, you say? What else do you know, oh, man who no longer listens at doors and windows?"

"Nothing, Mr Watters, I don't know nothing."

"Ah, that's a pity," Watters said. "You don't know about the robberies that pair plan next, then." He cast the idea out, hoping to catch some information.

"Not much, Mr Watters."

"Do you know what I heard?" Watters said. "I heard that you were back to your old games, Jim. I heard you were outside Ma Ramsay's brothel in Couttie's Wynd, staring in the windows."

"I never," Jim said, nearly dropping his brush. "I was just passing by. I never looked in."

"I heard that you played the Peeping Tom, Jim. What would happen if Ma Ramsay found it was you?" Watters allowed the idea to play in Jim's head for a minute. "She would send her bullies after you, Jim, and they would hand you to the girls." Watters shook his head. "I hate to think what they would do."

"I never saw much," Jim said. "Just a little bit."

"Of course, Ma Ramsay doesn't need to know," Watters said. "If I hear more about the jewellery robbery, I'd forget all about the Peeping Tom story."

"It was a local lad and a cracksman, Mr Watters. I know that, and there was a police officer involved. They looked at the house above first and then came back during the night and broke through the ceiling."

"You know more, Jim," Watters tapped the weighted end of his cane in the palm of his left hand.

"The policeman was a sergeant or a Lieutenant," Jim said. "He told the cracksman what to do."

"He was in charge?" Watters asked.

"Yes, Mr Watters. The cracksman was scared of him."

"Do you have any names?"

Jim shook his head. "No, Mr Watters, honest, I don't."

"I believe you," Watters pressed a shilling into Jim's hand. "Thank you, Jim, and I'm glad you've got yourself a steady job."

Jim looked at the shilling. "Thank you, Mr Watters," he said.

Watters looked around when a burly, heavily whiskered man emerged from the stables.

"Now, what's all this, Jim? You're meant to be working, not talking to every waif and stray that passes by!"

"Jim's doing a good job," Watters said. "He's not stopped working for an instant, and he was telling me how efficient your stables were."

"And who are you to judge?" the burly man asked.

"Sergeant George Watters, Dundee Police," Watters said. "We're always looking for a decent stable if our grooms are too busy."

The burly man touched his hat. "Oh, well, we provide a first-class service."

"So Jim was telling me," Watters said and strolled away, swinging his cane.

Three men then. One a returned ticket-of-leave cracksman, one a policeman who might be a sergeant or above, and the other a local thief. Watters pondered the unlikely trio. He would ask the prostitutes next, for the girls often picked up fragments of information from their clients.

———

Watters knew Ma Ramsay of old and entered her brothel without a qualm. He heard the noise of raised voices from upstairs, sighed, and mounted the steps. Why was nothing simple?

"What's going on here?" Watters cracked his cane against the wall. Ma Ramsay was trying to subdue an energetic young man who was shouting and gesticulating to a woman with a shock of black hair.

The man ignored Watters and grabbed hold of the woman by the throat.

"None of that!" Watters slashed the man's arm with his cane. "Leave that woman alone!"

The man started and stared at Watters. "It's none of your bloody business!"

"Dundee Police," Watters said quietly. "Stand back from that woman."

When the man blustered, Watters pushed him aside and pressed the end of his cane into the vee of his throat. "I said back off."

"He's refusing to pay, Sergeant Watters," the black-headed woman said.

"Pay the lady what you owe," Watters pushed his cane harder, "or I'll charge you with assaulting a lady, theft, and creating a disturbance in a private house."

"She's no lady! She's a common hoor!"

Watters slashed with his cane again. "Every lady deserves respect, you dirty-mouthed vagabond! Pay what you owe her and get out!" He reversed the cane and pressed the lead-weighted end against the man's forehead.

The man began to bluster again, saw the expression in Watters' eyes, and reluctantly extracted a handful of copper and silver coins from his pocket. "How much?"

Ma Ramsay selected a few coins, passed one to the black-haired woman, stuffed two inside her voluminous top and nodded. "Thank you, Mister. Now bugger off and don't come back."

The instant Watters relaxed his cane, the man swung his fist at the black-haired woman. Expecting that reaction, Watters blocked the punch and followed through, knocking the man backwards against the wall. As Ma Ramsay reached for her girl, the man lunged again, mouthing obscenities at the black-haired woman, and Watters lashed his arm with the weighted end of his cane.

"You're under arrest, cully! You're not treating a lady like that!"

"No!" Ma Ramsay shook her head. "Don't arrest him, Sergeant. I run a respectable establishment, and I can't have my customers leaving in handcuffs. It's bad for business."

Watters raised his eyebrows. He had expected that such events were an occupational hazard for any establishment in Couttie's Wynd. However, as he was about to ask Ma Ramsay a favour, he decided to agree.

"As you wish, Ma." He leaned closer to the angry man. "What's your name?"

"Herbert Balfour," the man said.

"Well, Herbert Balfour, apologise to the lady."

"Lady!" Balfour sneered until Watters cracked the lead-weighted end of his cane against his left knee.

"Apologise to the lady, Balfour," Watters said.

Balfour mumbled an apology, glaring daggers at Watters.

"Again, and louder," Watters ordered, raising his cane, and Balfour complied.

"I'm very sorry, Meg!"

"Now leave."

As Balfour turned away, Ma Ramsay delivered a hefty kick to his backside. "And don't come back!" she said.

"Thank you, Sergeant Watters," the black-haired woman said. "Nobody's ever called me a lady before."

"No? Well, you are a lady, Meg. I remember you from a previous case when you were helpful to me."

Meg glanced at Ma Ramsay as if seeking permission to speak.

Watters forced a smile. "If that fellow Balfour causes more trouble, let me know. Don't you usually have a trio of porters here to deal with men like him?"

"I had to get rid of them, and I'm looking for replacements," Ma Ramsay said. "What are you here for, Sergeant? And it's not for the good of our health."

Watters explained his purpose.

"I heard about the robbery," Ma Ramsay said. "Two men done it, one a cracksman and another who watched him."

"Watched him? Was the second man an apprentice?" Watters asked.

"No," Meg shook her head, so her black hair covered her face. "He was making sure the cracksman never kept anything for himself. I heard they worked for a third man, who had a hold on the cracksman. They were feared of him."

"Thank you," Watters stored that information away.

"If we hear anything else, we'll let you know," Ma Ramsay said. "

Hairy Meg lifted a hand as Watters left and mouthed 'thank you" again.

If I've done nothing else today, Watters thought, *at least I've helped one young woman gain some self-respect.*

CHAPTER FIVE

LIEUTENANT ANSTRUTHER STOOD INSIDE THE DOOR OF THE
Bell Street Police Office, watching as Watters returned from
his questioning. "You look like a man who failed," Anstruther
said. "What's on your mind, Watters?"

"That's Sergeant Watters, sir," Watters said, "and I haven't
failed."

"Oh? You were investigating the jewel robbery, weren't
you?" Anstruther stepped forward.

"That's correct, sir," Watters said.

"What have you discovered so far, if anything?"

Watters paused before he replied. "My informants have
told me there are three people involved, sir. They think one is
a professional cracksman, a returned ticket-of-leave man, but
the others they don't know."

Anstruther gave a small smile. "I could have told you the
thief was a professional, Watters."

"Yes, sir, I am sure you could."

"What the devil do you mean by that, Watters?"
Anstruther leaned over Watters, then moved away before
Watters held his gaze.

"I mean, you have experience in such matters, sir," Watters said. "Now, if you will excuse me, I must continue."

Why did I not tell Anstruther about the possible police involvement? Was it because I don't like the man? Or was it something else?

Duff and Scuddamore were waiting in the office, both trying to ignore the growing pile of paperwork.

"Did you find anything in the pawns?" Watters asked.

"We didn't find any of the stolen jewellery," Scuddamore took the role of spokesman. "The pawns knew all about the Sinclair robbery and said nobody had approached them that morning."

"The thieves are aware we'd check the pawnshops," Watters said. "I've sent Sinclair's list all around Scotland and some cities in England, so we'll see if that produces any results." He mustered a smile. "You know these things take time, lads. Keep trying, keep pushing, and something will happen. Even the smartest of cracksmen makes a mistake."

"Yes, Sergeant," Scuddamore said. "Duff and I put our heads together and compiled a list of any cracksmen with the skill to carry out these thefts."

Watters nodded. "He'd have to be able to scale walls and break into houses, hotels and jewellery shops as well as crack safes. That's a rare selection of skills."

"Yes, Sergeant," Scuddamore said. "We narrowed the list to eight, and some of them are already jailed or dead."

"Eight is more than I expected," Watters said. "I'm listening."

Scuddamore lifted a sheet of paper from his desk. "We have Arthur Cobb and Walter Abernethy. Owen Williams and Peter Hayes. Then there is John McLeish, Martin Lightfoot, Charlie Peace, and Nathan Johnston." Scuddamore looked up. "There might be more, Sergeant, but we can't think of them."

"Eight is quite enough to be going on with," Watters said. "Let's take these fellows one at a time. What do we know about Arthur Cobb?"

"He's a Londoner, Sergeant, never been known to leave the London area," Scuddamore said at once.

"It's doubtful he'd come up here then. We offer poor pickings compared to London." Watters said. "I think a major haul might tempt him, but not a few hundred guineas from Sinclair's jewellers shop."

"Lightfoot?" Watters asked.

Scuddamore grunted. "Went down for a seven stretch last year, but men such as him may break out."

They examined the list, with one or other of the detectives displaying their knowledge of the criminal fraternity as they discounted each man.

"That leaves Peter Hayes and Walter Abernethy," Watters said.

"We can discount Abernethy," Duff said. "He was transported for fourteen years some time ago. And Hayes is dead."

"Wait," Watters held up a hand. "You say Abernethy was transported?"

"He got fourteen years," Duff said.

"My informants told me the cracksman was a ticket of leave man. A Demonian returned before his time."

"That might be him, then," Scuddamore said. "Did Abernethy have any Dundee connections?"

"Find out," Watters ordered and snapped his fingers. "Abernethy, by God! Remember the biscuit crumbs on the floor? I'd bet a farthing to your pension, Scuddamore, that they came from an Abernethy biscuit."

"The cheeky rascal!" Scuddamore said with a hint of respect.

"Do you think he's telling us who he is?" Duff asked.

"Yes," Watters said. "Some of these cracksmen are proud of their housebreaking skills. Maybe Abernethy is one such." He became aware of Lieutenant Anstruther standing two desks away. "Can we help you, sir?"

"What's that you're discussing, Watters?"

"That's Sergeant Watters, sir, and we're discussing who the cracksman might be."

"He could be anybody, Sergeant. You'd be better trying to catch him rather than playing guessing games with names."

"We'll do both, sir," Watters promised. "Have you made any progress with your investigation? Did you think anything more about the biscuit crumbs you found?"

"Biscuit crumbs?" Anstruther turned sideways to view Watters through his right eye. "No, Sergeant. The crumbs were not relevant."

"I see, sir," Watters nodded.

"Lieutenant Anstruther," Scuddamore said when Anstruther withdrew to his private office on the floor above. "What was the false name of the Lieutenant who scouted the house above Sinclair's?"

"Kinghorn," Duff said. "Anstruther and Kinghorn are both towns on the south coast of Fife. Somebody else seems to be playing guessing games with names."

Watters shook his head. "Anstruther is not my favourite person either, boys, but he's not stupid enough to say he's a police Lieutenant when he visits a place he intends to burgle. I doubt that Anstruther's our man. I'd wager your pension again, Scuddamore, that our supposed Lieutenant is no policeman."

"Maybe somebody who could not come up to scratch in the force, Sergeant?" Duff hazarded. "Or an officer with a grudge." He looked around the duty room as if assessing every man present.

"That could be. In the meantime, see what we can come up with on Abernethy. I have to visit Mr Mackay." Watters stood up. "There'll be overtime tonight, lads, so don't expect to get much sleep." He glanced around the room. "And we'll keep this to ourselves. Don't let the word spread."

"You mean Lieutenant Anstruther?"

"I mean, we don't know if there's a police officer

involved," Watters said, "and I don't think there is, but we'll just go canny until we're sure."

————

Mr Mackay pressed his fingers together as he listened to Watters. "Walter Abernethy, you say." He nodded slowly. "I remember him. He was transported a few years back."

"Yes, sir."

"He was a professional thief," Mackay said. "We don't want that type roving around Dundee. I'll call a meeting and spread the word."

"We could set a trap for this fellow," Watters suggested. "Create a target so tempting than no self-respecting cracksman could ignore it and wait for him there."

Mackay mused for only a moment. "All right. I'll tell the men what's happening, and you catch this Abernethy fellow if it's him."

"Yes, sir."

"Do you have anything else for me, Sergeant?"

Watters hesitated. He did not like to withhold information from Mackay, a man he both trusted and respected, but he preferred to wait until he had more definite intelligence.

"We've nothing concrete, sir. My preachers, my informants, tell me that there were two or maybe three men involved."

Mackay's fingers tapped their devil's dance on the desk. "That's a start, Sergeant. You have numbers and a name. Dismissed."

Scuddamore and Duff listened as Watters outlined his idea. "Now spread the news," Watters said. "Not overtly, of course. Just a whisper here and there, a few hints to raise interest, and tickle Abernethy's fancy."

"Will Abernethy bite?" Scuddamore asked.

"I hope so," Watters said. "Either Abernethy or the man

who seems to control him. If we catch one, we should catch them both."

"What about the scuttling case?" Duff asked.

"That will have to wait," Watters replied. "I don't think we're finished with it yet, but Mr Mackay is more concerned with the cracksman."

"What's the plan, Sergeant?" Constables Boyle and Shaw hurried across the duty room, still eager despite the lines of tiredness that scored their faces.

"It's straightforward. We spread the word that the bank is delivering a month's advance of wages for the Waverley whaling ships, and we wait in his shipping office in Dock Street."

"Old Man Gilbride's Waverley ships? Muirhead's main whaling rival?" Boyle proved he was knowledgeable about current affairs in Dundee.

Watters smiled. "The very fellow! What better way of seeing if Muirhead is involved in the thefts than invite him to steal from his business rival?"

"You're a cunning man, Sergeant," Scuddamore said.

More devious than you realise, Scuddamore. If Abernethy falls for this, then we don't have a police officer involved. If he refuses the bait, then I will be more worried.

"One thing, boys," Watters said, "there were some men in Betty's Welcome, and they wondered who had stolen the donkey. They spoke to each other but wanted me to hear. Any ideas?"

Duff shrugged, while Scuddamore nodded.

"Aye, Sergeant, it's a joke against the police. I think it was in London that somebody stole a donkey, and the police failed to solve the case."

Watters nodded. "I see."

"There is an answer, Sergeant," Scuddamore said. "You say the man in the white hat because hatters use donkey skins to make white hats."

"Thank you, Scuddamore. You are a constant fund of information."

———

Dundee was quiet at two in the morning, with most public houses having long spilt their rowdy customers into the streets. Only a few men strode to their work or walked wearily home while the night-duty policemen watched for thieves. Watters entered the Bell Street Office and nodded to the sergeant on duty.

"Evening, Ruxton."

"You're working late, Watters."

"I've just a few odds and ends to tidy up while it's quiet." Watters signed himself in. "Is anybody else in?"

"Only me, a turnkey and a couple of constables."

Watters nodded and hurried upstairs to the duty room. The place was deserted and dark until Watters lit the gas and allowed the light to ease over the room. Watters thought there was something desolate about a near-empty room that was usually full of uniformed men.

After a few moments, Watters left the duty room and slipped quietly to the upper floors, where Mr Mackay and the lieutenants had their offices. He tried the handle of Lieutenant Anstruther's door, but the door remained fast.

Why lock your door within the police headquarters? What are you hiding, Lieutenant Anstruther? Watters had come prepared with his packet of lock-picks, so he knelt at the door and opened it within thirty seconds.

Closing the door, Watters lit the gas and kept the flame low, providing only a minimum of light. Anstruther's office was less than half the size of Mackay's, with a desk, two chairs, a stand-up mirror, and a bookcase filled with documents, books, and files. Watters moved straight to the desk, picked each lock, and opened the drawers one by one. He had no clear idea of his objective but wanted to either clear Anstruther of his suspicions or find something incriminating.

The top drawer held only stationary, pens and ink. The second contained a small revolver and ammunition, while the third was empty except for a leather-covered wooden box. Watters opened it carefully and stepped back when a pair of human eyes glared back at him.

"What the devil?"

Watters lifted the artificial eye carefully between his finger and thumb. It was beautifully made, coloured like a human eye and heavier than he expected.

"I didn't know you only had one eye, Lieutenant," Watters said. He shrugged. That would explain why Lieutenant Anstruther always kept his distance. It was not guilt but embarrassment over his glass eye.

Closing the drawer, Watters saw Anstruther's spare uniform hanging beside the mirror. He stepped across and, on a whim, lifted the coat. The trousers and jacket were beneath, with a pair of braces hanging down. Watters lifted them and grunted when he saw a brass buckle in place of the steel buckle that was regulation issue.

Watters left the room and returned to his desk downstairs.

CHAPTER SIX

PATROLLING THE PAWNSHOPS WAS THE MOST TEDIOUS PART OF A detective's duties, Watters thought, as he walked his allocated area around the maritime quarter, searching the pawns for stolen items from his list.

Watters' first call was at Mrs Flannery's, a small pawn off Dock Street itself. He knew Mrs Flannery as an honest woman, so he did not waste much time.

"Have you seen the latest list, Mrs Flannery?"

"I've only glanced at it, Sergeant Watters," Mrs Flannery said. "I don't welcome the criminal fraternity into my shop, and they know I'd report anything stolen."

"You're a good woman, Mrs Flannery," Watters lifted his hat as he left.

Watters' fourth call was at the Dundee Exchange Emporium, a much grander establishment with three polished brass balls hanging above the door and recently washed plate glass windows.

"You're back then, Sergeant?" The owner leaned over the counter, seeming quite relaxed in Watters' presence.

"I'm back," Watters scanned the shop, fully aware that the

owner was too canny to have any suspicious goods on display. "Anything for me today, Wullie?"

"Not today, Sergeant."

"Nothing you're willing to admit to, anyway," Watters said.

"I'm an honest man, Sergeant Watters!" Wullie spread his arms to prove his honesty.

Watters nodded. "Of course you are. Not like this professional cracksman causing all sorts of mayhem in Dundee."

Wullie, short, fat and with thick glasses, nodded. "I heard about him, Sergeant. We don't want his sort in town."

"No, we don't," Watters agreed. "How much do you know about him?"

Wullie assumed an air of complete innocence. "Not much, Sergeant. I heard he was here, that's all. He won't come into my establishment; everybody knows I never accept stolen goods!"

"You're one of the most honest pawnbrokers in the city," Watters said solemnly.

"Thank you, Sergeant," Wullie adjusted his glasses.

Watters nodded. "It's been months since I last found stolen property in here," he said, "and I know you'd tell me if anybody handed any in."

"I would," Wullie said.

Watters glanced over his shoulder as if nervous he may be overheard. "If you hear anything about this cracksman, let me know, will you? Especially now."

"Especially now?" Wullie leaned over his counter, seeking intelligence to pass on to his less reputable customers.

"Mr Gilbride of the Waverly Company is a bit concerned," Watters said and nodded. He did not need to say more.

"Ah," Wullie tried to look intelligent. "I see. Mr Gilbride."

Lifting his cane in acknowledgement, Watters left the pawnshop. He had planted the first seed. Now Wullie would spread it to the petty thieves who frequented his shop, and the news would spread up the tree to the upper branches of the criminal classes.

Swinging his cane at imaginary golf balls, Watters continued his patrol.

"Jim!" Watters hailed the furtive youth who tried to hide in a shop doorway.

"I wasn't doing anything, Mr Watters," Jim said immediately.

"I didn't think you were," Watters tapped Jim's leg with his cane. "How is your job doing, Jim?"

"I lost it, Mr Watters," Jim looked at the ground.

"I'm sorry to hear that, Jim. Why was that?"

"It was because I've no home, Mr Watters. I sleep in penny-a-night lodging houses, and Mr Arthur said he wanted somebody more respectable."

Watters frowned. Life was unfair to youths such as Jim. "I need a favour from you, James."

"A favour, Mr Watters?" Jim's eyes narrowed in avarice.

"Indeed. Have you heard any more about this cracksman in Dundee?"

"No, Mr Watters," Jim shook his head, causing his dark hair to flop around his head. "I would tell you if I had."

"Of course you would, James. You and I are chums."

"Yes, Mr Watters," Jim said. "We're chums."

Watters lowered his voice. "Between you and me, Jim, there's a strongbox full of advance wages in Dundee, and I'm a bit concerned that this mysterious cracksman will go after it."

"Wages, Mr Watters?"

"Yes indeed," Watters swished his cane again. "Some hundreds of pounds, I believe."

"Where are they, Mr Watters?"

"I can't tell you that, Jim," Watters said. "I can't tell anybody; I've already said more than I should."

Jim nodded. "Yes, Mr Watters. I understand."

Watters pressed a shilling into Jim's grubby hand. "Remember, if you hear anything, let me know right away."

"I will, Mr Watters," Jim said. "I won't let you down."

Watters walked on. He knew that Jim would sell his information in the Baltic Bar or Betty's Welcome to whoever was interested, and it would filter around Dundee.

"That's the ground prepared," Watters said to his men as they met in the duty room. "Within a couple of hours, all Dundee's criminals will know that Mr Gilbride is anxious and that somebody is hoarding advance wages. They'll put two and two together, and Mr Gilbride can expect a nocturnal visitor."

"Yes, Sergeant."

Watters sipped at his tea. "Now that we've told Abernethy what to steal, we must ensure the beat police are not too watchful." He raised a hand as Sergeant Murdoch entered the room. "Murdoch! Where will I find Boyle and Shaw?"

"Dudhope Street, Constitution Road and that area," Murdoch glanced at his watch. "If they're following the correct procedure, they should be in Dudhope Terrace in about ten minutes."

"Thank you, Murdoch; I'll find them later," Watters said. "These two want to be detectives, so we'll use them, boys."

———

Mr Gilbride ran his Waverly Whale Fishing Company from offices in East Whale Lane. Watters led his detectives to the office, spoke to a somewhat confused office clerk and then mounted the stairs to Gilbride's small but immaculate office on the upper floor.

Gilbride was an elderly man with silver hair and bushy side-whiskers on either side of sunken cheeks. He had a reputation for being a shrewd businessman.

"Which room will you allow us to use, Mr Gilbride?"

"One on the ground floor," Gilbride said. "We call it the spare room, and the sooner this fellow is caught, the safer we will all feel." He stood up, lifted his narwhal tusk walking stick, and pointed to the door. "Come along, gentlemen."

Watters inspected the spare room, small, with a barred window and a single entrance; it was suitable for storing cash. "Do you have a safe, Mr Gilbride?"

"I have two, Sergeant. A large, complex one in the basement strong room, and a small office safe."

"Empty the contents of the office safe into the larger one, if you please, Mr Gilbride, and bring the office safe in here. Allow your staff to see it enter the room and make a fuss about its security."

"As you wish, Sergeant Watters."

"Thank you, Mr Gilbride. The Dundee Police appreciate your co-operation."

Gilbride's barked orders brought a group of workmen with a sturdy hand barrow. Watters and Duff helped manoeuvre the square, steel safe from Gilbride's office to the spare room.

"Tuck it against the back wall," Gilbride said and ensured it was empty. "Thank you, men," Gilbride said.

Watters waited until the workmen had left the room. "May I have another moment of your time, Mr Gilbride?"

"Of course, Sergeant."

"You must know Mr Muirhead well," Watters said.

"I have known him these past fifteen years and more," Gilbride said.

"Could you tell me your opinion of him, sir?"

Gilbride looked irritated for a second. "I don't like to discuss such things, Sergeant. It's impolite to talk about a fellow behind his back."

"Would you say Mr Muirhead is an honest man?" Watters ignored the implied complaint.

"I have never found him less than honest," Gilbride said.

"And fair in his business dealings?"

"Scrupulously fair," Gilbride agreed.

"That agrees with my impression of the man," Watters said. "I think he is a hard businessman but honest."

Gilbride nodded. "Business is a hard world," he said. "The weak go under, and the men who depend on a weak manager for jobs will find themselves unemployed."

Watters smiled faintly at the neat way Gilbride had justified his business methods. "Would that apply to Mr Muirhead as well?"

"Mr Muirhead will do whatever he needs to gain financial success," Gilbride said, "as would any good man of business. He will not lie or cheat, but nor will he hesitate to take any advantage within the law."

Watters nodded. He was gradually building up a picture of Muirhead. "Thank you again, Mr Gilbride. Now we'll get you some attention and try to entice our cracksman friend to our trap. Come into my parlour, said the spider."

Watters had arranged for Eddie the Cabbie to bring his cab to the front of Gilbride's office. He stood beside the cab, with his detectives at his side.

"You remain here, Duff, and look inconspicuous. Scuddamore and I will bring in the wages."

"Yes, Sergeant," Duff said, grinning. He was probably the shortest policeman in Dundee and the broadest across the shoulders. He leaned against the entrance to Mr Gilbride's office, produced a pipe and lit up.

"Tayside Bank," Watters ordered Eddie and sat back. Without moving his head, he saw the group of loungers watching from the corner of the lane.

"We're being watched, Scuddamore," he said.

"Four of them, Sergeant," Scuddamore had given no indication of seeing anything. "Including Rab McGavin and Andy Taylor, Lochee weavers and part-time bullies."

"Good man, Scuddamore," Watters said. "They don't have the brainpower to be cracksmen, so somebody has sent them to watch old man Gilbride's establishment." He grinned. "We're making an impact."

Eddie drove them to the bank, where MacBride welcomed them in with a hearty handshake.

"Who are you setting up, gentlemen?" MacBride asked.

"A man who would rob you blind, sir," Watters said. "Please ensure your bank is safe this season. Take every precaution you can and then double them. This fellow has robbed jeweller's shops and hotels across the town."

"I will," the manager said. "I have warned my staff."

Watters and Scuddamore left the bank carrying a heavy strongbox, complete with a padlock, which they hefted into Eddie's cab.

"Who's watching us this time?" Watters murmured.

"Wee Owan MacMillan," Scuddamore said. "He's standing in the doorway of a close, smoking a clay pipe."

"He's a friend of Thiefy Campbell," Watters said. "I caught MacMillan breaking into a house last year, and the judge gave him six months. The criminal fraternity is aware of everything we do."

"I'd like to round the lot up and throw them in jail," Scuddamore said. "We know who they are; we could halve the crime in Dundee in one night."

Watters grunted. "A lot of people would agree with you, Scuddamore, but we need evidence of a specific crime before we arrest anybody."

"We're too soft with them," Scuddamore glanced out of the window. "MacMillan is following us."

"That's not surprising."

Duff was where they had left him, still smoking as Eddie drew up outside the office.

"We'll need your muscles, Duff," Watters called. "The box

isn't too heavy, but you look sufficiently formidable to frighten the Cossacks, let alone a Scottish cracksman."

McGavin and Taylor watched with interest as Scuddamore and Duff carried the strongbox into the building.

"I rather hoped they would try and wrestle it from us," Scuddamore said.

"Not with Duff here," Watters replied. "McGavin and Taylor are fine at hustling drunkards out of pubs and brothels, but that's their limit."

Mr Gilbride ushered them into the spare room, where the safe lay open. "In here, gentlemen."

Duff and Scuddamore laid the strongbox on the floor. "It will fit into the safe as it stands," Watters said. "Extra security." He grinned.

"What's inside?" Gilbride asked. "Nothing too valuable, I hope?"

"House bricks," Watters said. "If the cracksman manages to steal it, he'll get a horrible surprise."

"What now?" Scuddamore asked as they left the building.

"Now, we put two uniformed police on watch outside," Watters said, "and we observe from a distance."

"The uniforms will warn the cracksman off," Duff pointed out. "He won't try anything with a couple of constables there."

"The constables I have in mind won't be any threat," Watters said with a smile. "Our very own Boyle and Shaw."

"I thought Boyle was fairly intelligent," Scuddamore looked confused.

"He is sufficiently intelligent to act stupid," Watters said. "I have instructed them both what to do and provided an excuse to distract them from their duty."

"What's that, Sergeant?" Scuddamore asked as Duff laughed.

"You'll see," Duff said.

Sending Eddie away with instructions to come to Bell

Street in two hours, Watters led his men towards the Police Office, fully aware that half the criminals in Dundee would be watching him. Reminding Boyle and Shaw of their roles, he sent them to Gilbride's office.

"Now what?"

"Now we catch a cab," Watters said, "and keep the curtains drawn."

CHAPTER SEVEN

When Eddie arrived at the back door of the police office, Watters and the detectives boarded his cab.

"I'm getting a new cab soon, Sergeant," Eddie said. "I want a Hansom rather than this old-fashioned growler."

"There's less room in a Hansom," Watters said.

"Aye, but it's lighter, faster and more manoeuvrable. This old thing is clumsy, and Dundee's streets are getting right busy."

"You must be making good money, then, Eddie."

"Here you are, Mr Watters." When Eddie pulled up outside a semi-derelict building, Scuddamore and Duff disembarked to walk in different directions. Watters had chosen a suitable location for each detective to overlook Gilbride's offices.

"Thank you, Eddie." Watters said. "You know where to go next?"

"I have the address, Sergeant, Watters." Eddie touched his whip to the brim of his bowler hat.

"Take care of them."

"I will." Eddie cracked the reins and rumbled off.

Watters had chosen a location where he could see a

section of Whale Lane and the back of Gilbride's office. He settled down with a hunk of bread-and-cheese.

After all these arrangements, we had better catch Abernethy.

After half an hour, Watters saw Boyle and Shaw walk around the building, checking the doors and windows, as their duty demanded. They talked noisily, with Shaw lighting a pipe against regulations and Boyle pulling a newspaper from the pocket of his coat.

"Keep it up, lads," Watters said to himself as Boyle pointed out something in the newspaper to Shaw, who laughed, jabbing the stem of his pipe in the air.

They're playing their part well. Here comes the next stage.

The two women walked arm in arm along East Whale Lane. One carried a baby, while the other was a few years younger but very confident in her carriage. Watters watched anxiously, unsure if he had done the right thing.

The two women, Marie, and Duff's sweetheart Rosemary, began to talk to the two constables, distracting them from their duty. Boyle and Shaw played along, responding with laughter and loud voices, accompanying the women to the end of the lane, where Duff had concealed himself. Watters did not like the idea of Marie walking in the dark street, but with two uniformed police at their side and Duff and Scuddamore only a hundred yards away, he had reconciled himself. The idea had been Marie's, and once considered, she refused all Watters' arguments about the danger.

"You'll be there," Marie had reminded, smiling sweetly but with fire in her eyes, "and Constable Duff. It would take a brave Burker to face Duff!"

"You don't know what sort of men are out there," Watters said.

"I'm not as innocent as you seem to think!" The fire was growing hotter, and the sweetness diminishing as Marie's determination grew.

"You take care, then!" Watters surrendered while trying to have the final word.

Knowing she had won, Marie was gracious in victory. "You'll take care of me," she had said, dousing the flames with a smile.

Now Watters watched the police wander off with his wife and Rosemary, and then a man emerged from the shadow beneath a streetlamp. Medium height and dressed in dark clothing, he carried a carpet bag.

Got you, cully, Watters thought. *Get out of the street, Marie!*

Watters felt his tension rise as the man crouched beneath the back window of Gilbride's office. He watched as the burglar extracted a piece of cord and a length of metal from his bag.

I know that technique, Watters thought.

The burglar looped his cord around two of the bars on the window and twisted with the metal. After a few moments, the pressure forced the bars apart. The gap was not sufficiently wide to attract attention, but the burglar slipped his hand inside and carefully scraped out the putty from one pane of glass.

This fellow knows what he's doing.

Removing the pane, the burglar inserted his hand through the gap, unlatched the window and pushed it up. Only a small man could wriggle through the hole, but the burglar managed without difficulty. He pulled the pane of glass after him, placed a sheet of dark paper over the missing pane, pushed the two loose bars together and closed the window. With the dark paper looking like glass, only the most observant of passers-by would notice anything amiss.

Now, what will you do? Watters wondered. *You can't carry the strongbox out of that small space. And where is your companion? All my informers told me you worked with somebody else.*

Some cracksmen came supplied with a pony and gig, which they parked nearby. They would rob the premises, then run to the gig and drive from the robbery to their headquarters. Watters had Eddie's cab parked a street away just in case he was required. However, he had not heard the rumble of wheels on the cobbles nor the jingle of harness.

You're on foot, my friend, Watters said. *That means you are local.* Knowing that Duff and Scuddamore were watching the front of the building, Watters kept his concentration on the back window. He saw the faint glimmer of light inside the room, guessed that the cracksman was working by candlelight and smiled. *You're still there. Well, so am I.*

After twenty minutes, Watters saw the window slide open. The burglar pushed the bars slightly further apart and thrust his head outside, scanning the dark street. Watters withdrew an inch, although he knew it would take a good man to spot him through a half-closed wooden shutter.

Watters hardly heard the cracksman's low whistle. McGavin and Taylor responded, pushing a handcart across the cobbles, with one or the other checking around him with every fifth step. The cart was well greased, for it made little sound.

Using the same technique as the cracksman, McGavin and Taylor wrestled aside the window bars and then, quicker than Watters believed possible, manoeuvred them free from their stone base to create a much wider gap.

That will cost something to repair. I hope Mr Mackay thinks it worth the money because Mr Gilbride will send us the account.

As Watters watched, McGavin slipped through the gap and helped the cracksman carry the strongbox outside. Taylor stood watch, with his head darting this way and that, like a finch searching for a sparrowhawk.

Right, my lads, Watters said, as McGavin loaded the box onto the handcart. *I've got you now.*

Taylor threw a ragged blanket over the strongbox to disguise the shape, and all three thieves hurried along the street, with the cart making no noise at all. *You've done this before,*

Watters thought as he left his observation perch to follow the thieves.

Watters was experienced in following suspects, so even in the quiet streets, he managed to remain out of sight. He timed his steps to coincide with those of McGavin, so nobody would hear him and kept sufficiently far back to avoid detection. Taylor was the most nervous of the three thieves, watching everything and turning every dozen steps to peer behind him. Watters recognised the pattern and slipped into doorways or areas of shadow every ten steps, so there was no movement to alarm his quarry.

When they passed the entrance to Whale Lane, Watters stepped into the light for a moment, aware that one of his detectives, or one of the uniformed men, were expecting to see him. Watters had given instructions that the uniforms would remain in place to guard Gilbride's office while the detectives would follow him.

Taking the back streets and wending through a myriad closes and wynds, the thieves came to St Clement's Lane, a narrow street with crowded housing and the original base for Dundee's Police Office. Watters noted the three thieves were masters in avoiding the beat police's patrol routes and wondered if he should suggest that Lieutenant Anstruther or Sergeant Murdoch alter the times. Taylor slid into the shadows and pulled a blackjack from his sleeve, standing guard while the others tapped at a closed door. Watters noted the distinctive knock, rap- rap- rap, three slow then three rap, rap, rap, in quick succession.

When the door opened, McGavin and the cracksman lifted the strongbox and carried it inside. Taylor backed in last, still scanning the dark lane with his blackjack held ready.

Watters nodded as Duff and Scuddamore joined him, saying nothing. Watters held his cane firmly, with the lead-weighted end upward, ready to strike, and counted to ten, feeling the tension mount inside him. He nodded to Scuddamore, who moved up the lane to an area known as the Vault, searching for a back entrance to the house.

Still silent, Watters stepped to the door with Duff in support. The dark paintwork on the door was peeling to reveal a lighter colour beneath. Watters wondered how many layers of paint there were and how long it had been in place. He lifted his cane. Rap – rap – rap, three slow and then three fast taps.

Watters stepped aside and back, holding his cane ready to strike and reassured by the muscular bulk of Duff at his side. It was only a few weeks since a criminal had injured Duff in a fight outside Dundee, so Watters hoped his arm was fit to fight. A glance at him revealed the broad policeman standing quite relaxed with his staff like a toy in his massive fist.

Here we go. We're coming, Abernethy.

Watters heard voices from within the house, a low murmuring that increased in volume. He guessed the inhabitants were discussing whether to answer the door or not.

"Shall I break it down, Sergeant?" Duff asked, hopefully.

Watters glanced at his watch; he had allowed Scuddamore sufficient time to find a rear entrance. The tension was building up.

"Dundee Police!" Watters roared; he tried the door and found it locked. "Open up!" He nodded to Duff. "On you go, Duff."

Duff had two techniques for opening locked doors. One was a full-blooded shoulder charge, and the other a simple raised boot and mighty kick. He used the second method, and the door shuddered but held.

"They've bolted it," Duff said, took three steps back and charged. With his full weight behind him, Duff smashed open the door in a welter of splintered wood and wrenched-out bolts. Watters rushed in, cane ready. As he expected, Taylor met him with a swinging blackjack.

"No, you don't!" Watters blocked the weapon with his

cane, shifted his feet and punched Taylor, left-handed, in the throat, sending him staggering backwards.

As Duff recovered from his initial shoulder charge, Watters looked around. The room was small and had once been ornate, with a corniced ceiling and a large stone fire-place. Now, years of neglect had tarnished the cornices while patches of plaster peeled from the wall to fall on the bare floorboards. A single bed and a battered deal table with two chairs made up the only furniture, and the only other door at the back of the room was ajar.

McGavin and the cracksman crouched over the half-open strongbox, staring, while Owan MacMillan reached for a weapon.

"Dundee Police!" Watters shouted again as he pointed his cane. "You are all under arrest."

MacMillan snarled something incoherent, lifted a poker, and rushed at Watters, while McGavin seemed frozen to the spot. Only the cracksman had the sense to turn and flee.

Duff grinned as MacMillan banged into him.

"You'll have to do better than that, cully!" He threw the thief aside. MacMillan gave a mouthful of obscenities, grabbed the poker, and swung at Watters, who dodged.

"Bluebottle bastards!" MacMillan said and thrust the metal point of the poker at Duff's groin.

"Aye, would you, now?" Duff sucked in his middle and gave what looked like a casual swing that spun MacMillan against the far wall.

"I give up!" McGavin raised both hands in the air, realised that both detectives were fully occupied, dropped his arms and bolted through the door in the wake of the cracksman.

"Bugger!" Watters swore. "You take these two, Duff!" He was not particularly interested in MacMillan or Taylor but knew the operation would be wasted unless he caught the cracksman. The others were merely petty thieves, local ne'er-do-wells that the beat policemen could pick up any time.

Following McGavin, Watters ran through the door and looked around. He was in the house's back room, empty except for a small pile of clothes and minor artefacts that McGavin and his companions had undoubtedly stolen, and the only window was open.

Without hesitation, Watters lunged through the window. He was in an alley so narrow only one man at a time could squeeze through, and in the darkness, he could see nobody.

Which way did McGavin run? Watters looked right and left. *Choose!*

"Got you, my man!" Scuddamore's cheerful voice rang out. "Where do you think you are going?"

"Scuddamore," Watters shouted. "Did you get the cracksman?" The noise had awakened the neighbourhood, with lighted candles appearing at windows and querulous voices echoing in the echoing cavern of the Vault. A few of the braver inhabitants ventured out of their doors, armed with lanterns, and various weapons from pokers to broomsticks.

"Dundee police!" Watters shouted again. "Everything is under control! Please go back to your beds!"

"Can't you make less noise?" A man asked. "Some of us have work in the morning!"

Scuddamore appeared, holding McGavin with both arms twisted behind his back. "Good evening, Sergeant," Scuddamore said. "I found this beauty trying to run away. Do you want him?"

"Not particularly," Watters said, "but Perth Prison might. Did you get the other fellow, the cracksman?"

"Give me a minute, Sergeant, until I get McGavin secure." Scuddamore dipped in his pocket for his shangies, a foot-long affair of rope with a wooden handle that acted as simple handcuffs. He looped it around one of McGavin's wrists, attached it to his left arm and grinned. "Pray to step this way, kind sergeant of mine, and be careful because it's a tight squeeze."

Scuddamore had left the cracksman at the junction of the alley and the more spacious Vault, with his left wrist hand-cuffed to his right ankle. "I had to leave him here in case you needed help," Scuddamore explained. "I screwed my D pattern handcuffs on him, which is why I used the shangies for McGavin here."

D pattern handcuffs were so named because they were shaped like the letter D. They were cumbersome machines that the policeman had to work by screwing into place with a large key, encouraging many officers to use the lighter rope shangies.

"I may have keyed the D too tight," Scuddamore said, without even a trace of remorse in his voice. The D pattern had a fault that once the police officer fastened them, he could not adjust them, so the officer preferred to screw them tight rather than risking the prisoner slipping free.

"I think you may have." Watters lifted the cracksman bodily. He was small and light, with wide staring eyes. "Come on, you."

Watters took a deep breath, allowing himself some satis-faction. After a few hitches, his elaborate plan had worked. He had captured the cracksman and a trio of known criminals. He should be pleased with the night's work, but somehow, he felt a niggle of dissatisfaction. Everything had gone too smoothly, and something was wrong, although he did not know what.

CHAPTER EIGHT

DUFF HAD THE OTHER TWO THIEVES HANDCUFFED TOGETHER and sitting on the floor when Watters brought in Scuddamore's prisoners.

"Here we are then," Scuddamore said. "Such a cosy gathering!" He looked around the room. "What a collection of rogues in the nation and not a smile between the lot of them." He lowered his voice. "That cracksman is not Abernethy, Sergeant. He's too young."

Watters nodded. "I was thinking the same thing, Scuddamore. And where is the tall policeman? We have a lot of questions to ask these fellows."

With three police and four criminals crowded into the room, Watters felt it was more like a prison cell than a house. "You people will wonder what you stole," he said to the scowling prisoners. "Look." Producing the keys, he opened the strongbox and showed the contents. "Well done, boys. You're going to jail for four house bricks."

"And all the other robberies," Scuddamore reminded.

"Oh, yes, them too. Sinclair's the Jewellers and all the rest."

"I never did that," the cracksman spoke for the first time. Thin and slight, he had the prison pallor on his face.

"We'll discuss that at Bell Street," Watters said.

McGavin spat on the floor.

"That's the way," Scuddamore said, lifting him by the handcuffs. "On you come, my foul fellow."

Mr Mackay was already in his office when Watters brought in the prisoners. "Well, Watters," he emerged, grimly happy. "You caught them, then."

"We did, sir," Watters agreed. "One cracksman and three petty thieves." *And not one of them that looks anything like a policeman.*

Mackay cast his cold eye across the prisoners. "Three criminals by habit and repute and one face I don't recognise. Is that Abernethy?"

"No, sir," Scuddamore replied at once. "Abernethy will be older. I don't know this fellow."

"What's your name, my friend?" Mackay asked. "We'll find out anyway, so you may as well tell me."

"Abraham Hogg," the cracksman said at once. He straightened his back. "You can't pin the other thefts on me, sir, because I didn't do them."

"We'll see about that," Scuddamore said. "Come on, my beauty, and we'll take you to the interview room."

"No rough stuff," Mackay warned.

"No, sir," Watters said. "We'll be as gentle as a mother with a new baby."

"I tell you," Hogg said, "I didn't do any other jobs. I couldn't have because I only came out of prison yesterday morning."

That explained the prison pallor. Abernethy had returned from Australia, so he would have plenty of time on the sea voyage to gain a healthy colour on his face.

"I hope you enjoyed your freedom," Scuddamore said, "because you're going right back into the criminal hotel."

"Sir," Lieutenant Anstruther stepped into the duty room. As immaculate as always, he gave Watters a look that might have been of triumph. "There's been another break-in, sir."

"We know," Mackay said. "Mr Gilbride's office and Watters has caught the culprits." He indicated the four scowling prisoners.

"No, sir," Anstruther said. "A house in West Ferry and the thief stole a load of silverware." He gave Watters a sidelong look. "He made a professional job of it, too. He climbed eight-foot-high iron railings, cut out an entire pane of glass, carved a hole in the shutters to force off the keeper bar and opened the shutters without anybody hearing a thing,"

"He knew what he was doing, sir," Scuddamore agreed reluctantly.

Anstruther ignored Scuddamore's comments. His words were addressed to Watters, although he faced and spoke to Mackay. "He left his calling card, Mr Mackay."

Watters felt the blood drain from his face. Despite his success in arresting some unpleasant criminals, he knew Abernethy was still at large.

Mackay stiffened. "What calling card, Anstruther?"

"A biscuit, sir. An Abernethy biscuit."

"Oh, dear God." Watters felt all his guarded elation slide away. Walter Abernethy could not have been clearer. "He's taunting us, sir. He knows we know who he is, and he's laughing at us."

"And I have to find the money to pay for damage to Mr Gilbride's window," Mackay lifted the biscuit that Anstruther handed to him, snorted, and threw it into the pail that passed for a bucket. "We went to a lot of effort and expense to catch a few petty thieves. It was not a good day, not a good day at all, Sergeant Watters. I expect better in future."

"Yes, sir, Watters said.

Mackay stalked away, with Anstruther hovering for a moment longer.

"Your little games cost the police a great deal of money and some credibility, Sergeant Watters," Anstruther said. "I advise you to stick to proper policing in future, rather than trying to be clever."

"We took a cracksman and three rogues off the streets," Duff said, philosophically.

"The magistrate will throw out the case," Anstruther said. "Breaking into an empty room to steal a handful of bricks? I can almost hear the laughter now." He walked away, tall, dignified, and cold.

Duff called after him. "Catching four criminals would be a good day's work in other circumstances."

Watters shook his head. "Aye, Duff, in other circumstances, it would. In that case, we failed, and Abernethy is laughing at us." He saw the packet of Abernethy biscuits that somebody had placed on his desk and frowned. "And you can take that bloody thing away!"

Murdoch stood in the doorway, stuffing tobacco into his pipe. "I thought you might like them, George," he said.

Watters opened his mouth to reply, closed it, and sat down. He knew that Murdoch was trying to inject humour into a grim situation, but he was in no mood to laugh. Although he had taken a quartet of thieves off the streets, he was now convinced that a police officer was passing information onto Abernethy.

Then he remembered the brass buckle in Anstruther's office.

———

Watters was always glad to return home to Castle Street. He resented working overtime that kept him from his wife, but the consolation was the extra money that paid the rent and put food on the table. The sensation of putting the key in his lock was deeply satisfying, as was knowing he had no debts and some savings in the bank.

His house had three rooms, a bedroom, a living room, and a minuscule kitchen, with front and back windows to allow light. It was not large but compared to the houses in which most people in industrial Scotland lived, it was a small palace, and Marie kept it immaculate.

Marie's initial smile faded as she saw the expression on Watters' face. "Did you not catch him, then?"

Watters slumped onto his chair. "We caught the fellows who robbed Mr Gilbride's offices," he said. "Thanks to your help."

"Well, that's good, surely?" Marie sat opposite him.

"It should be good," Watters agreed, "if the men we caught were the men we wanted to catch."

"And weren't they?"

"No," Watters said. "We caught a cracksman and three wild men, but not Abernethy and his companion."

"Why is that?" Marie asked.

"Abernethy didn't turn up," Watters said. "I did all I could to catch him, and he evaded me with ease." He sighed, looking into the bright fire. "Too much ease." He explained about the Abernethy biscuit.

"The cheeky blaggard!" Marie said, with the hint of a smile pulling at the corners of her mouth. "Did you keep the biscuit?"

"I did not," Watters said.

Marie's smile broadened. "A pity, they're one of my favourites. They cure indigestion," she said. "And wind." She nudged him. "You caught four criminals, George. That's a good day's work."

"It's not good enough," Watters said. "I wanted Abernethy and whoever he is working with."

"Well, George, you didn't arrest him, and there's no sense

in moping over it," Marie adopted her wifely voice. "So, sit up, work out what went wrong and what you can do about it."

"I know what went wrong," Watters said. "Somebody told Abernethy about my plan, so when half the Dundee detective force and two of the finest uniforms were in one place, he struck somewhere else and left me a biscuit!"

"Somebody?" Marie raised her eyebrows.

"My informants warned me that a policeman calling himself Lieutenant Kinghorn helping Abernethy."

"I don't know an officer of that name," Marie said.

"There isn't one," Watters said. "But somebody, probably somebody in the police, informed Abernethy of my plan."

"And?" Marie asked.

"And what?"

"And what do you intend doing about it?"

Watters stared into the fire for a moment. "I am not sure," he said. "I must catch him, but I can't think how."

"You'll think of something," Marie looked up as the baby started to cry. "Oh, well, there goes our two minutes of peace."

"I'll go," Watters said, smiling.

Marie watched as Watters walked through to the other room. She had bought a dozen Abernethy biscuits from the local shop but decided not to produce them. She knew her man was not in the mood.

———

"Well, Watters," Mackay leaned back in his chair. "Your plan worked to an extent. We did get four unpleasant characters off the streets, but I fear we are no closer to catching Walter Abernethy."

"No, sir," Watters said. "It's possible that a police officer is involved."

Mackay stiffened in his seat as his fingers began their devil's tattoo on the desk. "Tell me all you know, Sergeant."

Watters related everything he knew without mentioning his suspicion of Lieutenant Anstruther.

Mackay listened, noting down the details. "Do you have a description?"

"Not really, sir. I know he is very tall."

Mackay sighed. "In the land of the blind, Watters, a one-eyed man is king. To the majority of people in Dundee, every police officer is very tall. You'd better do better than that."

"I will, sir," Watters did not mention Anstruther's brass buckle.

"This fellow calls himself Lieutenant Kinghorn," Mackay said when Watters finished. "Do you have any suspects, Watters?"

"No, sir."

Mackay's fingers returned to their frenzied tapping. "I hope you are wrong, Sergeant. Who else knows?"

"Scuddamore and Duff, sir. I thought it best not to tell Boyle and Shaw yet."

"I agree," Mackay said. "How safe are your detectives?"

"Perfectly safe, sir. They won't say a thing."

Mackay stood up and looked out of his window. "Leave it with me, Watters, but monitor the situation. How are your other cases coming along?"

"I haven't had time to look at the scuttling one again, sir."

Mackay's fingers began to drum on the window ledge. "Have you made a decision about the new detective?"

"Not yet, sir," Watters said. "I've set them a task, and I'll see which one gets the better result."

"What task?" Mackay's fingers stilled.

"These Fenian rumours, sir. Scuddamore found a poster advertising a Fenian outbreak in Dundee, and I sent them to find out more information."

Mackay's stilled his fingers and turned to face Watters.

"That's an important job, Watters. We don't want any of that Irish-Scottish trouble in Dundee. Do you think the prospective men are ready for that level of responsibility?"

"We'll soon find out, sir," Watters said. "In my opinion, if any group planned to cause trouble in Dundee, they wouldn't advertise in advance."

Mackay raised his eyebrows, and for an instant, Watters thought he saw some respect in the pale eyes. "You don't believe it's a genuine threat, then?"

"No, sir," Watters said.

Mackay's fingers drummed for another few moments. "All right, Watters. That's all. Dismissed."

———

Watters swung his cane like a golf club and looked for his two prospective detectives along Dudhope Street. When he heard the tramp of marching feet, he smiled. The sound brought back memories of his time in the Royal Marines and his few years as an NCO with the Volunteers before he concentrated solely on his police career. Resisting the instinct to salute, Watters watched the half dozen red-coated Volunteers march towards the town centre. They were mostly very young, probably still teenagers, hopeful that the glamour of the uniform attracted girls, with one older man with the stripes of a corporal in charge. As they marched, their bayonets bounced from their hips while gas light reflected from the barrels of their Enfield rifles.

"Good luck to you, lads," Watters said. "Let's hope you never have to fire these things in earnest."

He heard the Volunteers argue about some trifle, automatically opened his mouth to blast them into silence, and closed it again. Squabbles among Volunteers were no longer his business unless they disturbed the public peace.

"Fenians!"

Watters had nearly forgotten the Fenian scare. Now the word came to him, carried on some nebulous draught of air. He looked up, swung his cane again, and stepped into the shadows so he could hear without anybody observing him.

"They're Fenians, I tell you, come to storm Dundee."

Watters frowned. The speaker sounded very young. "Oh, dear Lord," he said when he heard a concerted yell from a score of voices.

A gaggle of children of both sexes and ages from ten to about fourteen charged along the street. They were all chanting, "The Fenians are here! The Fenians are here!"

What the devil is this? Watters asked himself.

When they came within twenty yards of the Volunteers, the mob of youngsters stopped and let loose a high-pitched yell. "Fenians!"

The Volunteer corporal stepped forward, presumably to ask the children where these Fenians were, only to flinch when a volley of stones rattled past him. "We're not Fenians!" he shouted.

"That won't work, Corporal," Watters murmured. He sighed, wondering how best to resolve the situation as the Volunteers retaliated by throwing back the children's stones. Within two minutes, Dudhope Street was a riot scene as children and Volunteers threw stones and insults at each other, with the growing number of children quickly in the ascendancy. When a group of older youths reinforced the children, the scene became more violent as they threw larger stones with more force.

A Volunteer yelled as a stone caught him on the forehead, knocking off his forage cap.

"We're not Fenians," the corporal shouted again, then staggered as a missile opened a cut on his scalp. "You wee buggers!"

"Enough!" Watters roared and strode forward, swinging his cane. "Dundee Police!" He may as well have called down the moon as the barrage of stones continued in both directions.

"He's a bluebottle!" One of the youths yelled, pointing to Watters. "A Fenian bluebottle! Get him!"

Watters ducked as a chunk of rock the size of his fist whizzed past his head. The youths shouted strange slogans as they followed their leader, pelting Watters as vigorously as they attacked the Volunteers.

"Dundee Police!" Watters stepped in between both groups, knowing he made himself more vulnerable. "Stop this!" He raised both arms. "Dundee Police!"

A stone clattered off the ground at his feet, and another cracked him on the arm. If he were in uniform, he might have been more effective, or he could have used his rattle to summon help. As it was, he was a lone voice in a rising volume of shouts and shrieks and a central target for the youths.

When a sudden rush by the youths prompted the Volunteers to band closer together, the corporal gave a hesitant order, and the men fixed bayonets.

"None of that!" Watters snapped, with a vision of bloodied and broken youths if the Volunteers charged. "Dundee Police! Put these damned bayonets away!"

"You're no bluebottle," one of the Volunteers said. "You're only an interfering bugger of a civilian. Where's your uniform?"

Watters strode forward and slashed his cane on the man's rifle. "You'll do as I tell you," he said. He staggered when a stone crashed onto the back of his head and then gasped as a bottle thumped onto his shoulder.

"Bayonets, men! Show them the bayonet!" The corporal shouted.

"No!" Watters roared, and the voice of authority finally stilled the Volunteers. Even the youths were silent for a moment, and then a tousle-haired redhead lobbed another missile, and the barrage started again. One of the Volunteers slid his bayonet in place with a sinister click. When other Volunteers followed his lead, the situation altered from dangerous to potentially lethal.

I'll either be a martyr or a hero here, but I must try and stop this madness.

Stepping towards the Volunteers, Watters grabbed the rifle from the nearest man. "Put that bloody thing down! You're in Dundee, not the North-West Frontier! You can't go around bayonetting people just because they throw stones at you!"

The other Volunteers crowded round, one or two nursing cuts and bruises, some angry and brandishing their bayonets at Watters.

What the devil do I do now?

"Corporal! Get your men under control. You're not here to fight children!"

The harsh police rattle was welcome as it sounded through the commotion, and two uniformed officers marched into the mob of youths, scattering them with sundry pushes and the odd slap to ears and heads. One swung his long staff at the youths' legs, pressing them back.

"Get along there!" The taller of the two said. "These men are not Fenians!"

Assailed from this unexpected direction, the youthful army frayed at the edges. They began to retreat, singly and then in small groups until the Dundee Police were in total control of the situation. The Volunteers stared at the newcomers, with the corporal unsure how to react.

"There is no Fenian threat to Dundee!" The taller of the two police shouted as the last of the youths ran away. "Tell that to all your friends." He approached Watters. "That was a Donnybrook, a regular Donnybrook. Are you all right, Sergeant?"

"Glad to see you, Constable Boyle," Watters rubbed the back of his head. He could feel a lump already forming there.

"I am glad you turned up. Things were looking decidedly nasty."

Boyle grinned, with Shaw like a shadow at his back. "We heard the commotion, Sergeant, and heard somebody shouting Fenians and thought we'd come along."

"You were just in time," Watters said. "Corporal, put these bayonets back in their scabbards and get on with your duty!"

"Yes, sir." The corporal muttered orders to his now-sheepish men. Watters watched the Volunteers shamble away, resisted the temptation to shout after them to march to attention, and checked himself for broken bones. Considering the noise and volume of stones, he was surprised that nobody was seriously hurt, with only a few cuts and bruises on either side.

"Sergeant," Boyle put a hand inside his tunic and pulled out a copy of the Fenian poster. "I found out more about this poster. Is this the right time to tell you?"

"No time like the present," Watters said. "What did you find out?"

Boyle stood at attention. "Shaw and I spoke to the people in Lochee and the Scouringburn, Sergeant, as you said. Most of the Irish folk knew about the Fenian Brotherhood, and some had even seen this poster. Nobody knew anything about an attack by the Fenians."

"Would they tell you the truth?" Watters asked. "People tend to lie to the police, even when they're in civilian clothes."

"Shaw can put on an Irish accent, Sergeant."

"Can you, Shaw?"

"Yes, Sergeant," Shaw said. "My mother was Irish."

"Good man. So is my wife," Watters said, wondering if there was more to quiet Constable Shaw than met the eye.

"Yes, Sergeant," Boyle said. "We were getting nowhere, and we decided to go to the source." He unfolded the poster and pointed to a small name at the bottom. "We went to the printer, Sergeant, that's his name there, James Valentine, and asked him who ordered the posters."

"Good thinking, Boyle," Watters said.

"Mr Valentine checked his accounts book and told us that a theatrical company paid for a hundred posters."

Watters looked up as a wind carried rain from the sea. Dundee had the reputation as Scotland's driest and sunniest city but still received its fair share of foul weather. "Did you follow your investigations through?" He wanted detectives who could act on their initiative rather than men who merely followed orders from above.

"Yes, Sergeant," Boyle said. "Shaw and I checked up on the theatre company, and they are producing a play in the Alhambra Music Hall."

Watters nodded. "Is it about the Fenians?"

Boyle smiled. "Yes, Sergeant. The Alhambra thought the poster would raise interest in the forthcoming play."

"Well done, Boyle, and you, Shaw. When your shift is finished, go back to the Alhambra, and tell the manager to remove all the posters. If they refuse, charge them with creating public disorder."

"Yes, Sergeant," Boyle said.

Watters watched the constables walk away and rubbed the back of his head. That cleared up the Fenian threat and showed him the mettle of Constables Boyle and Shaw. Boyle had waded into the youths without hesitating and had shown considerable initiative in investigating the poster. Shaw? Watters was not sure. Shaw seemed too quiet for a detective. *We'll see. It's early days yet, but I'd prefer a man with more fire.*

———

"Well, George," Marie leaned back in her chair, with the baby at her breast. "How is the case progressing?"

"Not well," Watters admitted. "We are no closer to catching the culprits than we were at the beginning."

"Don't bite!" Marie admonished. "Not you, George. I was talking to Patrick."

Watters smiled. "Maybe we weren't lucky that he was born with a tooth."

"I've never heard the like before," Marie said, looking down fondly at her son. "Did you know that some men are jealous of their children?"

"Jealous? Why?" Watters reached out to touch Patrick's shoulder. The baby gave a little gurgle of protest at being disturbed.

"Well," Marie jiggled her breast. "This was your exclusive territory until he arrived."

Watters smiled. "I think he has prior rights," he said. "As long as he doesn't bite too hard."

"He's biting now," Marie winced and changed sides. "Have you thought about how to progress with your case?"

"No," Watters said. "I am no further forward."

Marie looked up. "Do you know who this rogue officer is?"

"No."

"Who do you suspect?"

Watters considered. "I don't know," he said. "Some things point to Anstruther."

"Lieutenant Anstruther?" Marie asked, in case there were others in the force with the same name.

"The very man."

Marie considered for a while before replying. "Then you'll have to ensure he doesn't learn of your tactics." She looked up. "Are you sure you don't suspect Anstruther just because you dislike the man?"

"I'm not sure of anything," Watters said and explained about Anstruther's brass buckle and the broken buckle in Sinclair's.

"A broken buckle on its own signifies nothing," Marie said.

"I know." Watters reached for his pipe until Marie shook her head. "Don't smoke in front of the baby, George."

"Smoke's good for them. It clears their lungs."

"I don't believe that," Marie said. "Smoke makes me cough and stings my eyes, so imagine what it does to this wee man."

Watters sighed and put his pipe back on the mantelpiece. Sometimes Marie had the strangest ideas, but it was better to accept her foibles rather than argue.

"What's your next move, George? You always have some ploy up your sleeve."

Watters glanced at the baby, who had fallen asleep while remaining firmly attached to his mother. "I honestly don't know, Marie."

"You trust Scuds and Duff, of course." That was more a command than a question.

"I do. Duff can be too honest sometimes."

"It's impossible to be too honest," Marie said. "How about your two new men. Are they up to snuff?"

"I don't know about them yet. Boyle has promise, but Shaw is a bit shy, maybe even lazy."

Marie snorted. "Lazy won't last in the force," she said. "How about your informants?"

"They feed me scraps," Watters walked to the window and stared outside. "We don't have much of a view here," he said. "Only the houses across the street. I'd like a house with a view of the sea or the hills."

"Maybe some time," Marie said and shifted the baby slightly. "You can see the Old Steeple if you stand on the right and twist your head."

"So I can," Watters followed Marie's advice. The Old Steeple was central to Dundee, although it was a tower rather than a pointed steeple. It was the focal point of the City Churches and acted as a landmark for homecoming sailors and the home of the church bells that summoned the faithful to Sunday worship.

"I often look at the Steeple when you are on duty," Marie

said. "It gives me comfort." She eyed him, gently persuasive. "You must get a good view of the town from there."

"I've never been to the top," Watters admitted.

"I'd imagine," Marie spoke slowly, "that a man up there could see everything that was happening in the streets."

"He could," Watters agreed. "He could observe without being seen and send a message to somebody on the ground below."

Marie sat back, satisfied she had done her duty. Now her husband would water the seed she had planted and convince himself the idea was entirely his own. She held her baby closer. "But we know, don't we, my wee man?"

"What was that, Marie?"

"Oh, nothing, George. I was talking to Patrick. Mothers do such things."

CHAPTER NINE

AT 165 FEET HIGH, THE OLD STEEPLE DOMINATED THE centre of Dundee, although Watters found the 232 steps quite strenuous after a busy daytime shift. Watters and Scuddamore could see most of the town centre from the chamber at the top as they stood with their telescopes poised, scanning every street.

"Thank goodness the lamplighter will be here soon," Watters said as the evening light faded. "Or we'll be wasting our time up here."

Scuddamore laughed. "After all the effort to climb the stairs, too. I do wish we had more men, Sergeant."

"So do I," Watters agreed. "But we don't know who to trust. When I reminded Mr Mackay about Lieutenant King-horn, he saw my reasoning. We'll have to cope with the two of us, plus Duff down there on the ground."

Scuddamore gave a low chuckle. "Duff's not the fastest man on his feet, but once he gets something in his mind, he's the most determined."

Watters thought of Duff's spread of shoulders and depth of chest. "There are few criminals who could best him if he gets hold of them." He had wondered who to post at ground level. Scuddamore was undoubtedly the faster of his two detectives, but Duff was the more formidable if the culprits showed resistance.

They settled down, constantly moving to scan the streets. An occasional man, or group of men, walked past, going to overnight work, or returning from a late shift. Waters focussed the telescope on a tall figure and nodded when he saw it was the beat constable. Boyle worked methodically, checking the shop doors and windows to ensure they were locked.

"He's a good man, that Boyle," Scuddamore said.

"I've got my eye on him," Watters agreed. "He's more than just a body in a uniform. He's got a head on his shoulders."

"How about the other fellow, Shaw?"

Watters considered before replying. "I'm not sure about him, Scuddamore. He seems reluctant to push himself forward as if he's waiting for somebody to tell him what to do. He seems shy to me."

"Maybe he's only thoughtful, Sergeant."

"And maybe I'll inherit a fortune and live in a castle."

The lamplighter arrived to set a flame to the oil lamps that spread their flickering light across the principal streets.

"I've heard that sneak-thieves curse these lanterns," Scuddamore continued their previous conversation. "They make hiding much more difficult."

Watters smiled. "One young thief told me that street lighting is worth ten policemen," he said.

A group of young apprentices appeared, shouting to prove their manhood and singing a popular song as evidence of their youth. Watters focussed his telescope on them for a moment, then dismissed them as rowdy but harmless. Boyle stepped up to the apprentices, remonstrating.

"Good man, again, Boyle," Watters said again as the boys cursed the policeman and then moved away without singing. Boyle followed them to ensure they kept moving.

The youths retaliated, trying to intimidate Boyle by their numbers. He cuffed one across the back of the head and pushed them along the street, holding his staff in his left hand.

"Do you think Boyle needs help?" Scuddamore asked.

"I want to see how he handles the situation," Watters replied.

Boyle remained with the apprentices until they were outside his beat when he handed them over to Constable Spalding. The experienced Spalding shared a joke with the apprentices to defuse the tension and escorted them towards the Overgate, where they dispersed to their various homes.

"Boyle did well," Scuddamore said.

When a dark carriage rattled over the cobbles, Watters stiffened and focussed his telescope. "This could be our man," he said, for cracksmen often parked a fast carriage close to the scene of their crimes for a quick escape.

The carriage sped past, its wheels a blur and the driver using the whip more often than Watters liked.

"I know that chariot," Scuddamore followed its passage through his telescope. "It belongs to Muirhead."

"Are you sure?"

"Yes, Sergeant. He had a bit of a smash with a jute wagon a few months ago and damaged his rear wheel. See how the offside rear wheel is newer than the others?"

Watters altered the angle of his telescope. "It's slightly different."

"Yes, the carriage was hand made in Edinburgh, and the local coachworks could not quite replicate the fancy work of the spokes."

"What the devil is Muirhead doing out here at this time of night? It can't be business."

Scuddamore watched Muirhead's coach as it negotiated the narrow passage into the Murraygate. "He's not stopping, Sergeant."

"I don't think we've finished with the charming Mr Muirhead yet," Watters said. "With burglars using a foreganger line to enter jewellers and him driving his carriage through the streets at all times of night." He shook his head. "Scuddamore, look into the foreganger connection again. Talk to people at the whaling company and see if there are any identifiable marks. If I had another detective, I'd post him outside Muirhead's house to watch his movements."

"Yes, Sergeant," Scuddamore said. "You have Boyle and Shaw."

Watters considered for a moment. "They did well with your Fenian poster, Scuddamore. You may have an idea there." He frowned as something in the street below caught his attention. "Come here, Scuddamore. Something's happening."

Scuddamore joined him. "Where, Sergeant?"

Watters pointed. "Over there. You can just about make out movement in Fletcher's Close."

Scuddamore adjusted his telescope. "I can't see anything. Wait, yes, I can, Sergeant. It's a man crouching down. No, no, there are two men."

"Two furtive men at night?" Watters nodded. "I think we're onto something, Scuddamore. And is it a coincidence that Mr Muirhead passed a minute ago? Where's Boyle now?" Watters looked for the beat constable and checked his watch. "He's at the furthest end of his beat. These lads have timed it well. Come on, Scuddamore."

Leaving the telescopes to be collected later, Watters grabbed his cane and ran down the stairs with Scuddamore a few steps behind him. They had left the steeple door unlocked and dived outside to move, long-striding, in the direction of the suspected break-in.

Watters strode quietly, hoping to catch the burglars when they were busy, but one of the two men looked up as the detectives approached. Abandoning their tools, they fled in the opposite direction. All Watters saw were two men dressed in dark clothing, with their faces blackened to avoid recognition.

"Spring your rattle!" Watters shouted, with all pretence of silence ended.

Scuddamore already had the heavy wooden rattle in his hand and spun it, with the harsh grating audible a long distance in the quiet night-time streets. The two fugitives increased their speed as they ran, with the slightly slower of the two glancing over his shoulder at the pursuing policemen. Watters saw the gleam of eyes in the blackened face.

"Stop!" Watters shouted, knowing it was futile. "Dundee Police!" He did not see from where Duff appeared as the broad-shouldered officer joined the chase.

"They're splitting up!" Scuddamore warned as the two fugitives headed in different directions.

"Take the man on the right," Watters ordered, "I'll take the other." He knew that Scuddamore was the faster runner, and the fugitive on the right was gaining, while the man on the left was slower.

Watters' quarry slid into a close and clambered up a wall with amazing agility as Watters followed, losing distance with every step. "Dundee Police!" Watters shouted again in a hope-less attempt to slow the man down. The fugitive slid over the wall, vaulting like a champion athlete at the Highland Games. Watters followed, barking his knees on the rough coping stone, glad the owner had not cemented broken glass on top.

The far side of the wall was dark, with nothing visible and an atrocious stench of human waste. Watters crouched beside the wall, listening intently. He knew he would hear footsteps if the fugitive was still running and breathing if the man was in hiding.

"You're still here," Watters spoke in a conversational tone. "It's no good running or hiding. I have twenty policemen around the area. It's only a matter of time until we catch you."

The fugitive made no response, yet Watters knew he was there, standing or crouching in the dark and hoping Watters would pass him.

"I can hear your breathing," Watters said, wishing he had a lantern as the beat constables carried.

There was no reply. A cat howled somewhere, and then silence returned, thick and heavy, broken by an outbreak of voices in the dark. Watters recognised Duff's strident tones and hoped he was having more success.

"Did you hear that?" Watters said. "That was my men catching your accomplice. Now he'll get a lighter sentence while you'll get transported back to Australia, Mr Abernethy." Watters gambled that his guesswork was correct. "Oh, we know all about you, Walter. We've been watching you for some time."

With his eyes becoming accustomed to the dark, Watters looked around. He was in a small triangular courtyard with high walls on two sides and the cliff-face of a tenement on the third. Any access must be at the foot of the tenement wall, so Watters moved in that direction, hoping to block off his quarry. Unfortunately, the fugitive had the same idea and bumped into Watters in the dark.

In the confusion, Watters swung his cane, missed, and swore as the fugitive pushed him aside and dived for a rectangle of greater dark that was the exit from the courtyard.

"Stop that man!" Watters roared as he gave chase.

The doorway led to a narrow, curving passage off which doors opened. The fugitive ran silently, with Watters pounding behind him.

They emerged into the Nethergate, where streetlights cast shifting shadows and the wind slanted around the corners of buildings. "Stop, thief!" Watters shouted, fully aware that the burglar was faster than him. A stray dog passed him, tail between its legs and its head down. Watters saw the fugitive pass under a streetlight, with his soft shoes lighter than Watters' boots and making no noise on the paving stones.

"Stop thief!"

The fugitive moved faster, running in a straight line down the centre of the Nethergate. Watters knew he could not catch him and tried to recognise the man by his back view. He was young, in his late teens or early twenties, and very agile, but that description could fit many of the thieves in Dundee.

The fugitive dashed into a close and, by the time Watters reached the entrance, had vanished.

"Sergeant!" Boyle arrived, glancing up and down the street. "What's to do?"

"Down that close!" Watters panted. "One of our burglars!"

Boyle ran down the close, with the thump of his footsteps echoing in the dark. Watters followed, catching his breath, and fighting his lack of sleep. Working long hours and helping care for a baby was not the best combination for a man fast approaching forty.

Boyle's footsteps faded away, leaving an eerie silence in the close. Watters slid into the shadows, watching and listening, expecting his quarry to double back. The wind increased, with the rain no longer a drizzle but a blustering onslaught onto the beleaguered citizens of Dundee.

"I lost him, Sergeant," Boyle reported softly.

"So did I, Boyle," Watters said.

"Sorry, Sergeant," Boyle sounded disappointed.

"It can't be helped," Watters cursed quietly. "We'll get him next time."

Duff and Scuddamore arrived, looking disconsolate. "He escaped," Scuddamore said.

Once again, Watters' quarry had eluded him. Twice now, he had set a trap, and twice he had failed. Perhaps Lieutenant Anstruther was correct, and he should rely on the painstaking, inch-by-inch detective work rather than on his more unorthodox methods.

———

The draper's shop was a mess, with the desk splintered where the thief had smashed the lock.

"This doesn't look like the same culprit," Watters said. "That's not Abernethy's style."

"Maybe somebody else was working last night," Duff knelt beside the desk. "Whoever he was, he had no finesse, Sergeant. I think he used a chisel to force the drawer open here."

"Aye," Watters nodded. "Hardly the work of a master cracksman. More likely a youth after a quick couple of pounds to waste on drink and women."

"Money spent on drink and women is never wasted," Scuddamore murmured.

"Get working," Watters snarled. "These blackguards are making fools of us!"

The shop manager arrived, looking in horror at the chaos within his shop.

"What was stolen, sir?" Watters asked. "Did you have much inside the desk?"

"Only the float, Sergeant, a few pounds in silver and copper in case the early customers needed change." The manager checked his stock. "We're missing a coat, waistcoat, two shirts, and three sets of men's drawers."

"Is this from your stock, sir?" Scuddamore held up a pair of worn and grey men's underwear between his finger and thumb. "They're well used."

"They're certainly not ours," the manager said. "We carry the Smedley drawers from Matlock in Derbyshire. These?" He turned away. "Those are disgusting."

"I agree," Watters said. "I think the thief changed here, leaving his underwear behind and donning a new pair."

"The dirty bugger," Scuddamore said.

"Dirty bugger perhaps," Watters said, "but also a thief." He sighed. "No biscuit crumbs this time, Scuddamore, but keep hold of the drawers."

"Yes, Sergeant," Scuddamore said.

———

"Three burglaries last night," Watters said, fighting the anger that threatened to overcome him. "A hotel safe, a draper's shop and a merchant's warehouse."

"Yes, Sergeant," Duff and Scuddamore looked as unhappy as Watters felt. "We stopped the last, but Abernethy, if it was he, got quite a haul from the hotel."

"Not from the draper's, though," Scuddamore said. "He only got a few pounds there and a coat and waistcoat." He lowered his voice, "and nobody tipped off Abernethy this time."

That was because we didn't inform any other police officers.

"And we have a clue," Duff reminded.

"A clue? Is that what you call it?" Watters clenched his fists. "By the living Christ, we have ships sinking all over the sea and burglars robbing Dundee blind, and what do we have to show for it? We know by the scuff marks on the wall that there were two, with one taller or with bigger feet than the other. What else do we have?"

"A pair of drawers, Sergeant," Duff said.

When Scuddamore began to laugh, Watters silenced him with a sharp poke in the ribs. "I'm glad you find it amusing, Scuddamore. I have a good mind to round up all the known thieves in Dundee and have them drop their trousers so you can examine their drawers for a pair from Smedley of Matlock."

Scuddamore stopped laughing. He knew that Watters was capable of carrying out his threat. "Yes, Sergeant."

"Tea!" Watters said, and Duff poured out three mugs and handed them around.

"Duff, was the man you followed carrying a bag?"

"No, Sergeant."

"Nor was mine," Watters said. "I think they dumped the takings when they saw us, which means they'll return later. We will scour the surroundings." He sipped the tea. "Come on, boys, the thieves won't act with so many uniforms around, but let's set a wee trap for them."

Another trap? If this one doesn't work, I'll take Anstruther's advice.

"What's the plan, Sergeant?"

Watters swung his cane through the air. "I'll devise something," he said. "I'll have to think about it first."

———

"Where's Shaw?" Watters looked round the duty room. "Has anybody seen Shaw?"

"Here, Sergeant," Shaw lifted a hand from the chair on which he had been sitting.

"What the devil are you doing, Shaw?"

"Just having a wee rest, Sergeant," Shaw turned big eyes on Watters. With a nondescript face and limp, light brown hair, he seemed to lack any character.

Watters fought his impatience. He tried not to let his personal feelings interfere with his dealings with people. "I have a job for you, Shaw."

"Have you, Sergeant?"

"Stand up when you're talking to me!" Watters snapped, and Shaw reluctantly struggled to his feet. "Stand to attention!"

Shaw obeyed with a faint smile on his face.

"That's better." Watters moderated his tone. "I want you

to watch Mr Muirhead and note everything he does. I want to know when he leaves his house and when he arrives at his office, when he leaves and with whom."

"I might not know their names, Sergeant," Shaw said.

"Then describe them as best you can and try to find out."

"Yes, Sergeant," Shaw said. "Is this in addition to my beat patrols?"

Watters glanced at Murdoch, who sighed. "You can have him, George. God knows he's not much good anyway."

"You heard Sergeant Murdoch, Shaw. You're all mine."

"Yes, Sergeant."

"Get along and find Mr Muirhead."

"Yes, Sergeant." Shaw glanced at the clock on the wall. "Where will he be?"

Watters took a deep breath to blast the constable, realised that half the duty room was watching him and released it slowly. "It's working hours, Shaw. Mr Muirhead will be at work."

"Yes, Sergeant," Shaw ambled away.

"And get changed into civilian clothes!" Watters roared.

Murdoch grinned at him. "Now you see why I recommended him for detective duties."

"You recommended him?"

"Yes. Shaw's no good as a uniformed policeman, but he's so lazy he might make a good detective. He looks like he knows nothing, so he might blend into the crowd."

"Thank you, Murdoch," Watters said. "That was kind of you, pawning your failures onto me."

Murdoch laughed. "They're not both failures. Boyle is all right. He's a bit of a know-it-all but good at his job."

Watters shook his head and reached for his pipe. "Thank you, Murdoch. You've sent me a useless lazy bugger and a big mouth. Hardly the pride of Dundee, are they?"

"I had the choice of sending Shaw to you or booting him off the force. Now he's yours to mould into a useful member of the Dundee Police or some such nonsense." Murdoch handed Watters a quarter-inch of tobacco. "As for Boyle? He's a pretentious bugger with his Turkish cigarettes and airs and graces. If you can curb his arrogance, you might make something of him."

Watters grunted. "Aye, maybe." He stuffed Murdoch's tobacco into the bowl of his pipe. "At this minute, Murdoch, I could see you far enough."

Murdoch laughed, puffing furiously. "You'll get by, George. Now go and have a biscuit. I recommend an Abernethy."

CHAPTER TEN

"SERGEANT," SCUDDAMORE SCANNED THE DARK ALLEY, probing into the corners with the end of his staff. "Over there."

A pile of rubbish half-hid the leather bag, but Watters could make out the shape. "Leave it," he said. "Walk right past the bag as if you didn't see it. I'd wager a sovereign to a pound of cheese that the thief will return for it."

"Do you think he's watching us now?" Scuddamore asked.

"Possibly."

They walked on, shaking their heads in pretend disappointment. "We'll keep watch from there," Watters nodded to a window that overlooked the close. "That's Mr Spence's storeroom. He won't mind us using it."

"Yes, Sergeant." Scuddamore restored his staff to the long pocket inside his coat.

"Right," Watters said. "Move the uniforms away to give the thief a clear run but keep the beat officer on as normal to avert suspicion." He lifted his hand to summon a cab.

"Where are we going, Sergeant?" Scuddamore asked.

"Back here," Watters said. "But if Abernethy is watching, he'll see us leave and might come back for the bag. I doubt he'll leave it for long once we move the uniforms, or some wee vagabond will lift it and think he's gone to heaven!"

Eddie nodded as the detectives boarded his cab. "Where to, Mr Watters?"

"The end of the Overgate, Eddie," Watters said, "and let us out."

"That's only a couple of hundred yards, Sergeant."

"I know."

They left the cab quietly and slid into Mrs MacLeod's eating house. "We'll take it in shifts," Watters said. "I'll go first, and you take over in three hours, Duff, and then Scuddamore." He did not need to tell them to keep hidden, his men were experienced detectives.

Watters left Mrs MacLeod's by the back door. He was relieved to see the bag was still in place and a minute later took his position in the storeroom, standing a little back from the window so no passer-by could see him. He had not long to wait until the close became busy, with a horde of the curious wondering why the police had been so prevalent.

"It was a murder, I tell you," a large woman said. "Somebody murdered Mr Spence."

"It wasnae Spencey, eh," a thin-faced man shouted. "I seen him this morning. It was him the polis were after. He murdered his wife. Chopped her to pieces with an axe, and her such a decent wee soul too."

"If he murdered his missus, how come the polis never arrested him, eh?" Another woman asked, then answered her own question. "It's because they think he's going to murder somebody else, that's why. They're waiting to catch him in the act."

The crowd walked past, still arguing happily, and Watters settled down. Another man passed, smartly dressed in a topcoat and tall hat. He did not linger, but Watters saw his eyes pass over the pile of rubbish in the corner.

A young chimney sweep was next, with soot smeared

over his face and hands and a bagful of brushes over his shoulder. He walked up with a swagger, stopped right under the window to light a pipe, and muttered something to himself.

"Halloa; what have we here?"

Watters cursed and moved to the window.

Leave that bag!

Watters could do nothing as the sweep lifted the leather bag and hid it among his brushes.

Put that bag back, you blackguard!

The sweep glanced over his shoulder, turned around, and hurried back up the close.

"Bugger!" Watters said as all his plans collapsed. He ran from the storeroom into the close, "you there! That man! That sweep! Stop!"

The sweep looked back, saw a man running after him and fled, leaving a trail of brushes in his wake but retaining hold of the leather bag.

"Dundee Police!" Watters shouted. "Stop!"

The sweep increased his speed, just as Constable Boyle rounded a corner. Boyle took in the situation in a glance and chased after the fugitive. As Watters fell further back, Boyle lifted his staff, aimed, and threw it sideways, so it spun end-over-end through the air. It made loud contact with the sweep's legs, knocking him face-first to the ground.

"Got you, my bonny lad!"

Boyle grabbed the fugitive before he scrambled to his feet, whispered savagely into his ear, and was clamping on the handcuffs when Watters arrived.

"Well done, Constable," Watters said.

"Thank you, Sergeant," Boyle hauled the fugitive to his feet. "He's only my second arrest this year."

"He may be a very significant arrest," Watters said as Duff and Scuddamore pounded up, gasping for breath.

"I told you we're working in shifts," Watters said.

"We thought you might need us," Scuddamore replied. "Who's this beauty?"

"We'll see when he's washed," Watters peered at the sweep, trying to make out the features under the dirt. "I've never seen a sweep without a climbing boy before."

"Excuse me, Sergeant, may I get my lantern? I had to drop it to arrest this fellow," Boyle asked.

"Go and pick it up, or somebody will charge you for it," Watters said. "I don't know if this man was involved in the robbery, or he just saw the case and picked it up." He ordered Scuddamore to clear away the crowd that was gathering.

"Sergeant!" Duff sounded shocked. "The case is empty!"

"Of course, it's empty," Watters said. "You don't think I'd leave it full of loot as a gift for the burglars? I emptied it before I stood watch. The contents are quite safe."

Boyle arrived, fastening the lantern to his belt. "I was in the right place at the right time," he said. "I can get to like this police business."

———

Watters sat opposite the prisoner in the Bell Street interview room. "Right, my friend, the first thing we'll need is your name. Are you Walter Abernethy?"

"No." The man was too young to be Abernethy but might be the second thief. He was a slender, nervous-eyed man in his early twenties who twitched on his chair and looked towards the door as much as he did towards Watters. "What am I meant to have done?"

"Stolen a great deal of money," Watters said.

"I never stole nothing," the sweep turned his dirty face towards Watters. "I was just passing, and I saw the case lying there. I was going to hand it in to the bluebottles, and then you charged out of the closie shouting and yelling. I thought you were going to attack me, and I ran."

Watters grunted. The story was plausible, and without evidence, he could not arrest the man.

"What is your name?"

The man thought for a revealing moment before he replied. "Stuart Howie," he said at length.

"And what's your real name?" Watters asked.

"That is my real name," Howie said.

Watters sighed and tried a bluff. "If you co-operate, I will do what I can to keep your sentence to a minimum. At present, we have you for breaking and entering and resisting arrest. I can also add burglary and theft, which would at least double your sentence. If you are Abernethy, you'll be sent back to Australia for ten years or so, plus whatever the judge adds for breaking the ticket-of-leave terms and the burglary. So, do I call you Abernethy? Or some other name."

"Stuart Howie," the man repeated.

Watters looked up as Scuddamore entered the room, with Sergeant Murdoch at his side.

"MacPherson, the beat constable, found a bag of tools abandoned outside the shop our men were working," Scuddamore said. "Top quality London-made cracksman's tools including this," he placed an auger on the table at Watters' side.

"The burglars were trying the same technique as at Sinclair's and the hotel job, boring holes and pushing in a section to gain access. They were going through the outer door before they put an arm in to withdraw the bolts."

"Does the auger fit the marks from the other robberies?" Watters asked.

Scuddamore only hesitated for a second before he continued Watters' bluff. "It's a perfect match, Sergeant."

Watters faced the prisoner. "You might not be aware that every auger leaves a distinctive mark in the holes it bores. Now that Constable Scuddamore has matched this tool to the previous two robberies, we know you were involved, Abernethy."

"My name is not Abernethy," the prisoner said. "It's Stuart Howie."

Murdoch laughed. "Stuart Howie, my arse! You're James Connor. I arrested you last April for theft. You got six months then, and you'll get at least a seven-year stretch this time, my lad."

Connor paled under his soot and looked away.

Murdoch leaned over him. "I don't like you, Connor, but I wouldn't like to think of you suffering in Perth for half your life over another's misdeeds. If you help us, Sergeant Watters and I will see you only get eighteen months."

"I never done nothing," Connor insisted. "I just saw the bag and lifted it. Is it against the law to lift an empty bag?"

Connor opened his mouth to speak and closed it again when Lieutenant Anstruther pushed into the room, with Boyle at his side.

"What were you going to say, Connor?" Watters asked.

"Nothing, Sergeant," Connor glanced at Anstruther and away again.

"Is this your famous cracksman?" Anstruther asked.

"No, sir," Watters said, as Murdoch and Scuddamore left the room, taking Boyle with them. "This might be his accomplice. Sergeant Murdoch says his name is James Connor, a habitual thief."

"He's a nobody then," Anstruther said. "Did you find him stealing anything?"

"No, sir. He was lifting a bag that the thief used to store the loot."

"I saw the bag lying there," Connor said. "I was going to hand it in."

"Can you prove otherwise, Sergeant?" Anstruther asked.

"Not yet, sir."

"Take his name, search him, put him in one of the cells for

a couple of hours and release him." Anstruther ran a cold eye over the sweep. "But wash him first, for God's sake. I don't want any of my cells covered in soot or whatever that is."

"Yes, sir," Watters felt his case slipping away. "I would like to question him, sir."

"Didn't you hear me, Sergeant? Do as I say and get about your business."

"As you wish, sir," Watters stood. "All right, Connor. It's your lucky day, a free bath, a free lunch, and you're out of here."

A couple of sour-faced constables helped wrestle Connor to the outdoors yard, where one ordered him to strip, and the other worked the pump, filling a bucket with cold water.

"This will be the first bath in your life, Connor, eh?" one of the constables joked. "Get your bloody clothes off then, you dirty wee bugger."

When Connor protested again that he only lifted an empty case, the constables held him securely and stripped him naked.

"Wait!" Watters waited until the police had thrown a bucket of cold water over the cringing youth and were setting about him with hard-bristled brushes. "What's that?"

Sitting on top of Connor's pile of tattered clothes, the drawers were pristine white and obviously new, while a piece of string held his braces together beside the remains of a metal buckle. Watters smiled and lifted the drawers. At the top, a small label proudly announced the maker to be Smedley of Matlock.

"Hold him here, lads," Watters said. "I want to fetch something from the evidence locker. Don't worry about the cold. It will do him no harm."

Returning to the office, Watters searched in the evidence locker and hurried back to the courtyard to see Connor shivering and covering himself as he stood in a half-crouch.

"See what I found, Connor?" Watters held up the sliver of metal he had retrieved from the floor of Sinclair's. He pushed the fragment against the buckle of Connor's braces. "It's an exact fit," he said, with great satisfaction.

"What does that mean?" Connor asked.

"It means that James Connor, I arrest you for breaking and entering the Royal Hotel and Spence and Company in Reform Street, attempting to break into a house in the Nethergate and resisting arrest. There may be further charges to follow." He stepped back. "Carry on, constables. Scrub him well! Lieutenant Anstruther doesn't want his cells dirty. You can wash his clothes at the same time."

The constables dipped their hard-bristled brushes in the cold water and set to work with a will, with Connor yelling and cringing as they scrubbed him.

Watters watched for a minute before returning to his desk. *I saw Abernethy. The gentleman in the top hat and dark coat was Abernethy. He checked the leather bag was safe, then sent Connor to pick it up. I had Abernethy within two yards of me, and I let him escape. The net's closing on you, Walter. I'll interrogate Connor until I find out everything he knows, and then I'll have you, Walter Abernethy.*

Dawn was breaking before Watters finished his paperwork. He checked the cells, with a pink and tingling Connor ensconced in the cells beneath the police office. Haley, the turnscrew, had handed him in an extra blanket and some old but clean clothes.

"Yon Connor fellow looks a new man when he's all washed," Haley said.

"I hope he gets a good night's sleep," Watters slammed shut the spyhole. "I aim to interrogate him tomorrow. He's our link with Abernethy."

"Ah," Haley said. "The biscuit man."

"The very same," Watters held the turnscrew's gaze, daring him to say something.

When the turnscrew remained silent, Watters bid him a good night. Only when he walked home to Castle Street did he realise how tired he was.

Marie was already up, looking equally tired as she fed Patrick. "Busy night?" she asked.

"Busy enough," Watters said, collapsing into a chair beside the glowing embers of the fire. "We caught one of the burglars. Only the smaller cog, but it will rattle the cracksman and might lead to bigger things."

Marie was crooning a lullaby as she swayed to settle Patrick. "This little one was up half the night, so I'm trying to get him to sleep now. You'll have to fend for yourself, I'm afraid."

"You concentrate on the baby," Watters said. "I'll just get a few minutes rest before I do anything."

Five minutes later, Marie placed a cover over Watters as he slept. "Aye, five minutes or five hours, George. I wish your son would get to sleep so quickly."

CHAPTER ELEVEN

A HAMMERING AT THE DOOR STARTED WATTERS OUT OF SLEEP.
He stared around him, momentarily unsure where he was.
Marie was in the chair opposite, still holding a sleeping
Patrick, while the ashes were cold in the grate.

The hammering came again, more urgent than before.

"Sergeant Watters!" Scuddamore's voice sounded through
the closed door.

"What the devil?" Watters threw off the cover, rasped a
hand over his unshaven chin and staggered to the door.
"Scuddamore! What the devil do you mean banging on my
door?" He spoke in a hoarse whisper. "You'll wake the baby!"

"Sorry, Sergeant," Scuddamore said. "Mr Mackay said to
fetch you, Sergeant. There's been a development."

"There's been a what?" Still half asleep, Watters stepped
aside to allow Scuddamore to enter the house, pulling a cover
over Marie in case she was feeding Patrick. "We'll go through
to the other room, Scuddamore. Keep your blasted voice
down!"

"James Connor is dead," Scuddamore said the instant they
entered the back room.

"How?" Watters immediately switched from a tired family

man to a thinking police officer. "He was in the peak of health when we put him in the cell. How did he die?"

"I don't know, Sergeant," Scuddamore said. "The surgeon was with him when I left, and Mr Mackay said I should fetch you."

"Fetch me?" Watters glanced to the living room, where Marie was beginning to awaken. "I've hardly seen Marie this week."

"I know, Sergeant, but Mr Mackay said to fetch you."

"Aye, it's not your fault, Scuddamore. It's all part of the blasted job." Watters grabbed a hunk of bread, sliced himself some cheese and walked to the front door.

"Bye, George," Marie said sleepily. "Come again for another twenty minutes." She stood and carried Patrick to the bedroom, but the baby awoke before she crossed the threshold.

———

The cell was as Watters had left it, bleak, whitewashed and clean, with a single plank bed, a pail for a urinal, and a thin straw mattress. The only difference was that James Connor lay on his side, eyes and mouth open, dead.

"What happened?" Watters asked Doctor Musgrave, who was examining the body.

"I don't know yet. I'll have to perform a post-mortem. How was Connor when you put him in here?"

"Lively," Watters said. "He led us a merry dance."

"There's slight bruising on his legs and chest," the surgeon said. "Nothing that would cause any more than mild discomfort."

"That would have happened when Constable Boyle brought him down," Watters explained the circumstances of Connor's arrest.

Doctor Musgrave nodded. "Apart from that, I didn't find a

mark on him. I'll have to take him to my surgery. I'll have a report for you as soon as I can." He shook his head. "Who is his next of kin?"

"I don't know of any," Watters said. "I'll check."

"You do that and inform them what's happened," the surgeon said. "I do wish you police were more careful of your prisoners. You may think they are a bad lot, but they are all somebody's son or daughter, husband or wife. Human life is too precious to throw away, Sergeant."

Watters nodded. "I agree, doctor," he said. "I'll make enquiries about this unfortunate fellow."

Watters did not know Haley the turnscrew well. He was a tall red-headed man with a slight stoop.

"Connor was fine when I checked him at six in the morning," Haley said. "I brought him his breakfast, and he ate it with a fine appetite. He had the cheek to complain about the tea, and then at eight o'clock, his wife came to see him."

"Came to see him? Is it a hotel you are running, Haley?"

Haley did not seem concerned by Watters' question. "No, just a police cell block, Sergeant Watters. She was a nervous wee soul, too good for Connor, so I let her see him for five minutes, and then that was all."

"I'll speak to Mrs Connor," Watters said, already dreading the interview. "Did you allow anybody else to visit Connor? His cousin, perhaps? Or the lads he was at school with?"

Haley shook his head. "Nobody, Sergeant. The only other person was Lieutenant Anstruther." He looked away. "Mind you, Sergeant, I don't sit here watching the cell doors all the time. I sometimes take a turn outside to clear my head of the prison stink."

Watters nodded. The smell of a dozen men and women incarcerated in small cells with only a pail for hygiene purposes was not pleasant. He did not blame Haley for taking the occasional break.

"Do you think somebody could have entered the cells when you were gone?"

"It's possible, Sergeant," Haley nodded to the bunches of keys that hung on the wall of his cubicle. "All they have to do is lift the keys."

"Don't you lock your door?" Watters asked.

"What if there's a fire, Sergeant? Or some other emergency? I don't like the prisoners, but I wouldn't see them burned to death."

Watters nodded. "Thank you, Haley. I need to think about this."

Any police officer could have entered the cell to murder Connor. I am not an inch further forward. I can only hope Mrs Connor is six feet tall with arms like a circus strongman and a strong dislike of her husband.

Murdoch was off duty, but fair-haired Constable Menzies knew Connor well. "I didn't even know he was married, Sergeant."

"Could you get me his address?"

"It's up Lochee way," Menzies said, "Stanton's Close."

"Thank you."

"I have bad news, Sergeant," Duff entered the duty room as Watters sat at his desk, a mug of tea in hand and wondered how to break the news to Mrs Connor.

"Connor? It's bad news indeed, Duff," Watters agreed. "I don't like losing a man in custody. As well as the tragedy of a death, it leaves a hole in our investigation."

"No, Sergeant," Duff sunk onto a chair opposite Watters, "I mean that I have more bad news."

"What's that, Duff?" Watters fortified himself with another mouthful of tea.

"There's been another sinking, Sergeant."

"Carry on," Watters ordered, wondering what else could go wrong.

"Another of Mr Muirhead's ships has sunk in calm seas, Sergeant," Duff said. "This time, it was one called *Teresa.*"

Watters looked up. "I remember Muirhead showing me her model. She was a sail-powered coaster if I remember."

"That's right, Sergeant. She was carrying a cargo of potatoes and stones from Dundee to West Hartlepool."

"She was insured with the Dundee Maritime," Watters said, "and with the Scottish and English Mutual."

"That's right, Sergeant," Duff said.

"Were there any casualties?"

"No, Sergeant. She was lost on Tay Sands, and the crew managed to get ashore in the ship's boat."

Watters nodded. "Thank the Lord for small mercies. Was her cargo insured as well?"

"Yes, Sergeant," Duff consulted his notebook. "Mr Muirhead insured her freight, cargo, captain's effects, disbursements, and outfit stores."

"Who did Muirhead insure that lot with?" Watters asked.

"A new company to me, Sergeant," Duff said. "British United Insurance. They're a Liverpool company with branches all over the place. Muirhead insured her with the Dundee branch, in the Seagate."

"I'll talk to them." Watters put his mug down and reached for his hat and paused. "You said she sunk at the Tay Sands?"

"Yes, Sergeant."

"Get me the master's name and a list of the crew. Crosscheck them with the crew of *Toiler* and see if any man sailed on both vessels. We'll work on this while we wait for the surgeon's report on Connor's death."

———

British United Insurance occupied a small office on the second floor of a tenement in the Seagate. The clerk put his pipe aside when Watters entered.

"Sergeant George Watters of the Dundee Police," Watters introduced himself. "I am enquiring after the loss of *Teresa*."

"I don't blame you for that," the clerk said at once. "Damned cheek if you ask me. The fellow comes waltzing in cool as be-damned, insures her cargo and effects, and then three days later down she goes in sight of Dundee."

Watters laid his cane on the desk. "Do you suspect a crime?"

"You're damned right I do, Lieutenant!"

"Sergeant."

"Aye, Sergeant. We're here to run a business, not pay out to any damned scoundrel who wants to make a few pounds." The clerk was a middle-aged man with greying whiskers and hot eyes.

"May I see the documentation?" Watters asked. The signature read 'Keith Muirhead.' "Could you describe the man who signed this, please?"

"A damned scoundrel, that what he was," the clerk said. "A damned robbing scoundrel, trying to steal money from a reputable company such as the British United."

"Will you pay out?" Watters noted that the money was under a hundred pounds.

"Maybe," the clerk said. "But we won't be accepting Muirhead's company in future, and we'll pass that recommendation on to other insurers. The man is a bad risk, with two doubtful claims in as many weeks, and the police investigating both."

"I am only making routine enquiries," Watters said.

"You've already interrogated Mr Muirhead," the clerk said, "and you've spoken to his other insurers." He laid a finger at the side of his nose. "We insurers keep in touch with each other, you know. We know what we're doing."

"May I keep this?" Watters lifted the policy document.

"Return it when you are finished," the clerk said. "I'm putting Muirhead on my blacklist and recommending that others do the same. We don't hold by scuttling and fraud in the British Mutual, by God!"

Watters ignored the clerk's rant. "Has Mr Muirhead claimed his money yet?"

"Not yet," the clerk said. "Oh, he's a smooth-talking handsome man right enough, but that's not good enough for me."

"Describe him," Watters said.

"You've met him," the clerk said.

"Humour me," Watters said. "Describe Mr Muirhead."

The clerk lifted his pipe and clamped it between his teeth. "He's in his late thirties, maybe forty, well set up, with a smart line in clothes, as you'd expect from a businessman or a rogue. He speaks well, with a hint of Dundee in his accent."

"Tall? Short?"

The clerk mused for a moment. "Oh, he's tall, all right. Taller than average. Maybe an inch or so taller than you."

Watters nodded. "I am five foot ten. Thank you." He knew that insurance agents had to be shrewd judges of character, able to assess the men who came into their office. "Did you trust him?"

"He acted and spoke like a merchant and a shipowner," the clerk said. "But looking back, he was ill-at-ease, as if he was not quite who he said he was."

"Thank you," Watters lifted the documents. "You have been most helpful."

———

"So, Mr Muirhead is getting himself in trouble," Duff said.

"Either that or somebody is getting him in trouble," Watters placed the British United document beside the others. "The signatures match the Scottish and English but not the Dundee Maritime. I'd say the same man purchased the documents, and it was not Mr Muirhead."

"Why?" Duff said. "Why would anybody part with money for no reason?"

Watters poured himself another mug of tea. "That, Duff,

I do not know. Did you get my Articles of Agreement – my crew lists?"

"Yes," Duff handed them over. "There's *Toiler* and *Teresa.*"

Watters scanned the lists. "The crews are smaller than I expected," he said. "Only six men in *Toiler* and eight in *Teresa* and only Neilson the carpenter sailed in both." He looked up. "Maybe that's because one was a steam vessel and the other was sail-powered. The crewmen need different skills."

"What does that tell us, Sergeant?" Duff asked.

Watters scratched his head. "I don't know if it tells us anything," he said. "We have two vessels from the same company, both overinsured and both sinking in calm conditions without any rational explanation. We have an unidentified man who insured both vessels and others and paid for the additional policies, seemingly without any means of profiting by the sinkings. Why?"

"I can't see any reason, Sergeant."

"Nor can I, Duff. Men don't throw money away without reason. There is a purpose behind this, yet I can't think what." Watters finished his tea. "Maybe whoever scuttled the ships was not on board. Maybe he damaged them before they sailed."

"Is that possible, Sergeant?"

Watters put his mug down. "Maybe. You and Scuddamore interview the crews, get their opinion of what happened. I'm going to speak to Mackenzie, Muirhead's accountant. If there is any financial malpractice involved, he'll know all about it, or he'll be involved." Watters looked over the duty room. "Has anybody seen Shaw recently? I sent him to watch Muirhead, and I've not seen him since. Find him for me."

When Scuddamore and Duff hesitated, Watters glared at them. "Well? What are you waiting for? We have cases to solve! Move!"

———

William Mackenzie was a tall man with bright blue eyes and slightly dishevelled hair. He greeted Watters with a smile, offered him a glass of port, and settled back in his leather armchair.

"Now, Sergeant Watters. How can I help you?"

"Insurance claims, Mr Mackenzie, and the vessels *Toiler* and *Teresa*," Watters refused the port.

"Ah, yes, the mystery of the additional claims," Mackenzie smiled. "It's a strange one, isn't it?"

"It is. I believe that the Scottish and English Mutual paid out the best part of a thousand pounds for *Toiler*."

"That's correct, Sergeant," Mackenzie said.

"And you paid the money into a new account, which you opened yourself."

"You have done your homework, haven't you?" Mackenzie approved, sipping his port. "You are quite correct again."

"Bear with me, Mr Mackenzie," Watters passed over a slip of paper. "Could you write Mr Muirhead's signature here, please?"

Mackenzie's smile did not falter as he lifted his pen, dipped it in the inkwell on his desk and wrote K. L. Muirhead before passing the paper back to Watters. "That is Mr Muirhead's normal signature, Sergeant," Mackenzie said. "He always signs his initials followed by his surname."

Watters nodded. "Why did you open a new account for the money paid by the Scottish and English Mutual?"

"I thought there was some mistake, Sergeant," Mackenzie said. "I knew Mr Muirhead hadn't insured any of our vessels with that company – he uses the Dundee Maritime – so I was quite surprised when the cheque arrived. Rather than put it into the company account, I opened a new one and placed it there."

"You could have handed it back," Watters said.

Mackenzie's face assumed a pained expression. "Please, Sergeant Watters. The insurance company sent that money to

Mr Muirhead. Who am I to say what he should and should not accept? It's safe in the bank, and if the insurance company find they've made a mistake, then I'll refund them the same amount. In the meantime, it's earning Mr Muirhead a little interest."

"May I see the books?"

Mackenzie gave a sharp order to one of his junior clerks and, within five minutes, handed the bank book to Watters. "I'm afraid I can't allow you to view the company's accounts without a magistrate's permission."

"This will do for now," Watters said. The bank book was precisely as Mackenzie had described. He handed it back. "Thank you, Mr Mackenzie." Lifting his hat and cane, Watters left the office with the mystery as musky as ever, but Mackenzie removed as a possible suspect.

Watters swung at an imaginary golf ball as he walked back to Bell Street. He seemed no closer to solving either the scuttling case or the robberies, yet he knew that he had collected small pieces that, when added together, would help find a solution. He had two scuttled ships, with false insurance papers, and a series of robberies where the cracksman, Walter Abernethy, worked for an unknown third party. He had a dead thief, and possibly a police officer who was helping the cracksman, and a length of foreganger rope from a whaling ship.

Watters sighed. He would have to see Mrs Connor, but that might wait until the surgeon had finished the autopsy. That gave him time to visit the wreck of *Teresa*, providing the tide was right. He swung his cane, and in his mind's eye, the golf ball sliced off the fairway onto the rough.

I am missing something here.

CHAPTER TWELVE

SEAGULLS CIRCLED ABOVE AS WATTERS SAT IN THE STERN OF the dinghy, watching the waves rise around him. Mr Gall, the Broughty Ferry boat builder, had been happy to lease one of his boats to carry Watters and Duff out to the Tay Sands.

"I'll take you myself," Gall said. "God knows it's not often I get away from the office nowadays. There's so much documentation involved that I rarely put my hands on an adze, let alone a pair of oars." He left his office with alacrity. "Come on, Sergeant, and you too, Constable Duff. It's low water, so you'll be able to visit the wreck. With such heavy cargo, *Teresa* sunk at once."

"Stones, wasn't it?" Watters asked.

"Aye, building stones from Kingoodie quarry," Gall said. "Stones and potatoes. The saltwater will ruin the tatties, though." He handled his oars like the expert he was, guiding the dinghy onto the edge of the great curving sandbank that guarded the mouth of the Firth of Tay.

"Did you know Mr Muirhead?" Watters asked.

"I knew him as a customer," Gall said as his great hands manoeuvred the oars.

"What was your opinion of him?"

Gall shrugged. "A decent enough customer," he said. "Always late in paying his bills, but he always paid eventually. Not all do, you know."

"What did he buy?" Scuddamore asked.

"Whaling boats," Gall said. "Double-ended open boats to seat six men, light enough for the crew to chase the whales, yet sturdy to withstand the ice. David Livie and I compete for the whaling boat market. Livie thinks he builds the better boat while I know it's me." He grinned. "Muirhead always buys my boats, which is why I don't object to his late payment. He's a shrewd businessman, you see. He'll squeeze the last penny in interest from his money before he parts with it and take the last ounce of advantage in any business dealing. That's why he's such a success; no compassion in business yet not a trace of dishonesty."

"Thank you, Mr Gall," Watters said. All his informants said the same thing. Muirhead was an honest but hard businessman. Such a man would not be likely to scupper his ships.

Gall managed his oars as he approached the wavelets that broke on the sandbank. "We can't get any closer by sea, Sergeant. You'll have to walk from here," Gall indicated the wreck of *Teresa,* lying on her side in a depression. "She's a sad sight like that. Maybe Mr Muirhead will try to salvage her."

"Maybe he will," Watters said as he disembarked, with his feet sinking into the soft sand. Duff joined him.

"I reckon you've got a couple of hours at most, given the state of the tide," Gall said. "When it turns, don't delay. You wouldn't be the first to misjudge the tide here; she comes in fast and hard and from all directions."

"Thank you; we'll take care," Watters began to walk towards the stricken coaster, with Duff following and half a dozen seagulls wheeling above.

"I'll give you a hail when the tide turns," Gall shouted.

Teresa was about a hundred tons weight, a two-masted brig with a newly coppered bottom and fresh black paint.

"Muirhead takes care of his vessels," Watters said, running a hand over the hull. "These barnacles are fresh, and the seaweed is only last night's. All the stranger that he would pay for *Teresa's* upkeep if he planned to scuttle her."

"Either that or he was allaying suspicion," Duff said.

"That is a possibility," Watters agreed, walking around the vessel. He tapped the hull with his knuckles. "Sound as a bell, Duff. I can't see any rotted timbers, and no reason she should sink, except here." He stopped, bent closer to the hull, and pointed with his cane. "Look at that."

Somebody had drilled eight round holes through the hull below the waterline immediately behind the bow, each hole sufficient to be a significant leak.

"Once *Teresa* hit the Tay, the water would surge in here," Watters pushed the tip of his cane through each hole, checking to see if it penetrated the timber. "What do you think made these holes, Duff?"

"An auger," Duff replied at once.

"That's what I think, too," Watters said. "Now, why would anybody want to sink a ship except to claim insurance?" He walked around the sad wreck, shaking his head at the tangled mess of spars and rigging.

"At least we have a list of suspects," Duff said. "It must be one of the crew of *Teresa*."

Watters shook his head. "We can't be sure," he said. "*Teresa* was hardly out of the harbour when she sank. Somebody may have sneaked on board when she lay in the dock, bored the holes, and disappeared without being seen. He may even have bored them from outside."

Duff nodded. "That's not the case with *Toiler*," he said. "She was far out to sea when she sank."

"I agree," Watters said. "We'll concentrate on *Teresa's* crew. Take them one at a time and interrogate them." He looked at the stricken ship. "Wait here, Duff. I'm going aboard."

"What do you hope to find?"

"Anything," Watters shrugged. "Nothing. I don't know. To be frank, this case has me completely baffled. There seems no motive."

Teresa had an island - a central deckhouse to accommodate the master and mate - and a forecastle right forward where the crew spent their off-duty hours. As she lay on her side, water sloshed thigh-deep in both. A hundred items floated on the water while small crabs scurried over the surface and hid in corners of each cabin. Watters stumbled over the sea chests, now on their sides and with some burst open. While a search yielded nothing, Watters opened the hatch for the forward hold and swore when he saw the cargo of stones. The sinking had moved them, so the topmost stones had rolled sideways.

"I'll never shift all that," Watters said and eased open the hatch that led to the galley and cable locker. He expected the galley equipment and lines to be in confusion, but when he stepped over the sodden coils of rope in the cable locker, Watters could plainly see the holes bored through the hull.

"Both sides," he said, feeling the timbers for the circular holes. "Whoever bored these knew his way around a ship. He knew exactly where to make the holes and how much damage they would do."

When Watters emerged, sodden wet, Duff was sitting on the mainmast, smoking his pipe. "Did you find anything, Sergeant?" Duff asked quietly.

Watters grunted. "Only confirmation that the holes sunk her. I need your muscles, Duff."

"Yes, Sergeant." Duff looked pleased. "What do you want me to do?"

"Carry as many sea chests as we can to the dinghy. These chests contain everything the men possess, and they'll want them back. We'll do the fo'c'sle first, and then the officer's."

"The captain and mate will have more valuable possessions," Duff said.

"And the ability to replace them," Watters said. "The hands may be destitute without their chests."

"We'd better watch for the tide coming in," Duff said as the waves broke more heavily on the fringes of the sandbank.

"The quicker we move, the better," Watters opened the door of the fo'c'sle again, shook his head at the shambles inside and hauled out the first of the chests. Duff grabbed it, laid it on the sand, and returned for the next.

Gall raised his eyebrows as Duff walked across with a sea chest on his shoulder.

"Well done, officer," Gall said. "Or is that evidence?"

"It's a man's life." Lacking Duff's powerful physique, Watters struggled with the second chest and was grateful when Gall hurried across the sand to help.

By the time they got the six chests from the fo'c'sle, the tide had risen, cutting the sandbank to half its previous size, and waves were breaking from *Teresa's* hull.

"Best be on our way," Gall advised.

"I want to check the deckhouse," Watters said. "The master and mate will have left their belongings behind as well."

"The tide rises fast here," Gall reminded, "and my boat's already overloaded."

Watters glanced at the dinghy. The six chests weighed her down, so waves broke over the gunwale, splashing water inboard.

"We've time for one more trip," Watters said. "And I'll only take what's easily portable."

"You'd better," Gall called as Watters ran towards the wreck, with Duff a few yards behind. "I don't want to be held responsible for two drowned policemen."

Even in the short space of time since their previous visit, the tide had risen by six inches, so Watters was splashing in water when he reached *Teresa.* "You wait here, Duff," he ordered, "and I'll pass things out to you."

"All right, Sergeant," Duff said, stepping over the horizontal mainmast and adding tobacco to his pipe.

Watters wrenched open the deckhouse door and peered inside. The place was a mess, as he knew, with cots and charts, personal possessions and clothes, a compass and a boxed sextant all tumbled together. Aware how expensive a sextant was, Watters lifted the instrument with care and passed it out to Duff.

"Keep hold of that!"

"Got it, Sergeant!" Duff shouted.

There were other items, a telescope, a leather bag, a wooden box with initials carved on top, and all the time, the water was rising until Watters realised that waves were breaking on the deckhouse roof, and Duff was thigh-deep in water.

"That'll have to do," Watters said.

Duff gave his characteristic grin. "All right, Sergeant. It's getting a little wet here. I think I saw Neptune swimming past a minute ago, but it might have been a seal."

"Sergeant!" Gall was sitting in the same spot, "another few minutes, and it would have been too late. I'd come over for you, but these damned chests are weighing me down."

"Take us back, Mr Gall," Watters said.

With the dinghy so heavy, the return journey was slow, and darkness was approaching when they arrived at Victoria Dock. A score of eager hands helped unload the sea chests.

"Salvage, Mr Gall?" a one-legged man asked.

"Maybe," Gall replied. "If you had done your job properly, there would be no need of salvage." Gall nodded to Watters. "This lushy reprobate is Davie Lorimer, *Teresa's* shipkeeper."

"I'll speak to you later," Watters said to Lorimer. "I want to know where you were when somebody bored holes in *Teresa's* hull."

"I can answer that," Gall replied. "He was either lying

drunk in the fo'c'sle or sitting drinking in the Baltic," he motioned to the Baltic Bar, a seagull's call from the dock.

"I thought Mr Muirhead was a sharp businessman," Watters said as Lorimer limped away. "Why retain a useless drunkard?"

"Lorimer lost his leg on one of Muirhead's ships," Gall replied. "Mr Muirhead looks after his people."

A man who looks after his people is not likely to endanger them by scuttling his ships. All the evidence points to Muirhead being an honest man.

"You, fellow!" Watters waved to a porter with a handcart. "Take these chests to Bell Street Police Office."

Watters had the porter unload the chests at the police stables.

"I'll notify Mr Muirhead you're back," Scuddamore had spent all day taking statements from the crew of *Teresa* without finding anything new.

"Not yet," Watters said. "We're going through each chest first."

"I thought you were too kind, helping the tarry jacks," Duff said.

"We're the police, not a charity," Watters reminded.

The sea chests sat in a mute pile on the stables' floor, showing the sadness of shipwreck and the bleakness of a seaman's life. Some trunks were plain wood, others decorated with elaborate paintings of ships in full sail, while one was elaborately carved with a Greek key design and a near-naked woman.

"Somebody has skill," Duff said. "That's Aphrodite, I think, the Greek goddess."

Opening the chests one by one, the detectives sorted through the contents. Most held a sad collection of a few spare clothes, a pair of shoes to wear on shore and some tawdry souvenirs of a foreign voyage. One contained more, with four bird's feet, a sheath knife, a fid, marlinspike, and sail-maker's palm.

Duff lifted the birds' feet. "What the devil are these?"

"Albatross feet," Watters said. "Seamen in the Southern Ocean catch the albatrosses and make the feet into tobacco pouches, and sometimes cut off and dry the heads."

"Why?"

"To sell on land or give them as presents to people who are worthy of the gift."

Duff examined one of the feet. "I thought sailors held albatrosses as sacred. Don't they hold the souls of dead seamen?"

"Like the poet Coleridge wrote?" Watters asked with a smile. "No. If a man is washed overboard or is in an open boat, an albatross will attack them. They're predatory birds, and sailors think them fair game. I heard the French even eat the damned things."

Duff put the birds' feet down. "Strange creatures, seamen."

"Aye." Watters viewed the chests with their meagre contents. "Little enough to show for a lifetime's hard labour at sea," Watters said. "Seamen are merely ocean-going gypsies, rolling stones that collect no moss or anything else."

"Sergeant," Duff opened the final chest. "This is more interesting." He produced a collection of tools. "Hammer, chisels, saw, two adzes and an auger."

"An auger," Watters took the tool. "Now, that might be significant. We may have to return to the sandbank and see if the drill bit fits the holes." He glanced inside the chest, lifted a chisel, and returned it.

"This man might have been the ship's carpenter, of course," Scuddamore said.

"I doubt a small coaster would carry such a luxury," Watters told him. "I think we'll find who owned this chest and have a wee word." He examined the auger again. "There is still sawdust on the bit."

"That's what it's for, Sergeant," Scuddamore said.

"If we can match the wood on the auger with the wood on the hull, we might be a step forward," Watters said.

"How the devil do we do that?" Scuddamore wondered.

"We take a sample to a carpenter," Watters said. "Hercules Lowther, the ship's figurehead carver, will identify the wood immediately." He smiled. "We may be getting somewhere, Duff."

CHAPTER THIRTEEN

"It's still black out there," Scuddamore stared out of the duty room window.

"What was that, Scuddamore?" Watters held the length of foreganger as if the touch could convey a message.

Scuddamore returned to the desk and the pile of statements he was re-reading. "I said it's still black out there."

"Black," Watters repeated, still holding the foreganger. "Dear Lord, Scuddamore, you've given me an idea. When I was at the British Mutual, the clerk said he was putting Muirhead on the insurance blacklist and recommending that others do the same."

"I'm not surprised," Scuddamore said. "If Muirhead is making false claims, why should any insurance company take him on?"

"Or pay out," Watters said. "Scuddamore, maybe we've been approaching this the wrong way. Maybe it is not Muirhead scuttling his ships. Maybe it is somebody with a grudge against Muirhead."

Scuddamore frowned. "If he has a grudge, then why double insure the vessels? Surely that will mean Muirhead gains."

"Only at first," Watters said. "When the insurance companies all blacklist him, nobody would pay out. Mr Muirhead will lose his good name, as well as a great deal of money."

"That's devious," Scuddamore said.

"It's a possibility," Watters said, "but it still leaves us lacking a motive. Why would anybody hold a grudge against an honest man who looks after his workforce?" He looked around as the door opened.

"Sergeant Watters," Doctor Musgrave entered the duty room. "Is Sergeant Watters in here?"

"I'm here," Watters lifted a hand.

"Will you come with me, please?"

Watters joined him at the door. "What's the matter, Doctor?"

"I've finished the post-mortem of that unfortunate young man James Connor," Doctor Musgrave said. He looked over his shoulder as a group of uniformed policemen strode from the duty room to begin their day's duty.

"You look agitated, Doctor," Watters said.

"I am." The surgeon walked along the corridor and outside into the street. A brewer's dray lumbered past, with a plodding Clydesdale horse hauling the heavy wagon. "You see, Sergeant, Mr Connor did not die from natural causes."

"What happened?"

"He was Burked, Sergeant."

Watters nodded; he was not surprised that somebody had murdered Connor. When Watters left him, he was scrubbed clean, fed, and healthy, yet the following morning the turnscrew found him dead. "Burked? That takes some force."

The Edinburgh mass murderers Burke and Hare who had given the world the term "to Burke," which was a method of smothering. The assailant would usually come behind the victim, put one hand over his or her mouth and nose and press the bone of their wrist against the victim's throat. After a few moments, the victim would be dead. It was simple and effective, with the victim unable to make a noise.

"It does," Doctor Musgrave agreed.

"We know of only three people who saw Connor in his cell, doctor. Haley the turnscrew, Lieutenant Anstruther and Connor's wife."

"Then I am afraid that one of these three murdered him."

Watters sighed. "Would a woman have the strength to Burke a full-grown man?"

"That would depend on the woman," Doctor Musgrave said. "Is Mrs Connor a large, powerful woman? Such a woman can be as strong as any man."

Watters collected himself. "Could you see any reason why Mrs Connor should murder her husband?"

"I am a doctor, Sergeant Watters. You are the detective." The surgeon took two cheroots from his top pockets, offered one to Watters, smiled when Watters refused, and lit up. "I notice you ignore the possibility that Haley or Lieutenant Anstruther may be responsible."

"I find either possibility hard to believe," Watters said. He did not mention that his informants had indicated a police involvement.

Dr Musgrave inhaled deeply and blew out a cloud of tobacco smoke. "I know both men," he said. "I've known Lieutenant Anstruther since he was a young constable and the turnscrew since he joined the force, five, or was it six, years ago. Mr Connor's wife, I do not know. You'll have to see who has the motive to murder Connor or if anybody else slipped into the cell during the night."

"Thank you, Doctor," Watters said.

When Watters returned to the duty room, he remembered that Anstruther had been anxious to release Connor from custody, despite his possible guilt.

Why? Was it because Anstruther doesn't like me any more than I like him? Or was he hoping to get rid of a man who might identify him? Did Lieutenant Anstruther murder his associate in crime?

"Motive," Watters said to his detectives. "We need motive, means and opportunity. Here's a possible motive to think about. We suspect that there is a policeman involved in the robberies. If Connor had given him away under questioning, then that policeman would be in serious trouble."

"Yes, Sergeant," Scuddamore said.

"We do not know if Mrs Connor had such a motive." Watters looked over his men. "Nor do we know if she was physically capable of burking her husband. I will see her later today, probe for the motive and assess her strength."

"What shall we do?" Scuddamore asked. "We can't interview every member of the force."

Watters ignored the interruption. "Opportunity?" he said. "All three saw Connor alone in his cell. I want your thoughts, please, gentlemen."

Scuddamore spoke first. "If we've narrowed our police suspect to Anstruther and Haley," he said. "I think we should notify Mr Mackay of our suspicions, Sergeant. Neither of us has the authority to question a police Lieutenant."

"I agree, Sergeant," Duff spoke slowly. "Imagine if we accused either of them, and they were innocent."

Watters nursed his mug of tea. "You are right, gentlemen. I will leave any names out of my official report to Mr Mackay and tell him verbally. We will tell nobody else of our suspicions. Nobody at all – not even Rosemary, Duff."

"Yes, Sergeant," Duff said and added innocently. "Will you tell Marie?" It was no secret that Watters often discussed his cases with his wife.

"Marie already knows," Watters said. "I wish I had not told her, for a new baby is enough for anybody to cope with." He rose. "I have to see Mr Mackay. You two talk to Haley – that's the procedure – and examine Connor's cell. Interview the other prisoners, too, they might have heard or seen something. I don't like people murdering my prisoners."

———

Mr Mackay read Watters' report without any expression on his face. "You think that the robberies and the scuttling cases are linked, Watters?"

"Yes, sir," Watters said. "The whaling foreganger gave me the idea." He explained his reasoning.

"That's a very shaky peg on which to hang a theory, Watters."

"I know that, sir."

"We'll leave that aside just now," Mackay said. "What is your next move?"

"I have invited Mrs Connor into the police office so that I can tell her about the death of her husband, and I wish to revisit the site of *Teresa*'s wreck to see if the auger we found fits the holes in her hull."

Mackay pressed his fingers together in front of him. "Anything else?"

"My detectives have interviewed the crew of *Teresa* before they signed articles on a different vessel, and I hope to interrogate as many of the crew of *Toiler* as I can." Watters waited as Mr Mackay scribbled notes on a small pad on his desk.

"Do you have any theories about the scuttling, Watters?"

"Not yet, sir," Watters said. "I suspect that somebody has a grudge against Mr Muirhead, but who or why I cannot yet say."

Mr Mackay gave his characteristic bleak smile. "Do you believe that Mr Muirhead is innocent of scuttling, Watters?"

"I do, sir," Watters said. "When I played golf with him, he struck me as a sincere man, and his banker assures me he does not need to sink a ship for a few hundred pounds. His accountant, Mr Mackenzie, opened a special account for the extra insurance money and is ready to return it if necessary, which is hardly the action of a guilty man." Watters shrugged. "Everybody I have spoken to agrees that Mr Muirhead is a hard businessman but scrupulously honest."

Mackay began to drum his fingers. "Theories? Why would somebody pay good money on an insurance policy that pays out to a third party?"

"The only reason I can think is to damage Mr Muirhead's reputation, sir," Watters hesitated for an instant. "But as I said in my report, we saw his coach in the vicinity of the robberies, and that gives me cause for concern. I have posted a man to watch Mr Muirhead's movements."

"Who? Don't you need both your men with two ongoing investigations?"

Watters nodded. "I've posted Constable Shaw, sir. Sergeant Murdoch kindly agreed to take him off his uniformed duties."

"Lieutenant Anstruther will not like that, and Murdoch will be a man short."

"I know, sir," Watters said.

Mackay smiled again. "Why did you pick Shaw and not Boyle? I thought Boyle was the better of the two."

"Constable Boyle has shone so far, sir," Watters said at once. "He's mature, with a good brain, and he helped catch Connor with one of the neatest moves I have ever seen. That's why I chose Shaw. I thought I'd give him a chance to prove his worth."

"I see," Mackay said.

"There is one other thing, sir," Watters said, "and I deliberately left it out of my report."

"What's that?"

"I have mentioned the mysterious Lieutenant Kinghorn, sir."

"Somebody play-acting," Mackay said. "We have nobody of that name in the Dundee Police."

"I know, sir," Watters agreed and told Mackay about the three people who had visited Connor before his death.

Mackay's fingers were static, and then they pressed onto the desk, so the knuckles gleamed white. "I view such a possibility very seriously," Mackay said slowly. "I will keep an eye on these two without believing that either is guilty of betraying the trust I have in them."

"Thank you, sir," Watters said.

"And, Watters," Mackay continued. "I'd thank you to keep your suspicions to yourself."

"I will, sir."

———

Mrs Connor was a young, nervous woman in her late teens. She sported a fading black eye and looked from side to side as she entered the police office, seeming to be pleased when Watters greeted her with a handshake and an offer of a mug of tea.

"I'm afraid I have some bad news for you," Watters said.

"Bad news?" Mrs Connor cradled her mug like a shipwrecked sailor with a raft. "What bad news, Mr Watters, sir?" She seemed skeletal thin as she perched on her chair.

"It's your husband, Mrs Connor."

"Rab?" Mrs Connor's head snapped up. "What's that blaggard been up to now?"

"He's dead, I'm afraid."

"Dead?" Mrs Connor's eyes narrowed in suspicion. "I spoke to him just the other day. How did he die?"

Watters took a deep breath. "We believe somebody murdered him."

Mrs Connor's eyes widened slightly. "He won't come back?"

"No, Mrs Connor, he won't come back."

Mrs Connor leaned back in her chair. "Well, thank God

for that. Who murdered him, Sergeant? Tell me so I can shake his hand."

"We wondered if it was you," Watters said quietly.

"No," Mrs Connor shook her head, "although I've thought about it. Rab Connor's not worth swinging for."

"You were one of the last people to see him," Watters pointed out, "and it seems evident that you didn't enjoy the happiest of marriages."

"Happiest?" Mrs Connor's mouth twisted in a grimace. "I only married him because I was with child and didn't want to bear a bastard bairn. Then what happens? The wee one is stillborn, and I was left with that good-for-nothing." She stood up. "Well, if that's the bad news, Sergeant, I don't know what the good is."

"Sit down, please, Mrs Connor," Watters said. "I haven't finished the interview yet."

"What happens to the body?" Mrs Connor asked. "Does it go to the anatomists?"

Watters hid his surprise. "Mr Connor's body will be returned to you."

"Well, I don't want the damned thing. Look at my eye! That was my beloved Rab, damn his black heart. And look at this!" Before Watters could stop her, Mrs Connor peeled off her thin jacket and lifted her top, revealing an array of bruises of every colour from dull blue to bright orange.

Watters took a deep breath. "I see," he said. "Cover yourself up, please, Mrs Connor."

"Why?" Mrs Connor asked. "To hide Rab's shame?" Standing up, she turned around to display herself to the duty room. "This is what my husband done to me," she screamed. "This is the work of Robert Connor, so if any of youse killed him, thank you from the bottom of my heart!"

Watters gentled her back down and covered her up. "Have you seen a doctor, Mrs Connor?"

"A doctor?" Mrs Connor snorted in disdain. "Where would I get money to pay a doctor?"

"I'll arrange for you to see the police surgeon," Watters said. "Those bruises look unpleasant."

"I'm glad Rab's dead," Mrs Connor shouted, raising her top again. "He was a sneaky little bastard, cringing when he was with powerful men, slapping me around, and never doing anything on his own."

"Do you know who he was working with, Mrs Connor?"

Mrs Connor's mouth twisted in what might have been a smile. "Is that why you brought me here, Sergeant? Not to tell me about my dead husband, may he rot in hell, but to ask who he worked for. Well, I'll tell you all I know, Sergeant," Mrs Connor sneered the title, "and much good will it do you. He was there to ensure a cracksman did as he was told. He was spying on an honest thief and bringing his gains to another man."

Watters allowed Mrs Connor to rant. "Do you know who the other man was, Mrs Connor?"

"Damned if I do," Mrs Connor said. "I only know he was something important. An army officer or bluebottle Lieutenant."

"And the cracksman? Who was that?"

"You already know that. It was Walter Abernethy," Mrs Connor said, "and my brave Rab was to make sure he did his job and gave the takings to the man in charge. Abernethy got nothing." Mrs Connor's laugh held no humour at all. "And now my dirty, wife-beating bastard of a husband's rotting in hell where he belongs."

"Thank you, Mrs Connor," Watters said. "I'll take you to Doctor Musgrave."

Scuddamore laid the length of foreganger on Watters' desk and stepped back. "I've investigated this blasted thing, Sergeant, and it doesn't help us at all."

Watters grunted. "That's not what I hoped to hear, Scuddamore."

"I've spoken to the mates of two of Muirhead's ships and one of Gilbride's, and they all say the same thing. This rope is from a handheld harpoon, and modern whaling ships only use harpoon guns. This foreganger would not fit."

"Did you try it?"

"Yes, Sergeant," Scuddamore said. "I boarded one whaling ship of each company and inspected the guns. The gun harpoons have an attachment of a different shape to the handheld harpoon, and the foreganger is too large to slot through the aperture."

"Damn!" Watters said.

"Yes, Sergeant." Scuddamore moderated his tone. "When I asked the mates where a man might purchase such a fore-ganger, they said there was a sale of an old whaling ship called *Charming Amelia* a few years ago. She was the last Dundee vessel to use handheld harpoons, and the Greenlandmen – the whalers – reckoned her old-fashioned even then."

"Was there any connection with Muirhead?"

Scuddamore shook his head. "Not a whisper, Sergeant. Neither Gilbride nor Muirhead held a single share in *Amelia*. Some Welsh company bought her for the copper trade, and nobody knows what happened to the remaining whaling stores. They were probably sold off to ship's chandlers or pawnshops."

"Thank you, Scuddamore," Watters said.

This investigation was providing dead end after dead end. He had hoped that the foreganger might lead to Muirhead. Now he had only the wood chips in the auger and the sea chests, with a tenuous motive about a disgruntled man. His ideas were slipping away with little to show for them.

CHAPTER FOURTEEN

HERCULES LOWTHER, THE SHIP'S FIGUREHEAD CARVER, BARELY glanced at the auger that Watters placed on his counter.

"Could you identify these chips of wood?" Watters asked.

"That's pine," Lowther said. "Softwood," he sniffed it, then ran it through his fingers. "Canadian pine, I'd say, and from the deck of a ship judging from the smell of tar. Why do you want to know?"

"From the deck of a ship?" Watters asked. "Are you sure?"

"Sure enough," Lowther said. "The lower deck, I'd say, as there is very little salt on it."

"How about this?" Watters produced a sliver of wood he had cut from *Teresa's* hull.

"What do you reckon, Peter?" Lowther turned to the apprentice, who listened to everything that Watters said.

Peter Wallace grinned at Watters. "Halloa, Mr Watters. I'm still here!"

"I'm glad you're sticking to your apprenticeship, Peter." Watters had introduced Peter to Lowther the previous year.

"Come on, Pete," Lowther said. "What wood is this?"

Peter lifted the sliver, with his forehead creased in concentration. "It's foreign," he said. "Teak, I think."

"Teak it is," Lowther agreed. "Good lad."

"Thank you, gentlemen," Watters said.

"Did you think they were the same wood?" Lowther asked. "Teak is a hardwood, and pine soft. There is no comparison. Was the larger piece from a ship's hull?"

"*Teresa*," Watters said. "The vessel that came aground on the Sands."

"She was Country built then," Lowther said. "Built in India or Burma. They made good quality vessels of teak. Whoever bored the holes must have mighty muscles, for even with an auger, the wood is tough."

That is confirmation that I am looking for a powerful man, Watters told himself. *That's a small step forward. A powerful man who bored holes in Teresa, and a powerful man who murdered Robert Connor. However, the wood in the auger did not match the ship. My hope of an easy accusation did not last.*

———

Gall eyed Watters as he hired his boat. "You must like the seafaring life, Sergeant," he said. "The wind's kicking up a little." He gave a sour grin. "If you're interested in becoming a seaman, the Greenlandmen are recruiting. Muirhead's ships are having difficulty finding men this year."

Watters held up the auger from the sea chest. "I want to compare the holes in *Teresa* with this tool," he said.

"I see," Gall pushed off. "I heard she was scuttled. That's why Muirhead can't find men; they are scared to sail in case the ship goes down."

"I can understand that," Watters said. He took the oars and pulled into the Tay, with the wind pushing him to port and raising the tops from the waves. The sandbank was exposed again, with the wreck of *Teresa* in slightly worse condition than on his previous visit. Watters shook his head, knowing the vessel would gradually deteriorate. Already there were more barnacles, while a colony of crabs had made their home under the hull. Three seals voiced their discontent as Watters checked the holes in the hull with the auger.

"They're an exact fit," he said, with satisfaction, and headed back to Dundee. In the hour since his departure, the weather had worsened. Watters grunted as a wave broke on the stern.

"I'm back in the marines again," he said, calling on all his half-forgotten expertise to get back safely.

"You weren't long," Gall said.

"No," Watters held up the auger. "Do boat builders use these things?"

"All the time," Gall said.

"Do they come in standard sizes?"

"All sorts of sizes, with different diameters for the bit," Gall told him. "If that bit fitted the holes in *Teresa*, your man knew what he was doing. That's a professional's tool. No man could use it properly unless he was trained. A carpenter perhaps, or a boat builder or an engineer."

"I'll bear that in mind," Watters said.

On his way back to the Police Office, Watters advised Mr Muirhead that the sea chests were available for collection at the police stables, placed an advertisement in the local newspapers, and passed the word to Arbroath Betty.

"If you let your customers know, Betty," Watters said, "we have the sea chests from *Teresa* ready for the owners. They can collect them at the police stables."

Betty eyed him suspiciously. "Some of the lads don't like the bluebottles," she said. "They won't go to the Police Office."

"Tell the sailors that they're safe enough," Watters said. "We can't deliver the chests door to door; we're not a postal service."

The three regulars eyed Watters. "Aye," the bald man said. "Who stole the donkey?"

"Aye, who stole it, eh?" his battered companion said and laughed hoarsely, waiting for Watters to react.

"I courted then a Frenchie girl, she took things free and easy,
Then I found an Eskimo, and sure she is a daisy."

The scarred man held Watters eye as he sang.

Watters walked past the table. He did not have the time for banter. *I'll find your blasted donkey,* he promised himself.

———

"Sergeant," Scuddamore said.

Watters looked up from his desk. "Every time you have that look on your face, it's bad news, Scuddamore. What's happened?"

Scuddamore looked troubled. He looked around the duty room and lowered his voice. "I don't like to report this, Sergeant, but I think you ought to know."

"Spit it out, man!" Watters said testily.

"It's that fellow Shaw, Sergeant. You sent him to watch Mr Muirhead, yet I saw him in the Baltic Bar, drinking with a bunch of blackguards."

Watters quelled his surge of anger. "Maybe he was gathering information."

"Aye, maybe. I was checking the pawns, and later I saw Shaw playing football with a bunch of lads." Scuddamore looked away. "Sorry, Sergeant."

Watters grunted. "Don't be sorry for reporting facts. Why were you watching Constable Shaw?"

"I thought I'd better, Sergeant," Scuddamore said. "In case he was the Kinghorn fellow."

"You were right to tell me," Watters said. "Murdoch told me he's a lazy scoundrel."

"As long as that's all he is," Scuddamore said. "Shaw knew about your trap for Abernethy."

Watters breathed out hard. "Thank you, Scuddamore." He pushed aside the report he was writing for Mr Mackay.

"Yes, Sergeant." Scuddamore hesitated, "I don't like spying on other policemen."

"Nor do I, Scuddamore." Watters held Scuddamore's gaze until the detective constable apologised again and walked off.

"Straighten your shoulders, man!" Watters snarled at him. "You're a police officer, not some shambling tramp!" He glowered around the room as faces turned towards him. "And what the devil are you staring at? Get on with your work!"

————

Watters rapped on Mr Mackay's door and immediately entered.

"Ah, Sergeant Watters," Mackay ushered Watters to a seat. "The others will be here shortly. I wanted to speak to you alone first to see if there have been any developments in the murder case."

"Not yet, sir," Watters sat down. Mr Mackay had summoned the lieutenants and both detective sergeants to his office, which was a highly unusual procedure. "We've interviewed Haley and Mrs Connor, and I am convinced neither killed Connor."

"I spoke to Lieutenant Anstruther," Mackay said. "And there the case rests at present. You look agitated, Sergeant Watters," Mackay must have dressed formally for the occasion, for his high collar looked newly starched and bit into his neck, leaving a red mark, and his jacket and waistcoat were stiff with lack of use.

"I'm fine, sir," Watters said. "I just don't get much sleep at present."

"Ah," Mackay tried to smile. "The new baby, of course. How is young Peter?"

"Patrick, sir, and he's very well, thank you."

Mackay nodded, having unbent sufficiently for one interview. "Remind me what is happening with your other two cases, Sergeant, the scuttling and the robberies."

Watters gave a quick overview, with Mackay taking rapid notes.

"Do you have any further ideas, Watters?"

"I have a new theory, sir," Watters said.

Mackay ran two fingers around his neck to loosen his collar. "What's that, Sergeant?"

"We've had two scuttlings, sir, and yet Mr Muirhead has not benefitted from either."

Mackay nodded. "That's correct."

"I was talking to Mr Gall and some of the seamen down in Betty's Welcome in Dock Street," Watters said, "and they say the same thing. The whaling season is about to begin, and the crews are signing articles. Normally sailors are queuing up for a whaling voyage, but not this year."

Mr Mackay began to tap his fingers on the desk. "Do you think that's because of the scuttling, Watters?"

"Undoubtedly, sir. A ship sinking in the Tay, or off Arbroath, is bad enough, but a whaling ship going down in the Davis Straits, hundreds of miles from land is worse."

Mackay's finger tapping increased in pace and volume. "What is your theory, Sergeant?"

"I think the scuttlings are an attack on Mr Muirhead, sir." Watters unconsciously leaned forward to push his idea. "At least one insurance company intends to put Mr Muirhead on its blacklist, sir, making it harder for him to insure his ships. I think somebody is trying to discredit Mr Muirhead, or perhaps even to discourage men from sailing on his ships."

"Why would anybody wish that?" Mr Mackay asked.

"I don't know, sir. It's only a theory."

"A rival whaling company, perhaps?"

"I've spoken to Mr Gilbride of the Waverly Company, and

he respects Muirhead. I can't see him acting in such a manner."

Mackay's fingers began their devil's tattoo. "Neither can I. Let me consider your idea, Sergeant."

"That brings us to the murder, sir," Watters said. "I think the key to both cases is the mysterious police lieutenant."

"The man posing as a lieutenant," Mackay corrected swiftly.

"Quite so, sir. I suspect he murdered Connor to prevent him talking."

Mackay's fingers stilled. "That means we have a murderer at loose in the Dundee Police."

Both men looked up as somebody tapped at the door. Mr Mackay ordered them in, and Lieutenant Anstruther entered, followed by the quiet Lieutenant James Christie and Sergeant Donaldson, Watters' opposite number in the detective branch. Also present were Second Lieutenant Cathro, Sergeant Major John Hills, and Sergeants Ruxton and Murdoch. Two constables entered last, each carrying hard-backed chairs, which they placed in front of Mackay's desk.

"Come in, gentlemen, and take a seat," Mackay invited. He waited until everybody was seated and the constables had left. "I have taken this unusual step of bringing you all here because I wish to reorder the current arrangements."

In the ensuing silence, Watters heard the rumble of traffic outside the office and Christie's laboured breathing. Christie looked even more ill-at-ease in such surroundings than Watters felt, while Murdoch chewed at the stem of his pipe and winked at Watters, totally unconcerned at being in the presence of the great and the good.

"Gentlemen," Mackay continued. "You are all aware of the current situation in Dundee. We have had a murder in the police cells, which Sergeant Watters is attempting to solve, a professional cracksman targeting high-status addresses and a double scuttling. We also have a murder in Lochee, on which

Lieutenant Anstruther is working. I need hardly mention the trouble with mill workers in Lilybank and Scouringburn that Lieutenant Christie and Sergeant Donaldson are quelling."

"That's correct, Mr Mackay," Lieutenant Anstruther made himself spokesman.

"Sergeant Watters has informed me about his cases. Tell me about yours, gentlemen; you first, Anstruther."

Watters listened as each man outlined the progress of their investigations, although his mind was busy on the scuttlings and Connor's murder.

Mackay had been taking notes. "Thank you, gentlemen," he said. "As you seem to be on top of the industrial disputes at the mills, and Lieutenant Anstruther has nearly solved his murder, I am going to reorganise you to concentrate on Watters' three cases." He gave his smile that always reminded Watters of a cold wave breaking on the Caithness shore.

"I have a theory about the scuttlings, Watters," Mackay stopped his finger drumming and stood up, turned his back, and stared out of the window for a full minute before he continued. "Your idea has made me think. If somebody wanted to discredit Mr Muirhead, why stop at small, low-value coasters? If you were going to damage a shipowner, Watters, what type of vessel would you wish to sink?"

"The one with the highest value," Watters answered at once. He was aware that every man in the room was listening to him. Murdoch put his pipe aside, winked at Watters, and began to munch on an Abernethy biscuit.

"And if you were an insurance company and had already paid out on two vessels from the same company, would you be keen to pay out on a third?"

Watters shook his head. "I would not."

"Nor will the Dundee Maritime," Mr Mackay said. "Mr Muirhead would lose all his credibility with the insurance companies and the seamen." Mackay continued to stare out of the window. "Mr Muirhead has paid a great deal of money for his latest whaling vessel, gentlemen. If I were going to damage him, I would sink one of his new vessels, *Lancelot* or *Guinevere. Arthur*, Muirhead's other whaling ship, is older and less valuable."

"I see, sir," Watters said. "We had better set a guard on Mr Muirhead's vessels before they set out and check every member of the crew for a criminal background."

Mackay gave his bleak Caithness smile. "Yes, Sergeant Watters. We are going to do more than that. Mr Muirhead is desperate for men. We will put a couple on each whaling ship he owns."

Watters felt his heartbeat increase as he saw the inevitable outcome of Mackay's idea. "I see, sir. Will these men be looking out for the scuttler?"

"Exactly so, Sergeant Watters." Mackay sighed. "You have recently become a father, I believe."

"Yes, sir," Watters said.

"Congratulations," Mackay said. "The police service can be hard sometimes, Sergeant."

Watters knew what was coming next. "Yes, sir."

"I am sending you and another man on *Lancelot* and placing Scuddamore and Duff on *Guinevere*."

Watters took a deep breath. Although his service in the Royal Marines had taught him never to argue with a legal order, he felt a twist of anxiety for Marie. "Yes, sir. Can you ensure the beat constable looks in on my wife?"

"I'll do that," Mackay said.

Murdoch raised his hand, still holding half an Abernethy biscuit. "I'll look after Marie, George," he called. "My missus will call on her as well. We've got five little ones running about the house, and Eliza will enjoy another one."

"Thank you, Sergeant, Murdoch," Mackay said as Murdoch bit into his biscuit again.

Watters nodded to Murdoch, knowing he could rely on him.

"When are we sailing, sir?" Watters tried to keep the dismay from his voice.

"I can't say, Sergeant," Mackay said. "That's in Mr Muirhead's hands, or perhaps his shipmasters. You were a seaman before you joined the police, weren't you?"

"No, sir, I was a Royal Marine," Watters said.

Mackay grunted. "You were on board a ship in that debacle with the Americans a couple of years back."

"Yes, sir."

"You have experience at sea, then and will be quite at home on board *Lancelot*. Think of it as a little pleasure cruise, with pay." Mackay's smile faded. "Don't worry about the robberies, Watters. I will hand that case over to Lieutenant McQueen and Sergeant Donaldson, while Lieutenant Anstruther deals with the murder of James Connor."

"As you wish, sir," Watters tried to hide his sick dismay. He was leaving Marie when she needed him most. That mattered far more than catching Abernethy or the murder of James Connor.

"Don't think about the death of Connor, Watters," Anstruther called over. "I'll have that solved before you even leave the harbour."

———

Marie pretended to accept the situation. "As soon as I heard about the scuttling," she said, checking that Patrick was asleep, "I half expected Mr Mackay would send you to sea. Since we moved to Dundee, you're as much afloat as you're on land."

Watters allowed the exaggeration to pass. "I've asked Murdoch to look in on you from time to time."

Marie nodded. "Eliza will want to borrow the baby, anyway. Her youngest is three now, so she'll be getting broody." She looked up, forcing a brave smile. "I'll be all right, George. You take care up there in the ice."

Watters pretended not to notice the sadness in Marie's eyes and the deep lines of tiredness at the side of her mouth. He knew he was not the best of husbands.

"It's all right, George," Marie repeated, reaching out to touch his arm. "I'll be all right. You have your duty to do."

Watters nodded. A policeman's lot was hard on the wife, who never knew where he was, what hours he had to work, or if he would come home injured. "You're a good woman, Marie."

"Oh, nonsense," Marie said. "Get you gone, George," she pushed him away, allowing her hand to linger for a second too long on his shoulder.

Marie turned away to attend to Patrick, with her eyes bright with tears.

———

When the crew of *Teresa* came to claim their sea chests, Watters asked them to list the contents to prove they were the owners.

"Was that your first voyage on *Teresa?*" he asked.

With only one exception, the men shook their heads. "I sail on *Teresa* often, usually in the winter months," they said. "I usually go to the Davis Straits in summer."

"You'll be heading north again soon," Watters said.

"Not this year," two men told him. "Not with Muirhead's ships sinking every few weeks. He'll be hard-pressed to find a crew this season."

"Will you find another position?" Watters asked.

"Oh, aye. Old man Gilbride is hiring, and I heard a rumour that there's another whaling company in the offing."

Watters grunted. If the scuttler intended to scare the seamen from Muirhead's ships, his strategy was successful.

The carpenter was younger than Watters had expected, a middle-sized man in his thirties with a shock of fair hair and a ready grin. "Thank you for rescuing my chest, Sergeant," he said. "Without my tools, I'd never find work, and without work, I couldn't afford new tools." He lifted an adze and held it as delicately as he would a newborn baby.

"What's your name, Chips?" Watters already knew the answer.

"Neilson, Sergeant; Peter Neilson."

"You were in *Toiler* as well as *Teresa*," Watters said.

"That's right, Sergeant," Neilson placed his adze back in the chest as delicately as Watters held Patrick. "I seem to pick the unlucky ones."

"Did you know Mr Muirhead before you sailed on his ships?"

Neilson shook his head. "I knew him by reputation as a hard but fair man," he said. "I've never met him and never expect to." Neilson gave the typical Dundee answer. "He and I don't drink in the same public."

"You're not from Dundee, are you?"

"No, sir. I'm from Annan, down in the Solway Firth."

Watters found himself liking this open man, despite lingering suspicions. He decided on a direct approach. "You were the only man on board both *Teresa* and *Toiler*, and you are a carpenter with an auger that fits the holes bored into *Teresa's* hull."

Neilson looked confused. "Do you think I sunk these vessels, sir? I am a chippy, not a scuttler. Why would I sink a ship that employs me when I need a job?"

"A skilled carpenter will always find a job," Watters said.

"In theory, perhaps, sir, but a position isn't all that easy to come by nowadays." Neilson shook his head, smiling. "Me a scuttler? Well, that beats cockfighting!"

Watters pushed across the chest. He was suspicious of the carpenter, who had opportunity and means, but no motive that Watters knew. "I cannot argue with that, Neilson. Try and stay afloat in your next ship."

"I will, sir," Neilson seemed to bear no ill-will for Watters' questioning.

Watters was aware that seamen were nearly impossible to trace, for they could alter their names at will and hop from ship to ship and continent to continent.

"Do you live in Dundee now?"

"Until the next voyage, Sergeant," Neilson said.

And by then, I will be in the Arctic on Lancelot. I hope something turns up soon, or we'll never solve this case. I hope Marie is all right on her own.

CHAPTER FIFTEEN

THERE WAS ALWAYS A CROWD GATHERED WHEN THE DUNDEE whaling fleet sailed to the Arctic. Men, women, and children gathered along the quays of Victoria Dock and Camperdown Dock. They clustered in excited groups in every corner of the shore to watch the ships depart. Some were merely casual observers who liked to watch the spectacle, but most were wives and family, knowing they would not see their menfolk for months and may never see them again. The whaling industry was cruel to men and ships, with accidents and sinkings common. Barely a year passed without some whaling vessel lost to the ice.

Standing in the deck of *Lancelot*, Watters knew that death could claim him in a hundred different ways on a whaling voyage. It could come with a fall from a frost-slippery yard high above the deck or when the ice closed on a stranded ship and sliced through the double-thickened planking. It could come with a sudden fog when a boat's crew were separated from their mother ship or arrive with frightening rapidity in the swing of a whale's tail. It could come in a falling block from above or when a rogue wave washed the length of the deck and took an unwary seaman away.

On this voyage, Watters knew, the sneaking actions of a scuttler could also bring death, sending *Lancelot* down below the bitter ice.

No, I won't allow that to happen. I will watch every man on this ship.

With a crew of forty-four on board, Watters knew that guarding *Lancelot* would not be easy. His one advantage was his companion on board. Mr Mackay had sent Constable Boyle to help in the guise of an ordinary seaman.

Watters saw Boyle gather amidships with the hands, taller than most, as he waved to the crowd.

Thank God it's Boyle and not Shaw.

Captain Fairweather roared an order, and *Lancelot*'s single funnel belched out smoke. Men unfastened the hawsers that attached her to the quay, and the whaling ship eased out, with her figurehead of a mounted knight pointing the way.

Here we go, Marie, Watters thought. He did not need to search for her, for Marie had told him where she would be standing. She was in the front of the crowd, holding Patrick as her hat flapped around her head.

As *Lancelot* surged past, with her screw churning up the calm water and the crowd cheering, yelling, and the wives crying, Watters gaze met Marie's. There was no need for an overt display of emotion. Both knew how much they would miss the other. Watters raised his hand, holding Marie's eyes until *Lancelot* eased out of Victoria Dock, through Camperdown Dock and into the Firth of Tay. She anchored in the Roads and lay there, with Dundee to port and a flock of seagulls screaming around her three masts.

"What's happening?" Watters asked a rugged-looking elderly man.

"We're anchoring here until the crew is sober," the man said. Watters estimated him to be about sixty, but he may have been a lot older. Seamen often understated their age when they signed articles. "Look at them. Would you trust them if a wind blew up?"

Watters agreed. Those crewmen who were not reeling drunk from celebrations that morning were suffering from hangovers from drinking the night before. Even as he looked, one man made a lunge for the rail and spewed into the heaving waters of the Tay. "I see what you mean," Watters said.

The man smiled. "Aye, Captain Fairweather knows his job. He won't hazard his ship until the hands are fit, however much the owner grasps for pennies." He shook his head, "and with this crew of Greenmen and worse, God only knows what will happen."

Watters nodded to the Tay Bank, where the flowing tide covered the wreck of *Teresa*. "I wouldn't like to end up stranded on a sandbank a few miles from Dundee."

"Nor would I," the man said. He thrust out his hand. "I'm Urquhart, by the way. I'm the sailmaker on this ship."

"George Walker," Watters used the name under which he had signed articles. Urquhart's hand was hard as teak.

"Aye, Cap'n Fairweather will ensure we don't end up like *Teresa*, eh?" Urquhart said. "That was a bad thing, yon."

Watters nodded. "Aye, I heard the master miscalculated the tide."

Urquhart spat expertly with the wind. "Miscalculated the tide, my arse. She was scuttled by God."

"Scuttled?" Watters pretended surprise. "Who the devil would do that?"

"Somebody with a grudge," Urquhart said at once. "Or maybe Muirhead needed the money. He's a tight-fisted bastard that one."

"That's not a nice thought," Watters said. "As long as nobody tries to scuttle this ship."

"They'd better not," Urquhart said. "I'll keep my eye open for them, that's all. Captain Fairweather is taking no chances either. He checked every inch of our hull before we left Dundee and rowed around her in his launch to ensure nobody tampered with his ship." He grinned. "Mind you; it would take a lot to sink a Greenlandman with her double-planked hulls and steel bow plating!"

Watters agreed. "I doubt you could bore through her hull with an auger."

Urquhart laughed openly. "Not a chance, Walker! Her planking must be two feet thick or more and reinforced at bow and stern! No, I think we're safe enough in *Lancelot!*"

Watters smiled, although he wondered if he was going to waste four or five months of his life chasing a scuttler who was not on board. If Mr Mackay's theory proved wrong, and the scuttler targeted other vessels, a good portion of the Dundee detective force was unavailable to catch him.

"You'll have sailed in many vessels," Watters said, "One more voyage is nothing to you."

"I'm too old for sailoring," Urquhart said. "I thought I had swallowed the anchor years ago."

"What happened?" Watters asked.

Urquhart shrugged. "Life is not as you wish it to be. One minute you think it's all fair weather and a following wind, and the next, the storm hits, and you're all aback and nowhere to go."

Watters nodded. "There's a lot of truth in that."

"We'll be setting off soon," Urquhart said. "The Captain's looking up at the sails and testing the wind. I hope you're all prepared, Walker."

With his berth in the forecastle like the majority of the crew, Watters found it easy to blend. Every whaling ship carried a quota of Greenmen or first voyagers, men who had never been on a whaling ship before, but with the recent scuttlings, Muirhead's vessels had a higher number than usual. That situation benefitted Watters and Boyle, who were only two of a dozen Greenmen, over a quarter of the crew.

Watters' main concern was for somebody to recognise him, for he was well known as a police sergeant in Dundee.

"Don't shave for a few days," Marie had advised. "You'll look completely different with a hairy face."

Watters agreed, although the first few days saw him scratching madly.

"And don't practice your golf on board," Marie said. "People know you as the golfing detective."

"Do they?" Watters had asked.

Marie smiled. "I've watched you walking along the road, stopping to take a practice swing with your cane and walking again. If you do that on board, somebody will remark on it."

"I didn't know people watched me," Watters said.

"Be careful," Marie said. "And walk with a stoop. You're not in the Royal Marines anymore or the police. You always march as if you're on parade."

"Anything else?" Marie's administrations were beginning to irritate Watters.

"Yes," Marie said and kissed him. "That. Remember that nobody will expect to see a policeman on board. People see what they expect to see, so act as a seaman, and the crew will see a seaman."

Muirhead had supplied Watters with a plan of *Lancelot*, so he had an idea of the layout of the ship. However, what seemed evident on the plan was entirely different in reality, and when packed with stores and seamen, the interior of *Lancelot* was not easy to negotiate.

Lancelot left the Tay at dawn on the second day, with Captain Fairweather using the sails alone.

"Do you think steam-power will ever completely replace sails?" Watters asked Urquhart as they eased into the German Ocean.

"Steam kettles? I hope not. There is no skill in stoking a boiler. You see," Urquhart said, "the cut of a sail is crucial to the way a ship handles. I had a seven-year apprenticeship before I ever went to sea. Seven years in a sailmaker's loft, with a tyrant for a master and a belt across my lug to teach me wrong from right."

"It's a skilled job, right enough," Watters said.

"Aye," old Urquhart paused with his palm and needle. "Every able-bodied seaman can side seam, but cutting out a sail? That takes skill, and learning a skill takes time."

Watters nodded.

"Aye, cutting a sail is like tailoring, except with men's lives at stake. We have to take into consideration the shape and flow of the sail, the rounds and roping, the stretch of the canvas and shrinkage in dry weather."

Watters liked to hear an expert talk about his work, although he doubted whether he would ever need to use a sail-maker's craft.

"I used to dream about owning my own ship," Urquhart said, staring aloft. "I worked all my life for that, but," he shrugged, "look at me now. Over sixty years old and still the servant of another man."

The gale hit them an hour after they left the Tay. It was a typical German Ocean squall, ugly, fast-moving, and coming from two directions at once.

"You men," Masterton the mate shouted, "get aloft and bend a new lower fore topsail!"

Without the requisite skill to help, Watters could only watch and listen as the experienced Greenlandmen chanted at their work.

"Oh, blow my boys, I long to hear you,
Blow, boys, blow!
Oh, sing my boys, 'twill always cheer you,
Blow my bully boys, blow!"

"We have to be careful here," Urquhart said, jerking a thumb at the pencil-thin shaft that was the Bell Rock lighthouse. "If the wind blows us onto the Inchcape Rock, that's the Bell Rock's other name, we'll know all about it."

"Won't the captain use the steam engine?"

"Aye, maybe, but Mr Muirhead is purse-proud. He won't part with a penny he doesn't have to, and that includes using coal unnecessarily. He looks a merry old soul, but he's more like Scrooge than Old King Cole!"

Watters grinned, stowing the information away. "Is he really that bad?"

"Worse than that. The captain is feared to spend a penny more than he should. We're in for a starvation voyage, Walker, scant food and not much of it." Urquhart shook his head. "You know we get paid a fixed amount every month, plus a share of the oil money the ship makes for the blubber she brings back?"

Watters nodded. "I do."

"Well, the oil money and bone money – our share of the sale of the whalebone –can make up more than half our wages at the end of the season."

"As much as that?"

"Here's some free advice, Walker. Check your wages when they are paid. Muirhead's accounts are weighed, so the company keeps any extra, rather than sharing it with the hands. Muirhead's a stingy bastard, and that's on a good day."

The hands swayed the lower topsail aloft, with the words echoing around *Lancelot*.

"With a gallant ship and a bully crew;
Blow, boys, blow!
We're just the boys to pull her through,
Blow my bully boys blow!"

Watters watched them work, wondering which of the bully crew intended to scuttle the gallant ship and if they would pull her through the icy ordeal ahead.

"You look pensive, Walker," Urquhart said.

"I was wondering if any of these men planned to scuttle the ship," Watters said, honestly.

Urquhart shrugged. "Time will tell," he said. "Time will tell."

"Oh, blow my boys, no cause for growling,
Blow, boys, blow!
Though up aloft the wind is howling,
Blow my bully boys, blow!"

The sail rose, with the sweat dripping from the hands and the sea churning alongside. Watters saw the Bell Light slide astern as *Lancelot* made steady progress. Masterton, the mate, roared a succession of orders, and the hands raced aloft to bend the sail, fighting the stiff canvas as the wind tore it from their grasp. Down on the deck, Watters heard their swearing as they balanced on the footrope, braced themselves against the shifting, angling yard and fought to pass the rovings under the jackstay.

The squall returned, with a single monstrous wave crashed over the bow and swept the length of the deck.

"Hold on, Walker!" Urquhart warned. "One hand for yourself and one for the ship!"

Watters held on as the sea momentarily buried him, then *Lancelot* emerged, shook herself free of the water and bullied on.

"The sea must claim its own," Urquhart warned. "Just try not to be the sacrifice."

Watters saw Boyle at the opposite end of the deck. He seemed unconcerned by the gyrations of the ship and even managed to raise a hand to Watters.

Good man, Boyle, you're as good a seaman as you are a policeman. Murdoch did me a favour when he passed you over from the uniforms. I see a bright future for you, my friend.

166

"Oh, blow my boys, no finer weather,
Blow, boys blow!"

Watters knew he would never forget those few minutes when he and the sea were one, and *Lancelot* and her crew fought the storm. The words of the shanty remained in his head.

As Watters lay in his bunk that night, surrounded by the smells and sounds of the fo'c'sle, he pondered what he had learned. The hands considered Muirhead to be a parsimonious shipowner. That was interesting, as his fellow merchants believed Muirhead to be generous. The different viewpoint may have a bearing on the case. Perhaps some crewman resented being on short rations or having his oil money reduced. Watters watched the hands again. He now had a possible motive for the scuttling. All he needed was a culprit with the means and opportunity, yet for the life of him, Watters could not think how somebody could scuttle a double-hulled whaling ship in the open ocean.

———

"How long will it be before we are sunk?" Henderson was an experienced Greenlandman, a burly, bearded seaman with tattoos on both arms and a deep scar across his forehead.

"Why should we sink?" Crockatt was a first voyager, a nervous man with wide brown eyes.

"Muirhead is giving up his fleet," Henderson said, lying on his bunk with his booted feet on the donkey-breakfast mattress and his hands behind his head. "He's sinking them one by one."

"Why?" Crockatt looked around the dark fo'c'sle as if expecting Muirhead to appear with an auger any second.

"I don't know," Henderson said, making himself comfortable. "Maybe he's making more money from the insurance companies than whaling."

"Are you sure it's Muirhead?" Watters called across.

"Who else had access to his vessels?" Henderson asked.

"I don't know," Watters said. "I heard the scuttler was somebody who didn't like Muirhead."

Henderson shrugged. "If somebody hated him that much, they could blow his brains out or put a knife through him. Why go to the trouble of sinking his ships?"

Watters nodded. "I wondered that myself. But why are you on *Lancelot* if you think the ship might sink?"

Henderson pondered for a moment before he replied. "I like the life," he said slowly. "You either love the whaling trade or hate it, Walker. The loneliness outside the ship and the companionship within, the great vastness above and the northern lights, the freedom."

"How about killing the whales?" Crockatt asked.

Henderson grinned. "The toffs hunt deer and shoot pheasants on the Highland estates they stole from the people," he said. "The big game hunters go to Africa to shoot lions and elephants. We hunt the whales," he turned on his side to face Crockatt. "It's bloody work, but every whale and every seal increases our wages."

"How much profit will Muirhead make from a successful voyage?" Crockatt asked.

"Thousands and thousands," Henderson said.

"It's a lot to lose," Boyle said from the furthest corner of the fo'c'sle.

"Aye, and we'd better get some sleep. The weather will be rough tomorrow." Henderson closed his eyes.

Watters lay still a few moments longer, wondering about Marie. When he was sure everybody else was asleep, he slid from his bunk and ventured outside.

CHAPTER SIXTEEN

In the dark, *Lancelot* seemed a different ship, with the sound of the sea and the creaking of wood more prevalent. Watters had nearly forgotten how loud a sail-powered vessel could be as he glanced along the deck and slid below.

If the scuttler were on board and followed his usual pattern, he would sink *Lancelot* when she was near land, making the early days of the voyage the most dangerous. Whaling ships followed a recognised route, sailing coastwise to Orkney or Shetland, picking up fresh water and maybe a couple of extra hands, and then steering north. The old sail-powered ships would make a single trip, to the Greenland whaling grounds, between Spitsbergen and Greenland, or the Davis Straits, between Greenland and Canada. The more modern ships with auxiliary steam power typically made two voyages, the first to the Greenland Seas for seals, then returned to Dundee, unloaded the cargo, and sailed to the Davis Straits.

With parsimonious Muirhead refusing to allow *Lancelot* to burn her fuel, however, she was sailing directly to the Davis Straits, forgoing the sealing in the hope of finding an early capture of whales.

Watters headed for the forward part of *Lancelot*, the area the scuttler had holed in his two previous ventures. He moved slowly from compartment to compartment, listening for anybody else at large in the dark as he inspected the hull with the aid of a lantern.

I could be here all night and find nothing, he told himself, *or I might find a series of holes in the next minute. How the devil can somebody bore through a hull specifically designed to withstand the pressure of Arctic ice? The scuttler must be superhuman.*

Watters crawled forward, shining his lantern on the timbers of the hull, finding nothing. He was unsure whether to be pleased that *Lancelot* was in no danger or frustrated that he might be wasting his time.

He heard a slight noise, something different from the regular creaking of timbers, and closed the sliding shutter of his lantern. The darkness closed on him, thick and menacing as the ship waltzed to the tune of the sea.

The noise continued, a low rumble as if somebody was rolling a barrel across the deck. Watters tried to identify where the sound originated, but the alien environment of the ship disorientated his senses.

Behind him, Watters thought. The sound was somewhere astern. He moved silently, keeping his head down to avoid the low beams. The rolling continued, sounding like the metal hoops of a barrel passing over a wooden deck.

Who the devil is rolling a barrel in the dark? I must have a word with the cooper tomorrow.

"All hands!" Masterton's bellow reached even the deepest depths of *Lancelot.* "All hands on deck! Come on, boys, there's another damned squall coming!"

Swearing, Watters scrambled up to the main deck. The scuttler may be a potential threat, but at sea, the weather was more immediate.

———

"Sergeant!" Boyle whispered the word across the deck.

"The name's Walker," Watters hissed. "Be careful!"

"I think somebody just tried to kill me," Boyle inched closer as *Lancelot* battled her way northward around the knuckle of Buchan, with the expanse of the Moray Firth to port and the German Ocean throwing intermittent gusts of wind at them.

Watters and Boyle were on deck, working with paint pot and brush as the wind whined through the rigging above.

"What happened?" Watters asked.

"I was walking on the main deck last night, and a block fell from aloft," Boyle said. "I checked the rigging, but nothing seemed adrift, and I didn't see anybody."

"You wouldn't see in the dark," Watters said.

"Maybe somebody's guessed that we're policemen," Boyle said.

"Maybe," Watters said. "Keep alert and watch your back. Why were you on deck?"

"Checking for night prowling scuttlers," Boyle said. "I didn't see a damned thing. How about you, Ser- Walker?"

"I was below. I thought I heard something rolling about," Watters said. "I'll have another look when I get the chance."

"Whereabouts?"

"Forward, where *Toiler* and *Teresa* were holed."

Boyle nodded. "I'll check there when I get a chance."

"You're here to work, not yarn!" Masterton interrupted them, landing his boot on Watters' leg. "I've got my eye on you, you blasted lubber! Always poking around asking questions!" He kicked again. "Work, you lubber, or I'll teach you what work is."

Watters kept a hold of his temper, dipped the brush in the pot and continued.

Masterton watched, singing to himself,

"Now when I was a little boy, and so my mother told me,

That if I didn't kiss the girls, my lips would all grow mouldy."

An attempt on Boyle's life was not good, but at least it was confirmation they had chosen the correct ship. It was also a warning that the scuttler knew they were aboard.

———

"I didn't know you were on this ship," Watters said as Neilson grinned at him.

"Oh, yes. Mr Muirhead said he might need a carpenter," Neilson said. "Whaling ships are forever being damaged in the ice, with bergs falling on them, and pack ice squeezing them and all sorts of things." Neilson pointed to his chest. "Thanks to you, I have my tools."

Watters nodded. "Nobody must know that I am a policeman," he said.

"I guessed that," Neilson said. "Are you here to search for the scuttler?"

"I am," Watters said, wondering if Neilson was his man. The carpenter was sufficiently active to drop a block on Boyle from aloft and would know better than most how to sink even a stout whaling ship.

If I heard somebody below, and Boyle was attacked from aloft, does that mean there are two scuttlers on board?

Neilson began to sharpen a saw. "If I see anybody suspicious, I'll let you know."

"And tell nobody about me," Watters said.

"Not a word, Walker," Neilson said, still smiling.

That afternoon, Watters had the opportunity of watching Neilson at work as he created a new topmast out of a length of wood. The man's face was a picture of concentration as he used his adze to cut, shape and smooth the wood.

"I enjoy making things," Neilson said with a grin as he

examined his work. He took a deep breath. "God, I love the smell of new wood. Hold that end secure, will you?"

Masterton was not happy to have a crew with so many Greenmen and allocated them the jobs that took no skill. He had ordered Watters to help Neilson, while Boyle, being younger, was aloft.

"I know that face," Neilson said.

"Who?" Watters asked.

"That man there!" Neilson pointed with a stubby finger as Boyle clambered down from aloft, with Masterton raging at his lack of speed.

Watters swore. "Maybe in a different voyage?" His worst fear was of somebody recognising Boyle or himself as police.

"No," Neilson said as Masterton ordered Boyle aloft again. "It wasn't that." He shook his head. "I know him, though. It will come to me, by and by." He shook his head. "I've been sailing with Muirhead for a few years now, and this is the first voyage I wish I hadn't."

"Why is that?"

"Something is wrong on this ship," Neilson said. "I can feel it. *Lancelot* is not happy. I think she knows somebody plans to do her harm."

"*Lancelot* is a new vessel. That might explain how she feels." Watters knew that many seamen believed ships could be happy or unhappy.

"It's not that," Neilson returned to work, shaving the wood with his adze. "*Lancelot* knows what she's about." He glanced at Watters. "I'm glad you're aboard, Sergeant. The ship is scared." He ran a rough hand over the deck timbers. "Carpenters know wood, you see, and I can feel *Lancelot's* fear." He stood up and faced Watters. "Catch this bastard, Sergeant, or we'll lose another ship. And," he jerked his head to indicate Boyle, who was scrambling along the footrope as he held onto the mainmast, "I know I've seen that man before, but I'm damned if I know where."

———

"We'll have to be careful," Watters took Boyle aside. "Neilson, the carpenter thought he recognised you."

"He might have seen me on the beat," Boyle said at once. "Dundee is not all that big a place, Sergeant. Maybe it was the chippie who tried to kill me."

Watters grunted. After years in the police, he thought he knew men. "I don't think so," he said.

Boyle accepted Watters judgement. "I am surprised nobody recognised you, though. You're much better known than I am."

Watters stroked his beard. "People tend to see what they expect to see, and this simple disguise helps," he said. "And I've altered my stance. That was Marie's idea."

Boyle smiled. "All the boys say that Mrs Watters is part of the force."

"Do they? Well, the boys had better keep their opinions to themselves," Watters said, unsure whether to be pleased or irritated. "And you be careful. Keep out of Neilson's way if you can."

Marie part of the force? The police would be lucky to have her. Watters pictured her with Patrick on her knee, smiled, and shook away the image. Thinking of Marie would only weaken him, and he needed to concentrate on the case.

"A rolling sound from below?" Masterton glared at Watters as though he was a mortal enemy. "You're imagining things, man. You blasted first voyagers are all the same! You think the tiniest thing will sink the ship."

"I wondered what it might be," Watters persisted. "What with half Mr Muirhead's fleet sinking and stories about scuttlings."

"It's your imagination; that's what it is," Masterton said. "Now get back to work, you lazy lubber!"

Henderson gave the same reply, with additional expletives

as he gave his opinion of landsmen, first voyagers who asked stupid questions, and the world in general. Yet when Watters watched him, Henderson's eyes were thoughtful and later that day, he slipped below decks.

The storm came from the north, sending waves battering at *Lancelot's* hull. Again, Masterton called for all hands, and Watters scrambled aloft, balancing on a footrope as he struggled to control acres of stiff canvas.

"Fist it!" Henderson shouted. "Don't let it beat you!" He shook away the rainwater from his face. "This is sailoring, Walker! This is why you signed articles!"

As Watters struggled, he saw Boyle off to his right, furling the sail as if born to it. Watters grunted. Was there nothing that man could not do? He had only been on board a few days, and already he was acting like a prime seaman.

———

"Has anybody seen Boyle?" Masterton glowered around the fo'c'sle. "The bastard's lazing about somewhere rather than attending his duty."

"I saw him an hour ago," Crockatt said. "He was on the deck when that storm hit. I haven't seen him since."

Watters looked up, hiding his concern. "What's this fellow Boyle like?"

"He's the policeman Muirhead sent to spy on us," Crockatt said. "That tall bugger."

Watters did not have to pretend surprise. "I didn't know Boyle was a bluebottle." *Did everybody know about Boyle?*

"Aye, Crockatt said. "He's a spying bluebottle bastard. I hope the sea took him."

Watters said nothing as others in the fo'c'sle echoed Crockatt's words.

"Do you know him, Watters?" Masterton asked.

"We've spoken," Watters said, "but I can't say I know him." *Boyle will be below, checking on the sounds I heard.*

"Go and find him," the mate ordered.

"This is a queer ship," Henderson said. "Police spying on us and faces that don't belong. The sooner we return to Dundee, the better I'll like it."

"Aye," another experienced man said. "Too many Greenmen on board."

Watters grew increasingly anxious as he searched the ship.

"Boyle! Are you there?"

Boyle was not beneath decks, and nobody had seen him.

"The sea must have taken him," Henderson said. "The sea must have his due."

"Aye," Neilson nodded. "I knew there was something queer about that man. I never thought he was a bluebottle, though. I've seen him before somewhere, but not in uniform."

Henderson nodded. "Aye, I thought I kent his face the first time I saw him."

Watters said nothing, hiding his grief. Boyle had been a good man, a fine policeman with a promising career ahead of him. Now he was gone, vanished without a trace.

I can't believe the sea washed him overboard. Boyle was too athletic and sensible for that. I think the scuttler murdered him. What a bloody waste of a good man!

"Did you find him, Walker?"

"No, sir," Watters did not have to feign his concern. "I don't think he's on board."

Masterton swore foully. "We're undermanned as it is without hands throwing themselves overboard with the first puff of wind. Come with me when I tell the old man."

"Missing?" Fairweather shook his head sadly, so his white beard danced on his chin. "He was a Greenman, wasn't he?"

"Yes, sir," Watters said.

"The poor fellow must have fallen overboard," Fairweather said.

"Crockatt saw him on deck during that last squall," the mate said. "Maybe he lost his footing or misjudged the force of the wind or waves. It's easily done if you're not used to life on board."

"I'll enter it in the log," Fairweather said.

Watters felt sick. *I'll enter it in the log. Six words; that was all Constable Boyle was worth.* He had grown to like Boyle, for he was different from the average run of police officers.

"Don't look so despondent, Watters," Masterton said. "The sea takes its payment in human lives from time to time. Just be thankful it's not you."

"Yes," Watters said.

"You've served on a ship before, haven't you?"

"I was a Royal Marine," Watters said. "I've never been on a whaling ship."

"A Guffy, were you? Well, you'll learn," the mate said. "Don't take it so hard. Seamen live for today, for yesterday is gone, and we might never see tomorrow."

Watters nodded. He had lost messmates in the Royal Marines, but Boyle's death was unexpected. He returned to his duties, sick at heart.

———

"That's one gone," Henderson lay on his back with a Jew's harp in his mouth, playing a sad song that Watters didn't recognise. "There will be others."

"Do you think so?" Watters was dizzy from lack of sleep. He knew he could not continue to work by day and patrol the ship at night, while Boyle's death had robbed him of any relief.

Henderson strummed a few notes before he replied. "Undoubtedly," he said. "We have a done old man as master and a bitter ex-captain as mate. That combination doesn't work well at sea."

"I've barely seen Captain Fairweather," Watters said. "He seems thorough, though."

"Oh, he's thorough enough," Henderson spoke between spells at his Jew's Harp, "but he lacks fire. He won't take any chances, and that's undesirable when hunting the whales."

"He's not a man to scuttle his ship, is he?" Watters asked.

"Old Fair Weather Fairweather?" Henderson shook his head. "He's the most safety-conscious skipper you'll ever sail under, Walker. Now, Masterton?" He laughed. "Anything could happen with Masterton."

"Why is that?"

"Surely you've heard the stories?" Henderson sat up, putting his Jew's harp aside. "Don't you Greenmen do anything before you sign articles?"

"I haven't heard anything," Watters said, "except that Muirhead scuttled half his fleet."

Henderson did not accept the bait. "Jesus! Masterton used to be a captain. He skippered *Arthur* a few voyages ago, way up in Melville Bay, north of Disco Island in the Davis Straits. That's the stretch of ice and water between Canada and Greenland."

"And what happened?" Watters asked.

"*Arthur* rescued a couple of young Inuit from the ice, but before the voyage ended, the coonie – the woman – was pregnant, and Masterton was the father. She was only a bairn, and I heard that Masterton handed her to some Danish settlement in Greenland to look after. Old man Muirhead disapproved – he's a right Presbyterian is our Muirhead – and he said Masterton would never serve as a master in his fleet again."

Watters put the information aside. "Would nobody else take him on?"

"He sailed with a Peterhead company for a season but returned clean – that means he failed to catch a single whale – and came crawling back to Dundee. Muirhead's taken him on as Mate." Henderson shrugged. "Masterton's an angry man, or so I've heard."

The words remained with Watters. The mate was an angry, bitter man, but was he bitter enough to try and scuttle a ship? Masterton would have lost a lot of money and prestige by Muirhead's decision to remove him from command.

Masterton undoubtedly has a motive, and he'll have the skill, the means, to scuttle a ship, but would he have the opportunity?

As he scrubbed the deck under Masterton's blustering voice, Watters tried to work out Masterton's movements. As a whaling man, he would have been ashore when *Toiler* and *Teresa* sunk. It was entirely possible, even likely, that the holes in *Teresa's* hull were bored when she was in harbour. A man as resourceful as Masterton could have entered the docks to bore holes in *Teresa's* hull and could perhaps have weakened *Toiler's* bow plates. The pressure of the sea would have forced the weakened plates apart, eventually sinking the ship.

Watters nodded. He would add Masterton to his shortlist of suspects, purely on the evidence of hearsay and suspicion.

Am I grasping at straws here? Perhaps. Masterton is a tall man, such as my witnesses described Lieutenant Kinghorn. He has both motive and means, and maybe the opportunity as well.

Watters felt a sudden chill as Masterton's shadow fell across him. Was the mate capable of murder? He had been first to bring Boyle's disappearance to everybody's attention and was eminently capable of climbing aloft to drop a block on Boyle's head.

Watters continued to scrub, with his mind busy and images of Masterton wresting with Boyle on a stormy deck.

I must survive this voyage and prevent the scuttler from sinking Lancelot. I must bring Boyle's murderer to justice. For a second, a shaft of sunlight cast a shadow across the deck, and Watters saw a loop of rope swinging, like a gallows noose, across Masterton's throat. *Masterton or Anstruther? Masterton and Anstruther? What a combination that would be.*

CHAPTER SEVENTEEN

Six whaling ships sat in Bressay Sound in Shetland, with a host of smaller vessels and fishing boats bobbing on the sheltered water. Captain Fairweather allowed his men to go ashore while *Lancelot* took on fresh water and provisions for the forthcoming voyage.

Watters joined the laughing whaling men as they headed for the inns and pubs of Lerwick, Shetland's largest town. The veteran Greenlandmen men knew where the best publics were and guided the Greenmen, with a few veterans looking for the local women.

Lerwick was well used to whalers and other nautical visitors and welcomed them with open arms. Ever since the days of the Norse, and possibly long before, seamen had landed on these islands, and islanders had sailed to trade, plunder, and fish the seas.

"I'll see you lads later," Watters said as he slid away from the *Lancelots*.

"Where are you off to, Walker?" Henderson had a bottle of whisky in his hand and a song on his lips.

"I've somebody to see," Watters said.

"A woman!" Henderson said. "I knew you were no first voyager. Have you been up north before?"

"Not I," Watters said.

"It's a woman," Henderson shared his suspicion as if it were gospel truth.

"It might be," Watters said, breaking away and smiling at the ribald comments of *Lancelot's* hands.

Lerwick's streets were narrow and busy, with the houses stone-built against the weather and the sound and smell of the sea always in the background. It took Watters a few moments to find his bearings, and, checking behind him to ensure nobody was following, he slipped into the police office.

"And who might you be?" The duty sergeant eyed him up and down.

"Sergeant Watters of the Dundee Police," Watters said.

"Ah," the sergeant's attitude immediately improved. "We were told you might drop in."

"Have you any messages for me?" Watters asked.

"Only one," the sergeant was a slow-speaking Shetlander, with the high colour of a seaman or a farmer, and pale blue eyes that reminded Watters of Mr Mackay. He handed over the message and waited for Watters to read. "You were lucky," the sergeant said. "Your sergeant in Dundee sent a telegram to the Aberdeen, Leith and Clyde shipping company in Aberdeen, and the packet boat brought it to us. It only arrived yesterday."

"Don't you have a telegraph office here?"

The sergeant shook his head slowly. "Not yet. Maybe someday." He smiled. "The ships keep us in touch with the outside world."

Watters read the brief message.

"Robberies stopped. Marie and Patrick well. Murdoch."

Watters smiled; it was just like Murdoch to use an official telegram to reassure him that Marie was healthy. He did not know why the robberies had stopped, perhaps Abernethy had left for another city.

Or perhaps the man who managed Abernethy is on a whaling ship, ready to scuttle her? Masterton, perhaps?

"Is there a reply, Watters?" The duty sergeant was waiting with his pen poised over a sheet of paper. "I'll hand it to the master of the packet ship, and it'll reach Dundee by and by."

"Yes, please," Watters composed the reply as he stood in front of the desk. "Boyle dead, probably drowned. No further news." And he added, "love to Marie. Send that to the Dundee Police, please."

The sergeant did not blink. "I'll do that."

"Marie's my wife," Watters explained.

"I gathered that, Sergeant Watters." The sergeant read back the telegram. "I'll have that sent off today."

Watters left the police office with one burden lifted from his mind. Marie was healthy, and he had informed Mackay of the death of Boyle. Now he still had to find the scuttler.

Lifting a stick from the ground, Watters swung it like a golf club as he walked out of Lerwick into the wind-scoured countryside beyond. Walking helped him think, and he had a lot on his mind. Firstly, there was Boyle: had a wave swept him overboard, or had somebody murdered him because he was a policeman? Secondly, there was the possible identity of the scuttler. Apart from the rolling noise, which could be entirely innocent, Watters had detected no suspicious behaviour in *Lancelot*, but he still had a wary eye on Neilson and Masterton. The carpenter had the tools and opportunity to sink both *Toiler* and *Teresa*, while the mate had the motive and means. Thirdly, and constantly nagging at Watters mind, was the thought of leaving Marie alone with the baby. She had not signed the marriage certificate expecting her husband to abandon her in such a manner.

"The sooner I catch this bloody man, the better," Watters took a swing at a stone, sent it spinning over the field and swore again, remembering that Marie had warned him not to practice his golf.

Neilson or Masterton? Did one of them murder Boyle? I won't find out unless I mingle with the hands.

Watters found *Lancelot's* men happily making an inn bounce with their songs and laughter.

"Did you meet her?" Henderson dragged Watters beside him on a bench.

"That's for me to know and you not to find out," Watters said.

Henderson laughed as if Watters had said something very clever. "We've got our own woman here," he said. "We always visit before we head north, and this season we may need her more than ever."

"Need who?"

"Lizzie Flett," Henderson said. "Do you have a sixpence?"

"Yes," Watters fished out the silver coin.

"That'll do," Henderson said. "Come with me."

Lizzie Flett was a dark-haired, dark-eyed woman of medium height. She closed her fist on Watters' sixpence with a smile, rattled her large hoop earrings, and poured water from a jug into a small tin kettle.

"Sixpence for the wind, my man, sixpence for the wind."

Others from the *Lancelot* crowded around as Lizzie placed the kettle on the fire.

"Who are you?" Lizzie asked Henderson.

"Ian Henderson, Lizzie, Greenlandman from *Lancelot*."

"Let me see your hand," Lizzie examined Henderson's palm. "You are a man of the north," she said.

"I'm from Dundee," Henderson corrected.

"Your blood is from the north," Lizzie told him. "Your mother?"

"She was from Shetland," Henderson agreed.

"She is in your eyes," Lizzie said. "She is watching over you. Be careful of a mountain of ice, Ian Henderson."

"I will," Henderson promised.

The men surged forward, eager for Lizzie's advice. After a few moments, Lizzie pointed to Watters. "Let me see your hand."

Watters obliged as the whaling men crowded round to listen.

"You are not what you seem," Lizzie said, with her eyes more profound than any Watters had seen. "What is your name?"

"I call myself George Walker."

"That is not what I asked."

"No, but it's the only answer I will give."

Lizzie's eyes probed into Watters as she traced the lines on Watters' hand with her nail. "You are a seeker and will find what you seek and what you think is lost."

"That's cryptic," Watters said.

"I see danger," Lizzie told him. "I see a threat from a friend. You will meet danger under the single eye of the tall man. Beware the Cyclops, watcher."

"Thank you," Watters said.

The single eye of the tall man? What the devil does that mean? Was it mere gibberish? Who do I know with a single eye?

"My turn, Walker," a man pushed Watters out of the way and heard that his girl was missing him.

"I know what she's missing," Crockatt leered as Watters pushed Neilson forward.

"Here, Neilson, you get your fortune told." He wanted to see if Neilson was reluctant to have his hand read.

"Oh, go on, then," Neilson said, thrusting his hand out.

Lizzie pored over the lines. "You have a secret," she said at once.

"I have many," Neilson said.

"You have survived tragedy recently."

"Two shipwrecks," Neilson admitted. "And I don't want a third, thank you kindly!"

"Somebody disagrees," Lizzie said. She stepped back as the kettle boiled and studied the steam with her head on one side. "You have bought a favourable wind, seeker," she said. "Most of you will come back alive."

"Most?" Crockatt asked.

"Not all. There is danger in sudden brightness and danger in the dark. I smell death." Her deep eyes swept across the crowd, settled on Watters, and moved on. "There are questions to answer and a price to pay as men remain under the ice."

That could mean anything. Watters scanned the hands, knowing they were more likely to talk when drunk. Quiet men, loud men, young men boasting to look mature, and mature men wishing they were young again. All human life squeezed into the fo'c'sle of a whaling ship, and one may have murdered Boyle.

Watters saw Urquhart watching from a corner of the room, sipping at a glass of whisky, and smiling under his white beard. When Urquhart saw the direction of Watters' gaze, he lifted a hand in quiet salute and strolled closer, coughing onto the back of his hand.

"Do you believe in this fortune-telling stuff, Walker?"

Watters shook his head. "I find men's attitudes interesting," he said. "Lizzie's words are so ambiguous they could mean anything. Telling us there is danger from the ice when we're heading for the Arctic is a bit like saying it will be cold. I'm not sure about the one-eyed man, either."

Urquhart gave a slow smile. "And questions to answer? What might that mean?"

"Anything. A man can ask about somebody's wife or somebody's life." Watters knew that on board a ship, a man's private life was his own concern. If a man was a good seaman, honest with his shipmates and tried his best, that was enough. "Or maybe questions about a scuttled ship."

Urquhart nodded, coughed, covered his mouth, and wiped

blood from the back of his hand. "Life is never as we hoped," he rose, coughed again, and left the inn.

Watters followed, leaving the Greenlandmen to enjoy the boisterousness of the inn. *God knows they'll have little chance of enjoyment up in the Arctic.*

As Watters walked back to *Lancelot,* with the northern wind whistling through Lerwick's narrow streets, he stopped.

The single eye of a tall man? He remembered the box of false eyes in Lieutenant Anstruther's desk.

Lieutenant Anstruther only had one eye. Have I gone full circle, sailing north to leave the culprit back in Dundee? I know there are at least two people involved. Could it be Anstruther and Masterton as well as Abernethy? Have the robberies stopped because Masterton is away from Dundee?

————

Watters stirred in his bunk. He had thought it would be hard to adjust to the movement of a ship after so long luxuriating in a fixed bed shared with Marie, but he had slipped back into maritime life without much difficulty.

What had awakened him? Watters lay still, allowing his eyes to become accustomed to the dark of the fo'c'sle. He saw the sleeping figures of his crewmates and heard their laboured breathing in the tiny space, nearly devoid of air. One man was moving, creeping out of his bunk, and heading towards the door.

In the dark, Watters could not ascertain who it was. He waited until the man had left the fo'c'sle and followed, opening the door, and creeping onto the cold deck outside.

Lancelot sailed north and west with her engine quiet and her sails bending under the weight of wind. Watters crawled about the lower decks of the ship, keeping in the shadows. He listened to the creak of timber and the moaning of the wind in the rigging but heard nothing else. Watters was now familiar with the shipboard noises, which did not help him listen for the stealthy footsteps of the night-walker. He was aware the man might be innocently visiting the heads, but if so, he was lost.

Watters eased closer, creeping around the casks and boxes of provisions, and stopped when a stray shaft of moonlight fell on the face of the prowler. Crockatt.

What the devil are you doing, Crockatt?

Crockatt seemed to have no direction as he wandered around the ship, stopping at odd places. Watters followed, keeping quiet as Crockatt's behaviour became ever more erratic. After a tour of the ship, Crockatt headed back to the fo'c'sle. Watters gave him five minutes to settle and slid back into his bunk.

Crockatt is a Greenman, hardly likely to scuttle a whaling ship.

The wind dropped the following day, and Masterton bellowed for all hands. Watters joined the rest on deck, following the mate's orders.

"I saw you, Walker," Crockatt said as they hauled up the mainsail.

"You saw me do what?"

"I saw you sneaking about below decks," Crockatt said. "What are you up to? You're ayeways asking questions and nosing around."

"So are you," Watters turned the question around. "What were you doing, Crockatt?"

"Making sure nobody sinks us," Crockatt said.

"Work, you bastards!" Masterton roared. "Sing! Follow my words!" He shouted the opening lines of the shanty.

"Don't you see the black cloud rising?
Way haul away, we'll haul away, Joe!
Now when I was a little boy, and so my mother told me,
That if I didn't kiss the girls, my lips would all grow mouldy!"

The men joined in, with the Greenmen following the example of Henderson and the other experienced hands.

"I was searching for the scuttler," Crockatt said.

"Me too." Watters glanced aloft, where the mainsail caught the breeze and bellied out, pushing *Lancelot* deeper into the Atlantic.

Masterton stalked past, bellowing orders that saw the men run to various duties. Within half an hour, Watters found himself over the side, painting again.

Was Crockatt searching for the scuttler? Or was he trying to sink the damned ship? There are too many questions and not enough answers.

————

Lancelot passed Cape Farewell at the southern tip of Greenland in a fog so thick that nobody could see the land. Captain Fairweather ordered half a dozen experienced hands to look out for icebergs and other vessels. "Put a man in the chains with a lead," Fairweather called. "We don't know what's out here."

"Aye, sir," Masterton said. "Henderson, you're one of the few real seamen on this ship. For'ard you go and cast the lead."

The fog lasted three days, and then *Lancelot* emerged into clear weather, with the coast of Greenland a white smear to starboard and Davis Straits to port. They made good time heading north under sail alone as *Lancelot's* iron-shod bows cleaved through brash ice and frost glittered on the halliards and braces. Masterton or Fairweather sat in the crow's nest, searching for whales or ice, the experienced hands preparing the ship for hunting whales and teaching the Greenmen the intricacies of the trade.

"*Lancelot* is the carrier," Henderson explained, "and the whaling boats," he indicated the six small boats that hung on davits, ready for an instant launch, "are the hunters. When the man in the crow's nest spies a whale, we launch the boats and hunt it down."

Lancelot did not come across any whales until she was north and west of the whalers' rendezvous of Disco Island, halfway up the west coast of Greenland. Two whaling ships already sat under the snow-streaked hills, with *Guinevere* already waiting for *Lancelot.* Watters saw Duff from a distance as the respective captains met briefly, and then both ships sailed west into ice-slicked water and the whaling grounds.

"In a few weeks," Henderson said, "there will be a dozen ships here. Give Fairweather credit; he's got us here when the ice is thin."

"Thin ice or no ice," Crockatt said, "I'm still searching for the scuttler. If he wants to sink us, it will be here, where he can escape easily."

Watters agreed. He also slipped away to check *Lancelot* beneath the waterline without finding anything suspicious. Although he retained his doubts about Masterton and Neilson, he also wondered if he was on the wrong ship.

Maybe the scuttler is on Guinevere? If so, Duff and Scuddamore will cope. They are good men.

Within a week, Watters decided that he did not like whaling. *Lancelot* caught three whales within three days of leaving Disco Island, which meant long hours of intense effort, chasing the quarry through loose ice and biting blizzards. The kill was bloodier than Watters had expected, with the whaling guns sending their harpoons into the body of the whale. Then followed a terrible journey as the whale pulled the boats through the ice before the boatsteerer eased them sufficiently close for the harpooner to finish the animal with his lance.

The crew cheered at each kill, for the death of the whale gave each man a bonus. Each ton of whale oil melted from the whale's blubber added to their wages, as did each hundredweight of the whalebone or baleen from the mouth of the whale. Watters understood their elation, for money was always tight, and the whaler's wages paid the rent and put food in the mouths of their children.

The flensing was a horrible, messy job, using a winch to turn the whale as the hands stripped off the blubber and stored it in tanks that were integral to the manufacture of the ship. An elderly whaling man, known as the spectioneer, supervised the business, checking every stage through watchful eyes.

"That was a seventy-footer," Henderson said. "A whale of that size can make or break a voyage."

"It's all about money, then," Watters said.

"No whales, no profit," Henderson said as he cut the blubber into chunks before sending it down the canvas tube to the inbuilt tank. "If we hadn't caught any whales, the voyage would be a loss, and Muirhead would want to scuttle this ship next."

"Do you still think Mr Muirhead is scuttling his own ships?" Watters asked.

"Who else?" Henderson asked. "He stands to gain, and nobody else."

"We're a man short!" The spectioneer roared. "Where's that blasted Greenman Crockatt?"

Watters glanced around the deck. "Will I look for him?"

"Then I'll be two men short! Stay where you are."

Only when the flensing was complete did Masterton order the crew to search for Crockatt.

"Bloody Greenmen!" Masterton said. "If they're not throwing themselves overboard, they're catching Cape Horn Fever."

Watters had heard the term before. Masterton suspected that Crockatt was malingering to avoid work.

However, it was not long before somebody discovered Crockatt.

"They've found Crockatt." The news ran around the ship. "He's dead."

"Another death?" Henderson touched the whale's tooth he wore around his neck. "We should head back to Dundee now. This voyage is cursed."

Crockatt lay face down at the foot of a companionway with his skull splintered. Watters knelt beside the body, with his initial impression that somebody had battered the man's head in with a heavy object. He looked upward at the circle of faces as a dozen men watched him.

"I think he fell," Watters said.

"Aye, and I might be a prince of China," Henderson said. "Somebody pushed him. We have a murderer on board."

"I've seen murder before," Watters said. "Look at the angle of the body. This man fell down the stairs."

"Seen murder, have you, cully," Masterton said. "I thought you were a bit forward for a Greenman. So, you're a murderer, are you?"

"Not quite," Watters said. He pondered for a minute. Here he was, hundreds of miles from civilisation, with a dead body and perhaps a scuttler on board an Arctic whaling ship. "May I inspect the body?"

Masterton glared at him. "Are you a doctor?"

"No."

"The doctor will inspect him. You can get back to your duty."

In normal circumstances, Watters would have revealed his identity, but with Masterton as one of his prime suspects, he held his peace.

The law demanded that every Arctic whaling ship should carry a surgeon. *Lancelot's* surgeon was a youngster of nineteen who was raising money for his final year at Edinburgh Medical School.

"Crockatt died because of a severe contusion to the skull," the surgeon said.

"Man-made or natural?" Watters asked. "Did somebody hit him?"

The surgeon looked confused for a moment. "I could not say."

"Could you make a guess?" Watters asked.

"I'd say he fell," the surgeon said. "He was a Greenman. A sudden lurch of the ship could have unbalanced him. Or maybe somebody hit him with something long and heavy. It's hard to say."

"Thank you, doctor," Watters knew he would learn nothing more from the young doctor.

I am no further forward. We may have a scuttler on board, and Crockatt may have been murdered, although I doubt it.

Watters was returning to his duties when Masterton laid a heavy hand on his shoulder.

"Well, Walker? Did you learn anything from the doctor?"

"No," Watters shook his head.

"I didn't think you would. This voyage is the rummest I've ever sailed on." Masterton said. "Who are you?"

"Alexander Walker," Watters said.

"That may be your name, cully, but not who you are," Masterton's hand was heavy on Watters' shoulder. "You ask a sight too many questions for a Greenman. Who are you?"

"Sandy Walker," Watters said. "And I'm worried, Mr Masterton. That's two dead men in this ship so far and rumours of scuttling."

Masterton removed his hand. "If you find anybody endangering this ship, Sandy Walker, you tell me about it." He leaned closer to Watters, his eyes granite hard. "Do you hear me?"

"I hear you," Watters said.

"And if I so much as suspect that you're involved, I'll break your spine and maroon you on an iceberg," Masterton said.

Watters slipped his right foot back to give him more balance. "I wondered if you were involved," he challenged, holding the mate's gaze. He heard the creaking of the ship and wondered if Masterton would attack him.

"You're a strange one," Masterton said. "I don't understand you at all. I should kill you for that."

"We should work together," Watters' opinion of Masterton shifted as he read the mate's eyes. A scuttler and murderer would not have approached him in such a manner. "If I find anything, I will inform you, and you do the same for me."

"The devil, I will!" Masterton gave the correct answer for the mate of a ship to an insolent crewman. "Get about your duties, Walker, and don't get in my way again!"

Masterton is not the scuttler. I am sure of that. I'll keep watching and see what turns up. I feel something is about to happen soon.

CHAPTER EIGHTEEN

THE CREW MUSTERED AFT, AND CAPTAIN FAIRWEATHER READ the burial service as Crockatt's body was committed to the deep.

"Maybe the police will want to see the body," Watters had hinted, only for Masterton to refuse.

"The Dundee police have no jurisdiction here," he said, "and what will they see that the doctor has not already put in his report?" Masterton shook his head. "No, Walker, or whatever your name is, I won't have a dead body on board the ship. Crockett died at sea, and the sea will accept his body."

As the body, wrapped in Baxter's Number Six fine canvas and weighted at the feet with iron bars, slid into the sea, Watters remembered Lizzie Flett's words:

"There are questions to answer and a price to pay as men remain under the ice."

He watched the swirl as Crockatt slid under the water and said a short prayer. *Marie would like that,* he thought.

Murder or merely an accident? I doubt I'll ever know, but unless I find the scuttler, we'll all die here in this wasteland. Two men dead and not a step further forward

"Iceberg on the starboard bow!" The cry sounded from the crow's nest, the bucket-like contraption in which an experienced hand sat to watch for signs of whales or any danger to the ship. The Greenmen ran to the rails to view the iceberg as it loomed into view. As tall as the ship and twice as long, it eased serenely past, glistening white in a providential shaft of sunlight.

"Line the rail, lads," Masterton said, "Prepare to fend her off."

The veterans taught the Greenmen how to push away small bergs with long poles and watched as the ice giant floated past.

"There will be more ahead," Henderson warned. "We're heading into the ice now."

The thermometer had been low for days, with clear seas at Disco followed by a succession of snow and hailstorms that battered *Lancelot* and made the Greenmen curse they had ever signed articles for such a miserable voyage.

The old Arctic hands laughed at the wind that screamed through the rigging and the hail that hammered on the deck and taut canvas of the sails like rapid musketry.

"Welcome to our world, Walker!" Henderson said. "Crockatt and that other fellow, Boyle, will be in Fiddler's Green now, mocking us."

Watters knew that Fiddler's Green was the sailor's heaven, where the wind was always fair, and there was laughter, music, free grog and tobacco, and a willing woman for every drowned man. "I hope so," he said.

Boyle deserves no less.

With flying wrack obscuring the sun, Fairweather sailed by dead reckoning, knowing the ways of the Arctic, inching his way towards the prime whale-hunting grounds of the West

Water. After two days, the number of icebergs increased, with *Lancelot* sailing ever close to them.

"Winds strengthening, skipper," Masterton reported. "Coming from the south-south-west."

Captain Fairweather glanced aloft. If the wind strengthened further, it might blow them towards the bergs.

"Get the hands aloft, Mr Masterton. Furl the mizzen topsail."

Masterton shouted a volley of orders that had the men scrambling up the rigging to lessen sail.

"We could use the engine, sir," Masterton suggested.

"Not with the present owners, Mister Masterton," Fairweather said. "Mr Muirhead would shave an egg for its fur if he thought it would save him a farthing."

So it continued as *Lancelot* eased across Melville Bay, with Captain Fairweather setting the topsails when the gales eased and furling them when the wind strengthened.

Masterton kept the sailmaker and carpenter busy, demanding perfection in his ship. The mate inspected all their work, proving himself an expert at even the most intricate details of the craftsmen, as he checked the *Lancelot* from stem to stern every day and demanded instant attention to every minor flaw.

"You're searching for the scuttler," Watters said.

"What I'm doing is my concern," Masterton told him. "And none of yours. Get about your duty!"

After an abortive inspection of the ship, Watters looked over the rail. He did not like the ice in Melville Bay or the utter desolation of the Arctic sea. He could appreciate the beauty of the icebergs and the light nights when the sun was above the horizon, but the grey clouds hid everything. There was nothing in Melville Bay but snow, frozen sea, and ice. With intense cold and foul weather, he found himself longing to return to Dundee.

"I've been in some bad places in my life," Watters

muttered as he stuffed tobacco into the bowl of his pipe, "and this place is one of them. It's not as bad as the Dead Ned dreariness of West Africa with its fevers and slavers, but not far off." He looked around, suddenly aware he had been talking to himself.

"The coast of Dead Ned?" Masterton emerged from behind the shelter of the mainmast. "You're no first voyager, mister. Not if you know West Africa, and you're too damned opinionated. Who the devil are you? Out with it, man!"

Watters decided he had play-acted for long enough. "I am Sergeant George Watters of the Dundee Police, Mr Masterton."

The mate took a step back. "Well, damn me to hell on a Friday. You're a bloody Peeler."

"I am. Please escort me to Captain Fairweather, Mr Masterton. It's time to tell him the truth."

Captain Fairweather looked astonished when Watters introduced himself. "You say you are a policeman?"

"That's right, sir."

"Why?" Fairweather asked. "Why are you on board my ship, Sergeant?"

"After two of Mr Muirhead's vessels were scuttled, we suspected *Lancelot* might be in danger. I was sent on board to keep an eye on the crew." Watters decided not to mention Boyle. He could feed the captain information one piece at a time.

"Good God." Fairweather stared at Watters. "Mr Muirhead might have informed me."

"If he had done so," Watters said, "you would have treated me differently. The hands needed to accept me as a Greenman."

"I have been at sea for forty-seven years," Fairweather said, "and master for twenty-three years, without ever losing a ship. I won't lose *Lancelot,* by God."

Watters smiled faintly. "I'm glad to hear it, sir. I am here to help you keep your command."

Fairweather lifted his head as *Lancelot*'s movement altered slightly. "Scuttle my ship, will they? Is the scuttler on board, Sergeant?" Fairweather faced the mate. "Do you know about this, Masterton?"

"I have heard the rumours, sir," Masterton said. "I have been checking the ship at regular intervals."

Fairweather nodded, with his white beard bobbing at the end of his chin.

Watters broke a tense silence. "I don't know if the scuttler is on board, sir."

Fairweather had not commanded ships without learning to adapt to new circumstances. "All right, Sergeant Watters. How do you intend to find the scuttler?"

"I wish free rein to investigate," Watters said.

Fairweather lifted his chin, so his white beard pointed towards Watters. "I don't like the idea of a thief-taker on my ship, Walker."

"Watters, sir."

"Walker, Watters, whatever you are damn well called!" Captain Fairweather was finding it difficult to retain his temper. "You're a rum customer, and no mistake, coming on board my ship and demanding I do as you say."

"I'm not demanding anything, sir, except that you allow me to look for a scuttler. I will not interfere in your running of the ship."

Fairweather took a deep breath and glanced at the mate before he replied. "You have free rein, Sergeant Watters. All I ask is that you catch this scuttler. Mr Masterton will help you."

Masterton gave Watters a nod.

"Thank you," Watters said. "I'd like to inspect the area where Crockatt was found, please."

———

Watters glanced at the companionway. "What the devil was Crockatt doing here anyway?"

"I sent him down there," Masterton admitted at once. "Crockatt and I were trying to trace the scuttler."

Watters raised his eyebrows. "You could have told me."

"We suspected you," Masterton said with a twisted smile.

"Did he fall?" Watters looked up, where the steep companionway arrowed to the deck above. "Or did somebody smash his skull with a marlinespike?"

Watters shone his lantern on the deck to see the darker patch where Crockatt's blood had stained the timber. He glanced upwards and worked out the trajectory if Crockatt had fallen.

"He may have simply lost his footing," Masterton said.

"I think so," Watters said. "The injury was to the front of his head, which is consistent for a man tumbling face down. Who else might be down here?"

Masterton shrugged. "Not many people. The carpenter or sailmaker could have been checking their stores, or the cook, perhaps."

"That will be Neilson, who was on *Toiler* and *Teresa* or old Urquhart. The cook, I don't know."

"John Smith," Masterton said. "An old whaling man. I've known him for years."

"We'll speak to him in a few moments," Watters said. "The first time I was below decks, I thought I heard a rumbling, like kegs or barrels being rolled over the deck. Are there barrels stored here?"

"Yes," Masterton said. "In the storerooms in this section of the ship. Come with me." He led Watters to a small, heavily timbered area a few yards away. The lantern light bounced from the deck beams above and threw dark shadows into the hidden corners.

"That's a handy little space," Watters said.

Wooden boxes and kegs filled most of the room, with one noticeable gap on the left side of the room.

"What should be here?" Watters asked.

Masterton looked at the space and swore. "Gunpowder," he said quietly.

Watters traced the outline of the barrels in the dust with his foot. "I make it six kegs," he said. "What weight is in each?"

"Fifty-six pounds. Half a hundredweight." As first mate of the ship, Masterton would know every detail of the stores she carried.

"Three hundredweight of powder?" Watters would have whistled if he had been on land. Whistling at sea was not recommended as it called up the wind. "What are you planning to do? Start a war?"

Masterton shook his head. "No. If the ice closes in, we sometimes have to blow ourselves clear."

"I see. Three hundredweight of powder would make a nasty hole in the ship."

"It would send us to the bottom," Masterton said.

"We'd better find it, then," Watters said. "I wondered how the scuttler planned to sink a double-planked ship. I did not know you carried gunpowder."

"Every whaling ship does. Do you think the scuttler will set it off soon?" Masterton looked and sounded concerned.

"No," Watters said. "We're miles from anywhere. I think he'll set it off when we get close to land so that he can escape." He shook his head. "He's made a huge mistake in moving it when we're at sea. It's given us time to find the stuff and then locate him."

"This is your first whaling voyage, Sergeant," Masterton said.

"Yes."

"When next you go on deck, Sergeant, look around. You'll find you're not as isolated as you think."

"What do you mean?"

"Whaling ships work together, or at least in the same fishing grounds," Masterton said, "If *Lancelot* sunk, there will be other vessels within a few hour's sail or half a day's trek across the ice."

"I didn't realise that."

"Any whaling man would know that," Masterton said.

Watters nodded, although the statement, so casually said, had made his mind race. If any whaling man knew that *Lancelot* would be in company, then the ship was in great danger unless he located the gunpowder.

"The scuttler is probably an experienced whaler, then," Watters said. "We can discount the Greenmen."

That lessens the numbers considerably. If I take Masterton out of the equation, I have Neilson at the top of my list.

"We'd better get searching, Mr Masterton," Watters said. "You'll know this ship like the back of your hand. If you were to blow a hole in her, where would you choose?"

"I'd place the gunpowder down near the waterline," Masterton said slowly, "and amidships. *Lancelot* is more heavily reinforced in her bows and stern. The bows to break the ice, and her stern, in case of ice closing on her. She is trebled there – her hull is three planks thick – but only doubled in the remainder of the hull."

"What's amidships?" Watters asked and answered his question. "The engine room, except that the chief engineer would notice half a dozen kegs of powder. In the hold then, where we store the blubber."

"In the hold, or the cable locker, the paint store or the sail locker."

Watters nodded. "Any of the three would be a good place to put the gunpowder. Much of the cable is smeared with tar; the sails are dry canvas, and paint is highly flammable."

"Dear God," Masterton said. "If the powder blows there, *Lancelot* will burn like a torch! Come on, Watters!"

CHAPTER NINETEEN

MASTERTON WAS MOVING EVEN AS HE SPOKE, GLIDING through the ship and ducking under the low beams with more ease than Watters expected from such a big man. Watters followed, stumbling when *Lancelot* lurched before a heavy sea.

"In here," Masterton opened a low door. The smell of paint caught at the back of Watters' throat as he entered. Masterton scraped a Lucifer and applied it to the wick of a lantern that hung by the door. Yellow light pooled inside the cabin, revealing large tins of paint jammed together to keep them secure.

"There's little room for powder kegs in here," Masterton did not hide the relief in his voice.

"It will only take a single keg," Watters said. "With all this paint burning, *Lancelot* would have little chance." He began to move the cans, rolling them across the slanting deck.

"You carry on here," Masterton said. "I'll try the cable locker." He moved to the next cabin, and soon Watters saw lantern light shining from that doorway.

Watters moved a dozen tins, sufficient to enable him to see into the corners of the cabin. There were no kegs of gunpowder hidden there, only paint, tar, and boxes of brushes for the crew.

"We're safe in here," Watters called.

"Tidy up the mess," Masterton ordered.

"No time," Watters knew that Masterton would be obsessive about the smartness of his ship. "What's in the cable locker?"

"Cables and rope," Masterton said. His lantern illuminated the room with its neatly coiled lines of various lengths and thicknesses.

Watters lifted his lantern high and squeezed beside the mate, allowing the light to play along the lengths of rope as he traced the line of the bulkheads. "There's nothing in here," he said. "There's no room for anything in here." He lay on the deck, allowing the light to play on the cables, looking for non-symmetrical shadows or the glint of a barrel stave. "Everything's neat and orderly; nothing has been moved."

"Anything?" Masterton asked.

"Nothing," Watters said. "Only the sailmaker's loft now." He felt his hope fading even as the tension rose.

"If the powder kegs are not in the sailmaker's loft, then we'll need to scour the whole ship," Masterton stepped along the passageway. "That will alert the scuttler, whoever he is."

"I know," Watters said. "I'm not ready for that." He opened the door of the sailmaker's store and gasped. Where the other stores were squared off and orderly, in here, sails and long bolts of canvas were scattered around in no order.

"That's not right," Masterton said. "I'll have more than a quiet word with sails whether we find something in here or not."

"I know Urquhart," Watters said. "He's a quiet, elderly fellow. I can't see him leaving the place in shambles." He stepped inside, ducking under the low deck beams. "I believe we've found the place."

"I'll kill whoever did this," Masterton said. "By the time

I'm finished with them, they'll wish they had sat on a powder keg and blown it up."

Watters pushed a stack of Baxter's Number Three canvas to one side and held his lantern up high. "Here we are, Mr Masterton," he said. "Two barrels."

"Two? We're looking for six," Masterton said.

"Keep looking," Watters crawled onto one of the shelves. "I'll wager there are more hidden in here."

The canvas was heavy, and with so many bales opened and spread around, finding the barrels of powder took time. Masterton found the next keg, hidden within the folds of a bolt of Number Four canvas, and then the fourth keg a moment later.

"We have still got two barrels to find," Watters said.

"Better two than six," Masterton rolled the kegs to the middle of the locker.

"A hundredweight of powder can cause a lot of damage," Watters said.

Masterton swore. "We'd better find the damned things."

"If I was to scuttle this ship," Watters said. "I'd have two explosions, widely separated so the crew would not know which fire to fight or which way to run, and I'd have a boat or a raft ready."

Masterton nodded. "You've given this some thought, Sergeant." His mouth twisted into a smile. "You're not considering changing to the opposite side, are you?"

"One has to get into the mind of the criminals," Watters said. "So where would the least likely place be to place a keg?"

"Where nobody would notice it," Masterton said.

"Where on a ship would a keg be less noticeable?" Watters said. "Among others, of course."

"The galley stores," Masterton said and pointed to the four barrels of gunpowder. "What about these?"

"Put them in your cabin," Watters said. "But now we've found them, it's unlikely the scuttler will try anything. I wonder how Sails didn't see the scuttler moving into his locker." He swore softly. "Unless Sails is the scuttler! An experienced Greenlandman who knows his way around the ship. . ."

"Why?" Masterton asked. "He's an old, done man and a tradesman. Why sink *Lancelot?*"

"I was thinking the same thing myself," Watters said. "We'll find out when I question him."

Masterton pounded a massive fist into his left hand. "I'll come along to that interview."

"We have two kegs to find first," Watters said. "I doubt Urquhart will tell us where he's hidden them."

Leaving the recovered kegs in the mate's cabin, they hurried to the galley at the other end of *Lancelot*.

"What the devil?" Peter Neilson was inspecting lengths of wood below deck as Watters and Masterton hurried past. "What's the to-do?"

"Check your stores for kegs of gunpowder," Watters ordered.

"Check for what?" Neilson asked, stupidly, but Watters and Masterton were too busy to reply.

"Who's that?" Watters saw somebody in the darkness ahead. "Who are you?" He held his lantern high, so the yellow light created elliptical shadows among the deck beams. "Show yourself!"

There was no reply, merely the scuff of footsteps in the dark and the creak of timbers. Watters ran forward with his arm extended, flinging the lantern light forward.

"You, there!" He got a glimpse of something moving and then only darkness beyond the light as his quarry vanished.

"He's gone," Watters said.

"Probably nobody there," Masterton said. "Shadows in a ship can be deceptive. The galley's this way, Watters." He strode forward, ducking under the deck beams with the ease of a lifetime of practice. Watters followed, holding his lantern high and peering ahead, searching for the elusive figure.

"Here's the galley storeroom," Masterton grabbed the door handle. "Damn it to hell and buggery! It's locked!"

"Boot it open!" Watters was in no mood for niceties.

"You'll leave my door alone!"

John Smith was the cook and acted as the shipkeeper when *Lancelot* was in dock. An elderly man who had lost his left arm to the swing of a whale's tail ten years ago, he usually moved slowly but leapt from his galley when Watters and Masterton shouted outside.

"What the devil?" He echoed Neilson's words. "What's the to-do? You won't be booting in anything, my friend." Smith wielded a ladle, prepared to defend his domain against the mate, Watters, and anybody else.

"Gunpowder!" Masterton tried to explain. "We're looking for kegs of gunpowder."

"Well, I haven't got any," Smith said. "My boys wouldn't like it if I mixed gunpowder into their soup. Bugger off!"

"No," Masterton took a deep breath, "you don't understand."

"You're damned right I don't!" Smith lifted his ladle in a gesture of defiance.

"Somebody might have placed a keg of gunpowder into your stores," Watters said.

"Oh," Smith shrugged and lowered the ladle. "I'm sure I'll find it. You don't need it urgently, do you? Have the Russians attacked us, then?" He mustered a smile. "It's busy here this morning. I just chased somebody else away."

"I thought I saw somebody prowling around," Watters said. "Who was it, Smithy?"

"That's hardly your business, Greenman," Smith said, shaking his head to Masterton. "I don't know, three minutes on board, and he thinks he's important. Wait until we're in the ice proper, my boy. That'll learn you!"

"Who was it, Smith?" Masterton reinforced Watters' words. "We need to know."

Smith smiled again. "All right, all right, Mr Masterton. There's no need for the hurry. There's never any need to hurry up on the ice. Honestly, it's all rush and scurry nowadays. In my day, there was none of this hurry. We moved with the Lord's wind and were thankful to do so."

"Who was it, John?" Watters tried to persuade the old cook. "Get the key, for God's sake!"

The explosion took them all by surprise. Watters saw the flash a micro-second before he heard the sound and tried to duck as the bulkhead between the galley and the galley storeroom disappeared in a welter of fire and smoke. He was fortunate that the sturdy construction of *Lancelot* saved them from the worst effects of the blast, but the ship rocked, and thick smoke gushed into the galley and the corridor outside.

The force of the explosion threw Watters to the deck, where he lay, momentarily too dazed to think. For a moment, he was back in the Royal Marines, with a slave ship firing on them as it tried to escape the Brass River with its cargo of human misery.

He coughed in the smoke and coughed again, spitting blood. He felt pain in his right shoulder and leg, tried to rise, failed, and slumped back to the deck where the smoke was less dense.

Dear Lord, what happened?

There is danger in sudden brightness. Liza Flett had said.

"George!" That was Marie's voice, penetrating the fog of smoke that burned acrid in his throat. "George! Get up!"

Watters struggled to open his eyes, expecting to see the familiar surroundings of his bedroom in Dundee. Instead, he saw the rough deck of *Lancelot*, with splinters of burning wood and a layer of blue-white smoke.

"George!"

"Marie?" Watters pushed himself upright, staggered and grabbed hold of the bulkhead for support. He swore as he touched the hot wood, coughed again, and remembered where he was. "Jesus!"

The deck was ablaze, with orange flames licking from what had once been the galley stores and smoke filling the corridor.

"Masterton! Smith!" Watters looked around. Smith was dead, lying under a blazing beam with his head tilted at an unnatural angle and his hand still grasping his ladle. Masterton lay face down on the deck with little flames erupting from his trousers and jacket.

"Masterton!" Watters leaned over him, shook him awake and beat out the flames with the flat of his hand.

"What happened?" Masterton asked and broke into a paroxysm of coughing as he breathed in the smoke.

"The gunpowder!" Watters said. "We have to put the fire out before it takes hold."

Orange flames roared from the galley storeroom as the sugar caught fire.

"Water; there are barrels of fresh water with the galley stores," Masterton said.

Watters stepped back as an eruption of flames surged towards him. Swearing, he removed his jacket, wrapped it around his head and looked into the room. Orange flames and coiling smoke forced him to step back. "I'll try for the water kegs," he said. "You organise the pumps. Get hoses down here."

"Where's Smithy?"

"He's gone! Move!" Watters ordered.

Masterton nodded and fled, leaving Watters alone with the flames. He looked into the storeroom. Thankfully, the water kegs were piled near the entrance, and the scuttler had planted the gunpowder in the furthest corner, not quite against the hull. Watters knew that *Lancelot's* hull had been built thick enough to withstand the external pressure of the ice, but once the fire took hold, it would eat away at the timber. It was only a matter of time before the flames consumed the wood, and once the sea rushed in, *Lancelot* would sink. The scuttler would have won, and every man on board would be in danger.

Gasping at the heat, Watters thrust into the storeroom. Each water barrel had a bunghole near the bottom, from where the water could be released. Watters did not know whether that system was unique to Lancelot or if it was universal to all whaling vessels, and nor did he care. He grasped the nearest bung and tried to haul it out.

"It's too tight," he said, as the bung refused to move. "I'll have to knock it out."

The flames were spreading to the salted beef, so the smell of roast meat added to the acrid smoke and sickly sugar. Watters ran to the galley next door, ignored Smith's body, and looked frantically for a tool to help him remove the bung. He saw a wooden mallet among the litter on the deck, lifted it and returned to the storeroom, where the flames were even fiercer.

Come on, Masterton! What's keeping you? We need that blasted hose!

Lifting the mallet, Watters thumped it down on the wooden bung. His first stroke missed; his second only dented the wood, and then he had to step back as a flame surged towards him.

"I'm damned if I'll let a scuttler defeat me," Watters grunted and returned to his task. He lifted the mallet and hit again, this time knocking the bung out of the barrel, allowing fresh water to pour onto the deck.

"That's better!" Watters said, as *Lancelot* helped by heeling to port, surging the water towards the flames. Watters put his hands into the flow and splashed water over himself.

Now he knew the technique, Watters found the second bung easier to remove, and he continued until half a dozen barrels emptied their contents onto the storehouse deck.

"Watters!" Masterton's voice sounded in the corridor. "Stand clear!" He arrived with a working party and a canvas hose. "It's attached to a pump," Masterton began a technical explanation that did not interest Watters in the slightest.

"Just get the blasted fire out," Watters said, realising that his various burns were beginning to hurt abominably. He watched as the hands played a stream of salt water onto the flames, gradually easing the crackle and with the sugar the last to be doused.

"What a bloody mess," Masterton looked into the storeroom, with its smoking, charred boxes and barrels and the water sloshing back and forth with the movement of the ship. "I don't know how much we'll be able to salvage from that." He walked forward, splashing through the water, to inspect the bulkhead.

Watters joined him, ankle-deep in surging, filthy water floating with soot and charred pieces of meat. "Here's where the gunpowder blew up," Watters pushed at the wood. "We were lucky, the stores took most of the force. If the scuttler had placed it hard against the hull, it might have blown a hole large enough for a man to walk through, double planked or not." He swore. "I think the scuttler intended this explosion as a distraction, with the other kegs doing the real damage."

"You saved the ship, Sergeant Watters," Captain Fairweather arrived, looking worried.

"Mr Masterton and I did our best," Watters said.

"It's weakened," Masterton looked up when Captain Fairweather joined him.

Fairweather inspected the hull, frowning. "A damaged hull and half the stores missing," He shook his head. "I doubt we'll make the owners a profit this voyage."

"I reckon that was a single barrel," Watters said, "so there is still one barrel of gunpowder hidden somewhere on this ship, and the scuttler is still at large."

"Have you found out who it is?" Captain Fairweather asked.

Watters glanced at Masterton before he replied. "I think it's Sails," he said. "Urquhart the sailmaker."

Masterton nodded. "That's what I calculate, too. One barrel missing, and Urquhart is the culprit, although God knows why. I'll organise a ship-wide search." He looked Watters up and down. "You'd better see the surgeon, Sergeant. You're a bloody mess."

"The surgeon can wait," Watters said. "We must find that gunpowder." He only took a single step before he doubled up in a paroxysm of coughing.

"Surgeon," Captain Fairweather ordered. "We'll find the gunpowder."

CHAPTER TWENTY

THE YOUNG SURGEON GRINNED DOWN AT WATTERS. "THERE you are, Sergeant, all sorted. A few bruises and some superficial burns. Nothing that won't heal. You're a lucky man, you know."

Watters sat up impatiently without mentioning his dizziness. Catching Urquhart was more important than his health.

"Don't rush to get back to duty," the doctor said.

"Thank you, doctor," Watters put his clothes on again, wincing as the movement pulled at his injuries. He left the surgery at speed, staggered again outside the door, coughed out more smoke from his lungs and continued.

"Hey, bluebottle!" Henderson watched him from a distance. "When you've finished coughing up your ring, we're all aft."

Captain Fairweather surveyed the crew from his position at the stern.

"We have a scuttler on board," he said. "Somebody on this vessel tried to blow a hole in the hull." He allowed the words to sink in as the hands murmured to each other. By that time, the news had spread that the explosion had not been an accident, and rumours were rife.

Captain Fairweather motioned Watters to him. "You may know this man as George Walker. He is Sergeant Watters of the Dundee Police, and he is here to catch this scuttler."

Watters expected the murmur of discontent, suspicion, and unease from the crew. Policemen were not popular among seamen, possibly because the police had to arrest so many when roaming drunk and disreputable amidst Dundee's maritime quarter.

"Sergeant Watters and Mr Masterton saved the ship when the scuttler tried to send us to the bottom. We lost Smith, our cook and might have lost a great deal more men." Fairweather lowered his voice. "We might have lost the ship." He waited for half a minute before continuing. "We have a damned murdering blackguard on *Lancelot*. I want you all to tell Sergeant Watters everything and anything suspicious that you see. I want to know if you saw anybody running about the ship moving barrels of gunpowder or anything else, and I want this man caught."

Watters stepped forward to survey the crew. "I'd like to speak to Urquhart the Sailmaker, who, I notice, is missing from this gathering. If you find him, bring him to me. That's all." Watters tried to hide his anxiety, although he knew that the scuttler was still loose, and half a hundredweight of gunpowder was missing.

"Search the ship!" Masterton ordered. "I want that gunpowder found, and I want Urquhart in irons."

Watters helped as the hands scoured every inch of the ship from bow to stern. He heard their complaints and hoped he found Urquhart before they did.

"Blow up the ship, would he? The murdering bastard!"

"Aye, old Smithy's deid. He was a poor cook, but he didnae deserve to die for it."

"Auld Sails a scuttler? If I find him, he'll no be gaun tae the polis, I ken that, eh?"

The noise increased as the crew became frustrated at their

lack of success until the engineer shouted out. "Mr Mate! I've found your gunpowder!"

The words attracted a crowd, with Watters pushing through to the engine room. Masterton was there first, bellowing for the crew to "stand back, or by God, there'll be so many broken heads that you'll wish the ship was bloody scuttled!"

The chief engineer held up the keg of gunpowder. "Here you are, Mr Masterton." He ignored Watters completely. "Buried in my reserve coal bunker."

Watters shivered, imagining what would have happened if *Lancelot's* coal had ignited.

"Thank God for that," Masterton did not conceal his relief as he held the barrel. "Thank the good Lord. Is there any sign of that blackguard Urquhart?"

There was none. With the gunpowder safely stored in Masterton's cabin and the crew alerted to look for Urquhart, Watters felt some of his tension ease.

"Maybe Urquhart's gone overboard," Masterton mused.

"Perhaps he has," Watters said. "I hope not. I'd like to find out his motive."

"It doesn't matter now," Masterton said. "He can't do any more damage to the ship."

Now that Watters was no longer one of the crowd, he moved out of the fo'c'sle and took over the cook's quarters, while Masterton gave the cook's duties to a young Greenman who claimed to have once worked in a hotel kitchen.

The cook's quarters were tiny, dirty, and filled with opened boxes of biscuit and barrels of meal and flour. Watters spent an hour tidying up the cabin, tried to remove the resident population of insect life and continued his investigation by interrogating the crew, one by one.

As Watters expected, most of the hands were taciturn when he called them in. They were sullen under questioning, unwilling to help the police despite the danger to their ship, and answered Watters with monosyllables.

Nobody had seen anything suspicious. Nobody had seen Urquhart carrying kegs of gunpowder. Nobody had seen anybody leave their bunk except to go on duty, and nobody knew anything about anything.

With a pile of signed statements before him, and his notebook at his side, Watters leaned back and lit his pipe.

This case is full of dead ends and frustrations. Nothing seems to be complete. We solve a few crimes while the major criminals continue to elude us. Why did Urquhart try to blow holes in Lancelot? If I knew that, the whole case would come together.

———

"We need fresh water," Captain Fairweather said, "since you two gentlemen decided to pour most of ours onto the deck."

"Plenty icebergs around," Masterton pointed out.

Watters knew that maintaining a supply of fresh water was a skipper's nightmare, even without stray police sergeants knocking the bungs out of water barrels. He remembered being on the West Africa Squadron, patrolling for slaving ships and the ship's captain spreading sails above the decks to catch rain from the frequent showers. He remembered escorting landing parties and standing guard in case of attack by hostile tribesmen while the bluejackets filled kegs from streams. Fortunately, up here in the Arctic, icebergs were frequent.

Extending a telescope, Captain Fairweather examined each iceberg, shaking his head as *Lancelot* eased across Melville Bay towards the whaling grounds.

"We'll be lucky to make it across to the West Water," Masterton said. "I've got the hands at the pumps to keep the water level down. Urquhart did more damage than we thought."

"We don't have sufficient fresh water to make it home,"

Captain Fairweather said, without removing the telescope from his eye. "It's no good saving the men from burning only to have them die of thirst. Ah, there's one."

To Watters' eyes, the iceberg appeared no different to the scores of others they had passed, but when Masterton studied it, he nodded his approval.

"That'll do, captain."

"It must be half a mile long," Watters said.

"Aye, they come in all shapes and sizes," Masterton said.

Watters admired Captain Fairweather's seamanship as he manoeuvred *Lancelot* alongside the berg, which towered above them to many times the height of their mainmast.

"Ice anchors!" Captain Fairweather roared, and the hands fastened the specially shaped anchors to the iceberg. Within half an hour, *Lancelot* sat safely in the lee of the berg with the water flat around them and the hands admiring the island of ice.

"Do you know the technique, Watters?" Masterton asked.

"I don't," Watters admitted.

"We find a place where the ice on the berg is melting. Then we place hoses under the melting ice and fill the barrels. It's straightforward, and the water is as pure and sweet as you'll find anywhere."

Watters grunted his approval. "That sounds an ideal solution," he said. "It's a pity we can't pick up stores the same way."

Masterton smiled. "You heard the captain. We'll be heading home shortly, Sergeant. That explosion and fire weakened the ship. She'll be all right at sea, but the hull won't stand any pressure if we're locked in the ice."

"How many men will be on the berg?"

"As many as wish to go," Masterton said. "It's large enough to hold a small town, as you see, and it allows the lads to leave the ship for a few hours."

Watters glanced around the horizon. As well as a dozen

icebergs of various shapes and sizes, he saw the masts of five other whaling ships within a couple of miles. "I am surprised how close we are to the other vessels. If Urquhart is on board, he could nearly swim across."

Masterton shrugged. "The water's cold enough to freeze the nose of a polar bear, and Urquhart must be seventy if he's a day. He'd be a fool to try."

"I'll keep watch for him," Watters said.

"I'll have to leave you to it," Masterton said. "I have a ship to water." He gave a small smile. "If we're fortunate, we might find some seals on the berg and make a little money."

Watters watched as the crew filed onto the iceberg. The less fortunate trailed hoses and water barrels ashore under Masterton's critical eyes, while the rest roamed as if on holiday.

"They're thoughtless beggars," Watters said to Neilson. "Are you not going to join them?"

The carpenter shook his head. "This is the first opportunity I've had to repair the damage the explosion caused. Captain Fairweather has emptied the storeroom for me, so I will cut away the damaged timber and replace it as best I can." He jerked a thumb over the side. "We're tilting to starboard, which has lifted the damaged planking out of the water."

Watters nodded. "The best of luck to you, Chips." He strolled around the deck, trying to appear casual as he examined the ship. Fairweather always kept one whaling boat ready to launch, on bran as the whalermen called it, with whaling lances and lines and the harpoon gun ready with harpoons for the hunt. Designed to hold six men, the boat was too heavy for a single man to control. The other whaleboats were hanging from their davits, ready for a quick launch, while the captain's dinghy sat on the main deck, with a canvas tarpaulin protecting the interior from rain and spray.

Watters noted the position of the dinghy, very close to the

edge of the hull, so that one man should be able to launch her. He lifted the tarpaulin and looked inside. There was food and water sufficient for two days, a compass and a bolt of canvas for a cover.

"Mr Masterton!" Watters shouted, but the mate was on the iceberg. *Lancelot* was nearly deserted, with most of the hands taking the opportunity to stretch their legs on the massive iceberg.

"So, Mr Urquhart," Watters mused. "You're going to escape that way." He replaced the cover and stepped away, wishing he had brought his cane so he could swing it, a process that always helped him to think. "Where will you hide?"

Watters scanned the upper deck. *If I were Urquhart, I'd either escape now or try again. How would I do it? I'd sneak into the mate's cabin and grab a keg of gunpowder.*

Watters slipped below, hearing the hammering as Neilson worked on his repairs. The ship was eerily empty as he made his way aft to the mate's cabin, walking quietly and hoping for a glimpse of Urquhart.

Masterton's door was shut. Watters turned the handle and pushed it open. All six gunpowder barrels sat beside the bunk.

Thank goodness for that.

Something gritty underfoot caught Watters attention. He knelt, ran his finger over the deck and swore.

Gunpowder. I'm damned sure Masterton would have noticed if a cask was leaking.

Watters saw a thin line of black powder leading to the barrels and lifted them one by one. They seemed all the same weight, but on the top barrel, the cover was slightly loose.

Somebody has lifted the lid.

Watters prised the top open. The keg was full of white flour.

That devious little blackguard! Watters tempered his surprise with admiration. *He's taken out the gunpowder and left the keg. Nobody would know except for that spilt powder on the deck.*

The implications hit Watters.

We have a scuttler who failed but is at large on Lancelot. We have a boat ready with provisions and ships in the vicinity to which he can escape. We have a nearly empty vessel and a missing quantity of gunpowder; the situation is ready-made for another attempt. But where will Urquhart strike? Probably on the opposite side from the captain's dinghy and with a long enough fuse for him to light the thing and scramble clear. The captain's dinghy is on the starboard side, near the stern, so I'd guess the larboard side, forward.

With that thought, Watters swung an imaginary golf club and raised his voice slightly. "I think I'll have a turn on the iceberg and see what's happening."

There you are, Urquhart the Scuttler, the coast is clear. You do your worst, I'll do my best, and we'll see who comes up on top.

Stepping onto the iceberg, Watters sauntered away for two minutes, ensuring he was in open sight, and then turned and ran back on board. Without pausing, he slid down the companionway and made his way forward, ducking under the low deck beams. Deliberately avoiding using a lantern, he moved as quietly as possible and then stopped as Neilson began to hammer at something. The hammering stopped, allowing silence to return.

Somebody was ahead. Watters heard the slight scuff of feet on the deck. He stood still, listening, trying to peer into the dark, guessing that the scuttler was there.

A door opened, the creak of hinges faint but distinguishable. Watters stepped forward, placing his feet carefully on the deck, trying to control his breathing so nobody heard him. The wind must have been rising outside, for Watters heard it whining through the rigging, just as Neilson began to hammer a plank onto the damaged hull, with the sound echoing through the ship.

Watters moved forward again, using Neilson's hammering

to cover the sound of his feet. The hammering stopped, the door of the cable locker opened ahead of him, and somebody rushed out.

"Dundee Police!" Watters roared, more out of habit than anything else, and grabbed the man. In the dark, he could not see who he held, but his quarry struggled desperately, smashing something hard and heavy onto Watters' head. Watters winced, and his grasp slackened, allowing the man to slide away.

"Stop!" Watters yelled. "Is that you, Urquhart?" He was about to give chase when he remembered the man's reason for being down here. Watters knew he could either search for the gunpowder or chase the fugitive. There was no choice. If the ship was scuttled, some of the men here might die of exposure.

Yanking the door open, Watters dived inside. The keg was marked "Flour" and was hard against the hull, with a fuse glowing red in the dark. Watters dashed forward, plucked the fuse free of the keg, threw it to the deck and stamped out the flame.

Only then did the realisation hit him. If that fuse had been slightly shorter, the gunpowder would have exploded and, whatever damage it did to the ship, it would have blown him to pieces.

Oh, Marie, I nearly made you a widow before your time.

Breathing out hard, Watters ensured the fuse was dead and left the locker. He ran through the ship, aware that the fugitive could be hiding anywhere.

"Urquhart! I know it's you!"

Watters swore softly. He had to catch the fugitive. He ran to the upper deck, where Neilson was sawing a length of timber. "Neilson!"

"Halloa!" Neilson looked up.

"Did you see anybody run past just now?"

"Yes, somebody ran past. Why?"

"He's the scuttler. Did you see where he went?"

Neilson shook his head. "I'm too busy, Sergeant. I wasn't looking."

Watters glanced at the captain's dinghy, wondering if the fugitive would try to escape. A quick check assured him that nobody was hiding beneath the tarpaulin.

"He must have gone onto the iceberg."

For the second time in less than an hour, Watters leapt onto the iceberg. Groups of *Lancelot*'s men were roaming around, some actively searching for seals, most just talking, or smoking, or staring at the great pinnacles of ice that towered high into the blue sky.

"Did anybody see Urquhart come from *Lancelot* a few minutes ago?" Watters asked.

The seamen stared at him, wordless.

"He was the scuttler," Watters explained.

"*Lancelot*'s still afloat," one man pointed out. "He never scuttled anything."

"Did you see him?" Watters persisted.

"No," the whalers said.

"He tried to kill you," Watters tried again.

A man laughed, "So you say," and walked away.

Watters swore. He had frequently come across this attitude when men refused to help the police even when their livelihoods or lives were at stake. Even now, forty years after their formation, the Dundee Police were often viewed as a tool of oppression, something the supposedly respectable classes used to keep the less respectable under control. He raised his voice again. "Did anybody see Urquhart leave *Lancelot* within the past few minutes?"

Only the wind broke the silence as it howled around the peaks of the iceberg. Swearing, Watters stomped past the glowering Greenlandmen to find Masterton returning with a sledge laden with water butts. The men walking behind him were smoking and chattering as they returned to the ship.

"Did you see anybody come off *Lancelot* in the past fifteen minutes?" Watters asked.

Masterton shrugged. "I've had people coming and going all afternoon," he said.

Watters strode past the mate. The iceberg was the size of a small island, about half a mile long and three hundred yards wide, with peaks and troughs, level areas and sheer cliffs.

"I'm looking for Urquhart, the sailmaker," Watters shouted. "I need as many men as I can get."

The whaling men began a slow drift back to *Lancelot*. Only Henderson joined Watters.

"Come on then, bluebottle. For Smithy's sake."

They quartered the iceberg, walking within sight of each other as they paced from one end to the other, sliding on the ice, checking behind every pinnacle and protuberance.

The subdued cough caught Watters' attention, and he looked upward. Urquhart clung to a cliff of ice, trying to look as small as possible as he coughed on the back of his hand. The bright blood on his chin was apparent.

"Down you come, Sails. I think we should talk about an attempted scuttling."

CHAPTER TWENTY-ONE

URQUHART LIFTED HIS CHIN IN DEFIANCE AS HE SAT OPPOSITE Watters, with Fairweather staring at him in naked loathing.

"You tried to sink my ship," Fairweather said.

"I did," Urquhart responded. He looked even older in the gloom of the small cabin, with bald patches showing through the silver hairs on his head, but he sat as erect as a guardsman. He coughed, tried to hide the blood on his lips and coughed again.

"Why?" Watters asked. "You are a seaman. You know how dangerous sinking a ship can be and how many lives can be lost."

Urquhart did not flinch. "There would be no lives lost. Half the whaling fleet is within a few hours sail."

"You murdering hound," Captain Fairweather could barely contain his fury. Watters thought he was about to launch himself across the desk in the tiny cabin. "You wanted to sink my ship!"

"Crockatt is dead," Watters reminded. "And Boyle and Smith. You murdered them."

"Crockatt slipped and fell," Urquhart said. "Boyle?" He shrugged. "The sea took Boyle. That was nothing to do with me. I am sorry about Smith, but if you had not interfered, he would still be alive."

Watters' police instinct told him that Urquhart was lying. The man was too sure of himself, yet there was a slight hesitation before he spoke, and his eyes shifted away for a fraction of a second.

"We've plenty of time to discuss the murders of these three men," Watters said. "I am sure a jury will listen to all the details before the judge dons his black cap." He allowed Urquhart time to absorb the idea before continuing.

"How did you do it?" Fairweather asked. "You may as well tell us, Urquhart."

The sailmaker shrugged. "I had a spare key made for all the locked cabins," he said. "Access was easy."

Watters nodded. "You're a clever man, Mr Urquhart. What was your plan?"

Urquhart straightened in his seat. "I intended two separate explosions," he said. "A small explosion in the galley to draw the hands away from the larger one in the sail locker. That way, nobody would get hurt. By the time the fire reached the gunpowder in the coal bunker, you'd have abandoned *Lancelot*. The third barrel was only for insurance. When you found the barrels in my locker, I tried with what I had."

"You caused significant damage to my ship," Fairweather said.

"Not significant enough," Urquhart was not repentant. "I wanted to sink her. I would have succeeded too if your tame policeman was not here."

When Fairweather leaned across his desk again, Watters placed a hand on his sleeve.

"What Captain Fairweather and I wish to know is why, Urquhart," Watters said. "Why did you wish to sink this ship, and why did you sink *Toiler* and *Teresa*?"

Captain Fairweather rose once more, with his fists

clenched to dispense ready justice. "By God, I should charge you with mutiny and hang you here and now."

"I'd like to hear Mr Urquhart's motive first," Watters said mildly.

Urquhart leaned back, with his lips twisting into the bitterest expression that Watters had seen in any man. "Oh, I have a motive," he said hoarsely.

"What the devil have I ever done to you?" Fairweather asked in genuine perplexity. "I've always tried to be fair to my hands. I feed them well and don't drive them too hard."

"No, Captain Fairweather," Urquhart said. "I have nothing against you."

"Then what, and why?" Fairweather looked up as *Lancelot* shifted slightly, decided it was nothing dangerous and returned his attention to Urquhart.

"Muirhead," Urquhart said. "Keith Lancelot Muirhead."

"What do you have against Mr Muirhead that necessitates sinking his ships?" Watters asked.

"He ruined me," Urquhart said.

"Ah," Watters nodded, remembering the stories that Muirhead was a hard businessman. "Tell us more."

Urquhart looked from Watters to Urquhart and back. "You both know how ship ownership works. A ship is divided into sixty-four shares, with owners buying as little as one share or as many as sixty-four."

"We know that," Watters agreed.

"Men – and some women - buy shares as an investment; they want a share in the profits of each voyage." Urquhart looked at Fairweather. "I believe you have shares in *Lancelot*, Captain, while Muirhead is the major shareholder and managing owner of every vessel in his fleet."

"I have five shares in this vessel," Captain Fairweather said.

"I had twenty-five shares in *Charming Amelia,*" Urquhart said. "Do you remember her?"

"I remember her," Fairweather said. "She was an old sail-powered vessel that fished mainly in the Greenland Seas rather than the Davis Straits. She had a very young owner-master as I recall."

"Captain Richard Gow," Urquhart said. "The youngest master in the Dundee fleet and probably the youngest in any whaling ship. He was only twenty-eight, I believe and put everything he owned into *Charming Amelia*, even borrowing money from his family and the bank to buy her."

Watters did not hurry Urquhart. *Charming Amelia*? He remembered Scuddamore talking about her. *Charming Amelia* was the last vessel to carry handheld harpoons, and Abernethy's foreganger may have come from her stores. Watters took a deep breath. He had a connection between the scuttling and Abernethy's burglaries. Another piece of the mystery had clicked into place.

Urquhart coughed again and wiped away his blood. "It was the season of 1856 when we sailed north. Some people spoke of a possible Russian naval attack on the ships, as the Crimean War was at its height, but Captain Gow had no such qualms. Whales were hard to find that season, and we cruised the edge of the ice from Spitsbergen westward, capturing a few dozen seals but nowhere near enough to even pay the men's wages, let alone break even on the voyage. And then the lookout in the crow's nest sighted a whale."

Fairweather nodded; he was familiar with the scenario.

"There was another vessel close by, Muirhead's *Arthur,* and she also sighted the whale. Both ships sent out their boats simultaneously, with three boats from *Charming Amelia* and five from *Arthur*."

Fairweather nodded, imagining the scene. Watters remembered the frantic excitement when *Lancelot* chased a whale, with the men shouting hoarsely as they hauled at the oars, the boatsteerer trying to navigate the whaleboat behind the whale, and the storm petrels squawking overhead.

"The oarsmen pulled out into a sea of loose ice and small bergs, with the whale alternatively appearing and disappearing. One of *Amelia's* boats was first to close, with the boat-steerer ensuring the boat was safe from the flukes of the whale's tail. Our chief harpooner and mate, Andrew Buchanan, lifted his harpoon and thrust it in from only ten feet. I was on the starboard rear oar and saw Buchanan's throw, straight and true. The harpoon stuck in deep, and the boat's crew yelled, "A fall!' A fall!"

"Was it a hand harpoon?"

"Yes," Urquhart said. "Gun harpoons cost money, and we didn't have a spare farthing to scratch ourselves with."

Watters watched Urquhart's face as he talked, with the elderly sailmaker's eyes drifting away to the whale hunt and his body shifting as he once again rowed and hunted the whale.

"Buchanan hooked his foreganger around the billet head in the whaleboat, so securing the whale to *Amelia's* boat." Urquhart met Fairweather's eyes. "Our harpoon was first."

Fairweather nodded. "By law then, *Charming Amelia* owned the whale."

"That's correct, Captain," Urquhart said. "Buchanan hoisted a jack."

"That's the flag," Watters sought clarification.

Urquhart nodded. "Yes, Sergeant Watters. By hoisting *Amelia's* jack, Buchanan was announcing that the whale was her lawful property."

"Thank you, Mr Urquhart. Please continue."

"The whale pulled away, of course, towing the boat behind it. The whale pulled us at such a rate that the whale line screamed around the billet head. Willie Tosh, the linemanager, threw pannikins of seawater onto the billet head as the friction threatened to set the line afire. Each whaleboat holds six lines, but one by one, we used them up, although the boat was still attached to the whale."

Urquhart's eyes were distant as he recounted the scene.

"The whale was diving and twisting, and *Arthur*'s boats came alongside and fired in one of her harpoons."

"A friendly harpoon, as we call it," Fairweather murmured.

"Indeed, but less than friendly, as we later found out," Urquhart said. "The whale was still full of fight and struggled on, dragging the lines and boats behind it, until the lines of *Arthur*'s boat were also finished. The rest of *Amelia*'s boats lost the whale in the confusion of washing pieces and little bergs."

Watters nodded, drawing on his recent whaling experiences to picture the scene. He could see the whaling boats from rival ships, the ice all around, the beleaguered whale and the birds, squawking as they waited for the kill.

"Another of *Arthur*'s boats joined the hunt," Urquhart said. "And as our boat crept closer, with Buchanan ready to deliver the killing thrust, the second of *Arthur*'s boats raced to the whale, and a man named Sandy Kilner fired a harpoon deep into the whale. It raced away again, dragging all three boats behind it."

Captain Fairweather nodded without taking his eyes off Urquhart.

"Eventually, even that fighting whale tired and rested on the surface of the sea, with little floating pieces of ice all around and the three boats closing for the kill. In all the confusion, our jack had come off, and now there were two of *Arthur*'s boats and only one of *Amelia*'s."

Watters continued to scribble notes.

"*Amelia*'s harpooners killed the whale, with Buchanan thrusting in the final lance, but then everything altered. Sandy Kilner also shoved in his lance, and men from *Arthur*'s two boats swarmed onto the whale, stuck in their jack and claimed the whale."

Captain Fairweather nodded again, understanding the situation.

"Our boat's crew tried to fight them off, but *Arthur*'s men outnumbered us two-to-one. *Arthur's men* bored holes in the whale's tail and towed it back to their ship, leaving us battered, bloody and angry." Urquhart coughed up more blood, with his eyes focussed on the years-old drama rather than the captain's cabin.

Watters nodded, sympathising with Urquhart despite his recent actions.

"Captain Gow complained to *Arthur's* master, Captain Keith Lancelot bloody Muirhead, but to no avail. We came home clean – empty – so the voyage cost us everything we had and left us in debt. Captain Gow and I brought our case to the law."

Watters saw that Captain Fairweather was listening with more than professional attention.

"What did the court decide?" Fairweather asked.

"The High Court in Edinburgh heard the case," Urquhart said, "and both sides gave radically different versions of the story."

"They always do," Watters said.

"I've told you our side, the truthful side," Urquhart still sounded bitter. "The harpooner Kilner told a different story. He said that when *Arthur's* boat found the whale, *Amelia's* boat was not even in sight. Our advocate asked if *Amelia's* harpoon was not sticking out of the whale, and he admitted that it was, but without a line, so nothing attaching it to the boat."

"It was a loose whale, then," Fairweather murmured.

"Exactly so," Urquhart agreed.

"What does that mean?" Watters asked.

"A loose whale is open to anybody to capture," Fairweather explained. "If Kilgour thought the whale was loose, he was quite entitled to harpoon it for *Arthur*. Urquhart has already told us the whale had shaken off the jack. If *Amelia's* boat was still attached to the whale, then it was a 'fast' whale – fastened to the boat - and only *Amelia* had any claim."

"I see," Watters said. "So, the whole case rested on whether the whale was loose or fast."

"That's what the advocates decided," Urquhart said.

Watters noted that down. "How much money are we talking about here? What would one whale make in the open market?" He faced Urquhart. "Would that one whale have made *Amelia* a profit?"

Fairweather answered that question. "An average-sized whale of about fifty feet can make anything from £600 to £1100. The profit depends on the market for whale oil and bone, which fluctuates with demand, but prices rise with wartime demand or scarcity. In a year of poor catches, an average whale would make at least a thousand pounds, but in 1855, whalebone was around £300 a ton, and oil about £30 a ton."

"Our whale was seventy feet in length," Urquhart said. "We estimated about £1500 to £2000 that year- sufficient to pay our expenses and leave a profit."

"What did the judge decide?" Watters asked.

"He said that we were all liars," Urquhart said and adopted the tone of a High Court judge. "I never saw any class of men on whose evidence I had less reliance than on the depositions of sailors. At all times, under all circumstances, they are ever ready to claim that their ship was indisputably in the right."

Watters hid his smile. He understood the seamen's loyalty to their ship. In his opinion, men from any British army regiment would also argue black was white to prove their unit was always in the right.

"What else did the judge decide?"

When Urquhart looked up, Watters thought his eyes were as hard as anything he had ever seen in his life. "The judge, damn him to the pit of hell, decided that the crew of *Arthur* were telling fewer lies than our men. By that time, of course, the whale blubber had long been boiled into oil, and the baleen sold off. It made nearly £2000, and all the money went to Muirhead." Urquhart breathed out slowly. "And then Mr Shaw had to pay the legal costs. It broke him, broke the company, and broke me. We had to sell *Charming Amelia* to pay the legal fees, the debts, and the crew's wages."

Watters nodded. "I can understand your bitterness," he said, "but sinking ships, putting seamen in danger and murdering people is not the answer."

"I didn't kill anybody," Urquhart said, "and nobody was in danger."

"The court will decide that," Watters said. "I accept that Crockatt's death was an accident, but I believe you murdered Constable Boyle, while Smith undoubtedly died because of your actions."

"I murdered nobody," Urquhart said. "I don't know anything about Boyle and Smith was an accident. Muirhead is the murderer."

"Mr Muirhead won a controversial court case," Watters said. "He did not murder anybody. A judge and fifteen good men of the jury heard the evidence and decided in Mr Muirhead's favour. And that is where matters should end."

Urquhart coughed once more. "Do you see this blood?" he said. "I am dying of consumption. That voyage should have been my last, but because of Muirhead's greed, I had to return to sea, which is killing me. Muirhead is the murderer here."

Although Watters understood Urquhart's point, he quashed his sympathy. "I know you are not working alone, Urquhart. Somehow, you have inveigled Walter Abernethy to join you. If you tell me where he is and who else is working with you, I will speak in your favour at your trial."

Urquhart folded his arms in front of him and said nothing as blood dribbled down his chin.

"Is Mr Shaw the other man working with you?"

"Not unless he's come from beyond the grave," Urquhart

said. "He killed himself after the result of the court case. Muirhead killed him."

Watters swore silently, wondered if Urquhart was lying, decided to pretend to believe him and pushed on. Such a simple thing as a whale hunt had caused so many deaths and broken so many lives.

"You can't blame Mr Muirhead for that," Watters said, although he wondered what he would do if he had sunk all his money into a dream, gone into debt, only for a judge to hand everything to a rival. He would undoubtedly be bitter and seek something – possibly revenge.

Urquhart stared at Watters. "Muirhead was the master of the ship that stole our whale. He owned the company that took the case to court, and he did nothing when the Charming Amelia Company folded. He did not turn a hair when Richard Shaw drowned himself in the Tay and didn't even send a wreath to his memorial service."

Watters decided to leave any further questions until later.

"Not even a word of sympathy," Urquhart continued. "Hardly anybody came to the service. There was me and Deuchars, the mate. Nobody else."

"Deuchars, the mate? Where is he now?"

"Peterhead," Fairweather said. "He's master of *Northern Lights*, another whaling vessel." Fairweather looked up again as *Lancelot* gave another lurch. "Put your prisoner in the cable locker, Sergeant. We're going home."

Urquhart looked old and frail as Watters escorted him to the cable locker. As he stooped to enter, he spoke over his shoulder.

"I'm only the agent, Sergeant Watters. I'm only the tool, for at my age, and with my health, I've few days ahead of me whatever happens. The man you want is still in Dundee."

CHAPTER TWENTY-TWO

"WILL YOU TELL ME WHO HE IS?"

Urquhart seated himself on a coiled anchor cable. "No," he said. "I said I've only a few weeks or days to live, but I'd prefer to live them."

"Are you scared of your partner?"

"So should you be, Sergeant. I've seen him take on three Greenlandmen at one time and walk away unscathed. He'll break your back across his knee and smile at the memory."

"Aye, maybe so," Watters said, "but that's not your reason for keeping the name to yourself."

Urquhart leaned back, coughed, and smiled again. "I might die before we return to the Tay, Sergeant, or I might live to hang, but either way, I won't betray my loyalty. I'll die knowing that Muirhead will never learn who's hunting him down."

Watters thought of the whaling men of *Charming Amelia* and *Arthur* who lied for their ships. Such loyalty was expected at sea, but it made it hard for Watters to believe anything Urquhart said.

With Neilson's repairs holding her together, *Lancelot* limped back down the Davis Strait before the autumn brought back the ice.

Watters checked Urquhart every two hours, saw his prisoner weaken by the day, and hoped he would live to see Dundee. Despite Watters' questioning, the sailmaker said nothing more.

> *"Now when I was a little boy, and so my mother told me,*
> *That if I didn't kiss the girls, my lips would grow all mouldy."*

Masterton sounded cheerful as he joined Watters at the taffrail. "You've caught the scuttler and saved the ship," Masterton said. "You should be happy with the voyage."

"I'll be happier when I have the man behind it," Watters sucked at his pipe and blew smoke across the sea. "Urquhart admitted he's a follower, not the leader."

"You'll get him," Masterton said.

"There have been too many deaths," Watters said.

Masterton grunted. "The sea always demands his price. Do you see these birds?" he pointed to the flock of small birds that followed *Lancelot.*

"I do," Watters said.

"They're stormy petrels," Masterton said. "We call them Mother Carey's chickens. They look like nothing, but they are reincarnated seamen. Each one has the soul of a man lost at sea. One might be your friend Boyle."

Watters would have smiled at the fancy, but the situation was too serious. "I hope he's happy where he is. Boyle was a good man."

"So was Smithy," Masterton said. "I knew him well." He looked out to sea, watching the petrels. "I never sailed with Urquhart, but I'll wager he was a good man too, before the incident with *Arthur.* We don't know what's ahead of us, Sergeant, or what will change us."

Watters nodded. "Aye, but that good man's actions have led to the deaths of three equally good men, and he'll have to pay the price."

When one of the petrels flew close to Watters, seeming to look into his face, Watters sought for some resemblance to Constable Boyle. He saw none, for only a bird returned his gaze.

Boyle is dead and gone, and Urquhart is the cause, directly or indirectly.

Lancelot limped up the Tay on a glorious July morning, with Dundee bustling under a silver-and-pink streaked sky and a host of seagulls swooping around the ship. Watters scanned the city through Masterton's telescope, glad to be home as he searched through the factory smoke for Castle Street. Marie would be there, hoping to see him, for the telegraph would have sent news of their progress as they passed the ports in the north.

There was no fanfare to greet them as *Lancelot* berthed in Victoria Dock, no cheering crowds, only a group of porters and a trio of customs officials. Watters knew that within a few minutes, a score of carts would be alongside to take off the stored blubber and baleen, but in the meantime, *Lancelot* was only one ship among many.

"Home again," Masterton said.

"Home again," Watters had Urquhart's hands tied behind him as he gestured to the harbour police. "I'll hand this beauty over to the Bobbies first, tell the wife I'm home and get back to work."

"It's been interesting, Sergeant," Masterton held out his hand. "I am sorry about your colleague."

"Thank you." They shook hands, and Watters stepped ashore.

———

"George?" Marie stood in her nightgown with her hair an explosion and her feet bare. Watters thought she had never looked more beautiful. "When did you get back?"

"About an hour ago."

"Should you not report to Mr Mackay first?" Marie tried to straighten her hair.

"Blast Mr Mackay. You are more important."

Marie held out her arms. "I didn't expect you for hours yet."

"Well, you've got me now instead." Watters held her tight.

"I heard three men died on board *Lancelot*," Marie tried to sound brave as she pressed against Watters' chest. "I thought one might have been you."

"Yes. This is not the time to talk about that."

"Patrick's asleep." Marie held her man close. "I missed you, but that beard will have to go."

Watters smiled into her neck. "I'm home now," he said. "And the beard can wait an hour or so."

———

Mackay viewed the freshly shaved Watters across his desk. "It's a pity about Boyle," he said. "He was a good man."

"He was, sir," Watters agreed.

"He had the makings of a sergeant in him," Mackay said, which was high praise from him. "Do you think Urquhart murdered him?"

"I can't be sure, sir," Watters said. "I don't know why he would, although Boyle did mention an attempt on his life. Urquhart must be nearing seventy, and Boyle was in the prime of life." Watters shook his head. "I'm ambivalent about his death, sir. Perhaps Urquhart surprised him, yet I'm more inclined to believe the sea swept him overboard."

"Did you find any evidence of foul play?"

"No, sir." Watters shook his head.

Mackay's fingers began to drum on the desk. "No evidence and no motive, unless Urquhart discovered that Boyle was a policeman."

"That's the only motive I can think of, sir."

"Very well," Mackay said. "Perhaps it is only our suspicious police minds that seek murder in every accidental death. We'll leave it at that. I will arrange a memorial service for Boyle and see about a pension for his widow if he left one."

"He never mentioned a wife, sir."

"Look into it, will you, Watters? See if there any relatives we should notify about his death."

"Yes, sir. Now that we have a motive for the scuttlings, I'd like to check up on the fellow Gow."

"You said he was dead," Mackay said.

"Yes, sir, but he might have a relative who wants revenge for Shaw's suicide."

Mackay nodded. "Do that, Watters."

It was customary for whaling companies to pay a portion of seamen's wages to the wife or mother left on shore, so Watters approached Muirhead's whaling office to ask about next of kin for Boyle.

"Don't you police keep records?" The clerk asked.

"We have him as a single man with no relations," Watters said. "I thought I'd double-check."

"Don't you trust yourselves?" The clerk grumbled as he delved into his cupboard and returned with a large leather-bound book. "What was the name?"

"Boyle," Watters said patiently. "Richard Robert Boyle."

"Boyle," the clerk repeated. "Aye, here we are. Richard Boyle. Single. No relations. All wages to be paid at the end of the voyage." He looked up in consternation. "If he's no relations, to whom shall I pay the residue of his wages?"

"Don't you have a widow's fund? A fund for the widows and orphans of seamen who die in the company service?"

"Not officially."

"Then pay it into the unofficial fund." Watters knew that many shipping companies had semi-secret accounts for the bereaved, with the owners turning a Nelsonian eye to the practice.

"No wife, no siblings, and no parents." *Guinevere* had returned early after finding a rich haul of whales, and Scuddamore swore never to go back to sea. "A man of mystery, our late Constable Boyle."

Deaths on duty were not common in the Dundee Police, so there was a solemn air when Mr Mackay held a brief ceremony for Boyle. The local Church of Scotland minister gave a sermon that incorporated the love of God with an admonition for all policemen to live a moral life and give up the evils of drink. After the sermon, the men gave a short prayer and returned to duty.

"And that is the end of Constable Boyle," Scuddamore said. "A short ceremony and back to duty, boys."

"Not quite the end," Watters said. "Duff, I want you to go to his house and remove all his personal items. We'll keep them in storage here in case a relative turns up and then probably auction them off for charity."

"Yes, Sergeant."

"He lived in the Overgate," Watters scribbled the address and handed it over. "If you find any letters, see if he has a friend or relation. We may have missed somebody."

Duff nodded. "Yes, Sergeant."

"Back to business," Watters knew he sounded callous. He had witnessed the death of many colleagues in his time with the Royal Marines and knew that dwelling on such things only depressed people without helping the deceased in the slightest. "We have captured the scuttler, yet we know Abernethy is still at large. Urquhart is as tight-lipped as any man I've ever met, but we suspect the rope Abernethy used came from *Charming Amelia*. I can't work out why Urquhart and the mysterious Lieutenant Kinghorn should be robbing half of Dundee."

Lizzie Flett's words returned to Watters, "I see a threat from a friend. You will meet danger under the single eye of a tall man. Beware the Cyclops, watcher."

The only one-eyed man I know is Anstruther.

"The foreganger is a tenuous connection," Scuddamore said.

"It's all we have." Watters sipped at his tea.

"Sergeant," Duff looked around the Duty Room. "We also have the police connection."

"I haven't forgotten," Watters said. "I asked Murdoch if there had been any developments when we were away, and he said Abernethy was quiet for a month and then started again."

"He thought we were laying a trap for him," Scuddamore said.

"Quite likely."

Or Lieutenant Anstruther was ensuring I was out of the way before he began work again. The tall, one-eyed man.

"Scuddamore," Watters said. "Find out all you can about a fellow called Gow. He was the managing owner of the Charming Amelia Whale Fishing Company and committed suicide."

"I remember the name," Scuddamore said. "I can't remember him topping himself, though."

"Find out all you can."

"Yes, Sergeant." Scuddamore caught up with Duff as they left on their respective duties.

———

"Ah, Watters," Lieutenant Anstruther looked forlorn as he stood four feet from Watters. "I'm glad you're back."

"I heard that Abernethy's thieving again, sir," Watters thought that Anstruther looked every inch the tall, one-eyed man.

"Yes, I want you to look into a robbery at O'Toole's

jewellery shop," Anstruther kept his distance. "Find out if Abernethy might be involved."

"Yes, sir," Watters had no time to request information before Anstruther strode away.

Where the devil is O'Toole's Jewellery shop?

Duff interrupted Watters' train of thought as he walked ponderously across the duty room. "Boyle's house was empty, Sergeant," Duff said. "It was a rented house with nothing inside except the furniture."

Watters frowned. "Empty? Had somebody robbed it, do you think?"

"No, Sergeant. Everything was neat and orderly, shipshape as they say, and nobody had forced the door. It looked like the previous occupant had taken away all his belongings."

"Boyle was the previous tenant, and dead men don't do that," Watters said. "We haven't time for this now but go to the landlord and see if they cleared it up."

"I did, Sergeant," Duff said. "The landlord is a Mrs Flannery. She said she hadn't been near the place. Boyle paid his rent three months in advance and was a model tenant. She hadn't heard of his death."

"This isn't right. Dead men can't clear a house, and burglars leave a mess." Watters stood up, with his mind busy. "Speak to the neighbours, Duff, see if they saw anybody going in or out."

"What do you expect, Sergeant?" Duff asked. "A ghost?"

"I don't know what I expect, Duff. I have a robbery to investigate."

"I thought Inspector Anstruther had the robberies, Sergeant."

Watters gave a brief smile. "He has, but he needs our help." He thought for a moment. "I have another job for you, Duff."

"What's that, Sergeant?"

"I want a list of all the owners of *Charming Amelia*. If

Urquhart was seeking revenge on Muirhead, he was quite likely in partnership with another owner who lost money. I already have Scuddamore checking on Gow. And where the devil is Shaw? I haven't seen him since we returned."

"Nor have I, Sergeant," Duff said. "I'll get onto *Charming Amelia's* owners."

"And I'll find O'Toole the Jeweller."

"O'Toole's in the Overgate, Sergeant. I bought Rosemary's ring there." Duff coloured as if he had said too much.

Watters allowed himself to relax for a moment. "Good choice, Duff. Rosemary's a fine girl."

———

John O'Toole, the jeweller, greeted Watters with a mournful face and bowed shoulders. "Thank God you're here, Sergeant. They've taken all of my watches, the gold, silver, and even the cheap metal ones."

Watters sighed. "How many?"

"Fifty watches, Sergeant, new and old."

Watters took notes. "Do you have their identification numbers?" Each quality watch carried an identification number engraved on the back.

"Yes, Sergeant. I've made a copy of the list for you." He fiddled with a drawer under the counter and produced a handwritten list.

"Thank you, Mr O'Toole. That will come in very handy."

Mr O'Toole looked like he was about to burst into tears. "Some of my customers brought in watches to be repaired. They will be most distressed to have them stolen."

"I'll see what I can do, Mr O'Toole," Watters said. "I'll have a look around the shop."

O'Toole's shop was at the High Street end of the Overgate, with heavy shutters on the front and back window. With no apparent signs of entry, Watters examined the lock, which had only minute scratches around the keyhole.

"He didn't break in, did he?"

"I don't know, Sergeant," O'Toole said.

"Was there any damage? A broken window or door lock?"

"No, Sergeant," O'Toole said.

"He used a false key, then," Watters said. "May I see your key, sir?"

"Here it is."

Watters took the bunch of keys from O'Toole, examined them closely and picked off a fragment of putty from two. "There we are, Mr O'Toole. Somebody made an impression of your keys."

O'Toole looked astonished. "Who? Who and when?"

"Where do you keep them?" Watters asked.

"In the back shop, hanging on a hook," O'Toole said.

"Who has access?"

"Nobody except me."

"Do you have an assistant?"

"No."

"A wife?"

"I am not married."

Watters nodded. He could guess what had happened. While a customer distracted O'Toole, the cracksman or an assistant entered the back shop and pressed the keys into a pad of putty. For an expert, it would be the act of an instant. With the key's impression made, the cracksman would visit one of the many shady workshops in Dundee to have the key to O'Toole's shop cut from a blank.

"I'm going to have a look around, Mr O'Toole," Watters said. "If you stand clear, I'll get on faster."

Watters found the biscuit crumbs within three minutes. "Your burglar was named Walter Abernethy," he said. "He would work with another man, and he's been operating in Dundee for some months."

"Will you catch him, Sergeant? Will you get my watches back?"

"I'll do my best," Watters promised. "I'd advise you to get a couple of hefty bolts on the inside of your door, locked with padlocks, and in future, keep your keys in a safe, not hanging on a hook."

"Yes, Sergeant," O'Toole said.

"Did any of your watches have a watch bar?" A watch bar was a strip of metal attached to the watch and on which the owner could engrave his name.

"Yes, Sergeant," O'Toole said, still visibly upset. "Only two."

"Do you have a note of them?"

"Yes," O'Toole told Watters the names.

"Thank you. I'll get to work." Watters glanced again at the biscuit crumbs. He had arrested the scuttler, and now he could fully concentrate on Abernethy and Lieutenant Kinghorn.

Abernethy is still on the loose, but Scuddamore and Duff are on form. With luck, we'll get another break. The secret is to keep pushing on every front until something promising turns up. As for Abernethy? No criminal is infallible. When he makes a mistake, I'll be right behind him.

———

"Sergeant!" Scuddamore nearly ran across the duty room. "They never found the body."

"Which body, Scuddamore?" Watters guessed the answer.

"Gow's body, Sergeant. Gow was a champion swimmer, and when somebody found a pile of his clothes at Buckingham Point, the police thought he had gone too far and drowned." Scuddamore grinned. "I'll bet your pension to a queer farthing that he's still alive."

Watters took a deep breath. "Aye. I'll keep my pension. Well now, Scuddamore, I'd think Gow's still in Dundee."

Scuddamore smiled. "Do you think he's involved in the scuttling?"

"Without a doubt." Watters cut an eighth of an inch of tobacco and thrust it into the bowl of his pipe. "How about a relative?"

"No record of any relative, Sergeant."

"I think we're beginning to make some progress, Scuddamore. Now we shall seek out the late Mr Gow."

CHAPTER TWENTY-THREE

"I spoke to Boyle's neighbours," Duff reported. "They said they hadn't seen anything suspicious at all." He consulted his notebook. "Here's a strange thing though, sir. One lady said she saw Boyle a fortnight ago."

"I said we were hunting ghosts," Scuddamore poured out three mugs of tea. "Where's young Shaw? I thought he was the tea-maker now!"

"Tell me more," Watters ignored Scuddamore's complaint. "What did this woman see?"

"She said she saw Boyle enter the house with an empty canvas bag, like a seaman's bag, Sergeant, and leave with the bag full."

"That's our ghost!" Scuddamore said. "This woman saw a dead man."

"Be quiet, Scuddamore!" Watters said thoughtfully. "Duff, I want to talk to this woman."

Mrs Grady was middle-aged, neat, and had intelligent grey eyes. "I know what I saw, Sergeant Watters. I saw Mr Boyle entering the house with an empty bag, and when he left, the bag was full."

They sat in Mrs Grady's front room, with the smell of

beeswax in the air and every item of furniture gleaming. Mrs Grady sat erect, with her head held high and shoulders back.

"Is there any way you could be mistaken, Mrs Grady?"

"No, Sergeant." Mrs Grady said firmly. "I saw Mr Boyle."

"We believe that Mr Boyle, or Constable Boyle as we knew him, drowned some weeks ago."

"In that case, Sergeant, your beliefs are mistaken. I saw Mr Boyle only last Tuesday, as clearly as I see you now. There is nothing wrong with my eyesight, Sergeant."

On the wall behind Mrs Grady, the portrait of a handsome corporal in the Royal Scots stared out. At his side was a print of Florence Nightingale. Mrs Grady noticed the direction of Watters' glance.

"My late husband," she said, "and yes, Sergeant, I was one of Florence Nightingale's nurses."

"An honour to meet you, Nurse Grady." Watters stood, and, knowing he might appear foolish, he gave a smart salute. "Corporal George Watters, Royal Marines, but I was out before the Crimea business began."

Mrs Grady smiled. "Sit down, Sergeant Watters. I recognised you as a military man the moment you stepped through my door, and Mr Boyle is undoubtedly alive."

Watters was thoughtful when he left Mrs Grady's house. He swung his cane, humming a song as he considered the aspects of his case.

The scuttling seemed to be solved. He had caught Urquhart, who admitted scuttling *Toiler* and *Teresa* and trying to scuttle *Lancelot*. Urquhart had given a plausible motive, and as a trusted specialist, he would have the freedom to roam in any section of the ship. Watters did not doubt the sailmaker's guilt.

That left the significant problem of Walter Abernethy and his companion who posed as a police inspector, and maybe the mystery of Gow.

Watters swung his cane again, sending a small stone skidding along the street. Mrs Grady's belief that Boyle was still alive was unsettling, but she was an elderly woman, if as bright as a woman half her age.

I believe her. Or rather, I believe she thinks she saw Boyle.

"Mr Watters," the words came in a harsh whisper.

"That's me," Watters recovered his cane, ready to defend himself. "Show yourself!"

"Mr Watters," Jim appeared from a close mouth and sidled up to Watters, smiling.

"Good morning, Jim," Watters said. "What is it, my lad?"

"I heard something, Mr Watters."

"What did you hear, Jim?"

"Is it worth some silver, Mr Watters?"

Watters stopped walking. He had four regular preachers, or informers in Dundee, only one of whom he would trust more than an arm's length away. Jim was the least trustworthy and the least likely to approach him. "That depends what you overheard, Jim."

"I heard somebody was grazing turnips, Mr Watters."

Watters pretended disinterest as he swung his cane. Grazing turnips was thieves' cant - or thiefology as Jim would have said it - for stealing watches. "Turnips? I am no farmer, Jim."

"The ticking kind, Mr Watters."

"I see. There are many buzzers in Dundee, Jim. Some buzz on the fly, others on the stop." Watters used thiefology to make Jim feel at home. A fly buzzer was a pickpocket who stole from people moving, while to buzz on the stop meant to pick somebody's pocket while they stood still.

"Yes, Mr Watters," Jim looked up and down the street. An informer's life would be unpleasant if one of the criminal fraternity saw him talking to the police. "It wasn't a single buzzer, Mr Watters. It was a pile of supers."

Watters halted his pretence at nonchalance. A pile of

supers was a large number of watches. "Who and where Jim?"

"I heard it from a fellow boozy with too much lush, Mr Watters."

"A drunk? Was he reliable?"

"I dunno. I think so."

That was an honest reply. "What else did you hear, Jim?"

"The lush was boasting he gulled the cracksman and took a super for himself."

Watters hid his smile. That was the sort of break for which he had hoped. He knew there was no honour among thieves, although fear of the consequences would compel them to silence. However, thieves would follow their instincts to steal, even from each other, if they considered it safe. "Is that so? Did this lush have a name?"

Jim's hesitation informed Watters he had known the drunken man.

"You won't tell me," Watters knew Jim would only tell him a false name. "What else did you learn, my friend?"

Jim was becoming more nervous by the second. "The lush was boasting he was going to pawn the super. He said the bluebottles would know he had stolen it if they searched him, so he'd pawn it for a golden boy."

"A golden boy? It must be a valuable watch if the lush thought he'd get a sovereign for it."

"He said he knew a pawn down the Dockie." Jim shrunk his shoulders and tried to slink away as somebody walked towards them.

"Thank you, Jim," Watters pushed half a crown into his hand. "You did well, now run."

After Jim took a few steps, Watters roared, "you young scoundrel! You picked my pocket, you blackguard!" and ran after him, waving his cane.

That should impress your thieving chums, Watters thought as he allowed Jim to escape. A policeman was a prime target for a pickpocket, and now anybody who saw Jim with Watters would not know he was preaching.

So, somebody was selling a stolen watch to a pawn shop down the Dockie – that was Dock Street. Watters smiled grimly. He knew all the pawns, from the scrupulously honest to the downright criminal. Watters habitually toured the pawnbrokers in mid-morning, allowing the nocturnal predators time to unload their stolen goods. Today, Watters decided, he'd go twice. His morning inspection had yielded nothing, so he'd allow the pawnshops a few hours to reclaim any stolen goods from their hiding place and surprise them.

Wullie's was the third pawn that Watters visited. The proprietor looked up in alarm when Watters entered his premises. "Sergeant Watters!"

"Good afternoon, Wullie," Watters said. "I thought I'd come to see you again."

"Of course, Sergeant Watters," Wullie's smile was even more greasy than usual.

"I'm here about some watches," Watters glanced around the shop, searching for anything out of its usual place. "Somebody broke into Mr O'Toole's shop the night before last. Or rather they used a false key."

"That's terrible, Sergeant Watters," Wullie said. "There are some unpleasant people around nowadays."

"There always were, Wullie," Watters said. He sat on the counter, swung his legs over the top and slid down on the opposite side, beside Wullie. "You don't mind me joining you, do you?"

"Of course not, Sergeant Watters," Wullie said.

"Things look a lot different from this side of the counter, don't they?" Watters rapped his cane against the glass-fronted cases behind Wullie. "Is this where you keep all your most valuable stock? Or do you have another place, a strongbox perhaps, or even a safe?"

As Wullie stuttered, Watters strode to the small back room.

"I remember, Wullie, you have a secret compartment in here, don't you? I forgot to check it this morning."

"It's empty, Sergeant Watters," Wullie said, sidling beside him. "You're wasting your time."

"That's all right, Wullie. It's my time to waste." Watters ignored the rank smell of damp cloth in the back room. "Your secret place is beside the fireplace, isn't it?" He tapped the stones with his cane until one rang hollow. "Ah, here we are. Am I getting warm, Wullie?"

"It's empty, Sergeant Watters."

"Then I won't detain you long," Watters said. He used the end of his cane to lever one of the stones free, grabbed it with his left hand and placed it carefully on the ground. "Wullie! Look! Somebody's left you a present!"

"Oh, I forgot that was there, Sergeant Watters," Wullie said as Watters removed a gold Hunter watch, three silver watch chains and a collection of watch bars, both gold and silver. "You got me so flustered with your visit it clean slipped my mind."

"That's all right, Wullie," Watters said magnanimously. "Even a businessman such as you can't be expected to remember everything all the time. Where did these come from?"

"Different places, Sergeant Watters," Wullie said. "I'll just get my book."

Watters divided the watches into two piles, with the gold Hunter separate from the others. He examined it closely first, then laid it aside when Wullie came in.

"Is that watch genuine gold?"

"Genuine?" Wullie's laugh might have fooled a deaf baby. "No, it's only gold-coloured, Mr Watters."

"Are you sure? It's heavy," Watters said.

"It's electroplated lead," Wullie said. "A thin layer of gold."

"Ah," Watters pushed the gold Hunter away. "These silver watches are genuine, though."

"Yes, Mr Watters."

"Where are they from?"

"A Mrs Napier brought them in," Wullie sounded so confident that Watters knew he was speaking the truth.

"I wonder where she got them from. Leave me her address, will you?"

"Yes, of course, Mr Watters. Will that be all?"

"Not quite," Watters said. He examined the silver watches again and saw the name Napier engraved on all three, with the watch number beneath. It was the work of a moment to check the numbers with the list Mr O'Toole had given him. The numbers did not correspond.

"Your silver watches seem honest," Watters said casually. "I expected nothing else, of course."

"Yes, Mr Watters. Will that be all?"

"I'll just check your gold-plated watch," Watters said, "although I can't imagine why anybody would wish to steal such a thing. It won't be worth much."

"Only a few pennies, Mr Watters."

"I can't even see a number on the watch," Watters said.

"Maybe it's not worth putting on," Wullie said.

"No; somebody's filed it off," Watters showed the clumsy scratches on the back of the watch. "Quite spoiled the look of the watch. Now, why would anybody do that?"

"I don't know, Mr Watters," Wullie was looking decidedly uncomfortable again.

"Oh, well," Watters turned his attention to the watch bars. As he expected, three had the name Napier engraved beside the number. Ignoring them, Watters lifted the single gold watch bar. "This bar seems to fit into the plated watch," he said. "Yes, it does. Did they arrive together?"

"Yes, they did," Wullie said.

"That explains that, then," Watters said. "Somebody has

filed the name off this one, too," he said, "and the number."

"I didn't see that, Mr Watters."

Watters examined the watch bar more closely. "Ah! Whoever filed the number away has missed one. See?" Watters pointed to the underside of the bar. "The manufacturer has added an extra number. That's very thorough of him, don't you think?"

"Very," Wullie said, looking doleful.

"I'll have a wee check with my list and then be on my way," Watters ensured he was between Wullie and the door, ensuring the pawnshop proprietor could not escape. "Oh, my word, Wullie. The number matches one stolen from Mr O'Toole. I thought you were more careful than that."

Wullie looked so crestfallen that Watters nearly smiled. He gave him a few moments to think. "You'll have the name, though."

"It's in my book," Wullie said.

"Now, Wullie, I could arrest you for receiving stolen property, or I could ask you to help me," Watters said. "Who handed the watch in?"

"Billy Largo," Wullie read the name. "17 Fife Close, Fish Street."

"Thank you, Wullie. Did you issue him with a pawn ticket?"

"Yes," Wullie said.

"I'll go and have a word with Mr Largo," Watters said. "If I can't find him, I'll be back for you. I certainly don't know the name Billy Largo." Slipping the gold watch and watch bar into his pocket, Watters left the pawnshop.

Thank you, Jim. Your little tip might prove to be invaluable.

———

"I am Sergeant George Watters of the Dundee Police, looking for Billy Largo," Watters said to the thin-faced woman who answered the door in Fife Close.

"Who?" the woman looked confused. A man's voice sounded from the interior of the house.

"Who's that, Margaret?"

"It's some fellow looking for a Billy Largo!" the woman called back. "He says he's from the police."

The man appeared with a collarless shirt, and baggy trousers. "Who are you looking for, mister?"

"Billy Largo," Watters repeated.

"I don't know the name," the man said. "We're the Fergusons. Next door is auld Jock MacBride, and over there is Tam Glynn and his wife, Mary." He pointed to every door in the close, listing the occupants. "Somebody's given you the wrong address, mister, or the wrong name."

"Thank you, Mr Ferguson. My apologies for bothering you." Watters lifted his hat to Mrs Ferguson and returned to Dock Street, arrested Wullie Snell at the pawnshop and brought him to the Police Office.

"There's a surprise," Sergeant Murdoch said as he booked in Wullie. "How are you, Wullie? You've not been here for at least six months. Receiving stolen goods is it?"

"Yes, Sergeant Murdoch."

"You'll lose your license for good this time, Wullie. We're far too lenient with you."

Scuddamore came in with a pickpocket in tow. "No luck at the Overgate area pawns," he said. "I caught young Dippy Marjory as a consolation." He nodded to Wullie. "Good afternoon, Wullie. Welcome home."

"Wullie tried to sell me a false name, too," Watters showed Scuddamore the entry in Wullie's book.

"Billy Largo," Scuddamore smiled. "Now that's familiar."

"Do you know him?"

"I know who uses that name," Scuddamore said. "Largo is one of Thiefy Campbell's aliases. He also uses Thomas Aberdour, Murdo Reid, and Joseph Jackson."

"Thiefy Campbell?" Duff queried.

"He's a thief from Blackness," Scuddamore said. "A nasty wee creature, up to all the dodges."

"You said he used Thomas Aberdour as an alias?" Watters said. "Aberdour is in Fife, not far from Kinghorn."

"Just so," Scuddamore said. "But Thiefy could never pass as a policeman. Not even a blind man with no hands could mistake Thiefy for a copper unless the wee wretch grew six inches."

"Do you know his address?" Watters hid his elation. Jim's information had started a run of good fortune, with good policing helping.

"I know some of the addresses he uses," Scuddamore said. "Give me a minute to book this beauty in, and I'll come with you. Come along, my pretty," he pulled the pickpocket to Murdoch's desk. "This is Marjory Snodgrass, a snivelling little creature with ideas above her station. She dipped a flat and tried to run up the Wellgate Steps."

Snodgrass tossed her blonde hair, sniffed, and looked away.

When Scuddamore had deposited Snodgrass safely in her cell with the female turnscrew searching her for any more illicit gains, Watters checked on Wullie in the cell next door. He looked at Urquhart next, who lay on his side, coughing.

"Let's hope nobody murders either of these two," Scuddamore said. "Now for Thiefy Campbell. He lives off the Blackness Road."

"I've never met the lad, although the name is known," Watters said. "How does he work?"

"He's a nocturnal creature," Scuddamore said as they walked westward towards Blackness. "If we're lucky, we might catch him in his house before he sets out. Thiefy's normally a sneak thief. He was moulded in childhood, like so many of the criminal class. His father drowned at sea, and his mother died of cholera soon after. Young Thiefy, or Edward to give him his proper name, had no family, and by the age of five, he was already adept at snotter-hauling - stealing hand-kerchiefs."

"Poor wee bugger," Watters said. "He didn't have much chance, did he?"

"No. Like so many, his childhood moulded him into a life of crime. Now he is a thoroughbred professional thief. He usually works alone, but sometimes he can operate with others."

"Abernethy?" Watters asked.

"Perhaps. Thiefy has aspirations to be a gentleman. He steals gentlemen's clothes and parades around Reform Street to attract the ladies, but he can't hold onto his gains."

"My preacher told me he was lushy."

"Aye," Scuddamore said. "Drink is his downfall. Drink and a boastful mouth."

They reached the Blackness Road that stretched westward from central Dundee, and Scuddamore nodded to one or two of the people they passed.

"Agnes MacLear and John Black," he explained. "Mill workers and honest as the day is long."

"You were telling me about Thiefy Campbell," Watters prompted, watching a closed coach that passed amidst the loaded jute wagons and other works traffic.

"I've known Thiefy since before you came to Dundee, Sergeant. The first time I arrested him, you would be down in London, talking to her Majesty."

Watters grunted. "We don't drink in the same pub, Queen Victoria and I."

"Here we are," Scuddamore stopped outside a close. "He lives on the second floor."

"This is a respectable looking close," Watters glanced upwards at the clean tenement with its ranked, polished windows.

"As I said, Sergeant, Thiefy has aspirations above his class.

He wants to be a gentleman, like Mr Muirhead, or even Walter Abernethy."

Watters nodded. "Lead on, MacDuff."

The close was well kept, regularly swept, and smelled of carbolic soap and fresh paint. Scuddamore led the way with his footsteps echoing in the great cavern of the stairwell.

"Third floor, middle door," Scuddamore said. "And unless Thiefy fancies a thirty-foot drop to the ground, no way of escaping."

Watters nodded, noting the name above each letterbox and the gleaming clean astragals above the doors. "This is one of the best-kept closes I've seen in a long time."

"Decent folk in here," Scuddamore said. "This is my area, you see, and I keep it as free from people like Thiefy as I can."

The name Campbell was prominent on the door, carved in fine copperplate on a varnished wooden background.

"Here we are," Scuddamore stopped. "It seems almost a shame to disturb him."

"Almost," Watters said.

Rather than rap on the door, Watters produced his packet of lockpicks and opened the lock.

"I admire your skill at that," Scuddamore said. "If ever you leave the force, Sergeant, there's another career for you."

They entered the house quietly. It was clean, with rugs on the polished wooden floor and pictures on the wall. Of the three doors that opened from the central lobby, two were open and one closed. Watters glanced in the first room, a sitting room with comfortable chairs and a bookcase. The second was the kitchen, with an oaken table and four matching chairs, while jars and food containers filled the shelves. Early evening sunlight reflected from an array of brass pots and pans.

Thiefy lives in some comfort.

"In there," Scuddamore mouthed, jerking a thumb towards the closed door.

Watters turned the handle slowly, then shoved the door

open, with Scuddamore barging into the bedroom.

"Dundee Police!" Scuddamore roared. "You're under arrest, Campbell!"

As with the other rooms in the house, the bedroom was neat and well furnished, with a wardrobe, chest of drawers, two hard-backed chairs and prints on the walls. One of the two people in the bed screamed, and the other looked up in startled horror before sliding under the covers.

"You've nowhere to go, Campbell!" Scuddamore grabbed the man by the hair and dragged him naked from the bed as his female companion continued to scream, high-pitched.

Watters estimated Thiefy Campbell to be around twenty-eight, with the eyes of an old man and the body of a youth. He was slightly built and under average height. Watters grunted; Scuddamore was correct; nobody could think that Campbell was a police lieutenant.

"You dirty bluebottle bastards!" Campbell's companion shouted at the top of her voice. She flicked long blonde hair back from her face. "I'll bloody kill you!"

"Shoosh now," Watters comforted the woman. "We're not after you."

The woman stopped screaming and lunged at Watters, nails raking at his face. As naked as her companion, she yelled abuse as she tried to scratch out Watters' eyes. Grabbing her wrists, he held her at arm's length as Scuddamore ordered Campbell to dress.

"Watch that woman, Sergeant," Scuddamore warned. "That's Helen Montgomery, a notorious pugilist."

With Watters holding her wrists together, Montgomery was trying to kick, her bare feet flailing at Watters' groin. "Aye, she's a charmer," Watters said. "Behave yourself, Montgomery, or I'll arrest you for police assault!"

"Would you, now?" Montgomery screamed, nearly frantic with her frustrated desire to hurt.

"Get your clothes on, woman," Watters ordered, as Thiefy

Campbell slowly dressed, with Scuddamore encouraging him with hard prods with his staff.

"You won't arrest me!" Montgomery kicked again.

Watters' patience snapped. Turning Montgomery around, he shoved her hands inside the D handcuffs and screwed them tight.

"I cannae get dressed now, bluebottle bastard!" Montgomery screeched. "What are you gaunnae dae? Haul me oot naked?"

"This," Watters grabbed a blanket from the bed and threw it over Montgomery's body, tying it in a knot in front. "Now shut your teeth and behave."

Throwing Montgomery over his shoulder, Watters left the house, with Scuddamore urging the handcuffed Thiefy behind them.

"What's happening?" the respectable people of the close were at their open doors.

"Dundee Police," Watters explained, fighting the wriggling Montgomery, and hoping the blanket remained in place. He did not wish to shock the neighbourhood with a display of bare female flesh. "It's all under control."

"That's that quiet Mr Campbell," one silver-haired woman said. "He's such a nice, polite man."

"They're often the worst kind," Scuddamore said.

Watters hoped the respectable people did not understand the meaning of Montgomery's words as she screamed obscenities that should have blistered the paint from the walls.

Montgomery wriggled, kicked, and swore all the way back to the police office so that Watters was relieved to dump her in a cell under the gimlet eyes of the female turnkey.

"You've been busy the day, Sergeant," the turnkey said.

"Aye, this is Helen Montgomery, and she's all yours."

The turnkey gave a grim nod. "I know how to deal with her sort. You leave her to me, Sergeant Watters."

"We'll be back to talk to you, Thiefy," Scuddamore

warned as he escorted Campbell into his cell. "I think you've been keeping company with cracksmen and murderers. That's a bit above your level, isn't it?"

"Murderers?" Campbell sat on the hard bed, quite composed now he was back in a familiar environment. "I don't do murder, Mr Scuddamore."

"You can think about what you've done and who you work with," Scuddamore said. "We'll be back to talk to you later."

Watters summoned both the male and female turnkeys to him. "It's only a few months ago that one of my prisoners mysteriously died," he said. "I don't want such a mishap with either of these two." He slapped the weighted end of his cane into the palm of his hand. "When I return, I want them both hale, healthy, and hearty."

The turnkeys looked at him. Haley nodded, "Yes, Sergeant," while Nixon, the female turnkey, merely grunted.

"No visitors," Watters said. "None - and I don't care what rank they are or who they pretend to be. You have my orders, and you can tell that to anybody."

"What if Lieutenant Anstruther comes down?" Haley asked, "Or another policeman?"

"I don't care if it's Lieutenant Anstruther, Mr Mackay, or Queen Victoria herself," Watters said. "These are my prisoners," he winced as Montgomery began to scream threats and obscenities and kick at her cell door. "Nobody sees them until I return."

He called at the booking-in desk as he left. "Have you the most recent list of stolen property, Murdoch?"

"Here you are, George," Murdoch handed one over. Ten pages of dense print, it was the detective's Bible when searching for stolen property. "Good luck."

"Thank you," Watters sighed. Whatever else was happening, the day-to-day routine of the job must continue. If he had more men, he'd have more time to spend investigating. And where the devil was young Shaw?

CHAPTER TWENTY-FOUR

CONSTABLE SHAW SLOUCHED UP TO WATTERS' DESK, SLUMPED onto a chair without being invited and grinned. "I thought I'd better keep you informed of my progress, Watters."

Watters stared at him in disbelief. "Stand up until you're invited to sit, you little vagabond! And you address me as Sergeant!"

The force of Watters' words created a silence in the duty room. Shaw's smile vanished as he shot to his feet.

"Stand at attention! Who the devil do you think you are?" Watters roared, watching Shaw's face alter from lazy unconcern to shock.

"Sorry, Sergeant."

"I heard you were lounging about in publics and playing football with children when you should have been working," Watters was not prepared to allow Shaw off the hook yet.

"I was gathering information, Sergeant." A bead of sweat appeared on Shaw's forehead and rolled down his face.

"We're you indeed?" Watters controlled his voice. "Report, Shaw, and remain at attention!"

"I used the children to spy on Mr Muirhead," Shaw said. "I thought that the subject would be suspicious if he saw me all the time, but nobody notices lads in Dundee. So, some followed him, and others watched his house. The men in the public could see Muirhead's ships and told me whenever he visited them."

"I see," Watters nodded. "What did you find out?"

"Quite a lot, Sergeant," Shaw smiled. "I wrote Mr Muirhead's movement's down."

"Give me the gist," Watters said.

"Mr Muirhead is getting married, Sergeant. He visits his intended three times a week, returning home by coach at night."

Watters nodded. *That explained the coach. I never thought of Muirhead as having a private life.*

"Thank you, Shaw. Now write me a report with the relevant details and bring it to me with your notes. Off you go."

———

The people in the Blackness close were still discussing the afternoon's excitement with the husbands and wives that returned from their work.

Watters pushed through them, with Scuddamore at his back. "I am sorry, my friends," he said, "I can't answer your questions just now. I will only say that Mr Campbell is under arrest on suspicion of theft and Miss Montgomery on a charge of police assault."

"You might have allowed the young lady to get dressed," somebody said. "It was positively indecent the way you carried her out like that. I could see her leg right up to the knee!"

Watters nodded. "I'll bear that in mind next time a woman attacks me."

"You police are just brutes!" a middle-aged woman said. "I know Mr Mackay personally. I'll tell him to remove you from the force."

"I'm sure he'll listen to you, madam," Watters said. "Sergeant George Watters is the name."

Once again, Watters picked the lock, and they entered Thiefy Campbell's house. "Look for anything incriminating," Watters said. "Property that Thiefy might have stolen, money, anything."

"Yes, Sergeant, I know the drill," Scuddamore reminded Watters that he was an experienced detective.

"Thiefy lives well for a man with no occupation," Watters looked around the house. "Good quality furniture, a wardrobe of clothes and plenty of food in the cupboards." He placed the list of stolen property on the table. "Compare anything interesting to the items on the list."

"Yes, Sergeant," Scuddamore said.

After ten minutes, Scuddamore checked a silver finger-ring, found a match, and laid it carefully on the table. Watters added a silver pen engraved with initials that were not Campbell's, and within an hour, half a dozen stolen items lay beside the list.

"We've sufficient here to put Thiefy away for a seven stretch," Watters said. "Battling Helen Montgomery will have to do without her afternoon romps for quite some time."

"We are wasting our time visiting the pawns," Scuddamore said. "We should come to Thiefy's den first. He's a one-man danger to Dundee."

Watters nodded. "Aye, but we haven't found anything to connect him to Abernethy yet. These are all from Thiefy's personal endeavours, except for that single gold watch. I want something definite from Sinclair's or the hotel robberies."

Scuddamore opened the wardrobe and whistled. "He dressed well, did our Thiefy." He lifted the list and compared the various items of clothing. "Stolen from the Nethergate. Stolen from West Ferry. Stolen from Invergowrie. Halloa! What's this?"

The change in Scuddamore's tone alerted Watters. "What have you found, Scuddamore?"

"I'm not sure yet, Sergeant. I think there's a false back to this wardrobe. It seems very shallow now that I've removed all the stolen clothes."

Watters quickly measured the side of the wardrobe with his outstretched hand. "My hand span is 9 inches," he said. "I have three spans on the outside, and," he checked the interior, "two and a half inside. You're right, Scuddamore. There's a false back. Empty the whole thing." They threw the contents onto the floor in a confused pile of shirts, trousers, waistcoats, and jackets.

"Now we can see properly," Watters said, peering inside. "The wood inside the back is different. The wardrobe is of oak, with a beech back. There must be a way to move it." He ran his hand around the rim until he found a small opening. "Here's something." When he gave a quick pull, the back came off.

"Oh, clever Thiefy," Scuddamore said as he looked inside the concealed compartment. "What have we here?"

"Now we're getting somewhere," Watters felt his satisfaction grow. Jim's information was proving invaluable.

"That's a police lieutenant's uniform," Scuddamore lifted the uniform from its position at the back of the wardrobe. "Well, well, well. Thiefy Campbell, what have you been doing?"

Watters nodded grimly. "Some of the pieces are clicking into place," he said. "Is anything else in there?"

"Yes, Sergeant," Scuddamore said. "These!" He produced a pair of boots with enhanced heels and soles to make the wearer appear taller.

"How interesting," Watters said.

"Perhaps we have found our police lieutenant after all," Scuddamore said.

"Perhaps so," Watters said. "It blows my theory out of the water anyway."

"Were you hoping it was Lieutenant Anstruther, Sergeant?"

"I was only hoping to catch the culprit," Watters fenced with words, remembering Lizzie Flett's warning about the tall, one-eyed man.

"I thought it was Anstruther." Scuddamore continued. "Maybe it is, yet. Maybe he's working with Thiefy."

"Lieutenant Anstruther," Watters corrected. "Show some respect. We'll bundle all this up and take it to the office." He smiled. "It's been a good day, Scuddamore, and all thanks to a preacher called Jim and your local knowledge."

"It's good to know that the system works," Scuddamore pulled a pillow out of its case and piled the stolen goods inside.

"Keep the uniform on its hanger," Watters said. "If it's genuine, Mr Mackay will likely bring it back into circulation."

———

"Did Mr Mackay promote you, Scuddamore?" Murdoch asked when Scuddamore walked into the office carrying the lieutenant's uniform. "Should I call you sir?"

"Only if you bow at the same time," Scuddamore said, grinning.

Watters placed the pillowcase full of stolen property on the desk. "Have this lot booked in, please, Murdoch. It's all from Thiefy Campbell's place."

Murdoch glanced at the contents. "I know the address."

"There are more stolen clothes that we didn't bring," Watters put Campbell's keys on the desk. "We left them in a separate bundle on the table. If you could detail a couple of constables to bring them in, I'd be obliged."

"Do you think I'm your servant, George?"

Watters grinned. "If I were wearing that lieutenant's uniform, you would jump to my orders, never mind my requests."

"Aye, and if all my horses passed the winning post when they were meant to, I'd live in a palace in the Ferry," Murdoch said. "Where are you going?"

"Down to the cells," Watters said. "Come along, Lieutenant Scuddamore. Bring your new uniform."

Montgomery had quietened down and was lying on her bed. "She yelled for a bit," Nixon said, "until I went to speak to her."

Watters eyed Nixon, a middle-aged woman with years of experience dealing with recalcitrant female prisoners. "You managed to silence her."

"I did." The turnkey did not go into details, and Watters did not ask.

"I brought her some clothes," Watters handed them to Nixon. "A little more decent than a blanket."

The turnkey held them up and wrinkled her nose in distaste. "A little," she said. "Not much."

Watters moved on to Thiefy's cell. Thiefy was sitting on the bed with his head in his hands. He looked up when Watters and Scuddamore entered.

"I said we'd be back," Scuddamore said pleasantly. "And here we are."

Thiefy's gaze shifted to the Lieutenant's uniform and away again. He said nothing.

"Put this on," Watters passed the uniform over to Thiefy.

"Why?"

"I want to see if it fits," Watters said.

"It's too large."

"How do you know that without trying it on?" Scuddamore lifted Thiefy by his hair. "I don't like you, Thiefy. I don't like thieving little blackguards that break into other people's houses and steal things that folk have worked long hours to buy."

Thiefy gasped, trying to free his hair. "Let go, Mr Scuddamore."

Scuddamore lifted him higher, so Thiefy had to stand on tiptoes. "I think you were involved in a murder, Campbell. I dislike murderers even more than I dislike thieves. Now put on that blasted uniform before I lose my temper!"

Watters watched as Thiefy stripped off his clothes and put on the lieutenant's uniform. After only a few moments, it was evident that the uniform was many sizes too large, with trousers that wrinkled over his feet, arms that extended past Thiefy's hands and room within the coat for another small man.

"Try the boots," Watters invited.

The boots were about two sizes too large for Thiefy's feet. He stood slumped, looking ludicrous as Watters frowned at him.

"All right," Watters hid his disappointment. "We haven't found our false lieutenant yet. But we have found a link to him."

"And a man willing to preach on his old pals," Scuddamore said softly.

Watters nodded. "Yes. Thank you for the intelligence you gave me, Thiefy. It will lead us directly to Abernethy and the false inspector. Now get out of that uniform before you pollute it."

"I told you it wasn't mine," Thiefy said as he removed the uniform.

"The question is," Watters said, "whose is it?"

Thiefy shrugged. "I don't know."

"As you wish," Watters said. "We can either charge you with all the robberies, which will mean penal servitude for at least ten years, or we can spread the news that you helped us find Abernethy and then let you loose."

Watters saw Thiefy's face twist. "He'd kill me if you did that."

"Abernethy's no killer," Watters said.

"Somebody else is," Thiefy retorted.

"Probably," Watters tried to sound callous. "We'll let you think which you prefer, ten years penal or your old pal hunting you down." He lifted the uniform and left the cell, with Scuddamore slamming the door with a bang like the end of the world.

"I almost feel sorry for him," Scuddamore said.

"Don't bother," Watters held the uniform at arm's length. "He'd rob his granny of her last farthing and laugh at her tears. No, I have another plan for our Thiefy Campbell."

CHAPTER TWENTY-FIVE

"SERGEANT WATTERS!" MA RAMSAY TAPPED WATTERS ON THE shoulder. "I want you."

Watters blinked, surprised to see Ma Ramsay outside her home. She looked out of place in Dock Street, with all her gaudy finery exposed to the early autumn sun. "What can I do for you, Ma?"

"We've got trouble at my workplace," Ma Ramsay said, with shadows in her dark eyes. "Two of my porters have been beaten up, and the other didn't turn up for work."

"What's it about, Ma?"

"Hairy Meg," Ma Ramsay said. "Do you remember that fellow you sent away a few months back?"

"I do," Watters said, "Herbert Balfour."

"That's the man. Well, he wants exclusive rights to Meg."

"He wants to marry her?"

"Nothing like!" Ma Ramsay snorted. "He wants me to keep her for him and nobody else."

"And he attacked your porters?"

"Yes," Ma Ramsay said.

"Does he have a regular time for coming?"

"Saturday night after his work," Ma Ramsay said.

Marie will love me spending my Saturday night in a brothel.

"I'll look in," Watters promised, adding Ma Ramsay's to his list of distractions.

———

Shaw sat down beside Watters and handed over a thick sheaf of paper. "Here are my notes, Sergeant."

"Your notes for what?"

"You asked me to write a report on Mr Muirhead and bring you my notes."

Watters had almost forgotten issuing the orders. "Thank you, Shaw." He glanced at the densely written pages. "You've been busy."

"Yes, Sergeant."

"Spare me from reading through them all," Watters said. "Paraphrase Mr Muirhead's movements."

Shaw leaned back and stretched out his legs. "It's quite simple, Sergeant. He gets up at five-thirty and goes to work at six, either in Dock Street or East Whale Lane. Twice a week, he visits his ships and talks to his shipmasters, and twice a week, he visits Miss Alice Ross of Gowrie Grange."

"And who the devil is Miss Alice Ross of Gowrie Grange?" Watters guessed the answer but encouraged Shaw to give an accurate report.

"Miss Ross is Mr Muirhead's fiancé," Shaw said. "She is the younger daughter of Lieutenant-Colonel Arthur Ross of the Punjab Rifles and far too young for him."

"The devil she is," Watters remembered Muirhead's closed coach passing as he watched from the Old Steeple. "Why, the sly old dog."

"They're getting married soon," Shaw said. "You should read the Society column, Sergeant."

"And you should mind your lip, Constable," Watters said.

"Yes, Sergeant," Shaw said. "I meant no disrespect."

Watters eyed the young constable. "You did well, Shaw. There may be hope for you yet." He noted the surprise in Shaw's eyes. "Find Duff, tell him I sent you to assist him."

"Yes, Sergeant." Shaw saluted and left quickly, leaving his notes with Watters.

———

Saturday night was always busy in Dundee as working men and women relaxed and spent what they could afford of their meagre wages. Watters balanced his cane on his right shoulder as he strode to Couttie's Wynd with Duff at his side. He hoped he could sort out the problem quickly, for Marie had not been happy to see him leave.

Ma Ramsay put a hand on Watters' sleeve. "Thank you for coming, Sergeant."

"Our job is to protect people," Watters said. "If you could show us to Meg's room, we'll get into position nearby."

"This way," Ma Ramsay led them up a flight of stairs and along a narrow corridor, where thin wooden partitions gave each girl a modicum of privacy. Meg's room was near the far end, with a vacant cubicle next door. Meg stood outside, trembling with fear. She forced a smile as Duff winked at her.

"This will do," Watters entered the empty cubicle.

"The man Balfour is a brute," Ma Ramsay said. "He flattened my porters with ease."

Watters nodded to Duff, who stood in the opposite corner, with Meg between them. "With Constable Duff here," he said, "we have little to worry about. We'll wait in this room, and when Meg gives the signal, we'll appear."

Ma Ramsay gave Duff an appraising glance, from his lack of height to the breadth of his shoulders. "If you're sure," she said doubtfully.

Duff grinned. "You get along to your business, Mrs Ramsay. Sergeant Watters and I will handle your troublemaker." He shifted his balance from his left foot to his right. "Now, don't you worry about a thing, Mrs Ramsay. Nor you Margaret."

Hairy Meg shook her head. "It's Megan, Constable Duff. Meg is short for Megan."

"My apologies," Duff said. "We'll look after you, Megan."

Watters sat on the bed, pulled out his pipe, and began to fill the bowl. "Marie doesn't let me smoke in the house now," he said. "She thinks it's bad for the baby."

Duff smiled. "Women get the strangest of fancies, don't they?" He sniffed. "Somebody's been smoking in here, though. I recognise that aroma. It's not ordinary tobacco."

"God knows what people get up to in these places," Watters said. "It could be anything." He sniffed loudly. "You're right, Duff. I recognise the smell, too." He shrugged. "No matter. Let's hope this Balfour fellow's on time, and we can get home."

Balfour arrived precisely at eight. Watters heard his deep voice rasping in the building and his heavy tread on the stairs outside.

"Hairy Meg! You'd better not be with anybody else!"

"Ready, Duff?" Watters tapped the weighted end of his cane into the palm of his left hand.

"Ready," Duff stamped his feet on the floor. "I didn't tell Rosemary where I was," he whispered.

Watters hid his smile. "I told Marie," he said. "You'd better tell Rosemary when you see her next. If somebody else tells her you were in a brothel, it will be ten times worse."

They heard Meg squeal as Balfour stepped into her cubicle, and then Watters and Duff entered. Balfour held Meg by her long hair and had one hand lifted as if to slap her when Duff took hold of the man's arm.

"You don't treat a lady like that!" Duff growled.

"You're under arrest Herbert Balfour," Watters said as the man twisted and tried to punch Duff. "For attempting to assault a police officer," he winced as Duff caught Balfour's fist and threw the man against the wall. "And for assaulting a woman," Duff lifted Balfour from the wall, yanked his arms behind his back and screwed tight the handcuffs, "and for breaking into a house where you were asked not to return."

Meg watched, with one hand over her mouth. Watters was unsure whether she was enjoying the spectacle or was afraid.

Duff lifted Balfour with one hand. "If you come near this lady again," he growled. "I'll break every bone in your body."

"And I arrest you for rioting and blasphemy," Watters concluded. "If I think of anything else, I'll add it later." He lifted his hat to Meg. "I don't think this creature will bother you for quite some time," he said. "I'm looking for eighteen months at least."

"Thank you, Sergeant," Meg said, with her eyes bright. "If ever you fall out with your wife, don't hesitate to call by."

Watters gave a slight bow. "I'll bear your kind invitation in mind," he said and stopped as the drift of tobacco smoke came to him. "I recognise that aroma," he said. "Do you smoke, Meg?"

"I dislike that smell," Meg said. "I neither smoke nor drink. I don't use foul language either."

Watters stepped back as Duff shoved the manacled man from Meg's cubicle. "You're a decent girl, Meg. What brought you to this line of work?"

Meg shrugged. "It's a long story."

"Aye, everybody has a story. That tobacco smell is different. I've smelled it before."

"He was a gentleman," Meg said. "The customer who smoked that was a gentleman. A real gentleman. I think he was a ship's captain or an army officer or some such."

Watters frowned as his mind began to work. He sat on the edge of the bed. "Could you describe this gentleman to me, Meg?"

Meg's face altered. Her eyes softened, her mouth curved in

a smile, and she instinctively brushed back her mane of hair. "He's so handsome," she said, "tall and gentlemanly. He is a true gentleman, always polite."

"Turkish tobacco." Watters mind clicked. "That aroma is Turkish tobacco."

"Is it?" Meg asked. "He's the sort of man that I want to marry." Her face fell, "but no man will ever want to marry me, will they? I'm spoiled goods, I am."

"Nobody knows what the future holds," Watters said, sinking to his knees.

"What are you doing, Sergeant?"

"Looking for something," Watters said, running his hands over the cheap carpet. "Ah, here we are." He lifted the butt of a cigarette from the floor. "I will take this with me. Did your gentleman have a name?"

"Richard," Meg said.

"A last name?"

"I never give my last name and never ask for their's."

Watters nodded. "That's a fair point. Thank you for your help, Meg."

Reaching out, Meg held Watters' arm. "Thank you, Sergeant Watters, and you Constable Duff."

Watters strolled home from Couttie's Wynd, swinging his cane. He only knew one man who smoked Turkish cigarettes, and that was Constable Richard Boyle.

———

Duff placed a sheet of paper on Watters' desk. "That's the list of *Charming Amelia's* owners," he said. "Urquhart was the mate and held twenty-five shares. He was the sailmaker and put all his savings into the ship."

"I can feel sympathy for Urquhart," Watters agreed as he scanned the list. "Of the seventy-four shares, Urquhart had twenty-five. A fellow called Gow had another twenty-five, and the others had lesser numbers, from ten to a solitary share."

"Can you trace these owners?" Watters asked.

"I have found the addresses of most," Duff said. "But I haven't found Gow yet." He ran his stubby finger down the list. "This name may be of interest, Sergeant."

Duff's finger rested on the name Anstruther.

"There's that man again," Watters said quietly. "Ten shares. Maybe we'd better make a few more discreet enquiries about Lieutenant Anstruther, Duff." He held Duff's steady grey eyes. "And I mean discreet."

"Yes, Sergeant."

Watters nodded. He would trust Duff where discretion was concerned. While Scuddamore was a fund of local knowledge and could charm the birds from the trees with his handsome face and smooth manners, Duff was a methodical plodder. On the other hand, Scuddamore could be slapdash and say too much, while Duff would measure every word. In Duff's philosophy, every fact was a secret unless it was necessary to reveal it, and only then to a select few.

"Try and find this Gow fellow, and everybody with five shares or more," Watters decided. "I think we can discount the single share people; they'll have lost twenty or twenty-five pounds and whoever is targeting Mr Muirhead spent more than that on the insurance policies." He swung his cane two or three times. "I'll need a sample of Lieutenant Anstruther's handwriting, Duff, to compare it with the signatures we have."

"I don't like to investigate Lieutenant Anstruther," Duff admitted. "It's like stabbing him in the back."

"I feel the same," Watters said, "but it's our job. Keep it to ourselves, don't even tell Mr Mackay, and if this blows up in our face, I will take full responsibility."

Duff straightened his back. "It's my decision too, sir. I'm not hiding behind you."

"You'd never hide behind anybody, Duff," Watters said. "But think of Rosemary."

"Rosemary?" Duff's rugged, honest face creased in confusion.

"Aren't you going to marry her?"

"How did you know that, Sergeant? I've told nobody."

Watters leaned forward. "Because you'd be a fool not to, Duff, and you're nobody's fool. You also told me that you bought a ring. Now go and do your duty."

"Yes, Sergeant," Duff walked away.

Watters watched him for a moment, shaking his head, and returned to the plans he was formulating. He had a lot on his mind, with too many loose ends to splice together. Once he created an evidential rope, he would tie his case into a Gordian Knot that even the great Alexander could not part.

Couttie's Wynd was as dismal as ever, for even on a sunny evening, the tall tenements on either side limited the light. Jim was hiding in a doorway, trying to peer through a window where the curtain was partially open.

"You there!" Watters shouted, pointing with his cane. "What the devil are you doing?"

"Nothing, Mr Watters," Jim looked ready to flee or burst into tears.

"Nothing? You're loitering, loitering with intent!" Watters strode to the scared man. "Come with me, Jim Bogle. You're under arrest!"

"I wasn't doing anything, Mr Watters! Honest, I wasn't!"

"That's enough of that!" Watters grabbed Jim by the collar and marched him up Couttie's Wynd to the Nethergate. "It's a night in the cells for you, my boy and maybe another sixty to follow." He was aware of half a dozen people watching and knew word would soon spread that he had arrested Jim Bogle.

Murdoch sighed when Watters forced Jim into the police

office. "Is that another prisoner, George? You like to keep me busy, don't you?"

"This lad is a special case," Watters said softly as Jim wiped away his tears. "I don't want him booked in."

Murdoch frowned and put his pen away. "What are you up to, George?"

"You'll see." Watters frogmarched Jim into the interview room and pushed him onto the wooden seat reserved for suspects. He raised his voice. "Scuddamore!"

"Yes, Sergeant," Scuddamore had watched Watters' arrival.

"Two mugs of tea, Scuddamore. One for me and one for my nervous young friend here."

Scuddamore shook his head. "Are we giving them tea and biscuits now?"

"Yes, good idea, Scuddamore. Biscuits too. I think there's a box near my desk. Sugar and milk for young Jim's tea. Move!"

"Yes, Sergeant," Scuddamore threw a sarcastic salute and withdrew, glaring at Jim.

"Now, Jim," Watters said kindly. "You're not under arrest, so stop blubbering. I'm putting you in custody for a night or two, and you'll be perfectly safe, warmish and nearly comfortable."

"Why, Mr Watters? What have I done? I tried to help you."

"You were a great help, Jim." Watters looked up when Scuddamore appeared, slammed down two mugs of tea and a plate with four biscuits.

"Abernethy biscuits," Scuddamore said. "I hope you enjoy them. Is there anything else, Sergeant? A cake for the prisoner, perhaps? A velvet cushion?"

"Just less cheek, Scuddamore, and close the door behind you."

"Now, Jim," Watters said as Jim looked up from behind his

fringe of black hair. "You've to drink your tea and eat your biscuits."

"Yes, Mr Watters," Jim was shaking with fear. "What have you brought me here for?"

Watters pondered how much he could trust Jim, decided not at all, and drank his tea instead. "I heard there might be some trouble in Dundee tonight. You've heard of the Fenians?"

"Yes, Mr Watters."

"I heard a whisper that they'll be rioting tonight, so I thought you'd be safer in a cell. After all, you and I are chums."

"Yes, Mr Watters," Jim whispered.

"All right, drink your tea and come with me," Watters said. "I might be a little rough, but that's for your own good. Do you trust me, Jim?"

"Yes, Mr Watters," Jim said.

"Then do as I say and don't look so worried. Nobody will hurt you."

Bringing Jim down to the cells, Watters began to shout again, calling him all the names he could bring to mind. "Open a cell door!" he roared at Haley.

"Which one, Sergeant?" The turnkey was not used to Watters shouting.

"Any bloody one!" Watters kicked a door for effect. "That cell there!"

"Campbell's in there," Haley said.

"They'll have to double up, then! Is it the police cells you're running? Or a blasted coaching inn? Open the door!"

When Haley fumbled with the lock and opened the door, Watters grabbed Jim by the neck and arm and thrust him violently into the cell. "Get in there, you thieving wee bugger." He glared at Thiefy, who lay unmoving on his bed. "Company for you, Campbell. Two thieves together."

"I'll bring a mattress later," Haley said.

"You do that," Watters said. "And a blanket." He knew that Mr Mackay insisted that every prisoner should have a straw mattress and blanket at night. It was a piece of humanity that revealed the decency behind Mackay's stern exterior. "You behave yourself, Bogle! And don't try and pick Campbell's pocket!"

"You'll be all right, son," Haley whispered to Jim. "Don't mind his shine."

Scuddamore was at his desk, poring over lists of stolen goods. "That was a dirty trick to play on Jim," he said.

"You played your part well," Watters looked at his empty mug hopefully. "I'll use every dirty trick in the book to solve a crime and protect this city."

"Do you think it will work?" Scuddamore poured them both a mug of tea.

"I'm not sure. Thiefy is a canny man. He might see right through it, but Jim is genuinely scared of me, which might help. He's a natural preacher, so whatever Thiefy says, he'll tell us."

"Let's hope it's worth hearing," Scuddamore said.

———

"Is Lieutenant Anstruther on duty?" Watters asked innocently.

"The lieutenant's finished for the day," Murdoch knew the duty shift of every policeman, from the lieutenants to the lowest Johnny Raw.

"When will he return?" Watters asked.

"Murdoch did not have to check the rota. "Six o'clock in the morning," he said. "He's supervising an operation in the Ferry tomorrow. The Customs lads are worried about somebody smuggling tobacco from the Continent, with fishing boats bringing quantities ashore."

"Thank you, Murdoch," Watters said.

Scuddamore was listening at the door, half smiling as he chewed the stem of his pipe. "What's your plan, Sergeant?"

"Bring the uniform," Watters said.

"Lieutenant Anstruther keeps his door locked," Scuddamore reminded.

Watters smiled and produced his packet of lockpicks. "I know."

Watters unlocked then locked Anstruther's door and opened the shutters to allow the evening light into the room.

"Damn!" Watters said. "I had hoped there would be a spare uniform to compare."

"Over here, Sergeant," Scuddamore peered into the corners of the room. "Behind the mirror."

The uniform hung neatly on a selection of coat hangers, with the long coat outside and the rest underneath.

"Check the sizes," Watters knew that Scuddamore was adept with clothes.

"An exact fit," Scuddamore said after a few moments. "The uniform we found could have been made for the lieutenant." He smiled. "Maybe it was."

Watters stopped when light footsteps pattered outside the door.

"Anstruther!" Mackay's voice sounded, and he rattled the handle. "Anstruther! Are you in there?" There was a pause. "Confound the man! He's never there when I want him." The footsteps died away as Mackay mounted the stairs to his eyrie on the top floor.

"Check the tailor," Watters said. "Is there a name inside?"

Scuddamore checked. "Anstruther's is the official police tailor," he said. "Thiefy's hasn't got a label of any sort."

Watters nodded. "All right. We'll try to find the tailor. Not many would have the skill to make an exact copy of a police uniform. Are his boots there, too?"

"No, Sergeant," Scuddamore said.

"That would be too much to ask. There's one more thing I

need here," Watters walked over to the desk. The top was clear of everything except a blotter, inkwell and three pens.

"Don't look, Scuddamore," Watters said and picked the lock of the drawers. The top two drawers were no good, but the third drawer had copies of Anstruther's letters. Ignoring the most recent, Watters delved deep and withdrew two of the letters that contained Anstruther's signature.

"That'll do. Let's go, Scuddamore, and don't make a noise to alert Mr Mackay. I don't want him asking awkward questions."

———

The third tailor Watters visited examined the uniform with a critical eye. "It's well made," he said. "It's not one of mine." He looked up hopefully, "are the Dundee Police looking for a new tailor? I can give a competitive quote for as many uniforms as you wish."

"No," Watters said. "I want to find whoever made this uniform."

"Oh," the tailor sounded disappointed. He opened the jacket and examined the stitching. "Abraham Rivkin," he said. "I'd swear blind that's Abe's stitching. He's quite distinctive, you see."

Watters nodded. "Thank you." He knew Rivkin, the Jewish tailor off the Seagate.

Abe Rivkin worked long hours in his business, which he operated from the front room of his two-roomed house. He looked up when Watters entered and immediately looked nervous. Rivkin had emigrated from Eastern Europe, where a police visit could mean anything from the beginning of a pogrom to a demand for bribes.

"Mr Rivkin," Watters said. "I am Sergeant George Watters of the Dundee Police."

"Yes, sir," Rivkin bobbed in an obsequious bow as he

glanced at the room behind him. "You are welcome, Sergeant. What can I do for you?"

"You can stop looking so scared for a beginning," Watters saw two small children peering at him from the partially open door to the inner room. "I'm only here to ask your help."

"Anything I can help with, Sergeant Watters."

"This uniform," Watters placed the tunic on Rivkin's table. "I believe you made it."

Rivkin glanced at the stitching. "Yes, Sergeant. I made that."

"Could you tell me who it was for?"

Rivkin looked surprised. "It was for Lieutenant Kinghorn," he said at once.

"Did Lieutenant Kinghorn leave an address?" Watters asked.

"I'll check," Rivkin moved to the back room, clicking his tongue to move the children out of his way. He returned within two minutes, holding a small notebook in his hand. "Here we are, Sergeant Watters." He turned the book around and handed it to Watters. "Lieutenant John Kinghorn, Police Office, Bell Street."

"Thank you, Mr Rivkin," Watters said. "Could you describe the lieutenant, please? What did he look like?"

Rivkin screwed up his face with the effort of remembering. "He was a policeman," he said.

"Was he wearing a uniform?" Watters asked.

"No, sir," Rivkin said.

"Was he tall, short, blonde, dark-haired?"

"All policemen are tall," Rivkin was recovering some of his confidence. "Not blonde but light brown-haired."

Anstruther had light brown hair, thinning on top.

"How old would you say?"

Rivkin's face creased again. "He might have been forty."

Anstruther was forty-two.

"How many eyes did he have?"

Rivkin started at the question. "I did not look at his eyes."

"Thank you, Mr Rivkin," Watters lifted the uniform from the table.

"He was a very polite man," Rivkin continued. "A true gentleman."

With the lieutenant's uniform over his shoulder, Watters could not swing his cane as he walked back to the police office. The evidence was pointing towards Anstruther, but too many questions remained. Mrs Grady believed that Constable Boyle was still alive, and the discovery of the Turkish cigarette had rekindled that possibility while the mystery of Gow remained. Watters frowned.

I hope Jim brings me something valuable. I don't wish to arrest Anstruther, only to find him innocent.

CHAPTER TWENTY-SIX

"WELL, JIM," WATTERS SPOKE ACROSS THE BATTERED TABLE. He had released Jim from the cell and ordered him to appear at Betty's Welcome before the public's doors opened. "I'm sorry you had to spend two nights in the cells."

"It wasn't fair, Mr Watters," Jim said, tossing the hair from his eyes.

"You are right," Watters said. "It wasn't fair of me."

"I never done anything wrong."

"You got a warm bed and free food," Watters reminded, "and a talkative companion."

"Talkative? That was Thiefy Campbell," Jim said at once. "He was the lush I told you about."

"Was he?" Watters affected surprise. "The last piece of information you gave me was useful, Jim. Did Thiefy say anything else?"

Jim flicked away his hair again. "Maybe," he said.

"Maybe?"

Jim looked sideways at Watters. "How much, Mr Watters?"

"A shilling," Watters said.

"Five shillings," Jim demanded.

"Two shillings and it had better be worth that much." Watters slid a florin coin across the battered table then placed his open hand on top. "Come on, then, Jim."

Jim eyed Watters's hand, licking his lips. "There's something big on, Mr Watters," he said. "Thiefy was boasting of a big theft coming up. It's different from the rest, he said. Not the same kind."

"That's not worth threepence, let alone two shillings. Come on, Jim, tell all."

"He was sober, Mr Watters. Thiefy always says more when he's lushy."

Watters began to drag his hand back towards him, with the florin scraping across the table. "Threepence, so far, Jim."

"It's a wedding, Mr Watters," Jim said. "They're going to rob a wedding."

When Watters lifted his hand, Jim grabbed at the florin. "Which wedding?"

"I never heard, Mr Watters. Thiefy never said. He said that's for him to know and the bluebottle bastards to find out."

Watters saw Betty hovering in the background and knew she wanted to open the pub. "One last question, Jim, before Betty lets in the thirsty hordes."

"I don't know any more, Mr Watters," Jim whined, flicking the hair from in front of his eyes.

"Why do you infest Couttie's Wynd?"

Jim gave his greasy grin. "To look at the ladies, Mr Watters."

"Can't you get one of your own?"

"No, Mr Watters. I've never had a sweetheart."

Watters nodded and raised his voice. "I'll leave by the back door, Betty." He passed over a shilling. "You can allow your customers in, now."

Jim was first at the counter, displaying his two shillings as he ordered a dram.

"Here we are, Sergeant," Duff said. "All I can find about Mr Gow of the Amelia Whale Fishing Company." He laid a thin sheaf of paper on Watters' desk. "I checked his financial records with the bank and spoke to Mr Gilbride, Mr Muirhead, and the masters and shipowners."

"You've done a thorough job," Watters said. Every sheet of paper was headed and tabulated, with the points numbered in order of date. Duff had included a summary at the foot of each sheet.

"I might have found more, sir," Duff was not a man to accept praise.

Watters read the summaries first, knowing he would scrutinise the details later. "You've worked out his life story, I see."

"As best I could, Sergeant," Duff said. "There are gaps."

Watters grunted. "I'd wager there'll be gaps in everybody's life story," he said. "Gow was not a Dundee man."

"No, Sergeant. He came from Aberdeen."

Watters nodded. "And he was a military man."

"Yes, Sergeant. He served in the Frontier Wars in South Africa and the Crimea with the Corps of Royal Sappers and Miners."

Watters nodded, still reading. "Then he came to Dundee, served on a whaling ship and bought shares in *Charming Amelia*."

"Yes, Sergeant," Duff hesitated before volunteering information. "Mr MacBride, his bank manager, told me he borrowed money to invest. Mr MacBride advised him not to borrow too much, but Gow insisted. He had two good voyages at the whaling and thought he couldn't fail."

Watters lifted the sheet with Gow's financial details. "I see what you mean. I am surprised the bank allowed him to borrow so heavily. Mr Gow must be a persuasive fellow."

"Mr MacBride said he was, Sergeant." Duff hesitated again. "The Sundry Notes tell more, Sergeant."

Watters shuffled through the pile until he found the sheet headed Sundry Notes, which included descriptions of Gow and a subheading of Personal Notes.

"He was a tall, sun-browned man with a heavy beard and whiskers," Watters quoted. "Who told you that?"

"I compiled the description from what many people told me, Sergeant," Duff said. "The original descriptions are all there, with the names and addresses of the people who helped me."

Watters scanned the page. "I see Gow smoked Turkish tobacco," he said, "that would be from his time in the Crimea. And he was getting married?"

"Yes, Sergeant," Duff said. "He was engaged to a lady, but she broke off the arrangement when he lost all his money." He looked up. "She was Miss Alice Ross, Sergeant. The woman that Muirhead is marrying."

Watters closed his eyes. "I think you have found another motive. We'll have a word with Mr Gow very shortly," Watters said. "Do you have his address?"

"No, Sergeant. I have his old address, but after his company went under, he could not pay the rent. He left that house seven years ago, and I couldn't find where he is now."

Watters nodded. "Losing that whale bankrupted Mr Gow and ruined his life. I feel sympathy for the poor fellow."

"Yes, Sergeant," Duff said. "It's enough to turn anybody to a life of crime."

"I want you to find his current whereabouts," Watters said. "Urquhart planned revenge on Mr Muirhead, and I think Mr Gow also did. I'd put him on my list of suspects; he certainly had a motive. Now, the other matter."

Gow smoked Turkish tobacco, as did Boyle. The description fits both, except for the beard, and that is easily removed.

Dear God in Heaven! Is Constable Boyle our man?

Duff shook his head. "I haven't got Lieutenant Anstruther's signature or even a sample of his handwriting yet."

"That's all right, Duff. I managed to find that myself." Watters did not tell the straight-laced Duff how he had managed to obtain the samples. "Thank you for this."

Watters put the notes on Gow aside and concentrated on the sample of Anstruther's writing, comparing it to the signatures on the insurance documents. He grunted. "Can you see a similarity between these samples, Duff?"

Duff held both side by side. "I'd say they different people made them, Sergeant. Lieutenant Anstruther's writing is fancy, as if he writes with a flourish, while the other is smaller and neater."

"He might have disguised his writing," Watters mused.

"He might have, sir," Duff said. "But why should he when he's signing in a different name anyway?"

"Why indeed, why indeed," Watters said. "I can't see any similarity at all. Lieutenant Anstruther's letters are quite a different shape." He swore. "That's a dead-end, I am afraid. We can say that Lieutenant Anstruther did not forge Mr Muirhead's signature." He looked up. "That's quite a relief in a way, although it still leaves us with the mystery of the false lieutenant. A man who warned Abernethy of our plans and probably a serving policeman. We'll have to check this signature with every officer in Bell Street."

It's Boyle! Mrs Grady was correct. Boyle is alive, and he's been acting as Lieutenant Kinghorn. No wonder Abernethy could avoid our traps.

"That will make us very unpopular, Sergeant," Duff said.

"I know," Watters said.

"Unless we use the duty book, Sergeant," Duff suggested.

"I can volunteer for the remainder of Murdoch's shift," Watters checked his watch. "That will give me an hour, so unless we get a sudden spate of arrests, I'll have time."

"Sergeant Murdoch will think you're gone mad, Sergeant."

Watters smiled. "Murdoch thinks that already, Duff."

———

Murdoch left the duty desk almost before Watters finished speaking. "You're in charge, George," he said as he nearly ran out the door. "The missus will be surprised to see me home early."

Watters leafed backwards through the signing-in book, comparing signatures with the insurance document, looking at the shape of letters and writing style. He almost dreaded checking Boyle's signature.

I liked and trusted that man. Dear God, I even left him with Marie and the baby. Let me be wrong. Please let me be mistaken.

"Oh, Dear God in heaven," Watters breathed as he compared the writing. "They're nearly identical." He glanced around the room and sent a young constable for Duff.

"What do you think?"

"They're very similar," Duff said. "But Boyle's dead."

"And Boyle was one of us," Watters felt the sickness of betrayal. "We trusted him."

"We told him every detail of the trap we set for Abernethy," Duff reminded.

Watters stared at the signing-in book in dismay as he thought of the level-headed, clear-eyed Boyle. He fitted the description of Lieutenant Kinghorn, tall, broad, urbane, and Watters had a sudden memory of him hovering outside Connor's cell beside Lieutenant Anstruther.

"Boyle murdered Connor." There was no doubt in Watters' mind.

"Why?" Duff asked.

"We can ask him when we catch him," Watters said as his anger rose. "Boyle and Gow are the same person. Nobody attacked Boyle on *Lancelot*, he made that up to throw me off the scent, and he must have slipped off *Lancelot*, swam to Shetland and ferried himself back to Dundee. No wonder we didn't find any relatives as there never was a Richard Boyle. I don't like being gulled, Duff."

"You're not on duty here," Sergeant Ruxton stomped into the Police Office to take over Desk Duty. "Is Murdoch ill?"

"No, I just fancied a change," Watters said, vacating the duty seat. "It's all yours, Ruxton, and good luck to you."

———

"I always thought Boyle was too good to be true!" Scuddamore demonstrated an amazing gift of hindsight. "I'm not at all surprised."

"I wish you had told us earlier," Watters said dryly. "It would have saved us a great deal of trouble."

With his mind still busy with the implications of Boyle's betrayal, Watters forced himself to plot his next move. "Who do we know that's planning a wedding?"

"Mr Muirhead," Scuddamore said at once.

"And whose ships did Urquhart target?"

"Mr Muirhead," Scuddamore said again.

"I think we can safely say that Boyle and Abernethy will try to damage Mr Muirhead's wedding," Watters said.

"I still can't see the connection between Abernethy and Muirhead," Duff said.

"Boyle is the connection," Watters said. "I'm not sure how, yet, but Boyle is the connection."

"Can we discount Lieutenant Anstruther?" Scuddamore sounded disappointed.

"I believe so," Watters pushed Lizzie Flett's warning of the tall, one-eyed man to the back of his mind.

"Pity; I'd love to put the D's on him and screw them tight to pinch his wrists."

"Perhaps another time," Watters said. "With your information, Duff, and what our preachers have told us, we may lay Abernethy by the heels. He will surely lead us to Boyle, or Gow, or whatever his name is."

"What's the plan, Sergeant?"

"We lay a trap for Mr Abernethy," Watters said grimly. "And this time, the odds are in our favour. We know that Boyle is involved, we know the location of the crime that Abernethy is planning, and he doesn't know we know."

"This time, we'll lay Abernethy by the heels," Scuddamore lifted his mug.

"You're damned right we will," Duff said.

It was so unusual for Duff to swear that Watters nearly smiled. "Well said, Duff."

CHAPTER TWENTY-SEVEN

"HAVE YOU SPREAD THE NEWS?" WATTERS ASKED.

The detectives nodded, basking in the late evening sun. They always enjoyed visiting Broughty Ferry after the crowded, smoky streets of Dundee. Although the two towns were a short distance apart, they were opposites in wealth and attitude. While Dundee was an industrial town of hard-working mill girls, dockers and shipbuilders, Broughty Ferry had the reputation of boasting the wealthiest square mile in Scotland. The successful jute and linen merchants graduated to what had once been a simple fishing village, building palace-like mansions and living as if Dundee, where they made their money, was not even on their horizon.

"The preachers are primed?" Watters persisted.

"All primed, Sergeant," Duff said.

"Well, we'll just have to wait and see," Watters tapped the weighted end of his cane into the palm of his hand.

Joyeuse Garde, Mr Muirhead's house, was not as large as many others in Broughty but still magnificent by any standards. Situated on rising ground behind the town, it had a spreading garden of some two acres, in which the Scottish

Baronial building soared in a profusion of turrets, spires and corbie-stepped gables.

"This is some place," Scuddamore said. "I've always dreamed of owning a house like this."

"You'll need to change your occupation, then," Watters said. "You won't afford this on a policeman's wages."

"I might if I rise to get Mr Mackay's job," Scuddamore said.

Watters shook his head. "Mr Mackay is on about £48 a week. That's good money but well short of what you'd need for Joyeuse Garde."

"It's a queer name for a house, anyway," Scuddamore said.

"It was the name of Sir Lancelot's castle," Shaw murmured. "Our Mr Muirhead has Arthurian aspirations."

They sat behind a window at an upstairs room, overlooking the front garden, where the gravel driveway poured to the open wrought iron gates. About thirty yards from the front door, the driveway curved through a belt of trees, leaving a length disturbingly hidden from view.

"Here come the first guests now," Duff said. "A closed carriage, no less."

"You lads better get to your positions," Watters said. "Duff, you are with the servants; make sure Boyle doesn't see you. Scuddamore, you watch the back of the house. Shaw, you're patrolling the grounds, and I stay here in comfort and luxury."

The detectives moved to their respective positions, leaving Watters alone in the front room.

He watched as the closed coach disgorged its occupants onto the neatly raked gravel drive. A woman emerged wearing a wide crinoline with numerous flounces on the skirt and a slanted hat, and a gentleman in a pearl-grey jacket, and pinstriped trousers.

There's wealth in that coach.

Even from his perch, Watters could see the sun glinting on the gold Albert, the watch chain that stretched from one waistcoat pocket to another, a sign of prosperity to tantalise and tempt the itchiest of criminal fingers.

After the coach pulled away, another took its place, with Muirhead's efficient servants greeting each guest and escorting them inside Joyeuse Garde.

Watters scrutinised each guest, wondering if Boyle or Abernethy would try to sneak in disguised as a family friend or business associate. With so many jewels on display, a pickpocket would be in heaven, although Watters knew that Abernethy would consider himself above such a practice. A cracksman was in the hierarchy of criminality, above mere pickpocketing.

The third carriage to arrive was a hired gig, nearly out of place among the more exquisite vehicles of the rich. Watters nodded as Masterton emerged, looking flustered, and helped a small female into the house. When the light caught the woman's face, Watters saw she was an Inuit.

Well done, Masterton. So much for the tales that you abandoned your woman in the Arctic.

Captain Fairweather was next, with a smiling, ruddy-faced wife who spoke to the servants as if they were old friends and offered to help the groom care for her gig.

"You'll do for me, Mrs Fairweather," Watters approved.

The following vehicle was an open gig, with an elderly, white-haired man in black. The servants rushed to help him as he removed a large book from the seat and ambled up the stairs.

"That's the minister arrived," Watters said. "Now we're all set." He scanned the grounds again, hoping that Shaw was alert, for the next few hours were the most dangerous times.

By seven that evening, the flow of carriages had ended, and the guests filled the house. Watters heard the sound of loud, confident voices, the tinkle of female laughter and the clink of glasses. He had seen nothing untoward, no sign of any criminal activity and wondered if Thiefy had given Jim false intelligence.

As the sun sunk and evening shadows lengthened in the grounds, Watters saw Shaw shifting between the trees, a sliding shape searching for intruders. Mr Muirhead's outdoor staff were also active, watching as they went about their daily duties. Watters valued their help, although he knew a professional housebreaker would ghost past them unseen.

Mr Muirhead and his intended would gather the guests in Joyeuse Garde's Great Hall for the wedding ceremony, leaving the remainder of the house empty except for the servants. Watters was a sufficiently astute judge of human nature to know most servants would gather to watch the wedding and gawp at the display of glorious gowns and wealth in the post-wedding celebrations. By congregating in one place, the servants would leave the house vulnerable to any clever cracksman.

Watters had taken every precaution. He had checked every window was locked, with shutters in place. The back door was closed, locked, and bolted, and Watters had ordered lanterns to be placed every ten yards outside the house. "Light them at dusk," he advised.

Muirhead nodded. "I'll ensure the servants know."

"And move your valuables removed from the safe to an unmarked box deep in the cellars. Hide the box behind a crate of wine and amidst a group of similar boxes."

"Is the safe not the best place for them?" Muirhead asked.

"This fellow Abernethy looks at the most modern of safes as a challenge to his skill," Watters said. "Putting all your valuables in one place is like handing him an early Christmas present."

Muirhead only sighed. "What can I do?"

"Lock the safe securely, as you always do," Watters said, "and put a dog in the room."

"My gardener has two dogs," Muirhead said.

"They'll do," Watters agreed.

Shortly after seven, the noise levels decreased as the wedding began. Watters used binoculars to search the grounds in front of the house, knowing that Scuddamore was doing the same at the back, while Duff kept an eye on the servants and guests. Watters watched a footman slip outside the house, and moments later, the first of the lanterns flickered into life. Watters relaxed a little as the circle of lights surrounded the house.

Opening the door of his room, Watters heard the low drone of the minister's voice coming from the Great Hall. A ripple of laughter informed him that the minister had said, "You may kiss the bride," and Muirhead had responded with enthusiasm.

Miss Alice Ross, once Gow's fiancé, is now Mrs Keith Muirhead, but where is Abernethy?

A rumble of feet signified that the guests were leaving the Great Hall for Joyeuse Garde's reception rooms, allowing the servants to set up the tables.

Watters identified the sounds, checked his watch, and wondered again if Thiefy had deceived Jim or if he had misread the situation.

After the meal came the dancing, with the voices rising in volume as the drink and excitement took control. Watters hoped his men remained alert, for the noise would cover any movement by the cracksman. A rising wind sent the trees of Muirhead's garden swinging against each other, howled around the turrets and gables, and cracked against the shutters as the darkness intensified.

"It's blowing great guns," Watters said to himself. "Let's hope that does not complicate matters."

Peering out of the window, Watters thought he saw something moving on the far side of the bend, well beyond the pooled light from the lanterns. He concentrated, aware that the shifting trees obscured his vision.

"Something's out there," Watters said. Lifting a candle, he placed it in the window and lit the wick as a pre-arranged signal to Shaw.

The wind increased, whipping the branches, and sending the lanterns into mad jigs. Watters cursed silently as a frantic gust threw one of the lanterns to the ground, extinguishing the light.

If Marie were here, she would say the devil sent the gale to aid his works.

Another lantern crashed down, with the light flickering as the wind rolled it across the gravel until it came to rest five yards from its original position. Watters started as somebody tapped on his door.

"Sergeant," Duff looked tired and smelled of cooking from the kitchen.

"Has anything happened, Duff?"

"Yes, Sergeant. I've found an open window downstairs."

Watters grunted. "They were all closed and shuttered when I checked them earlier."

"Yes, Sergeant. I presume Abernethy must have bribed one of the servants."

Watters nodded. That was common practice when a thief wanted entry. Not every servant loved their master or mistress and allowing a thief into the house was an easy way of retaliating against a rebuke, restricted freedom, or low wages. "I saw somebody move outside. We can presume the thief, Abernethy or other, is already inside the house."

Duff nodded. "I'll alert Scuddamore."

"I'll come too," Watters said. "There's little point in watching outside now."

Scuddamore lowered his binoculars and looked around when Watters entered the room. "There's bugger all happening here, Sergeant," he reported, "except the gale playing merry hell with the lanterns. That's four extinguished now."

"Duff reports a window open downstairs," Watters said, "and I've seen movement outside."

"They'll be inside the house then," Scuddamore said.

Watters pondered for a moment, cursing that Abernethy had penetrated his defences so easily. "We'll get to Muirhead's study."

They moved across the house, their footsteps padding silently against the background of revelry from the celebrations. Watters halted them a few steps from the door. "Stay here." He put his hand on the door handle, turned it slowly and pushed. Two dogs lunged out, barking furiously, snarling, and curling back their lips to show their teeth.

"Jesus, I forgot about the dogs!" Watters backed away with Scuddamore joining him.

"It's all right," Duff stepped forward with both hands extended. "Come on, boys! We're no danger to you."

When one of the dogs lunged at Watters, snapping, Duff grabbed its throat and held it at arm's length. "No, you don't!"

The other dog backed away as Duff placed its companion gently on the floor and fondled its ears. "There you go, boy." He raised his voice. "I doubt our thieving friend has been in here, Sergeant."

The safe door was closed, and the room looked undisturbed.

"Look after the dogs," Watters sidestepped gingerly past them, "and I'll check."

The windows remained shuttered and closed, with no evidence of anybody having been in the room. "Put the dogs back inside, Duff." Watters watched as Duff ushered both now-subdued dogs back inside the study.

"Sergeant," Scuddamore said. "Listen. It's all gone quiet."

While the dogs had distracted the detectives, the music and singing had stopped. An eerie silence filled the house.

"Something's happened," Watters said. "Quietly now, lads, and follow me."

They descended the stairs, with Watters in the lead and the others following, their feet making little sound on the carpeted stairs. A deep voice sounded, the words lost in an echo, but the tone a definite command.

"Easy, lads," Watters said. "Something is badly wrong here."

"Bale up!"

The words meant nothing to Watters until a second voice reinforced them. "My colleague means hand over everything you have, gentlemen and ladies. We want all your gold watches, rings, chains, and cufflinks. All the money you have, and ladies, I want all your jewellery, necklaces, bracelets, rings, and earrings. Come along now!"

"Do you hear that?" Watters said. "Abernethy isn't after the safe, he's graduated to armed robbery."

"Aye," Scuddamore said, "and that other voice belonged to Boyle!"

CHAPTER TWENTY-EIGHT

"What the devil do we do now?" Scuddamore asked.

"We arrest them," Watters said. "We heard two voices; we know one is Abernethy, who is a cracksman and not normally violent. The other we think is Boyle, who may have been in the army," he gave hurried instructions. "I'll take Boyle. You two arrest Abernethy."

"I'd be better taking Boyle, Sergeant," Duff flexed his muscles, drawing his staff.

"No!" Watters said. He stopped outside the door leading to the hall, with his heart racing and his mouth suddenly dry. "I trusted that man, and I want to arrest him. Whatever we do, don't put anybody's lives at risk."

"Yes, Sergeant," Scuddamore agreed.

"On the count of three." Watters heard the murmur of voices from beyond the door, with one man's outraged protests. "One, two, three," he kicked open the door and ran into the hall.

Mr Muirhead, his new wife, and most of the guests crowded into the top half of the hall under the stairs. One guest was a dozen paces forward, in the process of placing his gold Albert on a table, which already glittered with a collection of watches, necklaces and other jewellery. Two men menaced the guests, both carrying revolvers.

Watters took all that in with a single glance. Of the two armed men, one was tall and broad, the other shorter and slighter, while thick blackening and handkerchiefs disguised both their faces.

Without stopping, Watters rushed at the taller of the men.

"Dundee Police!" Watters roared, moving at an angle to draw the thieves' fire away from the guests. For an instant, he was back in the Royal Marines, running at a slavers' stockade in the Brass River, with musketry cracking amidst the mist and his fellow Jollies shouting hoarse encouragement. "Drop the weapons." He was well aware that a nervous man might fire, while a professional thief was more likely to run or surrender at once.

His quarry did neither. The taller man kicked over a table to impede Watters' advance, swore and grabbed at the assembled valuables. Watters lunged forward, swinging his cane, and hit only fresh air as his quarry backed off.

"You're under arrest!" Watters shouted. He heard a confused noise behind him, the single report of a revolver and a hoarse shout.

"Help the police!" Muirhead shouted.

"No!" Watters jumped over the tumbling table. "Stay where you are!" The last thing he wanted was a horde of clumsy civilians getting themselves shot as they tried to intervene. "Leave this to us!"

Watters' quarry turned to run, with the revolver in one hand and a sparkling necklace in the other. He was fast, heading diagonally across the hall, kicking chairs over to impede Watters' pursuit, and saying nothing. Watters followed, stumbled over one of the spinning chairs, recovered, and moved on.

"Stop, thief!" He used the time-worn phrase. "You can't get away! I have men all around the building!"

Is that Boyle? I can't be sure. He's the same height and build. I think it is, but I'm not positive.

The guests had ignored his orders, with both men and women rushing forward, some to reclaim their possessions from the table and others hoping to catch the thieves.

Watters heard the revolver bang a second time, prayed that nobody was hurt and ran on. His quarry slid through the door of a cloakroom, with Watters only a few steps behind.

The second that Watters opened the door, the fugitive fired, with the report deafening in the confined space. He dropped involuntarily, and the bullet slammed into the wall above his head.

Watters rolled aside in case his quarry fired again, but when he rose, the shutters and window were open, and the gunman was leaping to the ground. Watters followed, ducked under the window, and arrowed outside, knowing a man framed by a window made an excellent target.

He landed on the path, swore as the gravel painfully burned his face, rose, and followed the gunman, who was vanishing into the swaying, wind-blasted trees.

"Bugger!" Watters swore and gave chase, hoping that Scuddamore and Duff had been more successful. He knew the wind would conceal any noise the fugitive made moving through the trees. He had to use his eyes, which, in the dark, was nearly impossible. A glitter of something on the ground attracted his eye, and he stooped to pick up the necklace.

"At least there's no booty for you this time, my friend." Watters stepped on cautiously, waiting for the report of a revolver, and the tearing impact of a bullet.

"There he is! God, but he's fast!"

That was Scuddamore's voice, with Duff's reply lost in the blast of the gale and swish of moving branches.

Watters moved on, aware his man had escaped but hoping for some stroke of luck. His quarry could either run through the trees and escape over the boundary wall into Broughty Ferry or remain hidden all night.

What would I do? I'd run into Broughty.

Leaving the trees, Watters returned to the drive to see a carriage parked on the gate side of the bend, with all three of his detectives there as Scuddamore clamped handcuffs onto their man.

"We got him, Sergeant," Scuddamore called.

"I've lost mine," Watters barely spared a glance at the prisoner. "Shaw, remain here, you two, come with me!"

The street beyond the garden wall was empty, and a cursory search revealed nothing. Watters hailed the beat policeman.

"Gunn! Did you see a tall man in the last few minutes?"

Gunn shook his head. "I've seen nobody all night, Sergeant. There was music in Mr Muirhead's house earlier and a couple of loud bangs."

"That was gunfire," Watters made a mental note to shake this constable up. "Keep your eyes open for a tall man."

"Yes, Sergeant."

Watters returned to the house, frustrated that his quarry had escaped.

"How did you catch this fellow?" He nodded to the prisoner. "I heard him fire at you."

"He fired into the air," Duff said. "He didn't try to shoot anybody."

"He got away from us," Scuddamore said. "I've never seen anybody move so quickly in my life. I'm fast, but he left me standing."

The prisoner watched them through deep brown eyes, listening to everything and saying nothing.

"Let's get him inside the house," Watters said, "and all these other people as well," he indicated the guests who milled around, talking loudly, brave now the danger was past.

———

Muirhead greeted Watters with an outstretched hand. "You caught one of the blackguards, Sergeant!"

"We did, Mr Muirhead." Watters showed the necklace he had picked up. "We retrieved this as well, although we'll have to retain it as evidence until the trial."

"And the other fellow?"

"He got away, I'm afraid," Watters said.

"You'll never catch him," one of the female guests said, and her husband gave a great bellow of laughter.

"Yes, you will," the husband said. "You'll catch him when the devil goes blind" He laughed again at his joke until Masterton shifted sideways and stood on his foot. Masterton's wife smiled, faced Watters, and winked.

The guests crowded around, staring at the prisoner, some demanding instant justice, others sharing their experiences of the crime.

"I'll need statements from you all," Watters shouted above the hubbub. "Please reclaim your jewellery and sit down." He glanced at Shaw. "You take the prisoner to Bell Street and book him in. We'll be all night here, so put this fellow in a cell and return here to help us."

"Yes, Sergeant," Shaw said.

"You," Watters addressed the prisoner. "What's your name?"

The man looked up. Some of the blacking had peeled from his face, and he had a fresh bruise on his left cheekbone, presumably gained during his arrest. "I am Walter Abernethy."

Watters felt a surge of satisfaction. "The biscuit man. We've been after you for some time, Abernethy."

Abernethy nodded and dropped his head. Smaller than average height, slight as a boy and with nondescript features, he looked like a man who would merge with the crowd.

"Take him away, Shaw." Watters sighed. He was not happy that one of his targets had escaped.

"All right, ladies and gentlemen," Watters said. "I am sorry to ruin your evening, but it's best to write these things down when they're fresh in your memories. The sooner we start, the sooner we'll finish." He nodded to Masterton. "You first, Mr Masterton." Watters led Masterton to the opposite end of the hall. "You may come too, Mrs Masterton."

Masterton's account confirmed that Abernethy pointed the pistol upwards, with no intention of shooting anybody.

"I heard that Mr Muirhead demoted you from master to mate," Watters said. "That would create resentment in anybody." He allowed the suggestion to hang between them until Masterton smiled.

"I was mate for one voyage, Sergeant Watters," Masterton said, "to allow Captain Fairweather his final fling on *Lancelot*. Mr Muirhead has appointed me her master for next season."

"Ah," Watters said. "Fo'c'sle rumours say otherwise."

Mrs Masterton laughed. "The whaling crowd like their rumours."

"They do," Watters agreed. "I am glad they are wrong. Please send up the next guest."

It was going to be a long night.

———

The detectives slumped around Watters' desk with mugs of tea sending spirals of steam into the air and exhaustion carving deep lines on their faces.

"Well done, lads," Watters said. "That was a hard shift, and we caught a prolific criminal. Give me details now, Scuddamore."

Scuddamore glanced at Duff before he started. "When we entered the hall, Sergeant, we saw the two gunmen on one side and the guests on the other. We knew you were going for the taller man, so ran to Abernethy."

Watters nodded, sipping at his tea. The memories were still diamond bright.

"Abernethy had his gun pointed at the guests, but I could see he was nervous. His hand was shaking so much I doubted he could find the strength to pull the trigger. He did, though. When he saw us, he pointed the revolver straight up and shouted that he wasn't going to shoot anybody. We dived forward. He fired and ran like a startled hare."

"He didn't fire at you," Watters said wearily, having heard the same account a score of times already.

"No, Sergeant," Duff said at once. "He fired straight upwards. I don't even think he meant to fire."

Watters nodded. "Carry on."

"He fell over a chair, and the gun went off. He dropped it and ran so fast we could not catch him," Scuddamore continued. "Right out the door, and then upstairs, with us pounding after him. Half the guests were screaming, and others were dashing forward, trying to get their jewellery, or maybe hoping to catch Abernethy, getting in our way and each other's way."

"Aye," Watters nodded. "They should have remained where they were."

"Yes, Sergeant," Scuddamore said impatiently. "Abernethy got out a window in the upper floor and scrambled down a waterspout. I tried to follow, and Duff ran downstairs and out the front door. We saw you charging into the trees, and Abernethy had vanished. We ran down the path to search for him, and there was a coach parked there."

Watters nodded. "That would be what I saw moving last night." Was it only last night? It seemed like a week ago.

"We thought we had lost him, but young Shaw had matters in hand."

"Shaw?" Watters raised his eyebrows. "Tell me more, Shaw."

"Well, sir," Shaw still looked nervous, biting his lower lip before he spoke. "I spent the night patrolling the grounds, as you told me. I must have been at the back of the house when the coach arrived. Anyway, I reasoned that it must belong to the thieves, or they would have driven right up to the house."

Watters nodded encouragement.

"So, I opened the door and remained inside. If you arrested the thieves inside the house, you wouldn't need me, and if they escaped, then I could catch them."

"And it was warmer inside the coach than in the garden," Watters said.

"That too, Sergeant. When I saw Abernethy running for the coach, I just waited for him, grabbed his arm, and told him he was under arrest. He was going to run when Constable Scuddamore and then Duff arrived."

"You did well, Shaw," Watters said. "You caught your man."

———

Watters crouched beneath the trees, examining the ground. "Take a cast of these footprints," he said. "Those are mine," he pointed to deep impressions in the mud. "But these are not."

Duff knelt beside him. "They may be the gardeners."

"I told everybody to keep away from this area," Watters said, "and these prints are fresh; see the edges? They've hardly crumbled. As they are in the same condition as mine, so I'd say they were made at the same time."

"Yes, Sergeant."

"A large boot, with evidence of wearing in the instep. That might be useful. We'll look at the coach next."

The coach sat in the same place, with a uniformed constable on guard. Watters opened the door and looked inside. "Can you smell that?"

Duff sniffed. "Yes, Sergeant. It's like tobacco smoke but different. It's perfumed, nearly."

"Exotic, isn't it?" Watters asked.

"Yes, and familiar, Sergeant," Duff said. "Megan's place had the same aroma."

"It's Turkish tobacco," Watters lifted a stub from the floor of the carriage. "Look at this."

Duff sniffed the dark stub. "That's the same," he said.

"Who do we know that smokes Turkish tobacco?" Watters answered his own question. "Why, Constable Boyle and Mr Gow, a veteran of the Crimean War and a man who resents Mr Muirhead for ruining his life."

"It was Gow, then?" Duff asked. "I could not recognise him with the mask and blackened face, but Scuddamore thought it was Boyle."

Watters smiled. "We've given Abernethy time to stew. Let's talk to him about our Mr Gow."

CHAPTER TWENTY-NINE

ABERNETHY SAT ON THE HARD BED IN HIS CELL, STARING AT the floor.

"Good morning, Abernethy," Watters greeted him. "How was your night?"

"I've spent better," Abernethy said.

"Aye, a police cell is pretty stark. You'd be expecting to live a life of luxury with all your thefts lately." Watters joined Abernethy on the bed, wrinkling his nose at the stench from the urine-bucket in the corner. "Come on, we'll speak in the interview room."

Abernethy walked like a broken man, round-shouldered and shambling. Watters pushed aside his sympathy, remembering the feelings of the man's victims.

They sat opposite each other in the interview room, with sunlight filtering through the high window and the muffled sounds of the police office intruding from outside.

Watters called in Duff. "This is Constable Duff, who you might remember from the other night. He will note down what you say." Watters expected Abernethy to close his mouth and refuse to talk.

"Did you catch that bastard Gow?" Abernethy said at once.

Watters did not allow the satisfaction to reach his face. "We will do," he said. "Why call him a bastard? Are you not companions in crime?"

"Companions?" Abernethy spat out the word. "He's a double-dealing blackmailing bastard."

"Who was he blackmailing?"

"Me!" Abernethy rose from his chair until Duff pushed him back down.

"Sit down, Mr Abernethy, please," Duff said.

"Why was he blackmailing you?" Watters asked.

Abernethy looked away. "It doesn't matter now," he said. "I'm an absconder. I was given a ticket-of-leave in Australia. I was no longer a prisoner in confinement, but the authorities said I wasn't allowed to leave the colony."

Watters nodded.

"Gow found out about me and forced me to steal for him."

"I see," Watters said. "How did he find out?"

"The bastard knew me from Australia," Abernethy said. "He was at the diggings there."

So that's where Gow disappeared to after his supposed suicide. He ran to the gold diggings in Australia.

Watters looked up as Scuddamore brought in two mugs of tea. He passed one across to Abernethy. "Did he say that unless you stole for him, he would preach to the police?"

"That's right," Abernethy said. "He recruited Connor and then Campbell to watch me. They were men without scruples or morals. They would sell their grannies for sixpence and drink away the proceeds."

"They're safely locked up," Watters said.

"I wish to God you had caught Gow."

"We will," Watters said. "Did he participate in your robberies?"

"No," Abernethy shook his head. "He had his creatures watching me while he stayed safe. He joined the police to spy on you."

"He was Constable Boyle," Watters said. "We know about that."

"He gave his creatures ten per cent of the takings," Abernethy seemed glad to speak, "and kept them in line with threats."

Watters glanced at Duff. "Did he murder James Connor?"

"Yes. Gow burked him."

Watters remembered Gow looking in when Connor was in the cell. "Are you willing to repeat that in court?"

"I'll give chapter and verse," Abernethy said. "I'll see him swing."

"If you help us," Watters said, "I'll try to get you a lenient sentence."

"I didn't come here to steal," Abernethy said bitterly. "I wanted an honest job until that bastard Gow recognised me."

Watters nodded. "The worst mischance possible for you, Abernethy." He frowned. "In that case, why leave the biscuits? You must have known we'd work out who you were."

"That was my pride getting the better of me," Abernethy said. "Sheer bloody vanity. We all have a weakness, you know. I like to boast with a Highlander's victory."

"A Highlanders' victory?" Watters asked.

"That's a victory in a battle the adversary doesn't even realise he's lost." Abernethy smiled. "When I scatter the biscuit crumbs, I am telling the world of my prowess without them even knowing."

"I have one more question," Watters said. "Why? Why did Gow go on a stealing spree? I think it was connected to a ship called *Charming Amelia.*"

Abernethy shrugged. "He didn't tell me," he said.

"All right. Duff here will stay with you while you write down everything you can, Abernethy. I want every detail you remember; anything that helps us convict Gow might alleviate your sentence. I can't do anything about you absconding from Australia, but if they call me to your trial, I will say I think you were a victim where the robberies were concerned."

Abernethy grabbed at the pen, dipped it in the inkwell, and began to write. "If you catch Gow, I'll speak at his trial and dance on his grave."

"That's the spirit, Abernethy." Unable to think sitting still, Watters grabbed his hat and cane and walked outside.

Gow and Boyle. Why would he embark on a spree of robberies? To gain money, of course. He had encouraged the scuttling to gain revenge on Muirhead. What revenge would he get by robbing a host of strangers?

Watters swung his cane with his mind working furiously, creating and rejecting theories with every step. *Was Gow only seeking to regain the money he had lost? Or did he have some other motive? If so, what would it be?*

If he sought revenge on Muirhead, what could he do?

Watters swung again, sending a pebble flying in a shot he would have been proud of on the golf course. The stone landed on the ground, bounced, and clattered against the wall of a mill.

If that had been on the ice, the stone would have skidded for another hundred yards.

On the ice. Dear Lord, how would Gow gain revenge on Muirhead? As well as sinking his ship and ruining his wedding, he could defeat him at his own game. He could purchase another whaling ship and return to the Arctic! That is what the thieving was for! Gow is raising money to buy a ship!

Where? Where would Gow buy a whaling ship? Would he buy an older ship and convert it? Or build a new, modern vessel like Lancelot?

If he did, would Muirhead or Gilbride not recognise him? Would the Dundee police not recognise him? Neilson, the carpenter, knew Gow but could not place him.

Watters hit another excellent shot, hoping that nobody was walking towards him.

There are other whaling ports beside Dundee; there is Hull and Peter-head. Where else could Gow hide? What makes Gow different? An ex-soldier who wishes to own a whaling ship, where might he be?

Down near the docks, perhaps?

Now desperate to work on his ideas, Watters took a final swing at a stone, turned, and hurried back to the Police Office.

"Halloa, George," Murdoch said. "What's the rush?"

"I need the telegraph," Watters said. He contacted the police in Peterhead, Hull and, for good measure, Aberdeen, Leith, and Liverpool, asking them to check anybody enquiring about buying a whaling ship. After that, he contacted the Dundee shipbuilding and boatbuilding companies.

"Here's Abernethy's statement," Duff pushed into the telegraph office.

Watters read through it. "Take that to Mr Mackay," he said, with excess energy burning through him. He had missed something, but what? He swore and began to pace the duty room.

I came in too early. I should have remained outdoors and let the walking soothe my mind. I missed something. What have I missed?

"Are you going to pace there all day, Sergeant? We're trying to work here." Constable MacPherson looked up from a form.

"I'm waiting for replies to my cables," Watters said.

"Well, wait somewhere else, can't you, Sergeant?"

Watters swore softly and left the duty room. He had to walk. He had to think. What had he missed?

Dock Street was a brisk ten minutes' walk away and Watters' second home. Maritime Dundee was his territory from the figurehead carver to the ropemakers, the Baltic Bar to the ships' chandler and tobacconist.

Watters stopped dead, with his cane in mid-swing. *Dear Lord, I am stupid. The tobacconist. Gow smoked Turkish cigarettes that would not be readily available in Dundee or elsewhere in Scotland, except in a tobacconist experienced in the strange fancies of seafaring men.*

Watters entered the shop, inhaled deeply of the mixed aromas, and smiled at the bald man behind the counter.

"Good afternoon," Watters said. "I am Sergeant Watters of the Dundee Police."

"I know who you are, Sergeant," the tobacconist said. "Are you here as a customer or a policeman?"

"A policeman," Watters said.

The tobacconist's eyes altered as all expression faded away. "What can I do for you, Sergeant?"

"Do you stock Turkish tobacco?"

"No, but I have the occasional order for it."

Watters nodded. "Have you had any orders recently?"

The tobacconist nodded, still expressionless. "Yes, Sergeant."

"Who ordered it?"

"I'll check." The tobacconist retired to his back shop and returned with a hard-backed notebook. He scanned the pages. "A Mister Mordred," he said.

That's a false name. "Did he leave an address?"

"Yes, of course, he did," the tobacconist said. "How else would I tell him that his order had arrived?"

"Thank you." Watters took the notebook and saw the name, Richard Mordred, with an address in Elliot, twenty miles north of Dundee.

Watters could not hide his smile. He knew that if he kept pressing, Gow would make a mistake. He was only human and, therefore, imperfect. The Turkish tobacco was his foible and his weakness, and it had led directly to him. Now Watters held all the advantages. All he had to do was pick his man up.

"When you see the fellow, could you ask him to pay his bill?" The tobacconist said. "He owes me seven shillings and sixpence."

"I'll ensure you get paid," Watters said. *The evidence has spliced my rope, and I'm going to catch you, Richard Gow.*

———

"Ah, Watters," Mackay looked up when Watters entered his office. "I have a message and a packet for you."

"Have you, sir?"

Mackay tapped his fingers on the desk. "It seems that when you caught Abernethy, you impressed a great number of people. Influential people, who decided you deserved a reward."

"Serving police officers don't accept rewards, sir," Watters said.

"No, they don't," Mackay said. "Is there a charity you'd like to help? The Workhouse perhaps, or the Industrial School?"

Watters thought for a moment. "I have one in mind, sir. A young lad who has helped from time to time."

Mackay passed over a small packet. "There are five sovereigns in there, Watters, and a letter of thanks from Mr Muirhead."

"I'll read out the letter to my men, sir. I'm sure they will appreciate it."

Five sovereigns reward from a collection of the wealthiest people in Dundee. No wonder they are rich, but I know who needs money.

"Now, Watters. Why did you wish to see me?"

"I believe I have located Mr Gow, sir."

"Is Gow our man?" Mr Mackay asked when Watters laid down his evidence, including Abernethy's statement.

"I am certain of it," Watters said. "He's in Elliot, sir, south of Arbroath." He waited until Mackay had scanned his report.

"Gow is Boyle? An ex-policeman?" Mackay shook his head. "For shame."

"We have the motive, the means and the opportunity for scuttling, housebreaking, murder, armed robbery and theft," Watters said. "We can add impersonating a policeman to the list as well – and welching on his tobacconist's accounts."

"Then we'll get him," Mackay spoke with great satisfaction. "I'll speak to the Chief Constable of Forfarshire, Watters, and you organise your men."

"We might need local help," Watters said.

"I'll arrange that," Mackay said.

"I'll find a map of the area," Watters said. "I don't want Boyle slipping away this time."

"No," Mackay's fingers began their habitual dance. "I'll arrange overtime and ensure you have everybody we can spare. Catch this fellow, Watters."

"I'll do my best, sir."

———

"George!" Murdoch approached Watters as he searched for a map. "We have replies to your telegraphs."

"From whom?"

"Nearly everybody," Murdoch handed Watters a small pile of documents.

"Thank you," Watters said. "I feel as if I'm drowning in paper in this job, Murdoch. Everything is documents and paper. I'm sure it wasn't always like this."

Murdoch laughed. "Get used to it, George. That's the future."

"God help us, then. We spend so much time writing and checking forms that we've no time for catching criminals."

Most of the replies were negative as the shipping companies reported no contact with Gow. The last two telegrams made Watters pause.

We recently delivered a launch of sturdy construction. Paid cash. Name given was Mordred. Might be your man. Signed Gall.

"Well now," Watters said. "That might be interesting."

A sturdy launch? Sturdy for the ice?

The final telegram was even more interesting. Ramage of Leith, an old-established shipbuilding company, reported an enquiry from a Mr Mordred for a three-hundred-ton steam-powered vessel suitable for Arctic whaling.

Got you, Gow.

Watters smiled in grim satisfaction as he consulted his Bradshaw for the train times to Elliot.

CHAPTER THIRTY

THE POLICE FILED ONTO THE EARLY TRAIN FOR ARBROATH IN the dark hours before dawn, each man carrying his staff and holding his tall hat under his arm. Unusually for the Scottish police, every fifth man sported an Enfield rifle. Because of the seriousness of the crimes, Mr Mackay took personal charge, issuing quiet orders that saw the officers fill the carriages.

"It's like a military operation," Duff approved.

"We're after an ex-soldier who did not hesitate to murder one of his own," Watters said. "We've whittled down his gang, removed his followers and the man who made him money. Now we're after him." He touched the butt of the revolver within his coat. "I don't want Gow to escape this time."

"No, Sergeant."

"Are you both armed?"

Duff and Scuddamore nodded and showed their firearms, while Shaw looked a little disgruntled.

"If you are chosen as a detective, Shaw, we'll allow you to carry a pistol as well. Until then, you can rely on your staff."

"Yes, Sergeant," Shaw said. "I've never even held a revolver, let alone fired one."

"We'll train you," Watters said. "Remember, if any

shooting starts, don't get involved. Keep out of the way and leave it to us."

Shaw nodded. "Yes, Sergeant."

The train started with a hiss of steam and rattled north, with the sea breaking to the right in a line of angry white. Out on the horizon, the Bell Rock Lighthouse flashed its periodic signal to warn mariners away from the Inchcape Rock while the riding lights of ships gleamed through the dark.

"Don't forget your places, boys," Watters said.

"We'll be all right," Scuddamore said.

"Duff, take Shaw under your wing. Ensure he does nothing rash."

"Yes, Sergeant," Duff said.

Watters touched the butt of his revolver again, held his cane, thought of Marie, and closed his eyes. He had made every arrangement he could, and now things were in the hands of God.

"Oh Lord, I will be very busy today and may forget you. Please do not forget me. Amen."

"What was that, Sergeant?"

"Nothing, Scuddamore. I was talking to myself." Watters stared at the darkness outside. "Now remember, lads, Gow lives alone. He has no servants and no wife, so any movement in the house will be him. The local police tell us he retires early and rises with the dawn, so we're going to catch him in bed."

The detectives nodded as the train rattled along the coast, emitting periodic bursts of steam. The sound of the wheels and the engine was strangely hypnotic, lulling Watters into a brief period of peace. *The calm before the storm,* he said, thought of Marie again and pushed the image aside. *I must concentrate on my duty and allow nothing to distract me.*

When the train stopped at Elliot, the police filed off in a long blue snake of tall men. As they emerged, each officer donned his hat, making them look somehow unreal in the swinging light from the station's oil lanterns. It was still dark and a cool wind, the harbinger of autumn, sliced in from the German Ocean, making men shiver and wish for the shelter of the Dundee streets. A ribbon of silver surf marked the boundary of land and sea.

"Here we go, boys," Watters said. "Good luck to you all."

"Good luck, Sergeant," Duff said, as Scuddamore checked the chamber of his revolver, and Shaw stared at the stars as if he had never seen them before.

Gow lived in a square, two-storey house named Mordred Cottage, a hundred yards from the sea, with the railway line at his back and the long beach in front. The riding lights of small craft gleamed from the sea, reassuringly friendly through the dark.

"Mordred was King Arthur's nephew," Shaw said. "He was the man who brought down Camelot and killed the king."

"I'd wager Gow named the place," Watters said.

Mackay stood on a handy crate on the railway platform and gathered the police around him. "Lieutenant Anstruther and Sergeant Murdoch, take your men and surround the house. Remain thirty yards away and don't let Gow see you." He gave quiet orders, and the police marched away, their blue uniforms making them nearly invisible in the dark and their rifle barrels protruding skyward from behind each marksmen's shoulder.

Holding up a gold Hunter watch, Mackay allowed the uniformed men five minutes to get into position. "All right, Watters. You and your men wake Gow up. I want a nice, clean operation with no casualties." He pressed his fingers together. "Have you organised the nautical reserves?"

"Yes, sir," Watters said. "They know what to do."

Mackay released his fingers. "Let's hope so. This Gow fellow is dangerous."

With his detectives behind him, Watters moved to the front of the house. Mordred Cottage faced east to catch the sun as it rose from the tossing waves. There were two doors, one in front and one at the rear, all enclosed within a third of an acre of much-neglected garden with a wind-twisted rowan tree extending its branches onto the slate roof. The garden gate creaked as Watters opened it, causing him to halt, for it was harder to see a standing than a moving man. When there was no sign from within the house, Watters stepped inside the garden.

The path was of Caithness slabs, moss-furred, partially overgrown with weeds and slippery with night-time dew. Watters tapped Duff's arm and pointed to the back door. Duff nodded and stepped around the house, bringing Shaw with him.

"Sergeant!" Scuddamore hissed.

"Keep quiet!" Watters whispered.

"Look!" Scuddamore pointed to the ground, where a providential shaft of moonlight gleamed on something metal.

Watters crouched down. "Dear Lord!" The vicious teeth of a mantrap waited for an unwary foot. Powered by a strong spring, the mantrap would snap shut on a man's shin, lacerating the skin, and possibly breaking the bone. "Watch your step, lads."

Moving with even more care, Watters checked the front step for further traps before he ascended. *The postman must hate coming here.*

German Ocean surf boomed on the sand and shingle beach, only thirty yards away. A seagull screamed, the call lonely in the dark.

Here we are, Gow.

Taking a deep breath, Watters nodded to Scuddamore and tried the door. As he expected, it was locked. He inserted his lockpicks into the keyhole, listened for the tiny click, turned the handle, and pushed. The door held tight, bolted at the top, middle and bottom.

Shaw appeared from the side of the house. "The back door's locked and bolted," he said quietly.

"We'll have to try this the hard way," Watters whispered, raised his cane, and rapped on the door. "Dundee Police!" he called. "Open up in there!"

There was no reply. The house remained as quiet as any grave.

Watters shouted again, with the same result. The seagull screamed again, closer now.

"Try the window," Watters ordered, and Scuddamore used the end of his staff to smash the glass of the nearest window, then shoved at the internal shutters until they broke. Inserting his hand, he unfastened the window and pushed up the lower half. The noise should have wakened half the neighbourhood but evoked no response from within the house. A dog began to bark in the nearby village of Elliot, setting off others, while the hush and crash of the sea were constant in the background.

"Lantern," Watters ordered, and Scuddamore lit a match and applied it to the wick of his bull's eye lantern. He adjusted the shutter, so only a narrow beam of light emerged, sufficient to guide them and no more.

"I'll go in first," Watters took a deep breath and slid inside, hoping that Gow was not waiting with a loaded revolver. "Dundee Police!" he shouted again. "We're coming in, Gow!"

Scuddamore was close behind him, darting the lantern light from side to side on the various items of furniture, a bust of Napoleon Bonaparte, and a selection of weapons on the wall. The light reflected from the blade of a sabre and a long Cossack Sashka.

"Dear Lord," Watters said again. "This place is like an armoury."

"Let's hope there are no mantraps inside the house," Scuddamore played the lantern light along the floor, finding only a red Axminster carpet on the dark floorboards.

"Open the front door," Watters ordered, "let some of the uniforms in."

The lack of response was unusual. Usually, a suspect would either cry innocence or attempt to flee. Younger suspects might hide under the bed or in a cupboard, but Gow was too old for such antics. Watters wondered if he was elsewhere, but if so, the doors could not be bolted from the inside.

Gow is in here, somewhere.

Scuddamore drew back the bolts of the front door, and two uniformed police stepped inside.

"Wait at the door," Watters ordered. "Only come if I shout for you."

The house interior was uncomplicated, with two large front rooms, a kitchen, and a storeroom on the ground floor, and four bedrooms above. A single staircase connected the ground and first floors, with a square landing halfway up, complete with a glass case containing a stuffed owl. Crossed swords decorated the walls.

"Open the back door," Watters said and waited until Duff and Shaw joined them inside the house before he ventured upstairs.

All four upper doors were closed, with no indication which might be Gow's bedroom. Indicating to Scuddamore to remain at the top of the stairs, Watters turned the first handle and pushed, stepping back quickly in case Gow burst out.

The room was empty except for a neatly made bed, a chair, and a chest. The next was the same, as was the third. The rooms were clean, tidy, and lacked all character.

Watters pointed to the fourth door, checked his revolver was handy and turned the handle. He glanced at Scuddamore and shoved open the door.

"Dundee Police!" He thrust inside, expecting resistance.

The room was empty, although the bedclothes were rumpled. The bookcase and neatly hanging clothes proved that Gow used this room while a sea chest sat beneath the window.

Scuddamore opened the chest and thrust aside tidily folded clothes. "Sergeant! Look at this!"

Two strong boxes lay in the bottom of the chest.

"That'll be the proceeds of Abernethy's work," Watters said. "Find Gow."

"He's not here," Scuddamore examined every corner with his lantern to ensure Gow had not shrunk into the shadows. "Where the devil could he be?"

Watters heard the sound first, a scraping from above. "He's in the attic!" He pointed to the small hatch that gave access from the upper landing. "Give me your shoulder!"

Scuddamore crouched and helped lift Watters to the hatch, which Watters pushed at, swearing. "He's blocked it from the inside!" He raised his voice. "You can't get away, Gow! We have the place surrounded."

"Smash the hatch, Sergeant," Scuddamore advised. "Break it in!"

"Find a ladder," Watters ordered. "This hatch is solid. A ladder, a chair or anything I can stand on."

"Sergeant!" Duff's roar sounded from the back door. "Gow's on the roof." There was the clatter of something heavy falling and a loud crash. "Ah, would you now!"

"Outside, quick!" Watters dismounted from Scuddamore's shoulders and ran outside, where a group of police officers was staring upwards.

"Be careful of mantraps!" Watters roared. "Mind where you stand!"

"He's throwing slates at us," one constable said as a slate exploded on the Caithness slab a yard away, shattering into a hundred fragments.

Watters glanced up and saw Gow as a tall, shadowy figure balanced on the apex of the roof. When their eyes met, Watters saw the hatred.

"Surrender, Gow, and you'll get a fair trial! You're only making things worse for yourself!"

Gow responded with a mouthful of obscenities.

"Well, somebody climb up there after him!" Watters ordered, just as another slate smashed at his feet. "Fetch a ladder!"

Watters strode to the rowan tree, wished he was ten years younger, and began to haul himself up the branches. "Give up, Gow!"

"Bugger off, Watters!" Gow appeared above Watters, balancing on the slates. From that angle, he seemed taller than ever.

"You're surrounded!"

Gow swore and threw himself into the tree, snatching hold of the topmost branches as he scrambled down. Watters grabbed at him, missed, and held on to prevent himself from falling as Gow descended as rapidly as a sailor.

"Stop that man!" Watters roared. He returned to the ground to see Gow brushing past a young constable, knocking another to the ground, and vaulting over the garden wall.

"He's getting away," Scuddamore followed, with his lantern light bouncing from the ground.

Watters heard a metallic snap and cry of agony.

"My leg! Oh, God, my leg!"

He glanced behind him, saw a uniformed constable on the ground clutching his trapped limb and swore. "Look after that man!"

Scuddamore was in front, with Duff trying to keep up. Shaw was moving towards the stricken policeman with his hands outstretched to help.

"Gow!" Watters roared, "You're with us!" He lengthened his stride and set off in pursuit.

The sun had tipped above the horizon, a silver-gold ball that sent long fingers of silver across the chopped waters of the German Ocean. Watters squinted into the light, watching Gow run across the rough grassland beside the beach.

"Come on, Scuddamore, you're the fastest man here."

Gow was a hundred yards ahead with his long legs gaining ground with every step. He glanced over his shoulder and then darted towards the shore.

"He's got a boat!" Watters shouted. "He's going for his boat."

"That was his escape plan," Duff panted.

Watters nodded, panting too hard to manage any coherent speech. "It's an onshore wind," he said. "He can't make any speed out there."

Gow had moored his launch beside a trickling burn, with the bow pointing to the sea. He unfastened the mooring rope, pushed the vessel into the stream without effort, grabbed a scull, and thrust out towards the first of the German Ocean rollers.

"He's getting away," Scuddamore shouted.

Watters nodded. "He won't get far," he said. "Lend me your lantern."

"My lantern?" Scuddamore handed it over.

Watters grabbed the lantern, stepped onto a large rock, and flashed a Morse Code message signalled out to sea.

"Who are you signalling to?" Scuddamore asked.

"The local police," Watters replied, squinting into the rising sun.

The reply came at once, and a succession of lights appeared around the bay. A few moments later, a metallic hail sounded.

"I guessed that Gow might go for his boat," Watters said. "Men like him have always got something up their sleeve."

The lights at sea congregated, moving closer to the land. Watters felt for his revolver. "With any luck, we'll have him, boys."

The rising sun strengthened the light, so Watters saw

Gow's launch try to escape, but the circle of fishing boats, with a policeman on each, baffled every attempt.

"They're pushing him towards us," Watters said. "He can't use sails in this wind and can't scull fast enough to escape. He'll be ashore in a minute."

"We've got him," Scuddamore said.

The launch appeared again, with Gow a lone figure in the stern. Watters strode down to the breaking surf.

"On you come, Gow. You have nowhere to go." Watters was aware of his detectives standing behind him and a double row of police waiting along the beach, some with their rifles ready.

"Well, bugger you, Watters," Gow stood at the stern of his launch, with the sun reflecting from the varnished hull and the stubby mast amidships. Behind the mast was a tall funnel, and Gow stooped and began to work with something.

"He's put an engine in the boat," Watters said.

"How the devil could he do that?" Mackay stood at Watters side, one hand holding his hat secure.

"Gow was in the Sappers," Watters reminded. "He's an engineer." He saw the first whiff of steam rise from the launch and worked at the lantern, sending a message to the police.

"Board Gow's boat!"

As the fishing boats closed in, Gow got steam up and began to move out to sea against the prevailing wind.

"He's getting away," Scuddamore said. "He's going to escape again."

CHAPTER THIRTY-ONE

"Shoot him," Mackay ordered, and half a dozen police rifles cracked, but although Watters heard the ping of bullets hitting the launch and saw the spark as a ball ricocheted off the funnel, Gow was untouched. The acrid whiff of gun smoke drifted across the beach.

"Where are you going, Sergeant?" Mackay shouted as Watters waded into the sea. "You can't swim after him."

Ignoring the Chief Constable, Watters tucked his cane into his belt and thrust overarm for the nearest of the fishing boats. The policeman in the stern stared, but a bearded fisherman threw out a line.

"In you come, chum," the bearded fisherman said as Watters clambered aboard. "Who are you, and what are you doing anyway?"

"Sergeant Watters, Dundee Police and follow that launch," Watters ordered.

"He's got a steam engine," the fisherman pointed out. "He can sail against the wind, and we can't."

"Then row," Watters pointed to the long oars that sat inside the open boat. "Row after him." He nudged the police constable, a man in early middle age. "Grab an oar and pull like the devil, man!"

"I'm no sailor," the constable looked dismayed at the prospect.

"You are now!" Watters shoved the oars into the man's hands, grabbed a pair himself and pulled mightily. "Steer after that steam launch!"

The bearded fisherman commandeered one of the policeman's oars while a younger fisherman steered, and with three men rowing, the boat made some progress.

"He's getting away, Sergeant," the constable said.

"Keep rowing," Watters ordered. "I don't know how much coal he has on board, and he has to keep the boiler supplied. We can row forever."

"Forever?" The policeman said.

"Bloody row!" Watters snarled.

Watters knew he would follow Gow as far as the coast of Europe if needed. He had not come this far for Gow to defeat him at the last hurdle.

I'll catch you, Gow! You inveigled yourself into my confidence, damaged the reputation of the Dundee Police and murdered one of my prisoners.

"Row, damn you!" Watters put all his strength into pulling at the oar. He knew he was tired and nothing like as fit as he once been. He did not care. He would row until he was exhausted and then row some more.

"He's still making ground on us," the bearded fisherman smoked a stubby clay pipe as he pulled at his oar.

"I don't care a damn," Watters said.

"The wind's shifting," the younger fisherman said a few moments later. "More easterly now, and it's kicking up the waves."

Watters could see the waves were steeper, breaking against the bow of the boat and sending spray and spindrift inside to splash against their legs. Glancing over his shoulder, he saw

Gow's launch rising and falling on the waves, with the wind blowing the smoke astern to smudge the surface of the sea.

"I can't row much further," the constable said.

"Row, damn you," Watters growled. "Row!"

"He's losing way now," the younger fisherman said.

Watters glanced over his shoulder again. Gow's launch was closer, with less smoke coming from the funnel and a cloud of steam blowing astern.

"He's losing steam, too," the fisherman said.

Watters remembered the ping of metal when the police marksmen had fired. One or more bullets must have pierced the boiler, and the pressure had enlarged the hole. The launch had slowed to a painful crawl, with Gow at the stern, working the scull.

"We'll catch him in ten minutes," the fisherman at the tiller said. "Unless he lands on the Inchcape."

The Bell Rock Lighthouse loomed ahead, tall and white as it thrust from the waves. At its base, the sea splintered in white fury against the green slimed Inchcape rock.

"The wind's caught him," the bearded fisherman altered the angle of his tiller, so the fishing boat steered away from the Inchcape. Watters could hear the boom of surf against the rock and saw the foaming white horror of the breakers.

"Stand by!" Watters roared. "We're coming to you, Gow!"

"Bugger you, Watters," Gow replied, standing in the stern of his launch amidst a cloud of hissing steam.

"You'll hit the rocks!" The bearded fishermen shouted. "We'll throw you a line!"

In reply, Gow levelled a revolver and fired.

Watters did not see where the shot went, for one man on a tossing boat on the German Ocean was unlikely to hit another, equally mobile, boat. "Don't be a fool, Gow!"

"Too late for that," the bearded fisherman said. "He's already a fool."

A wave lifted the launch and carried it closer to the Inchcape. Gow lifted his scull and tried to fend the boat from the rocks, only for the next wave to hammer against the hull, exploding in a welter of spray.

"He's gone," the bearded fisherman said. "He's capsized."

When the wave receded, Watters saw the launch on its beam end, with its keel pointing towards the fishing boat and the mast broken in two. "Where's Gow?"

"There he is!" The constable pointed. "He's in the water! That man swims like a salmon."

Watters knew that the sea covered the Inchcape Rock with twelve feet of water for twenty hours a day, so the period when anybody could walk on it was very limited. Even close up, it was hard to see where the rock ended, and the sea began, with only the tall white lighthouse as a guide.

Gow emerged from the sea, clambering onto the rock with his pistol in his hand. He looked backwards at the fishing boat, shook his gun, and shouted something towards the lighthouse.

"The keepers will look after him," the bearded fisherman said. "He'll be all right."

"They might not be," Watters said. "He's already killed one man. I don't want him murdering anybody else." He had the nightmare thought of Gow shooting the keepers and extinguishing the light, putting shipping in danger off this coast. "Take me as close to the Inchcape as you can."

"What?" Even the bearded fisherman looked surprised. "We avoid that rock, mister. We don't go close to the damned thing."

"If that man is loose on the lighthouse, he could do anything," Watters said. "Please take me as close as is safe."

"Nowhere is safe at that damned rock," the younger fisherman said. "That's why they built the lighthouse."

"I'll swim then," Watters said, eyeing the stretch of stormy water between the boat and the Inchcape Rock.

"Don't be stupid," the younger fisherman said and adjusted the tiller. "I'll take you as near as I can."

As they closed with the Inchcape, Watters could feel the vicious surge of the sea and see the menace. He remembered that scores, maybe hundreds of vessels, had been wrecked here, and he could imagine the fear and horror of a shipwreck in such a desolate place.

The younger fisherman took his boat within twenty yards of the Inchcape. "I can't go closer with this sea running," he said.

"Thank you." Watters slipped overboard without another word. He could not leave the lighthouse keepers alone with Gow.

The waves took hold of him the second he left the boat, pulled him under and turned him around. Watters struck out in the direction of the Inchcape Rock, hoping the sea would not dash him to pieces. He gasped as he broke the surface, saw a turmoil of broken waves, and heard the thunder of the surf, and then the sea tossed him contemptuously onto the Inchcape and withdrew, hissing.

Watters gasped, thankful he had landed on a bed of seaweed, saw a herring gull watching him and staggered to his feet. The lighthouse reared above him, its lower part green smeared with the sea, while one of the keepers stood on the steps that rose from a landing platform. Watters felt for his revolver and cursed to find he had lost it somewhere in the sea. His cane was also missing.

Damn it to hell! I've had that cane for years!

Gow was waiting for him, arms akimbo and his feet planted solidly on the rock, while the wind howled around them. "So here we are, Sergeant."

"Here we are," Watters agreed, shaking off excess water. "You could have made a good detective, Gow."

"That bastard Muirhead robbed me," Gow said.

"Urquhart told me the story," Watters watched Gow's face, waiting for an attack. "You were hard done by, for sure. The court will take that into account at your trial."

"You and I both know there won't be a trial," Gow began to move, stepping slowly towards Watters.

Watters remained still, content for Gow to come to him. He saw a trickle of blood on the man's face and a new bruise on his left cheekbone, probably made when the steam launch capsized.

"There's something I don't yet understand," Watters made conversation to calm Gow down. "Why did you help capture Connor? He was one of your followers."

Gow shrugged. "He was a common little thief. By arresting him, I helped gain your confidence."

"You murdered him."

"He would have blabbed," Gow said, "and then Muirhead would have got away scot-free."

Watters circled beneath the lighthouse, with the waves hammering on the rock.

"Give up, Gow. You know me. I'll ensure you get a fair trial and mention the circumstances."

"That's not the plan, Watters. I'll get away from you, buy a whaling ship and put Muirhead out of business." Gow lifted his revolver and tried to fire, but seawater or rough usage had damaged the weapon. He threw it at Watters in disgust.

"Now you've no weapon, Gow," Watters said.

"Nor have you, Sergeant," Gow responded.

Lifting a rock, Gow threw it, swearing. Watters stepped aside and closed, only for Gow to block his attack and throw him to the ground.

Watters gasped as he banged his head on the rock. He lay for a second, dazed.

Get up! He'll kill you if you lie here. Marie needs you.

Watters rolled sideways and saw his cane lying on the seaweed, cast up by the waves. Pushing himself upright, he dodged Gow's savage kick, grabbed the cane, held the flexible end, and swished the lead weight towards Gow.

"You won't take me, Sergeant," Gow sidestepped the cane

and threw a punch that bounced off Watters' shoulder and sent him reeling backwards.

Watters swung again, aiming for Gow's knee, hoping to incapacitate rather than injure, for he wished to take Gow back for a trial. He felt the shock of contact and heard Gow grunt, but then the taller man had closed, with his hands grasping for Watters' throat.

That's how Connor died. I'm not going the same way.

Watters jerked his head back and rammed up his knee, missing his intended target although managing to break Gow's grip. He stepped back, wielding the cane again.

Wordless, Gow came on with blood running down his face to drip from his chin and his eyes set like Aberdeenshire granite.

Watters lifted his cane, thrust for Gow's throat, and gasped as Gow landed a punch that staggered him.

Gow followed through, ducking Watters' next assault and launching a series of hooks, uppercuts and jabs that sent Watters backwards on the slippery rocks.

"You're four inches shorter than I am, Sergeant," Gow said. "Go back to your boat."

Too busy to speak, Watters blocked, weaved, and ducked, wincing whenever Gow landed a punch and waited the opportunity to retaliate.

Twice he thrust with his cane, only for Gow to dodge like a trained prize fighter. Watters felt a wave splash against his leg and realised that Gow had forced him back to the water's edge, and the tide was already rising, shrinking the rock minute by minute.

"Hey!" the watching keeper called. "What's happening down there?"

Watters used the momentary distraction to duck under Gow's next punch and ram the weighted end of his cane hard into his opponent's groin. He felt Gow stiffen and hit again, punching to the man's solar plexus.

As Gow doubled up, Watters brought his knee up with all his force, smashing Gow's nose. Gow yelled and crumpled to the rock.

Got you, you murdering bastard.

Watters knelt on top of Gow's writhing body, yanked Gow's arms behind his back and fastened the handcuffs in place.

"You're under arrest, Gow, for murder, shop breaking, theft, blackmail, housebreaking and police assault." He shook his head.

And all because one greedy whaling ship master stole a whale from another. What a waste of life.

"Who the deuce are you?" the lighthouse keeper was tall, with a weathered, intelligent face. "And who's that unfortunate fellow there?"

"I am Sergeant George Watters of the Dundee Police," Watters said. "And this man is my prisoner."

"Is he, now?" the lighthouse keeper said. "Well, you'd better get him inside the one-eyed man. The tide rises fast around here."

"The one-eyed man?"

The lighthouse keeper nodded to the lighthouse. "That's what I call the lighthouse. He stands tall with his one eye always on the lookout. You're fortunate, Sergeant, for the relief boat will be here with this tide and take us all back to the mainland."

The one-eyed man. Watters remembered Lizzy Flett, the Shetland fortune teller. Her prediction had come true. He had been in danger in the shadow of a tall, one-eyed man, and Lieutenant Anstruther was not involved.

"Come on, you," Watters dragged Gow to his feet. "We'd best get you to safety."

Now I have only one loose end to tie, and this case is closed.

CHAPTER THIRTY-TWO

JOHN MUNRO, THE FACTOR, PUSHED OPEN THE DOOR. "IT'S only one room," he said, "but we keep it clean."

Watters looked around. The furnished house in Fish Street was basic, with a simple bed, table and two chairs and precious little else. "It will do," he said. "I'll pay you two months' rent in advance."

Munro took the money and entered Watters' name in his notebook. "As long as your friend pays his rent, we won't have any trouble."

Watters tapped his cane against the table. "If he gives you any trouble, Mr Munro, you tell me right away."

"I'll do that, Sergeant Watters."

Watters shook Munro's hand and walked away, swinging his cane. He nodded to Eddie, who drove past on his cab, and turned into Couttie's Wynd. As he expected, Jim was loitering outside Ma Ramsay's.

"Come with me, Jim," Watters put a hand on Jim's shoulder. "I have something for you."

"I never did anything wrong," Jim gave his habitual reply as he tried to wriggle free.

"You never do," Watters said. He ran his eye from Jim's

ragged black hair to his ill-shod feet. "I think we'll have to make you respectable first."

"What do you mean, Mr Watters?"

"You'll see. Come along." Watters guided Jim to Mrs Flannery's, the most reputable pawn shop he knew, and selected a complete outfit of clothes, from underwear to a jacket and a nearly new pair of boots.

"I can't afford any of these, Mr Watters," Jim said.

"I'm paying," Watters assured him. "Help him fit them, please, Mrs Flannery," Watters said, "and check his pockets before he leaves."

Fifteen minutes later, Jim emerged from the back shop, red-faced and carrying a bundle of clothes. "What's this for, Mr Watters?"

"You'll see," Watters said. He picked a battered white hat from a stand. "And this too, please, Mrs Flannery."

"I'll throw the hat in for free, Sergeant Watters," Mrs Flannery said as Watters jammed it on Jim's head.

"Thank you, Mrs Flannery." Watters dragged Jim out of the shop and along to the Public Baths at the West Protection Wall. "In you come, Jim."

"What's this place?" Jim asked, recoiling from the austere walls. "Is it a prison?"

"It's a public bathhouse," Watters said, shoving Jim inside.

An hour later, with Jim shining clean and resplendent in his newly purchased clothes, Watters escorted him past the tide harbour to Victoria Dock.

"What's all this about, Mr Watters?" Jim asked.

"You'll see, Jim." Watters scoured the quay until he found a broad-shouldered man with a pheasant feather in the band of his bowler hat.

"I hear you're looking for a porter," Watters said.

"Aye," the man looked Jim up and down.

"Jim is available to start the day after tomorrow," Watters held Jim's arm to prevent him running at the mention of work. "If he gives you any trouble," he tapped Jim's backside with the whippy end of his cane. "Just refer him to me."

"My men never give me any trouble," the foreman said, rubbing the knuckles of his right hand into the palm of his left.

"Glad to hear it," Watters said. "Jim's been looking for regular work for some time. Now that he's got a house, he needs a steady job to pay the rent."

"I haven't got a house," Jim said.

"You have a house in Fish Street," Watters corrected him. "Now come with me."

Arbroath Betty sighed when Watters entered, with a nervous Jim in tow. "What's this, Mr Watters? There's not been more trouble, has there?"

"Not at all, Betty. I'm making a social call," Watters glanced around the room until he caught sight of the three regulars.

"He's still looking for that donkey," the bald man said.

"Have you found your donkey yet?" the scarred man said, and all three laughed.

Watters approached, dragging Jim behind him. "I've found it," he said. "Here's all that remains." Snatching the white hat from Jim's head, he placed it gently on the bald man's head. "The man in the white hat had it."

The bald man stared at him and began to laugh. "Well done, Sergeant Watters! You found the donkey!"

"Come on, Jim," Watters said. "The night is yet young."

"I never stole a donkey," Jim denied, as Watters led him back to Couttie's Wynd.

"I know you didn't, Jim," Watters said. "It's a private joke."

Ma Ramsay greeted Watters with a suspicious nod. "What's this, Sergeant Watters?"

"This is Jim," Watters said.

"Aye, he lurks in the Wynd, ogling my girls but hasn't the nerve to come in."

"He's not ogling today," Watters pressed a gold sovereign into Ma Ramsay's hard hand. "He's never been with a woman before. They frighten him."

Ma Ramsay nodded, bit the sovereign to test its purity and tucked it away inside her clothes. "Aye, I ken the type."

"I want him cured of ogling," Watters said. "Select your gentlest girl and show him everything. The best cure for a frightened ogler is to experience the real thing." He gave a small smile. "Hairy Meg will do nicely."

Ma Ramsay smiled. "Meg can cure a man of anything."

"But, Mr Watters," Jim would have run outside if Watters had not held him secure. "Mr Watters," he lowered his voice to an urgent whisper. "I don't know what to do!"

When Meg appeared, Watters passed her a sovereign. "This is Jim," he said. "He's never experienced a woman's company."

Meg eased herself to Jim and rubbed her curves against him. "It's your lucky night, Jim," she said and winked before leaning closer to him. "It's all right, Jim. You're safe with me."

"Mr Watters," Jim turned huge eyes on Watters. "I don't know what to do."

"You soon will, Jim. Here," Watters slipped a sovereign into Jim's pocket. That was the last of the reward money from Muirhead's wedding. "Have a good time, Jim."

———

"That's a good result," Watters said. "We removed a very prolific cracksman from the streets, captured a murderer, stopped a spate of scuttling and arrested a clutch of minor criminals. Gentlemen, we did well."

The detectives sat around him, stretching their legs out

and looking at the steaming mugs of black tea. "What will happen to Gow and Urquhart?" Shaw asked.

"That's for the fifteen good men of the jury to decide," Watters said. "We did our duty in arresting them." He sat back in his chair, reached for the whisky, and poured a generous tot into every mug. "There we are, gentlemen, a toast to us. Here's tae us!"

"Wha's like us?" Scuddamore asked.

"Damned few," Duff continued.

"And they're all deid!" they said together.

Watters opened a packet of Abernethy biscuits and passed them around. "And here's to a new tradition," he said. "An Abernethy to celebrate every success." He raised his tea to Shaw, "and welcome to the team, Shaw. Scuddamore will teach you how to make tea the way I like it."

Dear reader,

We hope you enjoyed reading *The Scuttlers*. Please take a moment to leave a review, even if it's a short one. Your opinion is important to us.

Discover more books by Malcolm Archibald at https://www.nextchapter.pub/authors/malcolm-archibald

Want to know when one of our books is free or discounted? Join the newsletter at http://eepurl.com/bqqB3H

Best regards,

Malcolm Archibald and the Next Chapter Team

NOTES

I based many of the events, adventures, and misadventures in this book on actual events.

Scuttling ships at sea was an abhorrent crime that was fairly prevalent in the nineteenth century. Of the two incidents in this book, the scuttling of *Toiler* was based loosely on the sinking of *William and Martha*, carrying paving stones and potatoes from Castlehill in Caithness to West Hartlepool in March 1892. The loss of *Teresa* was based on the scuttling of *Tryst* in October 1891.

Dundee was a whaling port from the 1750s to the beginning of the twentieth century. As with any other industry, whaling was open to various malpractices, including the theft of a whale. I based the theft in *Scuttlers* on a case in August 1829, when the Peterhead whaling ship *Traveller* and the Dundee vessel *Thomas* disputed a whale. On the day, *Thomas* came out on top, but the master and owner of *Traveller* took the Dundee whaling company to court and won the case. I gave more detailed particulars in my non-fiction book, *A Sink of Atrocity*, published by Black and White in 2012.

The Fenian scare was also based on actual events. The Fenian troubles began in the 1860s, and in October 1866, posters appeared in Dundee advertising a proposed Fenian invasion. The battle between local Volunteers and a gang of youngsters occurred, except without the police intervention.

Donald Mackay headed the Dundee police force from the early 1840s until 1876. A Caithness man, he was arguably the most successful of Dundee's early Chief Constables.

The case of James Connor, captured by his drawers, was inspired by James Gormally of Hawkhill. A youth with a lengthy criminal record, Gormally changed his underwear for a new pair while robbing Spence and Company in Reform Street in Dundee. That was in 1866, and the police traced him when they found the new underwear. The idea was so unusual I could not leave it out. Another thief, David Crockatt, was caught because of a broken braces' buckle in 1869.

The watch bar idea came from an Edinburgh case where the thief cut through the ceiling from the upstairs flat. He used a rope ladder to enter a jeweller's shop, and the police caught him through a watch bar with the watch number engraved on the back.

My professional cracksman was based partly on a thief who haunted Scotland in general and Glasgow in particular in the 1850s. He worked with a partner known as George Jackson, who claimed to be Canadian and used a great deal of equipment. In 1853 they targeted D C Rait in Buchanan Street, the largest jewellers in Glasgow, stole about £3,000 worth of jewellery and walked straight into the night watchman. The police chased and caught Jackson, but his mysterious colleague escaped.

The armed robbery at Muirhead's wedding was unusual for Dundee, so I borrowed some of the details from an 1866 robbery at Kirkton of Auchterhouse a few miles to the north. The criminals there had blackened their faces and carried weapons.

In nineteenth-century Scotland, habitual criminals often used false names. The idea was partly to confuse the authorities and partially to protect themselves from long spells in prison. The courts were more likely to award a harsh sentence to a known criminal than a first offender.

These examples are just a few of the very many criminal cases in nineteenth-century Scotland. Even a cursory study of the period brings to light a host of colourful characters and dedicated policemen. Yet time has added a gloss of romance to the events. For the victims, to be assaulted or burgled was just as traumatic then as it is now, and most career criminals lived a sordid life of brief periods of freedom between spells in jail. Indeed, for some, prison was the only real home they knew.

Sergeant Watters knew the criminal world, the good and bad, sad and vicious, so perhaps he will return with another case. Certainly, there was sufficient crime to keep him busy.

Malcolm Archibald.

Dundee and Angus, May 2021

Printed in Great Britain
by Amazon

65210752R00208